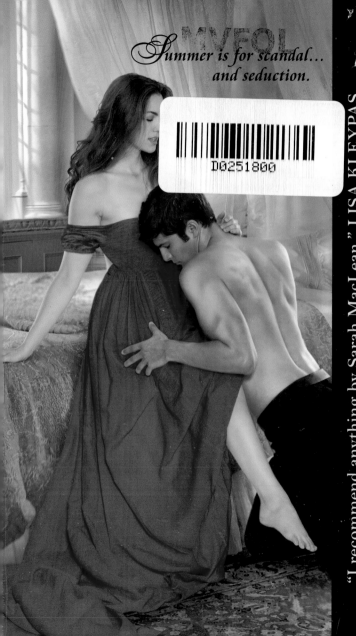

Summer is for scandal…
and seduction.

D0251800

"I recommend anything by Sarah MacLean." LISA KLEYPAS

"*B*e careful, husband, or you shall set tongues to wagging."

"I don't care what they think."

She knew better. "Nonsense. You've always cared what the world thinks. Too much."

He lifted a hand, and her breath caught at the anticipation of his touch. And then he was there, his warm fingers finding purchase on her cheek, as though they belonged there. "I did, once," he said, his voice like wheels on gravel. "I cared too much what they thought. And now, I seem to care too little. I seem to care only what you think."

It wasn't true, but she found she did not care. It was her turn to lift her hand. Her turn to set palm to cheek. Her turn to ravage.

And she did, feeling more powerful than ever when he exhaled, an edge of breath whipping over lips like memory. As though she'd burned him. She might have. They'd always been oil and flame. Why not let it happen? Just for a moment? Just to see if the combustion remained?

She arched up to him. Or he leaned down. It did not matter.

Romances by Sarah MacLean

SARAH MacLEAN

The Day of the Duchess

SCANDAL & SCOUNDREL, BOOK III

AVONBOOKS

An Imprint of HarperCollinsPublishers

THE DAY OF THE DUCHESS. Copyright © 2017 by Sarah Trabucchi. All rights reserved. Printed in the United States of America. No part of this book may be used or reproduced in any manner whatsoever without written permission except in the case of brief quotations embodied in critical articles and reviews. For information, address HarperCollins Publishers, 195 Broadway, New York, NY 10007.

First Avon Books mass market printing: July 2017
First Avon Books hardcover printing: June 2017

Print Edition ISBN: 978-0-06-237943-6
Digital Edition ISBN: 978-0-06-237946-7

Avon, Avon & logo, and Avon Books & logo are registered trademarks of HarperCollins Publishers in the United States of America and other countries.

HarperCollins is a registered trademark of HarperCollins Publishers in the United States of America and other countries.

FIRST EDITION

17 18 19 20 21   QGM   10 9 8 7 6 5 4 3 2 1

For soldiers in petticoats,

then and now.

The
Day of the
Duchess

Scandal & SCOUNDREL

Vol 3 / Iss 113, August 1836

DISAPPEARED DUCHESS DISCOVERED!

GOSSIP PERFUMED Parliament today when Seraphina, the Disappeared **DUCHESS OF HAVEN** returned from her *scandalous sojourn* to surprise Society and spar with her spouse on the floor of the House of Lords. The Long Lost Lady's parliamentary petition? **DIVORCE**!

By all accounts, **HOODWINKED HAVEN** has hied home, ceding the floor (but not the war) to his once lady love, **DANGEROUS DAUGHTER** and disdained duchess . . . now unwilling wife! The lady will *not be ignored, however.* She follows **furious,** vowing to end the marriage by *any means necessary.*

Is there **anything more salacious** than summer scandal?

MORE TO COME.

Chapter 1

***

DESERTED DUKE DISAVOWED!

August 19, 1836
House of Lords, Parliament

$\mathscr{S}$he'd left him two years, seven months ago, exactly.

Malcolm Marcus Bevingstoke, Duke of Haven, looked to the tiny wooden calendar wheels inlaid into the blotter on his desk in his private office above the House of Lords.

August the nineteenth, 1836. The last day of the parliamentary session, filled with pomp and idle. And lingering memory. He spun the wheel with the six embossed upon it. Five. Four. He took a deep breath.

Get out. He heard his own words, cold and angry with betrayal, echoing with quiet menace. *Don't ever return.*

He touched the wheel again. August became July. May. March.

January the nineteenth, 1834. *The day she left.*

His fingers moved without thought, finding comfort in the familiar click of the wheels.

April the seventeenth, 1833.

The way I feel about you . . . Her words now—soft and full of temptation. *I've never felt anything like this.*

He hadn't, either. As though light and breath and hope

had flooded the room, filling all the dark spaces. Filling his lungs and heart. And all because of her.

Until he'd discovered the truth. The truth, which had mattered so much until it hadn't mattered at all. *Where had she gone?*

The clock in the corner of the room ticked and tocked, counting the seconds until Haven was due in his seat in the hallowed main chamber of the House of Lords, where men of higher purpose and passion had sat before him for generations. His fingers played the little calendar like a virtuoso, as though they'd done this dance a hundred times before. A thousand.

And they had.

March the first, 1833. The day they met.

So, they let simply anyone become a duke, do they? No deference. Teasing and charm and pure, unadulterated beauty.

If you think dukes are bad, imagine what they accept from duchesses?

That smile. As though she'd never met another man. As though she'd never wanted to. He'd been hers the moment he'd seen that smile. Before that. *Imagine, indeed.*

And then it had fallen apart. He'd lost everything, and then lost her. Or perhaps it had been the reverse. Or perhaps it was all the same.

Would there ever be a time when he stopped thinking of her? Ever a date that did not remind him of her? Of the time that had stretched like an eternity since she'd left?

Where had she gone?

The clock struck eleven, heavy chimes sounding in the room, echoed by a dozen others down the long, oaken corridor beyond, summoning men of longstanding name to the duty that had been theirs before they drew breath.

Haven spun the calendar wheels with force, leaving them as they lay. November the thirty-seventh, 3842. A fine date—one on which he had absolutely no chance of thinking of her.

He stood, heading for the place where his red robes hung—their thick, heavy burden meant to echo the weight of the responsibility they represented. He swung the garment over his shoulders, the red velvet's heat overwhelming him almost immediately, cloying and suffocating. All this before he reached for his powdered wig, grimacing as he flipped it onto his head, the horse-hair whipping his neck before lying flat and uncomfort-able, like a punishment for past sins.

Ignoring the sensation, the Duke of Haven ripped open the door to his offices and made his way through the now quiet corridors to the entrance of the main chamber of the House of Lords. Stepping inside, he inhaled deeply, immediately regretting it. It was August and hot as hell on the floor of Parliament, the air rank with sweat and perfume. The windows were open to allow a breeze into the room—a barely-there stirring that only exacerbated the stench, adding the reek of the Thames to the already horrendous smell within.

At home, the river ran cool and crisp, unsullied by the filth of London. At home, the air was clean, promis-ing summer idyll and hinting at more. At the future. At least, it had done. Until the pieces of home had peeled away and he'd been left alone, without it. Now, it felt like nothing but land. Home required more than a river and rolling hills. Home required her. And so he would do this summer what he had done every moment he'd been away from London for the past two years and seven months, exactly. He would search for her.

She hadn't been in France or in Spain, where he'd spent the summer prior, chasing down Englishwomen in search of excitement. She hadn't been any of the false widows he'd found in Scotland, nor the governess at the imposing manor in Wales, nor the woman he'd tracked in Constantinople the month after she'd left, who had been a charlatan, playing at being an aristocrat. And then there'd been the woman in Boston—the one he'd been so sure of—the one they called The Dove.

Not Sera. Never Sera. She had disappeared, as though she'd never existed. There one moment, gone the next, laden with enough funds to vanish. And just as he'd realized how much he wanted her. But her money would run out, eventually, and she would have no choice but to stop running. He, on the other hand, was a man with power and privilege and exorbitant wealth, enough to find her the moment she stopped.

And he would find her.

He slid into one of the long benches surrounding the speaker's floor, where the Lord Chancellor had already begun. "My lords, if there is no more formal business, we will close this year's parliamentary season."

A chorus of approval—fists pounding on seatbacks around the hall—echoed through the chamber.

Haven exhaled and resisted the urge to scratch at his wig, knowing that if he gave in to the desire, he would become consumed with its rough discomfort. "My lords!" the Lord Chancellor called. "Is there, indeed, no additional formal business for the current session?"

A rousing chorus of "Nay!" boomed through the room. One would think the House of Lords was filled with schoolboys desperate for an afternoon in the local swimming hole instead of nearly two hundred pompous aristocrats eager to get to their mistresses.

The Lord Chancellor grinned, his ruddy face gleaming with sweat beneath his wig as he spread his wide hands over his ample girth. "Well then! It is His Majesty's royal will and pleasure . . ."

The enormous doors to the chamber burst open, the sound echoing through the quiet hall, competing with the chancellor's voice. Heads turned, but not Haven's; he was too eager to leave London and his wig behind to worry about whatever was going on beyond.

The Lord Chancellor collected himself, cleared his throat, and said, ". . . that this Parliament be prorogued to Thursday, the seventh day of October next . . ."

A collection of disapproving harrumphs began as the door shut with a powerful bang. Haven looked then, following the gazes of the men assembled to the now closed door to chambers. He couldn't see anything amiss.

"Ahem!" the Lord Chancellor said, the sound full of disapproval, before he redoubled his commitment to closing the session. Thank God for that. ". . . *Thursday, the seventh day of October next . . .*"

"Before you finish, my Lord Chancellor?"

Haven stiffened.

The words were strong and somehow soft and lilting and beautifully feminine—so out of place in the House of Lords, off limits to the fairer sex. Surely that was why his breath caught. Surely that was why his heart began to pound. Why he was suddenly on his feet amid a chorus of masculine outrage.

It was not because of the voice itself.

"What is the meaning of this?" the Chancellor thundered.

Haven could see it then, the cause of the commotion.

A woman. Taller than any woman he'd ever known, in the most beautiful lavender dress he'd ever seen, perfectly turned out, as though she marched into parliamentary session on a regular basis. As though she were the prime minister himself. As though she were more than that. As though she were royalty.

The only woman he'd ever loved. The only woman he'd ever hated.

The same, and somehow entirely different.

And Haven, frozen to the spot.

"I confess," she said, moving to the floor of the chamber with ease, as though she were at ladies' tea, "I feared I would miss the session altogether. But I'm very happy that I might sneak in before you all escape to wherever it is that you gentlemen venture for . . . pleasure." She grinned at an ancient earl, who blushed under the heat of her gaze and turned away. "However, I am told that what I seek requires an Act of Parliament. And you are . . . as you know . . . Parliament."

Her gaze found his, her eyes precisely as he remembered, blue as the summer sea, but now, somehow, different. Where they were once open and honest, they were now shuttered. Private.

Christ. She was here.

Here. Nearly three years searching for her, and here she was, as though she'd been gone mere hours. Shock warred with an anger he could not have imagined, but those two emotions were nothing compared to the third. The immense, unbearable pleasure.

She was here.

Finally.

Again.

It was all he could do not to move. To gather her up

and carry her away. To hold her close. Win her back. Start fresh.

Except she did not seem to be here for that.

She watched him for a long moment, her gaze unblinking, before she declared, "I am Seraphina Bevingstoke, Duchess of Haven. And I require a divorce."

Chapter 2

―――― ⌒⌒⌒ ――――

DUCHESS DISAPPEARS,
DUKE DEVASTATED

January 1834
Two years, seven months earlier. Minus five days.
Highley Manor

*I*f she did not knock, she would die.

She should not have come. It had been irresponsible beyond measure. She'd made the decision in a fit of unbearable emotion, desperate for some kind of control in this, the most out-of-control time of her life.

If she weren't so cold, she would laugh at the madness of the idea that she might have any control over her world, ever again.

But the only thing Seraphina Bevingstoke, Duchess of Haven, was able to do was curse her idiotic decision to hire a hack, pay the driver a fortune to bring her on a long, terrifying journey through the icy rain of a cold January night, and land herself here, at Highley, the manor house of which she was—by name—mistress. Name did not bestow rights, however. Not for women. And by rights, she was nothing but a visitor. Not even a guest. Not yet. Possibly not ever.

The hack disappeared into the rain that threatened to become heavy, wet snow, and Sera looked up at the massive door, considering her next move. It was the dark of night—servants long abed, but she had no choice but to wake someone. She could not remain outside. If she did, she would be dead before morning.

A wave of terrifying pain shot through her. She put a hand to her midsection.

They would be dead.

The pain ebbed, and she caught her breath once more, lifting the elaborate wrought-iron B affixed to the door. Letting it fall with a thud, the sound an executioner's axe, dark and ominous, coming on a flood of worry. What if no one answered? What if she'd come all this way, against better judgment, to an empty house?

The worries were unfounded. Highley was the seat of the Dukedom of Haven, and it was staffed to perfection. The door opened, a liveried young footman with tired eyes appearing, his curiosity immediately giving way to shock as pain racked Sera once more.

Before he could speak, before he could shut her out, Sera stepped into the doorway, one hand at her heaving belly, the other on the jamb. "Haven." The name was all she could speak before she doubled over.

"He—" The boy stopped. "His Grace, that is—he is not in."

She looked up somehow, her eyes finding his in the dim light. "Do you know me?"

His gaze flickered to her swollen midsection. Back.

Her hand spread wide over the child there. "The heir."

He nodded, and relief flooded her, a wash of warmth. She swayed with it even as his young eyes widened, drawn to the floor beneath them.

Not relief. Blood.

"Oh—" he began, the remainder of his words stolen away by shock.

Sera swayed in the doorway, reaching for him, this virtual child who had been so very unlucky in his post that evening. He took her hand. "He is here," he whispered. "He is abovestairs."

He was there. Strong enough to bend the sun to his will.

That might have been gratitude if not for the pain. It might have been happiness if not for the fear. And it might have been life if not for what she suddenly knew was to come.

Get out. She heard the words. Saw his cold gaze when he'd banished her from his sight months earlier. And then, somehow . . .

Come here. That gaze again, but this time heavy-lidded. Desperate. Hot as the sun. And then his whispers soft and beautiful at her ear. *You were made for me. We were made for each other.*

Pain returned her to the present, sharp and stinging, marking something terribly wrong. As though the blood that covered her skirts and the marble floor weren't enough of a herald. She cried out. Louder than she would have guessed, as there was suddenly someone else there; a woman.

They spoke, but Sera could not hear the words. Then the woman was gone, and Sera was left in the darkness, with her mistakes and the boy, the dear, sweet boy, who clung to her. Or she to him. "She's gone to fetch him."

It was too late, of course. In so many ways.

She should not have come.

Sera fell to her knees, gasping through the ache. Sorrow beyond ken. She would never know their child.

Dark-haired and wide-smiled, and smart as his father. Lonely as him, too.

If only she could live, she might love them enough.

But she was to die here, in this place. Yards from the only man she'd ever loved. Without ever having told him. She wondered if he would care when she died, and the answer terrified her more than all the rest, because she knew, without doubt, that it would follow her into the afterlife.

She clutched the boy's hand. "Tell me your name."

"Your Grace?"

She clutched his hand. "Sera," she whispered. She was going to die, and she wanted someone to say her name, not her title. Something real. Something that felt like it belonged. "My name is Seraphina."

The dear boy clung to her. Nodded. The knot in his too-narrow throat bobbing with his nerves. "Daniel," he said. "What shall I do?"

"My child," she whispered. "His."

The boy nodded, suddenly wise beyond his years. "Is there something you wish for?"

"Mal," she said, unable to keep the truth at bay. Unable to keep it from swallowing her whole. Just once more. Just long enough to put everything back to rights. "I wish for Malcolm."

𝒯he Duke of Haven threw open the door to the room where Sera lay, silent and still and pale, the force of the oak slab ricocheting off the wall startling those inside. A young maid gave a little cry of surprise, and the housekeeper looked up from where she held a cloth to Sera's brow.

But the Duke wanted nothing to do with the two

women. He was too focused on the surgeon at his wife's side.

"She lives," Haven growled, the words filled with emotion he did not know he could feel. But then, she had always made him feel. Even when he'd been desperate not to.

The surgeon nodded. "By a thread, Your Grace. She will likely die before nightfall."

The words coursed through him, cold and simple, as though the doctor were discussing the weather or the morning news, and Malcolm stilled, the full weight of their assault threatening to bring him down. Not an hour earlier, he had held his lost child in his hands, so small she did not even fill them, so precious he could not bear to return her to the maid who had brought her to him.

Instead, he'd sent the servant away, and sat in silence, holding the near-weightless body of his daughter, mourning her death. And her life. And all the things she might have been.

Knowing that, despite his virtually limitless wealth and power and position, he could not bring her back. And when he had been able to think beyond grief, he'd found solace in fury.

He would not lose them both.

Malcolm's gaze narrowed on the surgeon. "You misunderstand." He reached for the doctor, unable to stop himself. Lifting him by the lapels of his coat, the duke rained thunder down on the older, smaller, weaker man. "Do you hear me? She lives." The surgeon stuttered, and rage flooded Malcolm. He shook the doctor again. "*My wife lives.*"

"I—I cannot save her if she will not be saved."

Malcolm let go, not caring that the surgeon stumbled

when he hit the floor. He was already headed for Sera, coming to his knees at her bedside, taking her hand in his, loathing the cold in it, tightening his grip, willing her warm. He took a moment to look at her—she'd been gone for so long, and before that, he'd hated her too much. And before that, he'd been too desperate to notice what precisely he desired about her.

How was it that it took until now—until she was pale and still and on the edge of death—for him to realize how beautiful she was? Her high cheekbones and her full lips, and those sooty black lashes, impossibly long where they lay on her porcelain skin.

What would he give to have her lift those lashes? To look at him with those eyes that never failed to steal his breath, blue as the summer sky. He'd take them however they came—filled with happiness. With sorrow. With hatred.

He'd already given so much. So had she. What more did he have? What meager sacrifice could he offer? None. And so, in this, he would take without payment. He closed his eyes and pressed his lips to her cold fingers, limp and unmoving. "You shall live, Sera. If I have to pull you back from heaven itself. You shall live."

"Your Grace."

He stilled at the words, clear and emotionless, spoken from the door to the chamber. He did not turn to face the woman who stood there; he could not find the patience for it.

His mother's skirts rustled as she drew closer. "Haven."

Fury threaded through him at the title here, in this moment. Always a duke, never a man. How often had she reminded him of his place? Of his purpose? Of the sacrifices she'd made to ensure it for him? Sacrifices that made her one of the most feared women in Britain. A cut from the Duchess of Haven could ruin a girl before she'd even had a chance.

Not duchess. Dowager.

Malcolm stood, turning to face his mother, blocking her view of Seraphina. Suddenly, keenly, wanting her out of this room. Away from his wife.

He brushed past the older woman and the surgeon, pushing into the hallway beyond, sending maids scattering from their bent heads and hushed whispers. He swallowed the urge to bellow after them. To go against decades of training in title and position.

"You are being dramatic," she said. The greatest of all sins.

His heart began to pound. "My child is dead. My wife nearly so." Her gaze did not warm. He should not have been surprised by the fact, and yet it made him want to rage. But dukes did not rage. Instead, he met her cool blue gaze and said, "Your grandchild is dead."

"A girl."

Heat threaded through him. "A daughter."

"Not an heir," she pointed out, with cool dismissal. "And now, if you are lucky, you can begin again."

The heat became fire, rioting through him. Clawing up his throat. Suffocating. "If I am lucky?"

"If the Talbot girl dies. The doctor says that if she lives, she will be barren, and so she shall no longer be of use. You can find another. Produce an heir. One with better pedigree."

His gaze narrowed, the words difficult to understand over the roar in his ears. "She is Duchess of Haven."

"The title means nothing if she cannot produce the next duke. That's why you married her, is it not? She and her mother set a trap. Caught you. Kept you with the promise of an heir. And now it's gone. I would be less of a mother if I did not wish you free of such a cheap woman."

He chose his words carefully. "In this moment, you could not be less of a mother. You are a cold, heartless bitch. And I want you gone from this house when I return."

She raised one elegant brow. "Emotion does not become you."

He left his mother then, because he did not trust himself not to unleash every ounce of his unbecoming emotions upon her.

He left his mother and went to bury his daughter in the cold January ground, all the while praying that his wife would live.

When she woke, Sera was alone, in a room filled with blinding light. She ached everywhere—in bones and muscles and in places she could not name. In the place that had been so beautifully full of something more than hope, and was now so devastatingly empty of it.

She moved her hand on the counterpane, her fingers tracing over the softly worked, pristine linen to her stomach, tender and swollen and vacant. A tear spilled, racing down her temple, leaving a trail of loneliness as it slipped into her hair and disappeared. She imagined that it carried the last shred of her happiness.

Beyond the window, bright blue sky shimmered, clouded by nothing but the heavy glass panes. A bare tree branch in the distance appeared malformed, great black blotches upon it.

Not malformation. Crows.

One for sorrow. Two for mirth.

Her breath hitched in her throat.

"Tears won't bring it back."

Sera turned toward the voice, dreading what she would find there. Not her husband, but her mother-in-law, who seemed to make a practice of inhabiting rooms in which she was not welcome. Indeed, the Dowager Duchess of Haven was regularly present in the worst of rooms. The ones that destroyed dreams. The woman was a harbinger of sorrow. Even if Sera hadn't known in her soul that the child was gone, the presence of the dowager proved it.

Sera looked away to the window, to the sky beyond, bright and full of stolen promise. To the crows.

Three for a wedding. Four for a birth.

She did not speak. She could not find the words, and even if she could, she was not interested in sharing them with the other woman.

The dowager found enough words for both of them, however, drawing closer, speaking as though about the weather. "You might not like me, Seraphina, but you would do well to listen."

Sera did not move.

"We are not that different, you and I," the older woman said. "We both made a mistake trapping a man in marriage. The difference is that my child survived." She paused, and Sera willed her to leave the room, suddenly exhausted by the dowager's very presence. "If he hadn't, I would have run."

Running was a glorious thought.

Could she outrun it? The sorrow? The pain? Could she outrun him?

"There was no love lost in our marriage. Just as there is none lost in yours."

She was wrong, of course. Sera's marriage was all

love lost.. And now, as she lay alone in this blindingly white bed in this blindingly white room in this oppressively daunting home, she knew that her marriage would never be love regained.

Because there would never be love again. Not for Malcolm. Not for their child. Not for herself. She was alone in this room and in this life.

If only she could run. But he'd stolen her freedom just as well as he'd stolen her heart. And her happiness. And her future.

"You are barren."

Sera felt nothing at the words, which held no meaning in the moment. She did not care for the news of future, fantasy children, only for that of the child she'd lost. The child *they* had lost.

"He will need an heir."

He did not wish one. Hadn't he made it clear?

His mother either did not know, or did not care. "You cannot give it to him. Someone else can."

Sera looked away.

"If you wished it, I could help you."

She looked to her mother-in-law, into grey-blue eyes cold as the woman's soul. Sera did not pretend to misunderstand. She knew that her disappearance was all this hateful woman had ever wanted. The dowager had loathed Sera from the start—hated the circumstances of her birth, her father a commoner who had bought his way into the aristocracy and her mother, willing to do anything to climb, who had clawed her way up, crowing to all who would hear that her eldest had captured a duke.

Of course, Sera had believed him caught. Believed him hers. Wished it beyond measure.

But this woman—this cold, aging woman—had made sure that was never to be. In spite of the promise of a child. Because of it.

Until this moment, Sera had planned to stay. To win her husband's forgiveness. To defy the dowager's fury. But that was before. That was when she thought they might one day be a family.

When she had still harbored dreams of happiness.

Now, she knew better.

Thick skirts rustled as the other woman drew nearer. "You could run. Begin anew. Let him do the same."

It was madness. And still, she could not stop herself from saying, "What of our marriage?"

A muscle twitched at the edge of the dowager's lips. She sensed triumph. "Money buys everything. Including annulment."

Sera looked to the crows outside. *Five for silver. Six for gold.*

The dowager continued. "The absence of children will ease the way."

The words were a cold, quiet torture.

The absence of their child would never be easy.

"Name your price," the dowager whispered.

Sera was silent, watching the door behind the older woman, willing it to open. Willing her husband to return, filled with the aching sadness that consumed her. Desperate to mourn their child. Their past. Their future.

Willing to forgive her.

Willing to ask for forgiveness.

The mahogany door remained firmly shut.

He didn't wish it, and so why should she? Why shouldn't she close a door herself? Why shouldn't she choose a new path?

How much to do it? How much for a future? How

much to run? How much for a life, alone, pale in comparison to the one she'd been promised?

Alone, but *hers.*

She whispered the exorbitant number. Enough to leave. Never enough to forget.

Seven for a secret never to be told.

Chapter 3

DIFFICULT DUCHESS
DEMANDS DIVORCE!

August 19, 1836
House of Lords, Parliament

*H*e was as handsome as he'd ever been. She didn't know why she'd expected him to be otherwise—it had been three years, not thirty—but she had. Or perhaps not expected, but hoped. She'd harbored some small, secret dream that he'd be less perfect. Less handsome. Less, full stop.

But he wasn't less. If anything, he was more.

His face more angular, his gaze more consuming, he was even taller than she remembered. And so handsome, even as he came toward her, dressed in ancient parliamentary robes and the inane powdered wig that should have made him look like a child playing at fancy dress and instead made him look a man with a purpose.

Namely, removing her from the floor of the House of Lords.

He parted the similarly garishly appointed members of Parliament like a red velvet sea, encouraged by the hoots and jeers of those assembled aristocrats whose disdain she knew all too well from her former life. Men who could ruin a woman in a heartbeat. Destroy a family and a future. And do it all without thinking twice.

She'd loathed them all, and him the most.

But not for long.

She planned to put the loathing behind her now that she'd returned, ready to forget him. She'd imagined this moment for months, since before she'd returned to Britain, the entire plan designed to infuriate him to the point of agreeing to the dissolution of their marriage. For, if there was anything Haven loathed in the world, it was being played the fool.

Had that not been their demise at the start?

He approached, the massive chamber falling away along with the years. She'd been haunted by his eyes. Somehow not brown, not green, not gold, not grey, and somehow all of them at once. Fascinating and full of secrets. The kind of eyes that might steal a woman's wits if she wasn't careful.

Sera was careful, now.

Careful, and smart. She resisted the urge to back away from him, simultaneously afraid of what might happen if he touched her, and determined never to cow to him. Never to run from him again.

She was not the woman she had been when she'd left. She was returned with a singular promise to herself; when she left him this time, she would do so with pride. With purpose. With a future.

She had plans. And these men would not stop her.

And so it was that London's most powerful, assembled for the final day of the parliamentary session, witnessed Seraphina, Duchess of Haven's winning smile as she faced the duke of the same name for the first time in two years and seven months. Exactly. "Husband."

Another woman might not have noticed the slight narrowing of his eyes, the barely-there flare of his nose, the nearly imperceptible clenching of his square jaw. But Sera had once spent the better part of a year fascinated by the way this proud, unflappable man revealed himself in the infinitesimal. He was angry. *Good.*

"Then you remember me." The words were quiet and sharp. Of course she remembered. No matter how well she tried, she seemed unable to forget.

And she had tried.

She lifted her chin, keenly aware of their audience, and slung her arrow. "Don't fret, darling. I predict we shan't need to remember each other for long."

"You are making a spectacle of yourself."

She allowed her smile to widen. "You say that as though it is a bad thing."

One brow rose, superior as ever. "You are making a spectacle of me."

She did not waver. "You say *that* as though you do not deserve it."

She didn't expect him to reach for her, or she would have been prepared for what came when his fingers wrapped around her elbow, firm and warm and somehow unexpectedly gentle. Would have steeled herself for the assault of too long ago memories.

I've never felt anything like this.

She resisted the memory and slid her arm from his grip with a graceful force that he would feel and no one watching would ever notice. The duke had no choice but to let her go, even as he lowered his voice and spoke, the words barely there. "Who are you?"

It was her brow that rose this time. "You do not recognize me?"

"Not this incarnation, no."

Incarnation. It was not the wrong word, for she had been reincarnated. That was what happened to those who died and returned. It had felt like death, just as this morning, in this place, in all its heat and rancid stench made worse by the assembly of pompous masculinity, felt somehow, remarkably, like life once more.

"I could not taste freedom then."

His lips flattened. Before he could reply, a man shouted from the assembly beyond. "Oi! Haven! The chit's not allowed on the floor!"

Sera turned to the man. "My Lord Earl, I believe you meant to address me as Duchess."

The men assembled harrumphed and grumbled as the earl in question—now sporting scarlet ears—spoke to Haven. "Control your female."

Sera returned her attention to her husband, but did not lower her voice. "It is impressive that he believes you are able to do such a thing."

Her husband's eyes narrowed and Sera's heart began to pound. She recognized the look. An animal, challenged.

Let him come for her. She, too, had teeth.

"My offices. Now."

"And if I refuse?" She saw him realize her power. How many other wives could stand here, before God and husband and the House of Lords, and hold sway without fear of repercussions?

That was the secret, of course. If one did not fear ruin, one could not be threatened with it. As Sera had seen ruin in all its forms, had faced it and survived it, she did not fear it, and so he could not harm her. She'd been gone from London for nearly three years, her reputation in tatters long before she'd set foot in the carriage that had carried her away from the Haven estate on that long ago winter's day. It was remarkable, the power one held when one had nothing to lose.

At least, when one was *thought* to have nothing to lose.

And so she stood before the most powerful assembly in Britain, toe-to-toe with her husband, who had always held sway over her. Over her heart, and her hand, and her body, and her identity. Equals at long last. And she waited for him to make his move.

She did not expect him to smirk. "You shan't refuse."

"Why not?" she asked, uncertainty flaring, though she'd be damned if she'd show it.

"Because if you want a divorce, you will require my assistance to get it."

Her heart began to pound. Would he give it to her? The divorce? The freedom? Could it be so simple? Excitement flared. And triumph. And something else, something she did not wish to think on. Instead, she waved an arm in an exaggerated flourish. "By all means, Your Grace. Lead the way."

They left the main hall of the House of Lords to a cacophony of distaste and judgment. In the quiet hallway beyond, Haven came even with her and said, softly, "Was it worth the embarrassment? That scene?"

"You misjudge me if you believe me embarrassed by the opinions of those men," she replied. "I've suffered them before, and will again."

"And again and again if you get what you wish."

He meant the divorce. That she would never again receive social approval. He could not see that she did not care. "You mean, *when I get it*."

He stopped at a massive door, designed to loom and impress, and opened it, revealing the extravagant suite beyond, one reserved for the handful of dukes who chose to keep space at the House of Lords. The room was expansive and overwhelming, mahogany and leather and gilt, every surface inscribed with privilege and power.

She stepped inside, unable to avoid brushing past him, hating the way the barely-there touch rioted through her. And that was before the memories came.

She'd been here before. Sneaked in, cloaked and mysterious, to see him. To surprise him. Just as she'd surprised him today.

No. That day was nothing like today. It had been the opposite of today.

That day, she'd come for love.

She ignored the thought and spun to face him, uneasy as the door closed, the quiet *snick* like a gunshot. He tore the wig from his head, tossing it to a nearby chair with enough disregard to betray his outward calm. He worked at the fastening of the heavy robes, and she found herself unable to look away from that large, sure hand, bronzed and corded with grace and strength. When his task was complete, he swung the garment from his shoulders, the wave of the deep scarlet fabric distracting her, pulling her gaze up to his, where one dark brow arched in unsettling knowledge.

When the robes hung in their place by the door, he came farther into the room. "Where have you been?"

She moved to the massive window that looked east, to where the dome of St. Paul's gleamed in the distance. Crossing her arms over her chest with affected nonchalance, she replied, "Does it matter?"

"As you ran from me, and half of London believes me guilty of some kind of nefarious plot, yes. It matters."

"They think me dead?"

"They don't say it, but I imagine so. Your sisters don't help, glowering at me whenever we cross paths."

She inhaled sharply, hating the way her chest tightened at the reference to her four younger sisters. More loves lost. "And the other half of London? What do they think?"

"Likely the same, but they don't blame me for it."

"They think I deserved it. Of course." He did not reply, but she heard the reason nonetheless. She deserved it for trapping the poor, eligible duke into marriage, and not even having the decency to deliver him an heir. Ignoring the pang of injustice that came with the thought, she said, "And here I am, very much alive. I imagine that shall set tongues wagging."

"Where did you go?" The question was soft and if she hadn't known better, Sera would have thought it was filled with something other than frustration.

Her attention fell to a row of black crows perched on the roof of the opposite wing of the building, shimmering in the August heat. She took a moment, counting them before she answered. *Seven.* "Away."

"And that is all the answer I am to receive? I—" The reply was clipped and angry, but the hesitation was the thing that drew her attention.

She turned. "You?"

For a moment, he looked as though he would say something more. Instead, he shook his head. "So. You are returned."

"Ever more troublesome, am I not?" He leaned against his great oak desk in shirtsleeves, waistcoat, and trousers, long, muscled legs crossed at the ankles, a crystal glass dangling from his fingers, as though he had not a care in the world. She ignored the way her chest tightened at the portrait he made, and raised a brow. "You do not offer your wife a drink?"

His head tilted slightly, the only evidence of his

surprise before he straightened and moved to a nearby table adorned with a decanter and three crystal glasses. She watched as he poured her two fingers of amber liquid—he moved in the same way he always had, all privilege and grace, lifting the glass and delivering it to her with an outstretched arm.

She sipped, and they stood in silence for what seemed like an eternity, until she could bear it no longer. "You should be happy with my return."

"Should I?"

She would have given everything she had to know what he was thinking. "Divorce will give you everything you ever wanted."

He drank. "How did you ever guess that I longed to be plastered across the newspapers of London?"

"You married a Talbot sister, Your Grace." Five girls, infamous in the London gossip rags that had named them the Soiled S's, daughters of the Earl of Wight, once a coal miner with a skill for finding valuable stores of the fuel—skill enough to have bought himself a title. Earldom or no, the rest of the aristocracy could not stomach the family, loathing them for their remarkable ability to climb, labeling them celebrities for celebrity's sake. The irony, of course, was that their father had worked for his money, not been born into prestige.

How backward the world was.

"My destiny, then, a Dangerous Daughter."

Sera held back the cringe at the moniker—the one she'd inherited for them all.

You trapped me.

I did.

Get out.

"Not just any," she said, refusing to bend. "The *most* dangerous."

He watched her for a moment, as though he could see her thoughts. She resisted the urge to fidget. "If you won't tell me where you went, perhaps you will tell me why you have returned?"

She drank, considering the lie she would have to tell. "Did I not make myself clear?"

"You think divorce so easily obtained?"

"I know it is not, but you would prefer . . . this?"

He did not look away, his gaze so unsettling, seeming to see so much even as it hid everything. "We would not be the first to suffer a loveless marriage."

They had not always been so loveless.

"I've suffered enough." She spread her hands wide. "And, unlike the rest of the aristocracy, I have no reason not to end our unhappy union. I have nothing to lose."

He leveled her with a look. "Everyone has something to lose."

She matched it with one of her own. "You forget, husband. I have already lost everything."

He looked away. "I don't forget." He drank, and she watched the muscles in his hand tighten and strain against the glass, a small, secret, locked-away part of her wondering at it.

That part could remain locked away. She did not care what he remembered.

She cared only that he was a powerful man, with remarkable resources, and that the dissolution of their marriage was essential to the life she had chosen for herself. The one she had built from the ashes of the life she had left. "Let me be entirely clear, Haven," she said, forcing the formality. "This is our only chance to be rid of each other. To be rid of our past." She paused. "Or did you have another plan to exorcise the demons of our marriage?"

He exhaled, heading around the desk, as though he were through with the conversation. She watched him, considering the action. Imagining what he was thinking. "Did you?"

"I did, as a matter of fact."

Surprise flared. There were only three ways to dissolve a marriage. Hers was one. The others—"Annulment is not possible," she said, hating the thread of sadness that threatened at the words. At the idea that he might have pushed for it. There had been a—

There had been a child.

He met her gaze then. "Not annulment."

"Then you were intending to have me declared dead." It had occurred to her, of course. At night, when she thought about the possibility that he might desire an heir. That he might have changed his mind. That he might have decided another woman and another family were desirable.

There was only one way to clear the path to a new heir. With the exception of the fact that she was not dead. And one other minor issue.

"Four years hence?" The law required seven to have passed before a person could be declared dead. He looked away. "Ah. But you've the funds and the power to circumvent a little thing like the passage of time, don't you, Duke?"

His gaze narrowed. "You say that as though you do not plan to use those same funds to convince Parliament to grant us a divorce—something so exorbitantly costly that there have been, what, two hundred and fifty authorized? Ever? In history?"

"Three hundred and fourteen," Sera answered. "And at least at the end of my plan we are both alive. Was I to die soon? Am I lucky I arrived before the summer recess and not after it? When Parliament returns from summer idyll, rested and ready to disappear one duchess and make room for another?"

"It no longer matters, does it?" he said, the words calm enough to tempt her to rage.

It shouldn't have. She had one goal. The Singing Sparrow, her tavern. And with it funds, freedom, and future. None of which was hers until he cut her reins.

"So get to it, Sera. What is the reason for the dissolution of our once legendary union? There are limited arguments for divorce. What, then? Shall you tell my colleagues that I was intolerably cruel? Declare to all London that I am a lunatic? Perhaps you were forced to marry me? No," he scoffed. "Everyone knows you came quite willingly. Fairly tripping down the aisle to shackle yourself to me."

"What a silly girl I was," she snapped. "That was before I knew the truth."

His gaze narrowed. "And what truth is that?"

That you never wanted me. That you cared more for your title than for your future. That we would never be more than a passing, fleeting moment. That you wouldn't care when our family became an impossibility.

"It is no matter."

"I never lied," he said.

It was an echo of years earlier. *You lied.* She could still hear the words, as though he'd said them yesterday instead of three years ago, when he'd refused to listen. When he refused to believe.

Because she hadn't lied. Not when it was important. She raised her chin, defiant and defensive. "In this, *husband*, you do forget."

He set the weighted tumbler to his desk with an ominous thud, punctuating his movement as he came to her, a muscle twitching in his cheek the only indication of his irritation.

Sera willed her breath steady, her heart calm. She'd intended to infuriate him. She'd wanted to set him on edge. To make him wish her gone. To give her what she wanted. To set her free. She'd planned to be here. Planned to irritate. To leave him for the summer with the sourest of tastes.

She simply had not expected to be so trapped by the memory of him.

"I don't forget it, Seraphina. Not a moment of it. And neither do you." He drew closer, and she could not stop the step she took backward, toward the windowsill overlooking all London—the city that bowed to him as she once had. She took a deep breath, refusing to let him intimidate her.

And he did not intimidate. He did something much worse.

He reached for her, his fingers playing gently down the column of her neck, barely there, a whisper that she should have been able to ignore. "You think I do not remember you well enough to see it? You think I did not see the memories assault you when you stepped through that door? Into this room? You think I did not recall those same memories? The last time you were here? In this room?"

She swallowed, disliking the way he closed in upon her. "I don't recall ever being here."

"Lie to the rest of the world, Sera," he said, his fingers teasing over her shoulders. *She would not pull away. Would not let him win.* "Lie to me, even. About your past and your plans for the future. About where you have been and where you plan to go. But do not ever, ever imagine that I do not know the truth of your memories."

His touch reversed itself, returning to her neck, this time finding purchase, fingers curling warm and sure, his thumb stroking strong and familiar across her jaw, tilting her face up to his.

Marking her with the past.

With his words, soft as silk. "Do not ever, ever imagine that I do not know that you watched me remove those robes thinking all the while of the thickness of them. Of the softness of them against your skin. Of the way you once lay bare on them on this very floor. Of the way I lay there with you."

He was so close now, close enough to feel, to smell—leather and earth, as though he'd come in from the fields instead of the Houses of Parliament—intoxicating in his nearness even as his words stung.

Even as she told herself she did not care.

"I remember, Sera. I remember the taste of you, like sunshine and peace. I remember the feel of you, heat and silk. I remember the way you gasped, stealing my breath for yourself. Stealing me. The way you offered yourself as a prize. Making me believe in you. In us. Before I fell and you triumphed."

The insinuation that she had ruined them and what they might have had should not have surprised her, and still it did, moving her to find her words and strike her own blow. "It was never triumph. It was the worst mistake of my life."

Her aim was true. He released her. *Thank heavens.* "You received your title, did you not? And your sisters, the purchase they required to scale the walls of the aristocracy. And your mother, the voice to crow her triumph to the world. Her eldest trapped a duke."

Only because I never wanted anything like I wanted you.

She shook her head, hating him for being so close.

Hating herself for wanting him even as she wanted nothing to do with him. "I no longer want it."

He drew nearer, his eyes locked upon her, forcing her to tip her head back to remain his equal. "You should have considered that before you took it." Closer still, until she could feel the soft warmth of his breath on her skin. On her lips. "You think you have not ruined this place for me? This place that is for men of purpose? For history? For order? You think I am not in constant reminder of you? Of the future we might have had?"

It was a lie, of course. He didn't think of their future. If he thought of her at all, it was in anger and nothing else. But even now he toyed with her, searching for emotion. She'd always been his toy. Never his equal. She shook her head, refusing to be swayed by him. Refusing to be deterred from her goal.

"Enough," she said. "It's ancient past."

He gave a little laugh at that, devoid of humor. "Past is prologue, Angel. *I think of it every day.*"

Sera's lips parted on a silent gasp. He was close enough to kiss her, and suddenly she could remember, too. The feel of him. The taste of him. The way he had made her ache with want.

Except she was no longer that silly, stupid girl. She placed her hands flat against his chest, the strong, muscled ridges beneath his shirt stiffening at the movement, rippling as she traced them to his shoulders, her fingers teasing at the warm skin of his neck, tempting him.

He leaned in barely, nearly undetectable. Detected, nonetheless. Sera sensed victory. Her own whisper echoed in the room. "Your memory fails you if you think I have wreaked such havoc alone, husband. There were two of us on those robes. Two of us at Highley the day I trapped you. Two of us in London the day I begged you to release me—the day you swore you would take your vengeance for my sins by refusing me the only thing I ever wanted." She was proud of the steel in her words. Of how she could speak without her voice cracking. Without summoning memory of the child she'd lost, and the hope she'd lost in the same instant.

Proud enough to stand in her purpose and drive her point home. "But perhaps you do not recall the specifics as well as you think. Surely, it is difficult to remember all the times with me, as there have been so many other women since."

She reveled in his response, the way his head snapped up, his eyes—those beautiful, mysterious eyes—finding hers. He watched her, his anger clear, and she waited for his next move. Ached for it, even as she hated herself for doing so.

It had always been like this. Intense and evenly matched. Tempting beyond measure, even when it hurt.

"And so we get to it. Adultery." He rubbed a hand along the back of his neck as he looked away, exhaling on a soft laugh. "Unfortunately, this is London in 1836, and while you might think yourself a veritable Boadicea, wife, the law does not. My actions beyond our bedchambers are not grounds for divorce. You shall have to keep searching."

She picked at an invisible speck on her sleeve, affecting boredom. "Never fear, Duke. There is always impotence."

His lips flattened into a thin, straight line as Sera pushed past him, toward the door to the chamber, her heart pounding from his proximity, from memory and panic and something else she did not care to name. She released the breath she had been holding in a long, slow exhale as she reached for the door handle.

She turned back to find that he was now staring out the window, across the rooftops of London, the golden, liquid sunlight gleaming around him like a halo, marking his broad shoulders, his straight spine, his strong arms and narrow hips. She hated herself for noticing any of it. For remembering the feel of it. The warmth of him.

"Malcolm," she said, the handle already turning in her grasp. He stilled at the use of his given name, but did not look to her, not even when she said, proud and clear, "I feel I should point out that, while a husband's infidelities may not be grounds for divorce, a *wife's* are quite a different thing altogether."

And with her closing salvo, the Duchess of Haven left the Houses of Parliament, scandal in her wake.

Scandal, and a husband so irate, she imagined her divorce would come swift and without hesitation.

Chapter 4

SO-FINE SERAPHINA!
DOE-EYED DUKE MEETS HIS MATCH

March 1, 1833
Three years, five months, and two weeks earlier
Mayfair, London

"*S*urely there is nothing in the wide world worse than the first ball of the season." Haven pushed his way onto a small balcony at Worthington House, grateful for the cold, crisp March air, a welcome respite from the cloying heat and stench of the rooms inside, packed with more aristocrats than he could have imagined—all desperate to resume city life after months in the country, consumed with boredom.

"It's not so very bad," the Marquess of Mayweather replied, closing the door behind him.

Haven cut his friend a skeptical look. "It's impossible to move for all the debutantes and matchmakers within. They're slavering after us, as though we are meat."

Mayweather smirked. "There are, what, a half-dozen titles up for grabs this season? That is, young and able-bodied titles. A marquess and a duke on the cusp of middle age are prime cuts, Haven."

"Thirty isn't middle age."

The marquess moved to the balcony balustrade, setting his drink there and looking out over the extensive back gardens of Worthington House. "It's old enough for marriage to be on our minds."

Half the men of the aristocracy waited until their thirties to marry. Many until their late thirties. Haven wasn't a fool—he knew his bachelorhood was on borrowed time. He'd require a marriage and an heir soon enough, but Lord knew he wasn't interested in balls and long walks through Hyde Park to find it.

The idea was ridiculous. How many times had Haven heard Mayweather himself claim that heirs could be whelped any time? Unless . . .

"Christ," Haven said softly in the darkness. "You're caught." Was that a *blush*? "Someone has her pretty hooks in you."

The marquess looked away. "You needn't make it sound so mercenary."

"You said yourself that our titles make us meat."

"She doesn't think of it that way."

Haven would wager everything he had that the woman did just that. He raised a brow. "No, I'm sure not. I'm sure yours is a proper love match."

Mayweather scowled. "You needn't make it sound so improbable."

Not improbable. Impossible. Perhaps it was reasonable for others to assume their wives came to them with feeling. With desire. With more. But if that were true at all, it was for luckier men. For men born beyond the yoke of title and fortune and responsibility. Hackney drivers and street sweepers and sailors could marry for passion and even love. But men such as he and Mayweather? Dukes and marquesses, young and rich and titled? There was no such thing as love.

There was only duty, which required marriage, but if Haven knew anything, it was this: that men must enter marriage eyes wide open, aware of the disappointment the institution would no doubt set upon them.

Malcolm, Duke of Haven, knew it without doubt, as he was the product of that disappointment. How many times had his father looked past him, failure and something worse in his gaze? Not regret, though that was there as well. Something like loathing, as though he'd happily erase his son from time and space if it would give him back the life he'd once had. Haven had always imagined his father had been grateful when death came, and with it, freedom from the horrid reality with which he'd been saddled.

And then there had been the woman with whom the duke had been saddled. Haven's mother. Born without title or fortune, climbed to the highest rank in the land. Duchess. And the way she looked at her son, cool and aloof, with a hint of pride—not for the child she'd borne or the way he'd grown, but for her great deception, her legendary triumph. The title she'd thieved.

So, no. Haven knew his own life too well to believe that others might have it differently. And he faced his future knowing that if one expected disappointment, one could not be disappointed.

He approached his friend, putting his back to the balustrade and watching the golden light in the building beyond. "I'm simply saying that love is a great fallacy," he said. "Women are after certainty and comfort and nothing else. And if one is chasing after you, she is after your title, friend. Do not doubt it."

Mayweather turned to look at him. "It's true what they say about you, you know."

"What's that?"

"You're a coldhearted bastard."

Haven nodded and drank deep. "It doesn't make me wrong."

"No, but it does make you an ass." The words came from the dark stone staircase leading down to the gardens, clear and certain, as though the woman who spoke them made a practice of lying in wait for aristocratic men to say something for which she might chastise them.

Mayweather couldn't contain his surprised laugh. "From darkness, truth."

She replied to the Marquess. "If one of my friends said such things to me, my lord, I should make myself another friend. One with better manners."

Mayweather smirked at Haven. "It's not a terrible idea."

Haven squinted into the shadows, barely able to make out the female form there, paused halfway up the stairs, leaning against the exterior of the house. How long had she been listening? "Considering you're skulking about and eavesdropping on conversations to which you are not invited, I'm not sure your assessment of the state of my manners can be trusted."

"I wasn't eavesdropping."

"No?"

"No. I was listening. And I wasn't skulking. I was standing. The fact that you selected this precise moment to take refuge and deliver your—unsolicited, I might add—lecture on the wickedness of woman is a matter of my own terrible luck. I assure you, sir, I am witness to enough maligning of the female half of the population by virtue of being a living human. I did not need to eavesdrop for it."

Haven had to work to keep his jaw from dropping. When was the last time a woman had spoken to him like this? When was the last time *anyone* had spoken to him like this?

Mayweather laughed. "Whoever you are, you've rendered him speechless. And I'll be the first to say I thought that was an impossibility."

"A pity," she drawled from the shadows. "I had hoped he would continue his edifying dissertation: *Mercenary Manipulators, A Meditation on the Role of Women in the World*. It's positively Wollstonecraftian."

Finally, Haven found his tongue. "The men of London would be better off if they paid closer attention to my views on this particular issue."

"No doubt that's true," she teased, and he found he liked the warmth that flooded him at her words. "Do tell, good sir, how is it that you are such an expert on women's—what did you call them—pretty hooks?"

For a moment, he considered the idea of this woman's pretty hooks . . . of nails on skin. Teeth on lips. He pushed the thoughts away. He had not even seen her. He had no need of fantasy for a woman in the darkness. He shot his most disdainful look in her direction. "Experience."

She laughed, the sound licking over him like sin. He straightened. Who was she? "You are so very desired, are you? That you can spot a title thief at thirty paces?"

She moved as she spoke, ascending the steps. Coming closer. She wasn't near thirty paces away. She was ten paces away at best. Five, if he lengthened his stride.

His heart raced.

And that was before she stepped into the light, gleaming like a damn goddess.

He came off the balustrade without thinking, like a slavering dog on a lead. He did not recognize her, which seemed impossible, as she was dark-haired and pale-skinned, with eyes like sapphires. It was difficult to believe a woman this perfect—and this smart-mouthed—would go beneath Society's notice.

The mystery female hovered there, in the golden pool of candlelight, her gaze falling on Mayweather, making Haven wish his friend gone.

Making him jealous as hell.

"My lord, if I may, you should not listen to your callous friend. If the lady says she cares for you, believe her."

Mayweather forgot his brandy on the edge of the balcony and moved toward her. "She does say so."

"And do you care for her?"

"I do," he said, so earnestly, Haven wondered if his friend had ingested something poisonous.

She nodded with conviction. "Well then. Love is all that is required." And then she smiled, and Haven had trouble breathing.

Mayweather did not seem to have the same trouble with breath. Instead, he exhaled, long and dramatic and ridiculous. "That's what they say."

"Not everyone. Your friend believes that all women are in the market to steal a title."

Mayweather smirked. "He does have a particularly desirable title."

That cerulean gaze fell to Haven, curious and lacking in recognition, and so honest that it seemed as though he had been seen for the first time. "Does he? Well, then it shall be a lucky young fisherwoman who hooks him so prettily."

With that, she turned her back on him, as though he did not exist, and made her way for the door, as though she did not care a bit about him. As though she did not recognize him.

It was impossible, of course. It was some kind of

game that she was playing, to tempt him. And despite knowing it, he found himself tempted nonetheless. "I'm to believe you don't know me?"

She stilled and turned back, humor underscoring her words, setting him off-balance. "At the risk of sounding rude, my lord, I don't particularly care what you believe. As we've never met, I don't know how I would know you."

Mayweather barked a laugh, and Haven had the distinct urge to push his friend right over the balcony into the hedge below. "She has you there."

She did not *have* him. He was not to be had. "Your Grace," he said.

She blinked. "I beg your pardon?"

"You called me 'my lord.' It's 'Your Grace.'"

She smirked. "How did you know how thoroughly women adore being corrected by men? And over forms of address, especially. It is a great wonder that none of us have ever fallen in love with you." She dropped a little curtsy, the movement making him feel like a horse's ass. "Farewell, gentlemen."

And still, he could not stop himself. "Wait."

She turned back, beautiful and poised. "Be careful, *Duke*; I'll begin to think you're the one trying to get your pretty hooks in *me*."

The idea was preposterous. Wasn't it? "Your friends."

She raised her brows. "What of them?"

"You've never discussed me with them?" Was it honestly possible she had no idea who he was?

Her lips twitched with amusement. She was making a fool of him. No, he was making one of himself. For her. Like an imbecile. "I don't have friends; I have sisters. And I remain unclear on why they should know or care about you?"

Mayweather snorted at that, clearly enjoying watching him make a fool of himself. And still, Haven couldn't seem to stop it. He spread his arms wide. "I'm Haven."

She did laugh then. "Well, you certainly have a high opinion of yourself, Heaven."

Mayweather laughed and Malcolm became annoyed. "*Haven*. As in, Duke of."

There wasn't an ounce of recognition in her reply. "Fair enough. Then I take it all back. No doubt as a young and fairly handsome male specimen who happens to hold what sounds a proper title, you must be careful. The women, they must positively *flock*."

There. She finally understood. *Wait*. He blinked. *Fairly handsome?*

Who was she? Aside from being the single most maddening woman in all of Christendom, that was. She had turned her attention to Mayweather once more, dismissing Malcolm. "Good night, my lord. And may I say good luck?"

The marquess bowed low. "Thank you, Miss . . ." He trailed off, and it occurred to Haven that Mayweather was not so bad after all—if he discovered the girl's name, that was.

A grin spread wide and welcome across her face, and Malcolm felt the heat of it like the sun. "What a shock. It seems that *you* don't know who *I* am, either."

He blinked. "Should we?"

"No," she retorted, "I'm not *heaven*, after all . . ." Except she damn well seemed like heaven. But she was turning the door handle. She was leaving him.

"Stop!" he said, loathing the desperation in his voice. He could practically hear Mayweather's head snap around to stare at him, and suddenly, Haven didn't care a bit. Because she'd stopped, and that was all that mattered. "You can't leave without telling us who you are."

Her gaze glittered in the candlelight. "Oh, I think I can."

"You're wrong," he insisted. "How else will sad-sack Mayweather find you if everything goes pear-shaped with Heloise?"

"Helen," Mayweather interjected.

Haven waved a hand. "Right. She sounds lovely. Far too good for this imbecile. He's going to need your advice if he's to keep her."

"I beg your pardon!" the marquess protested, but it didn't matter. Because the woman laughed, bright and bold and beautiful, and all Malcolm wanted to do was to bask in the sound. In the warmth of it.

Instead, he offered her his most charming smile and said, "We shall begin anew. I'm Malcolm."

For the life of him he had no idea why he thought it necessary to offer his given name, which no one had used in twenty years.

Her brows rose. "I don't know why you should think I care about your given name, Your Grace, as I am female, and therefore already in possession of all relevant information pertaining to you." She switched into an awed whisper. "*You're a duke.*"

The teasing was back, and he loved it. She was remarkable. "Nevertheless, it is customary for women to introduce themselves to the men they intend to land."

She tilted her head. "I admit, I have not always moved in such high circles, but I am fairly certain that it is not at all customary for a woman to introduce herself to two strange men on an abandoned balcony."

"Not strange at all," he said. "Well, maybe Mayweather is. What with his obsession with Hester."

"Helen!" Mayweather interjected, drawing another small smile from the beauty.

"It seems we have an equal disinterest in given names," she said.

"If you wish it, I shall remember everything about her," he replied. "Mayweather, tell me something else about your Helen."

"She has cats."

He turned to his friend. "In the plural?"

Mayweather nodded. "Six of them."

"Good God. I don't imagine I shall forget that."

"I like cats," the angel said. "I find them intelligent and comforting."

Mayweather smiled. "As does Helen."

She matched his friend's expression. "She sounds lovely."

"She is. In fact—"

No. No more Helen. "In fact, you should go to her and tell her so," Haven interrupted, grasping at the music that drifted from the ballroom to the private balcony. Clinging to it. "And dance with her. Women like dancing." The angel's brows rose in amusement as he insisted. "Go, Mayweather."

For the first time in his life, the Marquess of Mayweather understood subtext. And he left the two of them alone, finally. Cloaked in darkness and chill, and somehow she made him warm as the sun.

Haven moved toward her. Wanting nothing but to be close to her. "Are you cold?" He let his voice go low, wanting to tempt her as she'd tempted him. Wanting her to desire him as he desired her.

But mostly, wanting her to stay.

She swallowed, and he could see the movement in her throat, his mouth watering with desire to press his lips there, to feel if her pulse raced as his did. To taste her skin, salty and sweet. When he raised his gaze to hers, he could see that she might allow it. That she was not unmoved. "It is time for my departure," she whispered.

The idea that she would leave, that he might never see her again, that he might never know her . . . it did things to him that he did not appreciate. So, instead, he said softly, "Do you?"

She tilted her head. "Do I like dancing?"

"Yes."

"I do, as a matter of fact."

"Would you like to? With me?"

Perfect white teeth flashed. Of course her teeth were perfect. Everything about her was perfect. "We can't dance. We haven't been introduced."

"Then dance with me here. In secret."

"No."

It was a game. He could feel it in his chest, the breathlessness of it. "Why?"

"It could ruin me. If we were found."

He stepped closer, close enough that he could pull her into his arms. "I would never ruin you."

It should have been a flirt. An empty, teasing trifle. Something men said to women to lure them into danger. But it wasn't. It was a promise. And more than that, it was the truth. He would never ruin her. It wouldn't be ruin when he married her.

He stilled. *Christ.* He would marry her.

He was going to marry this woman.

The realization should have filled him with terror. Not ten minutes earlier, he had decried the entire institution of marriage, suggesting that all women were gamesters and all men who thought otherwise lacked sense. But now, he was not filled with terror. He was filled with something entirely different. Something like joy. Like *hope.*

And, in the wake of *that* realization, he did pull her into his arms, this woman whose name he still did not know. She gasped, and he basked in the pleasure of the sound, which matched his own as he discovered what it was to hold the woman for whom he was destined.

They began to move to the music, quiet and distant, cloaking them in privacy. "I recall refusing to dance, Duke."

"Malcolm," he said, soft at her ear, loving her shiver at his name. "Tell me again, now that you're in my arms. Now that I'm in yours. And I'll stop."

He wasn't sure how, but he would.

She sighed, her lips curving into a little, lovely smile. "You're very difficult."

He could live in that smile. "I've been told that."

"I thought aristocrats were supposed to be accommodating."

"Not dukes. Haven't you heard that we're the worst of the lot?"

"And they let anyone become a duke nowadays, do they?"

He turned her toward the light, revealing her beautiful face. "If you think dukes are bad, Angel, imagine what they accept from duchesses?"

Her eyes went wide at the words, her lips pulling into a smile, full and lovely, all secrets and sin. "Imagine indeed." And he couldn't stop himself. He didn't wish to. He was going to marry her, after all. They would spend a lifetime kissing, so why not begin now? *Just a taste.*

She sighed as he closed the distance, and he heard his thoughts on her lips. "Just a taste."

She was perfect.

He set his lips to hers, fire spreading through him as she caught her breath, then sighed, low and sweet, as he gently licked over that full bottom lip, soft and sweet enough to make him ache. "Just a taste," he promised himself. Her. "Open for me, love."

And she did, letting him in, her lips soft and her mouth warm and welcome, tongue meeting his, tasting, tempting, teasing perfectly, as though they were meant for this. As though they had lived their whole lives to meet here, on this dark balcony, and set each other aflame.

There was nothing tentative in this beautiful woman, nothing timid or small. She was wild and passionate, and when she came to her toes, one gloved hand snaking up and around the back of his neck, reaching, pulling him down, pressing closer, offering herself to him, he recognized that it was not she who was ruined.

It was he.

He lifted his lips at the thought, turning her face to the light, looking down at her closed eyes, at her parted lips, the flush on her cheeks that spread lower, over the pale rise of her breasts. She was a portrait of pleasure.

Her dark lashes lifted, and what he saw there, mixed with desire and surprise, was his future. His wife.

Chapter 5

SERAPHINA SURFACES
ARMED WITH AMERICAN!

August 22, 1836
The Singing Sparrow
Covent Garden

"*So*, to be clear, you told him you were having an affair."

Sera set the box of tapered candles down and looked to the American leaning on the bar of The Singing Sparrow, Covent Garden's newest tavern. She'd discovered Caleb Calhoun in a similar tavern in Boston, Massachusetts, half a day after her ship from London had made port.

She'd been in search of real, warm food—something better than the cured meat and pickled veg that had played the role of sustenance during the month-long transatlantic journey—and she'd been pointed in the direction of The Bell in Hand tavern, three doors down from the rooms she'd let while she considered her next move.

The American had come off his chair when she'd entered, looming large alongside a handful of other, less imposing and more dangerous characters, making himself her protector that day. And the next. And the next.

And soon, he wasn't simply an American, but her employer. Then, her business partner. And then, the dearest friend she'd ever had. Soon, the only person in the world who knew everything about her, and the only one who demanded nothing of her.

That he was also the only one who kept her honest was one of his lesser points at this particular moment. Nevertheless, she soldiered on. "I did not tell him that."

Sera did not like the way Caleb leveled her with a frank green gaze, as though it were a perfectly simple question and she'd provided an unacceptable answer. "I didn't!" she insisted. "Not really."

"Not really," Caleb repeated. "Sera, I don't like the idea of being murdered by some aristocrat without warning."

"Do you think many people enjoy the idea of their own murder?"

He cut her a look—one she imagined brothers reserved for their most insufferable sisters. "There are days when I am not opposed to the idea of yours. Particularly if your lovelorn duke is coming after me."

"I assure you. He is not lovelorn." He'd looked the very opposite three days earlier. He'd looked positively unmoved that she'd turned up.

Caleb grunted.

Sera ignored the tacit disagreement. "It's not as though I named a man and provided physical description. I simply suggested that if he wished to divorce me on the grounds of adultery, I would not be opposed to such a solution."

"That's the kind of semantic argument an English-woman would use."

She cut him a look. "I *am* an Englishwoman."

"No one ever said you couldn't try a bit harder to throw off the yoke, darlin'."

"Please. Everyone knows that half the divorces granted by Parliament are done so after husbands and wives collude. I am more than happy to play the adulteress if it will help get me this place."

Which it would. The moment the marriage was dissolved, The Singing Sparrow was hers, and she could begin anew. Without the past and the ghosts of it that haunted her.

"All they have to do is see you slinging a drink or two, and they'll all believe you're properly fallen," Caleb replied.

"A girl can dream." She toasted him and drank. "I'm not a very good duchess, am I?"

"I don't know much about duchesses, but what I can tell you is that you're nothing like you were when you wandered in off the street like a lost lamb, so there's hope for you yet," he allowed, crossing his arms over his wide chest. "But returning to the topic at hand, you implied we were having an affair."

"I did not. I simply stated a fact. If he *inferred* such a thing . . ."

Caleb laughed. "Then he simply did what you'd intended. And when he discovers who landed on the docks beside you . . . I'm at the receiving end of the duke's wrath. And then we shall have to fight. And then—" He waved a hand dramatically. "We shall have no choice but to be at war again."

"You do realize that you are not an ambassador of any kind, do you not?" Sera lifted the box of candles and weaved between the tables scattered throughout the empty tavern, straightening the chairs. "I can't be responsible for what the man thinks, Caleb," she said, the words loud enough to travel through the empty room. "But I can say that I don't imagine he'll care enough about my actions in the last three years to be much trouble."

Caleb gave a little disbelieving snort. "That's bullshit and you know it."

Sera ignored the coarse language. "If he is angry, it will have nothing to do with you, and everything to do with how I've ruined his precious legacy. Again. I wouldn't worry about your face. Which isn't really that handsome," she teased. "No one likes a broken nose."

"Every woman likes a broken nose, kitten. And besides, I can take any toff who comes my way." Sera smiled at the words, and at the description of her husband, who, despite being the most aristocratic man she'd ever known, was decidedly un-tofflike. Caleb continued as she ascended the steps to the little stage at the far end of the room. "In fact, I look forward to seeing the bastard. I'd like to teach him a lesson."

Sera reached up to remove the stubs of beeswax candles in one of the enormous candelabra flanking it. "Unfortunately, Mr. Calhoun, I highly doubt you'll have a chance to meet him."

"He'll come looking for you."

"Care to wager?" she teased. "Fifty dollars says he's left town with the rest of London, and I shall have to seek him out to get my tavern."

"I think you mean the rest of London's spoiled, moneyed set." Caleb opened a small, secret compartment in the bar and lifted out a box of tobacco and papers, making a show of rolling a cheroot. "The lords of the manor head home to check on their serfs?"

Sera laughed softly. "Something like that. Though

escaping the stench of London is likely a more accurate description of what's happened."

"Bah," Caleb scoffed. "The stink of a city is how you know it is alive."

She headed for the matching candelabra on the opposite side of the stage, replacing candlesticks with precision. "You would make a terrible member of the aristocracy."

His laugh boomed through the room. "I've no doubt of that, love. You've got yourself a bet. Fifty dollars says your man walks through that door by week's end."

She didn't like the certainty in her friend's voice. As though he'd already won the bet. And she liked his next point even less. "Either way, Duchess, it's time we get to work, don't you think? You need that man to agree, and you need this place to be the best Covent Garden has ever seen, so the moment it is yours, it is legend. So, how do you get his agreement?"

She'd have to see him again, even if she didn't want to. Even if she didn't want to face him, handsome as ever and somehow entirely changed.

Caleb added, "We've been here for seven weeks and I'm already itching to get back on American soil."

She looked up, squinting into the darkness. "You could go, you know. You don't have to . . ."

She trailed off, not knowing how to finish. Caleb had done so much. He'd protected her when he found her, broken and alone in a city—a country—a continent— she'd never known. And he'd helped her find her feet again. Her strength. He'd given her reason to smile again. And then he'd given her purpose. And when she'd decided it was time for her to return to England and begin anew, he'd packed his bags without hesitation.

Sera shook her head and repeated herself. "You don't have to."

He lit the cheroot, and the orange tip glowed in the dimly lit space. "And yet, here I am. A remarkable man, don't you think?"

She raised a brow. "A model of modesty, most certainly."

"So. When do we serve your idiot husband his ass?"

She laughed at the words, spoken with unadulterated glee. "I feel that you might not get that opportunity."

"You don't think he'll give you the divorce?" She could see his wide, furrowed brow even from a distance. "Then you return with me, and start fresh in Boston."

If only it were so easy. If only she'd been connected to the city across the sea—bustling with new victory and the promise of a young country. She'd come to love Boston for its hope and its people and Caleb. But it had never been London.

It had never felt like home.

She picked at the round, heavy candle stub in her hand, extracting the wick and rolling it between thumb and forefinger, watching the black char mark her skin. "He'll give me the divorce," she said, knowing that Malcolm likely wanted nothing more than to be rid of her. "But I imagine he'll do so with a fair amount of punishment."

Caleb came off the bar then, moving toward her, broad shoulders and wide jaw that marked his rough, colonial upbringing long before he opened his mouth and revealed his uncultured accent. He was an animal in a cage here, in this world governed by rules he found at best inane and at worst unconscionable.

"You don't deserve his punishment."

She raised a brow. "I left him, Caleb."

"He left you first."

She smiled at that. "Not in any way that mattered."

"In *every* way that mattered," he scoffed.

She sighed. "Duchesses don't leave," she explained for the dozenth time. The hundredth. "Certainly not without providing an heir."

Not even when an heir was impossible.

"They should do when their husband has exiled them," he replied. "Remaining is bollocks."

"No, it's British."

He cursed round and vicious. "Yet another reason you lot deserved the ass-kicking we gave you."

"You should find passage on the next ship out. You've a life to return to." She tried for humor. "You're not getting any younger, friend. It's time to find a woman who will put up with you."

"As though that will ever happen." Of course, it would. Caleb Calhoun was one of the most charming men Seraphina had ever known. He stopped at the edge of the stage, looking up at her, his green eyes serious. "I keep my promises, Dove. I'll see you through the divorce. I'll see this place successful and yours. And then I'll leave, and happily accept my monthly proceeds."

She grinned. "I shall sleep well knowing that my money will come as a comfort."

"*Our* money, partner."

Within a month of meeting, Sera and Caleb had purchased another Boston pub, and another and another. Between his instinct for location and hers for what made a tavern impossible to leave, they'd put several of Boston's longest-standing establishments out of business before deciding that London would be their next conquest.

They'd purchased the pub within forty-eight hours of disembarking on the banks of the Thames, after setting their sights on Covent Garden—a neighborhood dominated by a pair of brothers and chock full of low, dark taverns said to host a floating underground fighting ring. Though Sera and Caleb had no interest in competing with a fight club, they did see opportunity for a proper pub in the area. Something like the pubs that were taking Boston and New York by storm. Something with entertainment.

The Singing Sparrow was the obvious answer. An equal partnership between the two, or as equal as one could be while Sera was married. Which was to say, it was an equal partnership between Caleb and Sera's husband, though the Duke of Haven was blissfully ignorant of this particular holding. Under British law, however, married women could not own property or business. Their husbands owned everything . . . including them.

Divorce was the only way Sera would ever own this business—the only thing she'd cared about in nearly three years, and the key to her self-sufficiency. To her freedom.

The only way she'd ever take back the life he'd stolen from her.

The life he'd chased her from.

Get out.

Tears came, unbidden. Unwanted. How many times had she remembered his words—the cruel disavowal in them, the aloof disdain, as though she were nothing to him—and drawn strength from them?

How often had she vowed to claim her future even as he owned her past?

And somehow, a half an hour with him erased all the strength she'd worked to build. She took a deep breath and looked away, into a dark corner of the pub. "I'll be damned if he'll make me weak again."

Caleb did not hesitate. He never did. It was a failing of his being American. "He can only make you weak if you allow it." Her gaze snapped to his. "You stand strong and remember why you're here. And if he punishes you, you punish him right back. But I'll tell you one thing, if he's all you've described, he's going to give you a fight for the divorce."

For all he knew about her past, he had never witnessed it. She shook her head. "He hates me." The words were honest and real—words she'd clung to every time she'd doubted herself in the last three years. Which was often.

"That doesn't mean he doesn't want you."

Memory flashed, Malcolm's fingers running over her skin earlier in the week, the shiver of anticipation that came with the touch, the way Sera had ached to lean into it. To the memory of it. To the way those fingers had once made her sing.

To the way they had made her feel for the first time in years.

Not that she was interested in feeling.

And besides, "Want isn't worth the trouble."

"God knows that's true," Caleb said, dry as sand. "But no one has ever said men cared for the truth." Though he hid it well, Caleb nursed his own broken heart. A lost love, never to be regained. "I don't know much, darlin', but I know that you deserve better than whatever that dandy aristocrat could have given you."

What a good man Caleb was. Decent and proud and with a heart bigger than any she'd ever known. She sighed. "Why couldn't it have been you?"

He shrugged a shoulder and took another long puff at his cheroot. "Timing."

She smiled. "If only you'd been here three years ago."

He gave a little laugh. "I could've used you there five years ago."

Sera reached for her friend's face, placing her hand on his strong, stubbled cheek, tilting his chin up until his gaze met hers. "If you could erase it—all of it—all of her—would you?"

He did not hesitate. "Hell yes. You?"

His hand came to cover hers at his cheek as she let herself consider the question. She'd lost so much. Her love, her life, the promise of her future. So much loss that her heart ached even at the hint of the thought of it.

If she could take it back, she would. Without doubt.

Caleb saw the answer in her eyes, and squeezed her hand in camaraderie. He lifted his chin in the direction of the center of the raised platform. "Show me how it feels up there, Sparrow."

She turned in a slow circle on the stage, trying to put the events of the last day from her mind, wanting to lose herself here. "I am not painted." She never sang without her disguise—even in Covent Garden, someone might recognize a Dangerous Daughter.

"There's no audience."

"Another reason not to sing."

"Pah," he said. "You don't need an audience."

She smiled. "It helps."

"Sing for me, then."

"I've an excellent one for you, as a matter of fact." She placed one fisted hand on her waist and listing to the side, belted out a raucous verse from a song she'd learned from the sailors on the ship that had returned her to London. *"Let every man here drink up his full bumper. Let every man here drink up his full glass."*

She stopped, but Caleb didn't laugh. Instead, he waited, arms crossed, for her to finish. She straightened. *"And let us be jolly and drown melancholy, drink a health to each beautiful, true-hearted lass."*

He nodded. "You shall own London's hearts in mere weeks. What else have you got?"

She hadn't planned to sing. Not honestly. Not from her heart. But she did then, sliding from the shanty into another, less playful melody, slower, filled with the melancholy she'd just vowed to drown. *"Oft in the stilly night, ere slumber's chain has bound me, fond memory brings the light of other days around me."*

The song was Caleb's favorite and one of hers, as well—a tribute to memory and childhood and love and loss. And when she sang it, it was always about the life she might have had, if only things were different. The life she allowed herself to consider only in slumber.

There were few places better than an empty, dark tavern to sing, the notes clear in the silence, unhindered by clinking glasses and wild chatter and scraping chairs, the melody finding purchase in the dark corners of the room, fading to whispers, making memories in the walls to be recalled by strangers.

She closed her eyes and let herself fill the room. And for a few, short moments, the Sparrow was free.

Caleb did not applaud when she finished. He simply waited for her to return to the moment, and then he said, "The bastards who spout shit about it being better to have loved and lost have either never loved or never lost."

She laughed at the crass words and came toward him. "Shall we drink to that?"

"With pleasure." He dropped his hands to her waist and lifted her from the stage.

Her feet had barely touched the floor when the main door to the tavern opened, letting in a flood of late-afternoon sunlight. Caleb's gaze flickered past her to the imposing figure in the doorway. "You owe me fifty dollars, Duchess."

She caught her breath as the looming shadow growled, "Get your hands off my wife."

Chapter 6

―――――――― ⌇ ――――――――

CALHOUN CLOCKED; TORY TOFF
TOSSED FROM TAVERN

January 1835
One year, seven months earlier
Boston, Massachusetts

The Duke of Haven had barely found his footing on American soil before he was headed for the line of taverns overlooking the wharf. Salt and cold hung in the night air, clinging to the uncomfortable wool of his greatcoat, heavy and full of the lingering smell of weeks at sea.

There was a time when he would have made straight for an inn after interminable nights aboard a frigate in an uncomfortable berth, unable to find sleep or an inch of dry air, his nights spent pacing the deck of the ship, staring at endless black sea and sky made star-bright with the bitter cold.

There was a time when he would have left the ship and gone instantly in search of a warm bath, fire, and bed.

But that was before he searched for her.

Before he'd spent months crawling the cities of northern Europe after she'd left, certain she'd fled Highley for passage on a ship to Copenhagen, believing her sisters when they'd offered their suggestions for her destination. Oslo, Amsterdam, Bruges.

He'd forgotten that, however much his wife loathed him, his sisters-in-law loathed him far more. That was, until the one he'd nearly ruined had taken pity on him and told him the truth. "She might have left us, Duke, but she left you first. And we shall honor that wish above all."

Damn women and their loyalty. Did they not wish her found? Did they not see she could be in danger? Did they not see what might come of her leaving? She could be—

He stopped the thought. She wasn't dead. If she were dead, he would know. Even now, after all they'd been through, after all the sorrow and hate, he would know if she were dead. But gone was nearly the same. Worse, perhaps, because of the lingering, flickering, barely-there promise of it. Because of the memory that came with it, impossible to forget. He couldn't forget an instant with her. Not since the night he'd stepped from a crowded ballroom to a balcony in search of fresh air, and there she'd been. As though she'd been waiting for him.

And so she had been.

It wasn't a trap. It was all real.

Her words echoed in the cold wind. He hadn't believed them. And now, he didn't care if she'd been waiting for him. He could only hope she waited for him now. Here.

It was a year since she'd left, nearly to the day, and he found that as the time passed he only became more dogged in his search for her. It did not help that the anniversary of her leaving marked a different anniversary— one that brought an ache to his chest that could not be relieved. An ache he knew she felt, as well. He could not bring back their child. That, Haven knew, just as he knew there would never be another.

But he could love her well, and out loud. He could mend what he had broken. And that might be enough.

Would. It would be enough.

It took him longer than it should have to find the tavern he sought, The Bell in Hand, through the twisting, turning labyrinthine streets of the unfamiliar city. It did not help that his accent and clothing revealed his home country; it seemed many Americans were uninterested in aiding an Englishman—and so Haven was grateful they did not immediately identify his title.

He'd traveled half the world for her—older, more venerable, more powerful countries. He was not about to let America keep him from her.

He pushed into the smoky tavern, assaulted immediately with dim lights and the din of men on their way into their cups. Not only men. There were women, too, laughing and drinking deep of their tankards, and Haven tracked them with eager eyes, searching for one woman in particular. His woman. His wife.

It was a full room, and poorly lit, and he could not be immediately certain she was not there. There was a woman, he'd been told. Voice like a summer songbird. Dark hair and a perfect face that had the rumor mill thinking she was French—weren't all beautiful women French?—but it was possible she was English. She'd appeared from nowhere three months after Sera had left him. They called her The Dove.

He'd imagined her just inside this door, alone, frozen in time and space. Close enough for him to capture her by the waist, toss her over his shoulder, get her back to the boat, and spend the entire journey home apologizing to her. Winning her back. Loving her to distraction.

But dreams were not reality. Seraphina was not in this room. Haven purchased an ale and, putting his back to the bar, considered the assembly. The timing was right. Perhaps he was desperate. Perhaps he was mad. But the timing was right, and it seemed right. She was dark and beautiful, tall and elegant, and she sang like an angel.

His gaze fell to a doorway at the back of the room, hinting at more space, promising more people. Promising her. He headed for it. Might have reached it, if not for the heavy hand that came to his shoulder.

"Looks like you've lost your way, toff."

Haven shrugged off the hand and turned, one fist curling at his side, ready for a fight. An American stood inches away, an inch or two shorter than Haven, but an inch or two broader. It had been a few years since Haven had felled someone of this size, but he had been a top fighter at Oxford, and had little concern for the skill returning if necessary.

Before he could speak, the American added, "You aren't welcome here."

Haven's brows rose. "You disapprove of men with funds to drink?"

Something flared in the American's gaze. Something like recognition, tinged with something like loathing. "I disapprove of Brits who don't know their place." The American nodded to the door. "Find somewhere else to drink."

Haven emptied his tankard and set it on the bar, then extracted his purse and removed several coins. Extending them to the other man, he said, "Give me five minutes in the other room. I shan't break anything."

The American stared long and hard at the coin before taking it. Haven resisted the urge to smirk. Every man had a price, and it seemed as though this man's was rather low. The American flashed a row of straight white teeth. "Well, if you're paying for it. What are you looking for?"

Haven looked toward the door. "A woman."

The American grunted. "We're not a brothel."

"I'm looking for a specific woman," Haven said. "A singer. I'm told she sings here."

The other man nodded. "You're talking about The Dove."

"She is here." The words came on a wave of relief. Haven's heart beat stronger and faster. It was she. He knew it without hesitation. He turned to the doorway, his only thought getting to her.

The hand again, at the same shoulder. This time firmer.

This time, Haven swatted it away with force, turning again. "Touch me again, and I will not hesitate to touch back."

"With that response, I'm not letting you get near her."

Malcolm took a deep breath. Willed himself calm. Failed. "Where is she?"

"What do you want with her?"

"To—" He stopped. To bring her home. To start anew. To find what they had once had. To find more. "To talk."

"Who are you?"

I'm her husband. How long had it been since he'd said that word? It felt, somehow, unwelcome until she'd returned it to him. He hesitated over his reply.

The American did not hesitate. "Cat got your tongue, Red?"

A collection of laughter followed the words, and Haven imagined he'd been insulted, as though it hadn't been half a century since the redcoats fought in Boston.

I'm a goddamn duke! he wanted to scream, but he knew it would do him no good. There were few doors such a statement could not open in Britain, and yet here it would likely make things worse.

"I'm a friend."

The American's unsettling green eyes narrowed. "That's a lie if I've ever heard one."

The words were low enough that they should not have been heard by any but Haven, but they seemed to silence the room nonetheless.

And that's when he heard her.

"When I remember all the friends, so link'd together, I've seen around me fall, like leaves in wintry weather; I feel like one who treads alone."

He'd know the voice anywhere. The way it curled like liquid smoke through the room, sad and soulful, touching minds and hearts and making men sit up and pant. He remembered her singing in his arms once before. Before she'd betrayed him. Before he'd betrayed her.

He met the American's gaze, the other man's green eyes flickering away the moment they met him. Past him. To the door to the back room. Haven saw the nervousness in them, even as he saw the barely-there shake of the other man's head.

She was there.

And he would tear the place down to find her if he must.

Curse on his lips, he turned and started for the room, the crowd suddenly thicker, less fluid. He threw shoulders and elbows to get men out of the way.

"Wait!" the American shouted from behind, catching him by the sleeve, then the arm, leaving him no choice.

Haven turned, the punch already flying. Connecting with a wicked thud, the other man's nose giving way beneath his fist.

"Christ!" The other man buckled, hand flying to his nose, blood immediately covering his hand.

Haven had broken it, and he had no regrets. The American could hang, for all he cared. Shaking the sting from his hand, he said, loud enough for the room to hear it, "Anyone who gets in my way receives the same."

He turned on his heel, and the path to the back room opened, bodies eager to clear it. He had to get to her. He would apologize. Make her believe him. Make her believe that they could start anew.

But he had to get to her.

He pushed through the doorway, eyes adjusting to the dimmer light, finding the poorly lit stage at the far end of the room as applause and whistles rang in his ears. It took him a moment to see the woman standing there for what she was—pretty and dark, with a wide, welcoming smile.

Not Sera.

The woman waved her hand in the direction of a man with a fiddle at one side of the stage, and he began to play a rousing jig of sorts, at which point she lifted her skirts to show her ankles in red stockings, to the pleasure of the assembled crowd.

Haven watched for what seemed like forever, not believing.

He could have sworn he'd heard her. He would have known that voice anywhere. A girl pushed past him, tray laden with ale. He stayed her movement with a touch. "That woman. The dancer. Who is she?"

Her gaze followed his. "The Dove."

The words, so uninterested, so direct, were a knife to his heart.

The Dove wasn't Sera.

It was never his Sera.

Chapter 7

~~~~~~~~~~~~~~~

SPARROW SINGS TO CITY'S SOUL

*S*he'd been in Boston.

He'd traveled half the world to find her, the echo of that song curling through him in that godforsaken tavern in that godforsaken city an aching reminder of his failure.

Regret slammed through him.

He should have searched more. Should have torn the damn place apart. But he'd felt the disappointment so keenly, been so thoroughly overwhelmed by the futility of the search, by his anger—at Sera for hiding so well, at her sisters and his own mother for aiding her so thoroughly. And at himself, for his inability to find her.

Except he had found her.

It had been her, all along.

And it had been this goddamn American, too.

Haven's gaze fell to the other man's now crooked nose, the pleasure he might have found in having been the instrument of the feature's demise overwhelmed by the fury that this man was touching Sera. Laughing, happy Sera. Comfortable in her skin.

When was the last time he'd seen her that way?

How often had he remembered her that way?

Countless times. As many times as he'd remembered the way she sang, so out of place with the dark, empty tavern down a dingy Covent Garden lane. Because she sang like an angel, achingly beautiful, full of sorrow and longing and truth. And as he'd stood in the doorway, watching her, the ache had returned, though it had never been far to begin with.

He'd ached for her for years.

She filled him, stifled him, stole his breath, marking his chest with her lilting, sad song, as surely as if she'd extracted a blade and carved it herself, drawing blood like a siren.

And then she'd turned away, giving all that beauty to another man, and laughed, the sound—free and light and damn perfect—a harsher blow than the music. He remembered every time she'd ever laughed with him, making him twice the man he was. Ten times it. Making him a king. A god.

There was nothing in the wide world like his wife's laugh.

He hated that she gave it to another.

And then the American put his hands on her. Lifted her from the stage with such ease that there was no question that he'd done it before. That he'd touched her before. That he was allowed access to her.

Jealousy raged through Haven, fury in its wake.

There was no way she was leaving him for an American.

There was no way she was leaving him, full stop—but the American did add insult to injury. Particularly when Haven considered the fact that the other man was broader, bolder, and possibly handsomer than Haven was, broken nose aside.

Not that any of that mattered. She was his wife. And

he would not stand by while another touched her. In fact, if the damn Yank did not remove his ham hocks with all deliberate speed, Haven was likely to remind his opponent just how well he could break a nose. As soon as he navigated his way through the tables and chairs to reach them.

As though she heard the thought, Sera moved in front of the other man, and Haven tried not to notice the way the action stung, whipping envy through him—the vision of his wife protecting another man. A man who continued to touch her with a certainty that could mean only one thing. Possession.

He'd known she was here, with an American. He'd been prepared for the idea that they were lovers. But the visual of it was a wicked blow.

"Ah," the American drawled. "The duke arrives."

"The *husband* arrives," Haven replied, unable to bank the anger in his tone. And then, to his wife, "We are yet married, Seraphina."

How was she so utterly calm? "Not in any way that matters."

In every fucking way that mattered.

She added, "The silly laws of this nation may make me your chattel, Duke. But I will never play the role. I should think the last three years would have made that point well."

He resisted the urge to spirit her away and show her just how well he could claim her. To make love to her so thoroughly that she screamed to be his. To lock her away and show her how well the role of wife could suit.

Instead, he took the nearest seat, at a low table in the dark corner, knowing she wouldn't be able to see him as well as he could see her. Desperate to regain the upper hand, he willed his voice calm. His muscles still. Even as he wanted nothing more than to tear the tavern to pieces. "I shan't be cuckolded," he said.

Her spine straightened. "If only I had been able to say the same."

Shame came, hot and unpleasant. He resisted it, redoubled his conviction, directing his attention to the American. "Remove your hands."

For a moment, he wasn't sure the other man would respond in any way but to level him with a long, superior look, one that Haven imagined had been taught to every young man in the colonies with a loathing for the king. After several seconds, however, he let go of Sera, spreading his hands wide with a too-loud laugh. "Far be it from me to suffer the fury of a husband scorned."

"That door should have been locked," she said, released from the touch of her lover. Sera headed to the bar at the end of the tavern, seemingly uninterested in the masculine posturing in which Haven could not help but engage. As though he were a much younger man. A much stupider one.

Not so much stupider.

He directed his scorn to the other man, who touched his wife with such casual comfort that there was no doubt of their intimacy.

She'd been unfaithful. He shouldn't mind it. Shouldn't have been surprised by it. After all, it had been years.

And he had been unfaithful, too.

Once. And not like this. Not with emotion.

Lie.

There had been emotion. The action had been full of anger. Full of punishment. All for Sera. Sera was the only woman who had ever had his emotions. Not that she would believe it.

Not that she would care.

"Don't worry, Caleb," she was saying, "Malcolm doesn't believe himself scorned. For that to be the case, he would have had to have wanted the marriage from the start."

He had wanted it. He'd wanted her.

He stayed silent as she moved around the bar to place a small glass on the counter and pour a healthy drink into it. "How did you find us?"

Malcolm hated that *us*. The way it cleaved her to another man. Instead of answering her, he asked a question of his own. "What in hell are you doing here?"

She raised a brow. "Here, London?"

There had been a time when he'd enjoyed her playing the ingenue. When it had made him feel a dozen times the man. No longer. "Here, in a damn pub."

"We prefer the word *tavern*."

We. "Call it whatever you like, but it's a pub in the heart of Covent Garden, inhabited by a duchess with newfound skill in drinking."

The American laughed, and Malcolm hated him a little more. "Should have called it The Drunken Duchess!"

And then Sera was laughing and Mal had the distinct desire to burn the place down. "I am deadly serious, Seraphina. Why are you here?"

She leaned back against the far wall, arms crossed over her chest, glass dangling in one hand. "I was born here."

"No, you weren't."

She lifted a shoulder. Let it fall. "I was born in a coal town in the North Country, and reborn in Boston. Covent Garden's a proper third to the trio, don't you think?"

He narrowed his gaze on her. "You're daughter to an earl."

She smirked. "And you are the one who was so very

insistent that my father's title didn't count, Your Grace. A title won at cards makes no kind of blue blood, not even when won from Prinny himself."

The words stung with memory. "I never—"

She stopped the lie with a wave of her glass. "More importantly, Haven, why are *you* here?"

To rescue you.

Another lie. This woman didn't need him. In all the time he'd sought her, he'd imagined her fearful. Weak. Ruined. This woman was none of those things. There was nothing cowering about her. Instead, she was all strength.

She was nothing like the woman he'd met on that long-ago night outside the Worthington ball. Except . . . she was. That woman had been bold and brash. She'd stood up to him. She'd drawn him in like a warm flame on a cold night. And for weeks afterward, her smart mouth had tempted him as much as her warm body had.

And then he'd discovered the truth—that none of their courtship was real—and she'd changed. She'd quieted. She'd dimmed. She'd paled.

She'd become someone else, entirely. Because of him.

And now, here, with years' distance between them, that simpering, quiet bride was gone, returned to the strong, bold woman she'd once been. Stronger. Bolder.

More beautiful.

Not because of him. In spite of him.

There, in the dark tavern, watching her sing, watching her drink, watching her stand up to him, the truth whispered through him. He might have spent three years attempting to find and save her, but she did not need saving.

"Why are you here?"

The answer was simple enough. "We're not through."

Her brows shot up, the surprise there in direct op-position to her calm words. "We are, as a matter of fact. We were through two years and seven months ago. Before that. Or do you not remember turning your back on me the moment our vows were spoken? Shall I remind you? Shall I remind you of the way you did it again, in front of an entire garden party? Of what you did after that? With another?"

Of course he remembered.

He remembered it every night, struggling to sleep, desperate to reverse time and stop himself. To tell her the truth instead of the lie his pride insisted upon. If he had, would everything have been different? If he had, would they be happy now?

"How did you know where to find me, Haven?"

"I didn't," he said.

"You're surveying all the taverns in London? And simply happened along?"

"You cannot imagine the world simply ignored the spectacle you gave Parliament. You were seen leaving the House of Lords in a carriage belonging to an Ameri-can." He stood, affecting a calm he had not felt in three days, and approached, tossing a look to the man in ques-tion. "Caleb Calhoun of Boston. Known pub owner, gambler, and general scoundrel."

Like an ass, the American bowed. "I like to think of myself as more a specific kind of scoundrel."

Malcolm raised a brow. "And which kind would that be?"

"The one the ladies adore."

Mal's fists clenched, itching to find purchase once more upon the American's face. "Careful, Calhoun, or you shall find something more than your nose broken."

Recognition flared in the other man's gaze, which flickered to Sera and back to him. And Haven saw the truth. Sera didn't know he'd come for her. The American had never told her. If he had, would she have faced him? Would she have let him win her back?

He opened his mouth, prepared to tell her all. To win her here and now.

And then she said the American's name.

"Caleb." The name was soft, her voice filled with the worst kind of censure—the kind laced with love.

Regret and doubt shot through Mal. She couldn't love this man. Not when she'd loved him once. She had loved him once, hadn't she?

He pushed the thought from his head, hating it and the way it made him waver. Changed the topic. "Calhoun owns two properties in London. One is a residence. I went there first, only to be told the duchess was not at home." He looked at the American, taking in his crossed arms and his smug smirk. "She's through living with another man, by the way."

The American's brows rose, his gaze sliding to Sera, who sipped calmly at her drink. "I do enjoy the fact that you think either you or Caleb has a say in what I do."

"The other is a new tavern, barely weeks old, already praised for the nightly entertainment—whatever that means. Spends his days here, with a woman. Tall, dark, beautiful." He drew closer, hating himself for coming here. Wishing he could leave her. Wishing he could take her with him. "I hope you wear a mask."

"Why? Are you afraid I'll ruin your reputation?" She paused, then said, "Go home, Duke. There is no reason for you to be here."

No reason but that he had not drawn a full breath for

two years and seven months, and now, air had returned, fresh and welcome. And all he wanted was to breathe it in. "It's only natural I be concerned."

She narrowed her gaze on his. "You will of course understand why I don't for one moment believe you were actually concerned."

The American offered her a small grunt of encouragement, and Haven's jaw set. Irritated with their audience, he drew even closer to her, nearly touching the narrow bar protecting them from each other. He repeated, softly, "We're not through, Sera."

She looked over his shoulder. "Caleb."

He loathed the other man's name on her tongue, loathed the trust in the breathy word. The faith. Faith she'd never given him.

Faith he'd never earned.

He turned to face the American, aware that men might be willing to kill for Sera. But the other man had not moved. He stood at a distance, hands on his hips, a soldier ready to strike.

"Leave us," Seraphina finished.

For a moment, Haven thought she was speaking to him. He should leave. It was best for both of them.

But, suddenly, he was ready to do battle.

There was no battle to be had, however, because she was looking at Calhoun, the calm, quiet American who seemed willing to give her everything for which she asked. Just as Malcolm once had.

The American's brows rose.

Sera nodded.

And that was enough. Calhoun turned and left the room like a fool. No. Not a fool. A king. Because in that decision to leave without looking back, there was an unfathomable amount of trust, born of the knowledge that when he returned, she would be there, waiting for him.

Another thing Malcolm had once known himself.

Calhoun made his way from the room, the curtain through which he had pushed still swaying behind him when Mal said, "So the American is your lapdog? Goes where you tell him?"

"He trusts me," she said. "'Tis a glorious luxury in a man."

The words at once shamed him and infuriated him.

"What do you want? Covent Garden was never your haunt. And even if it was, you always made an impressive effort to avoid any doorways I might darken."

"That's not true," he said, wishing they were anywhere but here. "I remember a few times I wanted to be nowhere but with you."

"That was before you decided you wanted nothing to do with me," she said.

You lied, he wanted to say. *You lied and then you left.* But it wasn't so simple. The truth ended with, *I chased you away.*

He should leave her. Give them each freedom from the other. How many times had he told himself he should stop looking for her? How many times had he been unable to do so?

And now that he'd found her, he knew he'd never be able to leave her.

"Why are you here, Malcolm?"

The name shivered through him. She was the only woman who'd ever called him by his name. He'd not even been Malcolm to his mother, for whom he was nothing but triumph—the future duke. But Sera always seemed uninterested in the title.

Even when it seemed the title was all she'd been interested in.

And now, hearing his name on her lips for the first time in years, he was at once desperate for the sound of it—for the man he'd once been in the shadow of it—and filled with anger for the way she wielded it. Soft and lilting and entirely too personal.

As though she were his wife in truth.

He gritted his teeth. Answered her question. "I'm here to fetch you."

"I've no interest in being *fetched*," she said.

"Then you shouldn't have come back."

"I came back to set us both free." She drank again, finishing the amber liquid in the small, heavy glass. "I've plans. A life to live. I could have disappeared forever."

"Why didn't you?"

For a moment, he thought she might answer. The truth was there, suddenly, shot across her face. But he couldn't read her the way he'd once been able to. And then she said, "I suppose I thought you deserved better."

It was a lie.

He didn't deserve better; he deserved much, much worse.

Which meant only one thing. She was hiding something.

His gaze narrowed on her. "Better, as in public embarrassment as a cuckold? Better, as in a wife who so loathes me that she finds divorce more palatable than a dukedom?"

She smirked. "You say that as though I have any claim at all to the dukedom. You made it more than clear that I was not welcome in your world, Your Grace."

"You left before—" He stopped himself from finishing the thought.

A long moment passed, emotion absent on her face. "I left before you could send me away, like unwanted property."

"I wouldn't have—"

"Of course you would have. And I didn't want it. I didn't want the anger. I had enough of that myself. And I didn't want the regret. I had enough of that, too. And what else was there? Pity? No, thank you. I wished for a future free of all that. And you should, as well."

The words rioted through him. He hadn't wanted to send her away. He'd wanted to keep her forever. He'd grieved for her, dammit. For years. He'd grieved for what they might have been. And when she'd left—he'd never admit this to anyone—he'd pitied himself.

She lifted a flint box and came around the bar, making for the stage. "We're through here, Duke. Go home to your estate and plan your bright future. Leave me to mine, and think of how lucky you are that you are being offered a second chance. Find a new duchess!" she offered, as though the idea were an excellent one. "And when October comes, bring the petition for divorce to the floor. Paint me an adulteress. And let's get this business done."

Dammit, he didn't want another future. He wanted the one that had tempted him all those years ago. Her future. Theirs. He'd sought it, dammit, the world over. He wanted to scream the truth at her. That he'd been in Boston. That he'd searched the Continent. That he hadn't slept in two years, seven months. That he'd only ever wanted her.

And he might have, if it hadn't seemed that she wanted nothing to do with him.

"You wish your adultery to be made public?" He was riveted to her grace as she began to light the candles on the stage.

"The House of Lords certainly won't allow the dissolution of our marriage to be on your actions, and I would not be the first wife to bear such a brunt in order to get what she wishes."

But it was not what he wished. He wished the opposite. A marriage in truth.

"The powerful collude, Duke. They connive and they scheme to get what they want." She looked to him, inscrutable. "And the proof of it is how well they suspect it in others."

He didn't care if she'd schemed. Not anymore.

"I want my divorce," she said. "I've a future before me."

"With your American?"

She did not reply, and he watched her as she lit the candles, golden light spreading like starlight through her mahogany curls, her words echoing through him.

He wanted to be her future. Which meant he'd have to win her.

Find a new duchess.

He approached her once more, weaving through the tables.

She met his gaze, unwavering. Proud. "Leave, Haven. Caleb won't be happy if we open the doors and you're here. There's nothing worse for business than a duke."

Find a new duchess.

"I'll leave on one condition," he said, the words coming as quickly as thoughts formed.

She lifted a brow.

"Come with me."

She laughed, low and long and somehow full of knowledge, as though she knew what he was to do before he knew himself. But then, it had always been that way between them. "And what then?"

"Come to the country. You give me six weeks. Until Parliament is back in session."

She turned back to the candles. "What is this, some grand plan to woo me again? As though we are in some kind of romantic novel?"

Yes.

He was smart enough to stay quiet.

"We're not in a romantic novel, Haven. This is not a love story."

"Because you are in one with your American?"

"Because I've no desire to be in one. Ever again."

Again. He would think on that word another time. Cling to it. "Fine," he replied. "But you are in a marriage with me, and you vowed to obey."

She leveled him with a look. "And you vowed to honor."

"This is my offer. Six weeks, and you get your divorce." It was a lie, but he'd cross that bridge when he got to it.

Her gaze narrowed. "What do you intend to do with six weeks of my company?"

"I intend to put it to good use," he said, the answer coming even as he spoke it. "I intend for you to find your replacement."

He heard her sharp intake of breath, and it was his turn to feel self-satisfied. To feel as though he'd won. His turn to smirk.

"What does that mean?"

"Just what I said," he replied. "You come to the country and spend six weeks seeking your replacement."

"You want me to matchmake you."

He enjoyed the disbelief in her words, the way it helped him to regain his footing. "You must admit, it would save me a great deal of effort."

She narrowed her gaze. "You do not think such an arrangement would be . . . impractical?"

"Not at all."

"Oh, no. I'm sure it would not be at all awkward for the poor poppets eager for the attention of a duke to be closed into a country house, playing charades with his first wife—whom he is about to divorce."

"I think it would be much more likely that they would find it a relief. After all, if we are able to coexist, perhaps I can avoid the worst of the divorce."

One sleek brow rose. "You do not think that your dukedom will be a balm to your wretched reputation?"

"I should like them to have proof that I have not mistreated you."

"Mistreatment is not only external."

Guilt slammed through him, punctuated by the memory of the sound of the carriage door slamming shut as he sent her away. Of the sound of her tears on the day she returned. Of the sound of the silence that fell when she left him for good.

Not for good, though.

She was back.

He swallowed the emotion and met her gaze. "You want your divorce, do you not?"

She watched him as she seemed to consider her words. Finally, she said, all calm, "I do."

"Find your replacement, Sera. And it is yours."

It was a mad plan. Pure idiocy. And he would have been unsurprised if she'd told him so. Still, he held his breath, waiting for her reply, watching the way candlelight flickered over her skin, casting her into light and shadow, a remarkable beauty.

But she did not tell him so. Instead, she nodded her agreement. "Now leave."

He gave her what she wanted and left without a word, making preparations to woo his wife.

Chapter 8

_____ ✒ _____

SEASON'S SLOWEST SCANDAL: TIME MARCHES FOR TICK TOCK TALBOT!

April 1833
Three years, four months earlier

"*B*eethoven?"

Seraphina looked up from the pianoforte to find her sister Sophie across the conservatory, a piece of music in one hand, an expectant look on her face.

Sera wrinkled her nose. "Too bombastic."

Sophie returned to the stack of music. "Hymns?"

"Too pious."

"Children's ballads?"

Sera shook her head.

"Mozart?"

"Too . . . Mozart," Sera sighed.

Sophie cut her a look. "Oh, yes. No one likes Mozart."

Sera laughed and toyed at the keys of the piano, playing a little impromptu tune. "Thomas Moore."

Sophie rolled her eyes. "It's always Thomas Moore with you. Honestly, if I didn't know better, I'd think you wished to marry him." She lifted a well-worn piece of music and walked it across the room, squeezing herself onto the little tufted bench where Sera already sat and setting the page to the ornate music rack.

Sera reached out to lovingly smooth the paper. "If he weren't double my age and married to an actress, I'd be inclined to do just that, honestly." She fingered the keys, finding the opening notes to the song, loving the way they washed over her. She didn't need the sheet music. Not for this, or any of the other pieces from Thomas Moore.

She closed her eyes and played from memory while her sister replied, "Nonsense. You'd never give up your perfect duke."

Sera went warm at the words and missed a note. "He's not *my* duke."

Except she rather thought he was. Even if she did not think of him as a duke at all. He wasn't a duke. He was Malcolm. *Her* Malcolm. All smiles and touches and kisses like a promise. And every one of them for her. They'd seen each other dozens of times in the six weeks since they met, in public and private, and every time, it had felt as though it was the two of them alone. Like magic.

"I should like him to be my duke," she said softly.

"Then he shall be." Sophie turned the page of the music even though Sera did not need it as she let the music take over.

She sang. "*'Tis the last rose of summer, left blooming alone; all her lovely companions are faded and gone . . .*" The song always made her ache. "*No flower of her kindred, no rosebud is nigh, to reflect back her blushes, or give sigh for sigh.*"

"Lady Seraphina Eleanor Talbot!"

She stopped playing.

Sophie looked to her. "It sounds as though you are in trouble."

And the door to the conservatory burst open, flying back to connect with the wall beyond, revealing the Countess of Wight, formerly Mrs. Talbot. Their mother.

The countess brandished a newspaper in one hand, holding it high above her head like a heraldic banner, though the panic in her eyes indicated that the banner in question was in no way triumphant.

Sera's remaining three sisters followed close on the countess's heels, the warning in their respective wide-eyed gazes a clear indication that something had happened, and it was not a good something. Sesily, the sister closest in age to Seraphina, was shaking her head dramatically over their mother's right shoulder, while Seleste and Seline, numbers three and four of the quintet, appeared to be aiming for meaningful stares.

Though Sera could not for the life of her divine what meaning those stares were meant to have.

And then the countess spoke, outrage shaking the words from her. "Has he had you?"

Sera's jaw dropped at the crass question. "What?"

Seline and Seleste gasped their shock as Sesily's eyes went wide. For her part, Sophie went stick straight, immediately reaching to take Sera's hand. "Mother!"

The countess did not look at her youngest daughter, focused entirely on her eldest. "Now is no time for propriety. Answer the question."

Sera was speechless.

Sesily—darling, loyal Sesily—leapt into the fray. "Have you gone mad, Mother? Who are you even referring to?"

The countess did not hesitate. "The Duke of Haven. And now that is clear, let me ask again, and you would do well to answer me, Seraphina. Has he had you?"

Sera closed her mouth. "No."

The countess watched her for an interminably long silence before Sophie stood. "They are in love."

The countess laughed, high and shrill and unpleasant. "Has he said so?" The question landed like a blow. Sera pressed her lips together, and her mother read the answer without it having to be spoken. "Of course he hasn't."

The countess turned away with a violent twist. "Dammit, Sera. What have you done?"

She shook her head. "Nothing!"

Her mother looked over her shoulder, morning sunshine cascading through the window highlighting her disappointment. "You think I was not young once? You think I cannot see that lie?"

Sera stood, fists at her sides. "He cares for me."

"He cares for what you're giving him."

"Mother." This, from Seline. "You needn't be cruel."

"It seems I do, though," said the countess. "Because it's never occurred to any of you that you might be taken advantage of." She swung back toward Sera, already crossing the room, fast and furious. "Half the season is gone, and he's not courting you."

He was though, wasn't he?

Before she could argue the point, her mother pressed on. "He hasn't spoken to your father."

She opened her mouth. "He will."

"No, Sera. He won't. He's had six weeks to do so. He's had six *years* to. You expect me to believe that after six years of seasons, of being disdained by pompous aristocrats with more money than heaven itself, of scraping for invitations and pleading for attention, the *Duke of Haven* has taken a liking to a Soiled S?"

Yes.

It didn't matter that they'd all struggled to find suitors who weren't impoverished or untitled. It didn't matter that she and Malcolm had never discussed their future. He'd promised her he wouldn't ruin her on that first night, on that balcony.

He wanted her. She knew it.

She wanted him.

"It's true."

The countess shook her head, and for a moment, Sera saw sadness in her mother's gaze. Sadness, and something like pity. "No, Sera. No one has such luck." A pause. Then, "The papers say you've been indiscreet."

"I haven't. We haven't."

Except, they had. There had been the time in the carriage. And the stolen moments at the Beaufetheringstone Ball. And the time when she'd snuck into his offices at Parliament—but nothing had happened.

Well, nothing serious. Nothing irreversible.

Her mother did not believe it. "Let me be plain. Are you still a virgin?"

Her sisters gasped as she said, "Mama!"

"Save your shock for another, Seraphina. Are you?"

"Yes."

"But he's come close." Sera hesitated, until the countess barked, "Seraphina."

"Yes!" she snapped, turning on her mother. "Yes. And I wish he had. I wish I weren't."

Lady Wight's eyes went wide as Sera's sisters gasped. "He's not going to marry you."

"Why not?"

"Because all five of you have been out for years, and not one of you has come near a duke. They think us *cheap*. They think us unworthy of their names and their titles." She waved a hand at her sisters. "Seleste might become Countess of Clare, but only because the earl is virtually a pauper and your father's money is worth more than the shame we bring upon a title. But mark my words, not one of them will find marriage if you let yourself be ruined by this duke."

Seleste's face fell at the words, and Sera hated her mother in that moment. Even more so when she continued. "Haven might as well be a star in the sky for all you shall reach him and not get him. The season is six weeks old and you've seen him, what, a dozen times?"

Twenty-six times. But Sera remained quiet. She didn't have to speak. "More than that, likely, what with all the sneaking about you girls have been doing while I was looking the other way." The countess brandished the newspaper high. "The gossip rags were not looking the other way, Seraphina. Do you know what they say about you?"

Sera's heart was pounding. "They have nothing to say. I've been careful."

The countess laughed, the sound humorless. "Not careful enough, Tick Tock Talbot."

She set the paper onto the music rack, covering the song there.

Dreams of duchessdom doomed to disappointment . . . Time trips timidly despite dozens of aristocratic assignations . . . Tick Tock Talbot hopeless to hook Haven . . . though a tempting taste (tart-like, even)!

Sera's cheeks were blazing.

They hadn't been careful. There had been the hundreds of glances across crowded events, his wicked winks and her soft smiles and all the secrets they'd told without even speaking. And there had been the dozens of little touches, grazes at her elbow, fingers down her arm, the way his hand lingered in hers when they were allowed to greet each other in public. The warm day the previous week, when they'd walked in Hyde Park and he'd helped her over every tiny rock and stick, his touch a slow sinful slide.

They hadn't been careful.

"A tart," her mother explained, as though Sera could not read the insult herself. "They call you a tart. And that's not the worst."

It was absolutely the worst, Sera should have said. But she could not find her voice.

Not so, her mother. "The worst is the horrible moniker."

"Soiled sister?" Sesily interjected from her place in the corner. "That comes from Papa. From coal. It has nothing to do with Sera."

"It has everything to do with her now, but that's not the one I'm referring to." Her mother's words came from a distance, through the rushing sound in Sera's ears. Through shock and anger and embarrassment. "Sera knows which one I mean."

Sera nodded, then whispered, "Tick Tock."

"They're mocking you. The way you wait for him, time passing you by, another season half-over, and not even looking to eligible men. Men who might have you. Tick Tock Talbot." The countess threw up her arms. "And they know you've given him everything."

Sera looked to her mother. "Not everything."

"Oh, Seraphina," the countess said, her exasperation clear. "It doesn't matter if you've done it. They think you have. You're ruined, girl. And he's one of the richest dukes in Britain."

"We—" She swallowed. "He wants me."

"I've no doubt of that." Her mother shook her head, the words gentling. "But if he had plans to marry you, darling, he would have come and seen your father. Instead, he's taken advantage of you. He's saddled you with a horrid name and he's saddled your sisters with ruin by association." She paused and drove the point home. "*You've* saddled them with it."

Sera looked to her sisters . . . the Soiled S's, never welcome in society, always the subject of scorn and speculation. Seleste and her impoverished earl. Seline, too smart for her own good. Sesily, too brash to ever be a proper aristocratic lady. And Sophie, poor, quiet Sophie, whom the whole world thought plain. Who would care for them?

The countess broke into her thoughts. "There's another man. One who's willing to marry you. To get you out from under this horrible gossip. Perhaps, if you marry him quickly, Tick Tock Talbot will be forgotten. The Soiled S's will be forgotten. Perhaps, if you marry him, you can save your sisters their embarrassment."

"That can't be the only way," Sesily blurted out.

"No!" Seline said.

"Mother—" Sophie spoke. "Sera shouldn't have to marry for us."

The only one who remained silent was Seleste. Seleste, who was being courted by an impoverished earl. The best title the Talbot sisters could hope for. Far below that of a rich, perfect duke.

A rich duke who had never said a word about marriage.

Her mother spoke again, cold and serious, for Sera alone. "You will stop this embarrassing chase. You will find a man who will marry you. And you will marry to secure your sisters' futures and your own. This season, before the gossip mill ruins you forever. Because marriage is how women win." She turned to the rest of her daughters. "It's time you girls see that. Your father's title will never garner you the respect you deserve. And you haven't a brother to protect you. Someday, Papa shall be gone, and you shall have to fend for yourselves and to do that, you shall have to marry. And the only way you'll do that well is for your sister to tidy up the mess she's made."

Had she made a mess? Was it true?

She looked from one sister to the next, each wide-eyed with sorrow and something else. Something star-tlingly like fear.

How she loathed this world and the way it preyed upon women.

Tears came, hot and angry, and she loathed them as well, for their weakness. Why was it that men's rage came in a flurry of fists, while women's came on a flood of tears?

The countess watched her for a long moment, not looking to her other daughters when she said, "Now out, all of you. Leave us."

Her sisters hesitated, bless them, each one looking to her, waiting for her to agree to their departure. She nodded, loving them, knowing what she would do. Pre-pared to walk away from the man she loved for them. Prepared to, as her mother had said, clean up her mess.

Sophie pulled the door closed behind her, leaving Sera and the countess together. After a long stretch of silence, Sera dashed away her tears and set a hand on the pianoforte, as though she could draw strength from the instrument. She took a deep breath. "Who is the man you wish me to marry?"

Silence stretched between them before her mother ap-proached, reaching for her daughter and placing a hand to her cheek, the soft kidskin like a firm promise. "I wish you to marry the man you wish, Sera. But a duke—"

Tears came again, and Sera could not hold them back. "I don't care that he's a duke. That was never of interest."

"I know."

"He is Malcolm. I wish for Malcolm."

The countess shook her head. "But Malcolm is Haven before all, my dear."

Sera closed her eyes, everything suddenly, startlingly, painfully clear. "He won't marry me, will he?"

"No," said her mother, and Sera opened her eyes at that, meeting her mother's dark brown gaze. "No, he won't."

The longer she resisted the truth, the longer she put her sisters in danger. Without marriage, they were all lost. It was her duty as eldest daughter to ensure that never happen.

And then her mother said, quietly, "Unless . . ."

Sera's heart leapt. She'd do it. Whatever it was.

If it ended with her sisters safe and Malcolm hers, she'd do anything.

Chapter 9

SOILED SISTERS' SUMMER SIEGE!

"Thank goodness. She's brought food."

Seraphina turned away from the window of the coach when her youngest sister, Sophie, Marchioness of Eversley, announced their arrival at their childhood home. She smiled at the pronouncement—Sophie had always been fond of food—and it was nice to know that some things did not change.

"It's only two hours to Highley, Sophie."

"One cannot be too careful," her sister replied as the door opened, revealing their middle sister, Sesily, armed with a wicker basket. "Do you have pasties?"

"I don't, as a matter of fact," Sesily said, setting the basket on the floor and pushing it into the carriage before she lifted her skirts and set foot to the step. "Move in, girlies."

Sera pressed closer to the far side of Caleb's largest carriage, which he'd happily relinquished to ferry her and her sisters to the country. To Haven.

She'd put off the travel for several days, imagining, she supposed, that he might forget their agreement. She would have put it off longer if she could have, but Haven had sent word to The Singing Sparrow that if she did not arrive today—ten days since her *parliamentary performance*, as he referred to it—then he was going to return and fetch her himself.

There were many things Seraphina Bevingstoke had vowed never to do again, but certainly being publicly called to heel by a man was chief among them. And so she'd gone to Caleb and made arrangements to be absent from the Sparrow for several weeks. And then she'd packed her bags. But not before summoning reinforcements.

"Ow!" Her middle sister, Seleste, threw an elbow. "There's no room, Sesily!"

It seemed that even the largest carriage they could find no longer made for comfortable passage. Even with the windows cracked open to relieve the heat.

Sera sighed. "We're going to have to make room. Sesily has to fit."

"Make her sit on the floor," Seline, the fourth of the fivesome, suggested from the opposite bench of the carriage, waving a fan wildly. "Late to coach, snug as a roach, no?"

Sera laughed at the echo of their father's rule for their childhood travel. It was improbable that five children and two parents ever made for comfortable passage, but they'd done it. "There are two problems with that line of thinking. First, we are considerably larger than we once were when someone could reasonably fit on the floor. And—"

"And Sesily's bottom is considerably larger than it once was?" Seleste chimed in.

Everyone laughed as Sesily winked and said, "I rarely hear complaints about the size of my bottom."

That much, Sera believed. Sesily was far and away the most voluptuous of the five Talbot sisters, and far and away the most coveted. But Sesily embraced scandal even more than the rest of the sisters, did and said whatever she liked and remained unmatched because of it—despite routinely having men slavering after her.

"No doubt the male half of London is afraid of being sat upon. Sit over there," Seleste replied, pointing to Sophie and Seline.

"No. Sophie needs space. She's increasing."

"I knew I chose well," Seline bragged from her seat.

"She's not increasing in the next two hours!" Seleste protested, even as she pushed in, pressing Sera closer to the door.

"We don't know that!"

Sera inhaled deeply, attempting to make herself smaller, but even as she did, she could not find discomfort in the moment. If there were anything in the wide world that could keep her from thinking of the next six weeks of her life, it was the whirling dervish of her four slightly mad, entirely maddening, utterly wonderful sisters.

With a final push, eliciting a frustrated groan from Seleste, "Close the door, William!" Sesily called out to the footman beyond. "Quickly, before we explode from here and cause a scene!"

"Oh, yes," Seline said, dry as sand. "No one would expect that of us."

Once that was done, everyone in the carriage released a long breath and Seleste said, "Is it possible to be crushed to death in two hours?"

"Oh, please. You're about as wide as a twig," Sesily said. "It's impossible to squash you. Push over."

"There. Is. No. Room!" Seleste protested.

Sesily sighed. "Need I remind you what happens when I am not comfortable in a carriage?"

A collective groan rose from the rest of the occupants, and Sera laughed. "That was the second reason why she couldn't sit on the floor."

"If you vomit upon me . . ." Seleste warned.

"I'm simply saying that you would do well to remember that your kindness could mean the difference in trajectory. And with Sophie with child . . . one never knows what might sympathetically follow my own unfortunate projection."

Seline wrinkled her nose and looked to Sophie. "Don't you dare."

Sophie shrugged, a twinkle in her eyes, her fan flying through the air. "One does never know."

Seleste groaned. "Remind me again why we are all in this carriage when we all have husbands and carriages of our own?"

When Sophie, Seline, and Sesily spoke, it was in unison. "For Sera."

Seleste nodded and sighed. "The things we do for sisters."

Sera looked to the window, unable to speak for the knot that formed in her throat at the words. She had been gone for three years. She'd left without a word, without stopping to tell her family—whom she had always loved beyond reason—what had happened. She'd dashed a note through her tears on the Bristol docks, telling them only, *She did not live. I'm for America.*

And once in Boston, she had not written, too afraid of what setting pen to paper might release. Sorrow. Grief. Regret. She'd stayed away, and they'd lived their lives. But when she'd returned, they had not hesitated. They'd resumed their loyal devotion, as though she'd never left.

Even though she'd missed so much. Two marriages. Four children. Birthdays and balls and scandals and so much that seemed at once less important and infinitely more. Her chest tight with emotion, Sera inhaled sharply in the silent carriage, nothing but the clattering wheels on the cobblestones to cover the sound.

Sophie leaned forward, reaching across to place her hand on Sera's skirts. "Sera."

Sera shook her head, unable to find words.

"You needn't say anything," she said. "We are beside you."

Sera looked to her sister, the one she remembered holding as a baby. Dear Sophie, who had always been the quiet one. The unassuming one. Out of place. Except never unassuming. When it came time to show loyalty, it was Sophie who was always willing to fight.

It had been Sophie who had pushed Haven directly onto his ass in a fishpond when they'd happened upon him at a garden party with another woman. Believing Sera had betrayed him. Believing she had lied, and not only in omission.

It had been Sophie who defended her, even as she had not defended herself.

The actions had ruined Sophie's reputation summarily. One did not strike a duke without repercussions—not even a duke to whom you were related. And still, her sister had not hesitated.

And truthfully, the image of Haven waist-deep in a fishpond was not unwelcome on Sera's darkest nights.

But Sophie was wrong. Sera did have to speak now. If only to say, "I am very happy to be . . ." She trailed off, uncertain of the end of the sentence. It had seemed possible that she might finish with *home*.

Certainly, a scene such as this, crowded into a carriage with her sisters—who had once known her best in the world—had been home. But things had changed. And then there had been a time—fleeting and disastrous—when home had been wherever Haven was. And then there had been the hope of home again, lost with the child that had been so full of promise. Now, the truth—home was a strange, ephemeral thing. Was it possible that no one ever honestly knew its embrace?

No. Home wasn't what made her happy in that moment.

She forced a smile. Looked at each of her sisters in turn. "I am very happy to be with you."

That much was the truth. Even as they trundled toward Highley, where she would match her husband to another. As though it were a perfectly ordinary thing for a wife to find her replacement. As though it did not sting that he had clearly been planning to replace her all along.

Not that it should matter. And it didn't. Not really. It was just pride.

That was it.

She looked to the window again.

"So . . ." Sesily began, and Sera prepared for the question, knowing that she had no doubt unlocked a deluge of them. And it was only fair, was it not? They were here, piled into a carriage with virtually no information about whys and wherefores, simply because she had asked. Certainly they deserved some answers.

She looked to Sesily who, of course, was the first to leap into the breach. Sesily had never in her life kept quiet when there was something important to be said. "Yes?"

"Is Caleb very handsome?"

There was a beat as the question fell into the carriage, surprising everyone. Seleste grinned. "You've finished with the men of England, then? On to America?"

"I'm not unwilling to consider the possibility."

"Mother will go mad if you marry an American!"

Sophie said. "Remember how furious she was when Seline married 'that horse breeder'?"

"First," came Seline's exasperated reply, "Mark is not just any horse breeder. He's richer than half the aristocracy."

"Which means virtually nothing," Sesily interjected. "Everyone knows half the aristocracy are poor as church mice."

"Second . . ." Seline pressed on, "Mother knows better than to interject herself into another marriage. It hasn't gone terribly well in the past. We're headed to the country to secure Sera a divorce, for God's sake." It was difficult to argue that. "Which brings me to third, Mother will be thrilled beyond words to see Sesily married to *anyone*. Even a barkeep. From *America*." The last was said the way one might pronounce a dread disease. *Plague*. Or *leprosy*.

"Not a barkeep, per se," Sera said, softly.

They all heard her nonetheless, Sesily's wide grin, the only indication that they were eager for her input. "Which brings me back to the important question at hand."

Seline spoke at the same time. "Pub owner, then."

"We prefer tavern," Sera said.

Sophie shot forward again. "*We*." She looked at the others. "She said *we*."

"Bollocks," Sesily said, reaching for the narrowly cracked window at the side of the coach and pushing it open as far as it would go—unfortunately, not far enough to move the air in the conveyance. "I suppose the more important question is not whether Mr. Calhoun is handsome, but rather if he is claimed."

Sera shook her head. "He is not."

"Handsome?" Sesily teased. "Pity."

"Claimed." Sera laughed, enjoying the feeling, rare and welcome. "He's quite handsome, as a matter of fact."

Sesily's eyes lit up. "Excellent!"

"You are certain he is not claimed?" Seline asked thoughtfully. "You haven't—"

Sera shook her head. "I haven't."

"At all?" Seline said, full of disbelief.

"At all."

"You know none of us would judge you if you had," Seleste leapt to say.

"Of course not. What with how awful Haven must have—" Seleste said, cutting herself off before she could finish the sentence, the result of their sisters' combined, pointed stares. "Never mind."

Except he hadn't been awful.

She didn't say the words. Hated that she even thought them. But in all the years that she had been away from him, she had not taken a lover. And thinking of him had been why.

"Well," Sesily said. "Is he big and brutish? Warnick-sized? I should not turn away someone Warnick-sized."

The outraged gasps and snickers around the carriage pulled Sera from her thoughts. "The Duke of Warnick?" If she recalled correctly, the Scotsman had inherited a dukedom years earlier and never came to London. "Is he in Society now?"

"Rarely. He's King's dearest friend," Sophie said, referring to her husband with a wave of her hand. "And married to one of our dearest friends. You'll meet Lily soon enough. She promised they'd be back in town in the autumn."

"Oh," Sera replied, unable to find other words. Hating that a whole person had entered their lives while she'd been gone. It was a silly thought, of course. No doubt dozens of people had done just that. And besides, she had Caleb, didn't she?

"You'll love her," Sesily said. "Everyone does."

"Everyone thinks she's a proper scandal," Seline said, looking to Sera. "She sat for a nude painting while you were away. It put Sesily's dramatics to shame."

"Well. *We* love her. We love anyone with a scandalous past." She grinned. "That's why we like *you* so much, Sera. Now. To the point. Is he very large?"

Sera smiled. "Very."

Not as tall as Haven. She ignored the thought.

"Excellent."

"And very brash. Hates Englishmen."

Sesily smirked. "Then he shall loathe Haven."

"He already does." She paused, then added, "He's a good friend."

Sesily watched her for a long moment. "You deserve one of those."

She wasn't sure she did, honestly.

"We shall all get along perfectly, then," Sesily said. "Is he joining us?"

"No," Sera answered, too quickly, nearly revealing the lie in the truth. Caleb was not joining them. He was to stay in London to keep the Sparrow in order. But that did not mean that Sera was leaving the tavern entirely. "He's not."

"Sera, we believe you *haven't*." Sesily offered an exceedingly clear hand motion, eliciting several snickers. "But is it possible that . . . you *wish* to?"

All the world, so interested in her sexual exploits. And none understanding that she hadn't any exploits. That she didn't want them. Ever again. "It's not possible. Caleb is not joining me. You are. And that's that."

A pause again. And then, "Does Haven know *we're* joining you?"

Sera hesitated, and the silence stretched through the carriage. "Not . . . exactly?"

"Well. There's that, then," Sophie said, matter-of-factly. "I did wonder why he had been so willing to open his doors to me. Considering . . ."

Seline laughed. "Considering the last time he saw you, you put him on his ass in a lake."

"It was a pond," Sophie pointed out, primly. "An *indoor* pond."

"Oh, yes. That's much better," Seleste said.

Sophie waved away the jests and looked to Sera. "So, we might be turning right back round once we get there?"

"I'm not spending a minute longer than necessary in this carriage," Sesily moaned. "It's hot and miserable in here."

Seleste pressed closer to Sera. "Oh, no."

"I'm beginning to feel ill," Sesily said.

"I don't even have to look out the window to know we've left the city, then. It's only a matter of time before Sesily casts up her accounts." Seleste turned to Sera. "Someone told the driver that we'd likely be stopping and pushing her out the door?"

"I wasn't quite so unfeeling as that, but yes."

"Unfeeling. She's a grown, adult human and she can't ride in a carriage without being ill."

Sesily groaned, and Sera thought she looked a bit green. "I don't know how your earl puts up with you."

Seleste smiled. "He likes a challenge."

"Don't look out the window, Sesily," Sera offered.

"Ugggh."

"In all honesty, Ses . . ." Sophie changed the topic,

reaching down for the basket Sesily had brought with her. "If not pasties, what is in the basket?"

"Not food."

Sophie sighed.

"Didn't you have breakfast?" Seline said.

"I did. But surely it's lunchtime now."

"It's half past nine."

"Oh."

"Good Lord. Your state is making you hungrier than usual, isn't it?"

Sophie nodded, reaching for the basket. "Eating for two and all that. You are sure there are no tarts in here? Fruit? Bread? *Oooh. Is there cheese?*"

"Uuuughhh. Don't say cheese."

"Never mind. I shall look myself." Ignoring Sesily's groan, Sophie worked the latch on the basket.

Sesily sat straight up. "Wait! Don't—"

A wild yowl rose from the basket, followed immediately by Sophie's shriek of surprise as she leapt back and a massive ball of white fur shot out onto Seleste's lap. Seleste shrieked as well, her arms coming to protect her face, as the animal clambered up her torso to reach the back of the bench, arching its back and clinging to the narrow space.

"What is it? What is it?" Seleste shot across the carriage, one hand clapped over her eyes, and planted herself between Seline and Sophie, eliciting a chorus of disapproval from the previously comfortable duo.

"For God's sake, Seleste," Seline said. "Stop screaming."

Seleste stopped screaming.

Sophie found her voice. "That isn't cheese."

The cat let out a low growl.

"Now we'll never get him back in the basket," Sesily whined.

Sera began to laugh. The laughter came long and welcome, in great, heaving gasps. Seline caught it next, and then Sophie. And soon, the trio was unable to stop, the ebb tide of laughter swiftly overtaken by another rise, and another, until they'd lost complete control of themselves.

"It isn't funny!" Seleste protested. "The thing attacked me!"

The thing in question hissed.

The carriage slowed, and a tap came at the roof. "My ladies? Is all well?"

"And now the coachman thinks we've all gone mad!"

Sera found breath enough to call out, "All is quite well, thank you!" before Seline and Sophie collapsed into laughter once more, bringing her along with them.

When it had once more receded, Sesily spoke, one hand over her eyes. "If I did not feel as though the insides of me were soon to be outside of me, I am sure I would find this whole scenario terribly diverting."

Sera swallowed an inappropriate hiccup of laughter. Sesily's motion sickness was not amusing. "Sesily," she said, attempting calm collectedness. "Why did you bring a"—she smirked, unable to stop the amusement—"cat?"

"Why not? People bring animals to the country," she said with a weak wave of the hand.

"Of all the mad—" Seleste interjected. "Animals like horses! Like hounds! Not cats!"

"Why not cats?" Sesily asked.

"Because it's not as though you can saddle up a cat and ride out for the afternoon, or toss it a stick. They're terribly antisocial."

"Not Brummell." They all blinked as the enormous white cat in question meowed and bumped his head against Sesily's chin. "Brummell is all charm."

"Oh, yes. That's the very first descriptor I would use."

Brummell narrowed his yellow eyes at Seleste and meowed in what could only be described as feline affront.

"Brummell," Sera said.

"Quite."

"I, for one, think he does his namesake proud," Sophie said.

"Thank you," Sesily said. "Seeing as the rest of you are paired off, I thought it was only right that I be allowed a handsome gentleman suitor of my own." She paused.

"None of us are paired," Seleste pointed out.

"Not in this precise moment, but you're practically songbirds the rest of the time. Like squawking doves."

"Doves coo," Sophie pointed out.

"Whatever." Sesily waved a hand. "Perfectly paired. Like a damn oil painting."

"Sounds a terribly boring painting," Seline said.

"Enough. You *know* what I mean."

And Sera did know. "I am not paired like a dove."

Sesily looked to her. "Then why are we headed to your husband?"

"Because he's forcing me to go there."

"Just as he forced you to return to London? As he forced you to storm Parliament and demand a divorce?"

"Sesily." Sophie's gentle warning went ignored.

"Just as he forced you to leave?"

Defensive, Sera narrowed her gaze on her sister. "What are you saying?"

For a moment, it seemed as though Sesily might answer the question honestly. As though she might say all the things that she must have been thinking. That they all must have been thinking. Instead, she sighed and leaned her head back against the seat. Brummell took that moment to climb down from his perch and settle on her lap. "Only that it seems you are poking a bear, Seraphina. Why else arm yourself to the teeth?"

"How have I armed myself?"

"How else does a Dangerous Daughter arm herself?" This, from Sophie. "With the rest of us."

Like that, the humor was gone from the moment, and Sera was returned to the present. To the fact that she was not simply out for a summer's ride. To the fact that she was headed to the country, to the place she'd once loved as much as she'd loved its master.

The place where she'd lost herself. Left herself. The place she'd fled to begin anew.

Not anew. Again.

"And a cat, it seems," Seleste added.

Sera ignored the attempt to lighten the mood. "I owe you all so many answers."

Sophie shook her head. "You do not owe us anything. But if you would like to tell us what you desire, we are here to help you get it."

Except they could not give her what she desired. They could not return her to the past, or catapult her into the future.

They could not restore what she had lost, or gift her with the only thing she could imagine would heal her wounds. Or make her forget she'd ever been married.

The only person who could do that was her husband, ironically. And so she careened toward him. To find her replacement. And fetch her divorce.

She would get her freedom. She would own the Sparrow. She would sing, and live a new life. And she would move forward.

She did not deny it seemed slightly easier with her

sisters at her side, because of their loyalty. And there, in the shifting, clattering carriage, filled with stifling heat and an ornery cat, she resolved to tell them the truth.

"I have not been with Caleb." Lord knew why she began there. But it seemed an important point. "I haven't been with anyone since . . ."

Her sisters nodded. Understanding.

They didn't understand, of course. But she appreciated the effort.

"Well," said Seleste. "Once you've received your divorce, you'll find another and build a life. Husband, children, the whole lot."

They didn't know. This was the secret she kept. The one she'd fled and would never forget.

"When I left, the day I left . . ." she trailed off. Tried again. "I cannot have another child."

The silence in the coach was deafening, and Sera hated it. Hated that her sisters, who never seemed to be at a loss for words, could not seem to find them.

She looked up, refusing to cower. Sophie's eyes glistened. Seleste's mouth was ajar, her shock clear. Even Seline, the least emotional of them all, seemed horrified by the confession. Sera nodded. "Now you know. My future—it's not a family." Still, silence reigned. Sera looked to Sesily, wanting the confrontation that only a sister could give. "Come now, Ses. Not even you can find something to say?"

Sesily met her gaze without hesitation. "You didn't deserve any of it."

Six words, and somehow no one had ever said them. Sera had never even thought them. And now, there they were, like a perfect, welcome wound, stealing her breath. She pressed her lips together, regaining her composure. "No one does."

Sesily nodded. "God knows that's true. But you didn't. And I think you ought to know it."

Without a reply, Sera looked out the window, surprised, somehow, to see the chimneys of Highley peeking over the horizon. "We are nearly there."

Her heart began to pound.

The last time she'd been in a carriage approaching Highley, she'd barely noticed the house, the way it rose up in stunning, stately magnificence, speaking to the venerability of the dukedom to which it belonged. It was massive—a sprawling estate house with grounds that spread over hundreds of acres of lush green countryside.

It was designed to impress. To intimidate. To separate the haves and the have-nots. She'd at once loathed it and loved it, because it was this place that had sired her husband, as though he'd sprung not from man, but from manor.

When she'd tempted Malcolm to smiles here, she'd felt more powerful than at any other time in her life.

She touched her fingers to the window, leaning toward it, imagining she could catch the sweet smell of the earth beyond. Imagining she could catch the past. The future it had promised.

She shook her head.

That future wasn't possible. But that did not mean that a new one wasn't.

A new one, where she was free. Where she cared for herself. Where she succeeded on her own merit and not the whim of her aristocratic husband. No matter how different he seemed. And he did seem different, though she could not put her finger on how.

She supposed she was different as well.

Different enough to know she must stay the course.

The carriage slowed to turn up the miles-long drive,

swaying mightily on the less traveled ground, and Sera returned her attention to her sisters, each watching her, an assemblage of soldiers in corsets and petticoats. Awaiting their orders.

She looked from one to the next, each proud and prepared. She could not help her smile. "He's going to be livid when we all pile out."

"Good," Sophie said, and Sera marveled at her strong, proud youngest sister. At the way she'd grown and blossomed. "I have rarely made the Duke of Haven's life pleasant, and I don't intend to begin now. He's a massive debt to pay."

The house came into view, and she instantly noticed him, standing alone at the top of the steps leading to the main entrance. She stiffened, and Sophie peered out the window. "Good Lord. Is he waiting for you?"

"No doubt he was afraid I would not heed his summons."

"He's proper horrid," Seline said.

"There's still time for us to turn the coach around," Seleste offered.

For a moment, Sera considered it.

"Do you think he's been there all morning?" Sophie asked.

"Possibly," Sesily groaned. "No doubt he's made some deal with the devil for endless stamina."

Seraphina might have thought to thank heaven for her loyal sisters, each more willing to skewer Haven than the last. But she was instead transfixed by the man.

It looked as though it was somehow reasonable that he'd been standing on his steps all morning, still and strong—perfectly turned out in pristine coat and trousers, boots polished to looking-glass shine—as though he would happily remain there until nightfall. Longer, if need be. Sera hated how calm he looked, as though it were perfectly normal for a duke to linger at the entrance to his estate, awaiting his guests.

Not guests.

His wife.

The mistress of the house.

There had been a time when he had waited there for a different reason. Because he could not bear another minute without her.

She couldn't help the little huff of laughter that came at the thought.

The carriage came into the rounded drive, and his gaze found hers through the small, mottled window. She resisted the instinct to look away. As it pulled to a stop, he came forward and Sera's brow furrowed. What was his game? Where was the requisite liveried footman to scurry in and open the door with an aristocratic flourish? The Haven she'd known would never have dreamed doing a servant's work.

Not true. He'd performed this exact task once before.

Her brows went up in question, and he raised an insolent brow, as if to say, *You dare question me?*

She changed her mind. This man was not so different from the Haven she had known. She could not wait to see his response when the door opened and he was faced with all five of the Soiled S's. No. He'd never called them that. He'd always called them the other name. The worse one. The Dangerous Daughters.

"Sera?" Sesily asked.

"Hmm?" She did not look away from him. She couldn't. He was always more handsome in the country, dammit.

She didn't like being off-kilter. Didn't like the sense that all this was about to go pear-shaped.

"Does Haven like cats?"

She looked to Sesily, already coming to the edge of her seat, Brummell in arms, as though she was prepared to do battle. Sesily was often first into the fray, even when she was green at the gills. "I don't know. But I doubt it."

"Excellent," she said.

Haven opened the door, and Sesily flew from the carriage, thrusting the panicked cat into his arms. "Hold this!"

Surprisingly, he did, somehow controlling his own shock as he failed to control the animal, which immediately went wild, hissing and clawing and flailing to be free.

All while Sesily cast up her accounts upon the duke's perfectly polished boots.

Sera's hand flew to her mouth, as though she could capture her astonished gasp. As though she could hide the pleasure that edged through it. She couldn't.

His head snapped up at the sound, and he met her eyes, at once furious and shocked beyond words. Sera lowered her hand, revealing her grin, wide with the realization that everything had, in fact, gone pear-shaped.

For him.

Chapter 10

─── ✒ ───

DANGEROUS DAUGHTER DOWNS DUKE!

April 1833
Three years, four months earlier
Highley Manor

*M*alcolm couldn't believe his good fortune.

She'd come. He'd asked her to come, and she had.

He bounded down to the carriage, ignoring the cool April wind, looking up to the coachman as he opened the door and pulled out the steps. "You weren't followed, were you?"

If she'd been followed, she'd be ruined. And he did not wish her ruined. He only wished her his. Privately. There was no privacy to be found in a London season.

"No, Your Grace," the driver said, his tone barely edging into offense. "Followed your directions to the letter."

Haven was already looking into the coach, breath catching as skirts appeared, a deep berry red, the color of desire. And sin. And love. The color of love.

He reached for her hands, gloved in the same wicked color, disappearing into a perfectly tailored grey traveling cloak, buttoned high up the neck with utter propriety.

He hated that coat, and vowed to remove it just as soon as she was inside this house. Just as soon as she was on solid ground—the ground that would soon be theirs.

Just as soon as he asked her to marry him.

She grinned up at him. "I hope you understand how well I trust you, Your Grace. Some might say that accepting an hours-long carriage ride to Lord knows where, alone, is a terrible idea."

He lifted her gloved hand to his lips, wishing the fabric gone. Wishing her warm skin against his. *Soon.* "Your trust is valued beyond measure, my lady."

Her gaze slid past him to the manor house. "This is an impressive cottage."

He didn't turn to look at the massive structure, at the cold stones, hundreds of years old, that had seen generations of dukes before him. He lowered his voice to a whisper, barely recognizing himself when he said, "I wish it were a cottage."

Her eyes lit with teasing pleasure. "What then? You, a humble shepherd? Me, a rosy-cheeked milkmaid?"

Settling her hand into the crook of his arm, he led her up the stone steps and through the enormous entryway, empty of servants. He'd given them the day, and in that, taken it for himself. He did not have to play the duke. Not ever with Seraphina. He spoke low at her ear, nevertheless. "Is that what you'd like?"

She looked up at him. "Shepherd, woodcutter, butcher, rat catcher. Whatever you choose, that's what I'd like."

He believed her. Had there ever been anyone who had wanted him first, and his title second? Not any of the women who chased after him at balls throughout London . . . not any of the men who angled for his friendship and his financial backing . . . not even his mother.

Indeed, his mother had only ever wanted the title. The child required to secure it had been an inconsequential aside.

But Seraphina, she wanted *him*. Not the title.

He guided her into his private study—the only room in the house where he felt truly comfortable—where a fire burned in the hearth. "Rat catcher?" he asked, turning her to face him as the door closed behind them, her nearness relaxing him, warming him.

She smiled. "They can be terribly useful."

"And what of you?" He pulled her close.

Her hands came up, around his neck, her fingers sliding into his hair, and he fought the urge to close his eyes and bask in the touch.

"What would you like me to be?" she asked, her beautiful blue eyes meeting his, seeing into him.

He didn't want some fantasy version of her. He didn't need it. She was the fantasy. Heart pounding, he shook his head. "Whatever you wish to be," he whispered. "Whatever makes you happy."

"A seamstress then," she whispered, her gaze falling to the weave of his topcoat, one hand sliding down to stroke the fabric. "Mending clothes by candlelight, singing in the window, waiting for you to come home."

He'd take that life. Trade everything for it. For any life she would give him. But he wouldn't have to.

"What would you sing?"

She smiled. Then, God help him, she sang. Like heaven. *"Here lies the heart and the smile and the love, here lies the wolf, the angel, the dove. She put aside dreaming and she put aside toys, and she was born that day, in the heart of a boy."*

He pulled her close, unable to do anything else. Unable to look anywhere but into her beautiful blue eyes, unable to think of anything but the sound of her. The smell of her. The feel of her. "I didn't know you could sing."

She blushed. "All well-bred young ladies are required to do so."

Not like that. His arms tightened around her. "But you're not a lady. You're a seamstress in the window. With the most beautiful voice I've ever heard."

She sighed at the thought. "Only in my dreams."

He shook his head. "Try another dream."

She laughed, the sound filling him with light, as it always did. "I'm rubbish at this game, it seems."

"No," he said, setting his hand to her chin, tilting her face up to his. "You are quite good at it. But I've a better picture to paint."

Her brows rose. "Do you?"

"You're a duchess." Her eyes went wide at the words, and he saw the desire there. Not for the title. For him.

She wanted him.

He continued. "You're perfect and so far beyond my reach that I daren't even look at you." He did look at her, of course. "I daren't even think of you." The flush returned, and he ran his thumb across the pink skin of her cheeks. "I certainly shouldn't touch you." Her lips parted, and he couldn't resist leaning in, closer, thanking heaven that they were alone. "Most definitely shouldn't kiss you."

"Nonsense," she said, coming up on her toes. "What is the point of being duchess if I cannot insist upon kissing?" She closed the distance between them, and he groaned his pleasure as she gave herself up to him, soft and sweet and perfect, tasting of mint. She always tasted of mint, as though she were in a constant state of readiness for him.

He licked past her lips, delving into her mouth, sliding and stroking and tasting until she gave herself to him, to the moment, to the illicitness of it. And then she was matching him, stroke for stroke, and his hands were at the fastening of her cloak, making quick work of it, pushing it over her shoulders and down her arms. She didn't hesitate to help him, and he considered it something of a miracle when he pulled away, leaving them both panting.

She blinked up at him. "Malcolm?"

He closed his eyes at the name, at the pleasure that rioted through him when she spoke it. Shook his head. "I didn't intend for this—"

She smiled. "I did."

The bold, brash words were too much. Who was this woman? How was she so brave? So sure? How did she control him so well? How did he want it so much?

And then she whispered, "We haven't much time."

She was right. She had to return to London in scant hours. He'd brought her here to have a moment with her, without prying eyes and clamoring gossip. Not to take her, but to ask for her.

He should have gone to her father. Asked properly. He was a duke, dammit. There was a process for the asking of a hand in marriage.

But he didn't want others in this. He wanted her, alone. Honest. His, not because of titles or business or finances or land or because her father decreed it. It did not matter what an old man wanted. It mattered only what she wanted. What she chose.

And she was choosing him. She was the only person who had ever truly chosen him.

There was time enough to ask her father. He wouldn't say no. No one turned away a dukedom.

But what if she did?

His heart pounded even as she smiled, curious, and reached for him, one red-gloved hand sliding down his arm, leaving fire in its wake. "Malcolm?"

He captured it. "What did you tell your mother? Your sisters? How did you escape them?"

Later, her hesitation would consume him. But in the moment, he barely noticed it. "I told them I was visiting an ill friend. That I would be gone for the afternoon."

He nodded. As excuses went, it was not perfect, but it was not horrendous. It bought them an hour. Two, perhaps. Enough time for him to ask her. Enough time for him to make her say yes.

What if she didn't say yes?

He ran a hand through his hair, suddenly unsettled. Doubt was not an emotion with which he was familiar.

"You've never been to my home," she said, pulling him from his thoughts.

"I—" He stopped, not knowing what to say.

She shook her head. "It doesn't matter."

Mal had the distinct impression that it did. He didn't want to sit on an uncomfortable settee and suffer the smirks and stares of her mother and sisters, the ones that marked him as nothing more than a title. The ones he suffered whenever he was in public—a bachelor duke, like a bull to market. He met Sera's eyes and told her the truth. "I'm too greedy for you," he said. "I want you for me, alone. I want to be yours, alone."

A pause, silent and thoughtful as she considered him. It felt as though she could see into him. She took a deep breath then, letting it out, as though she'd made a decision.

And she had.

"Well," she said soft, serious. "I am here. Sans chaperone. As requested."

He had no right to make such a request. She should never have agreed. But she wanted him just as he wanted her. He knew it every time he looked into her eyes, every time he caught her gaze across a ballroom, hundreds of people keeping them from each other.

He knew it now, when she reached for his face with her free hand, the kidskin there blocking her touch—making him wish she weren't wearing the gloves. "I am yours," she whispered. "Shepherd, duke, rat catcher . . ." She shook her head with a smile. "Whatever you wish."

He lowered his forehead to hers.

"Yours to do with as you wish," she whispered.

His breath came on a tide of pleasure.

She would say yes.

But if he made love to her, she would have to say yes.

And then his lips were on hers, and she was his. In his arms, his fingers working at the fastenings of her bodice, making room for their touch, reveling in the little sighs and gasps she offered—each another gift, just for him. Private.

Christ, he loved the privacy of this. The idea that no one knew that she was his. That no one imagined this moment. That even after today, when all the world knew that they would be matched, this afternoon was theirs alone. Shared with no one.

And then her bodice was open, and she was bared to him, and her fingers—those damn gloved fingers—were guiding him, and he was tasting her warm, smooth skin, his name on her lips like a prayer.

This was how it would be forever.

No titles. No demands. Nothing but them, together.

Happy. Wanted.

Loved.

He slid his hand down to the hem of her skirts, reaching and finding the impossibly smooth skin of her leg beneath. She wasn't wearing stockings. She was magnificent. He ran his teeth over the skin of her breast, knowing, somehow, that the edge would set her aflame. Her gasp set him in motion, moving lower, even as her skirts slid up, her thighs opening without hesitation, as though she knew what he planned.

As though she wanted it even more than he wanted to give it to her.

And she did. He knew it—reveled in it as she arched up, offering herself to him, giving in to him. And he took it without hesitation. Without guilt or shame.

She was here, they were alone, and this was for them and no one else. Not her parents, who would no doubt crow their marriage to the world, nor the gossip rags that would immediately track their every move.

No one knew what she allowed him to taste that afternoon, in his private study, with none but the walls to witness.

No one knew what she allowed him to touch.

What she allowed him to take.

No one heard her little gasp of pain, the sighs of pleasure that came afterward, the way she fell apart a heartbeat before he followed her, splintering from the pleasure of their secret, perfect love.

Just as he did not hear the door to the study open.

Just as he did not hear the shocked murmurings from the women assembled beyond.

Just as he did not realize what had happened, until Seraphina went stiff beneath his touch, pushing him off her, scrambling backward, trying unsuccessfully to cover herself.

Until the Countess of Wight barked out a horrified "Seraphina!" followed by, "You brute! Remove your hands from her person *immediately*!"

He did. Instantly. Not yet knowing that it was the last time he'd ever touch her with complete trust. Not yet understanding the full scope of the situation. "My lady," he said, immediately retrieving his coat to cover Seraphina—to protect her. Sera first. Always. "You misunderstand."

"I understand you are a bounder, Haven. The worst kind of cad."

"Not the worst kind," he said. "I intend to marry your daughter."

Even with the disastrous events of the afternoon, the words lightened him. The brash countess would surely settle once she heard that. It wasn't the most ideal of circumstances, and he and Sera would likely not be able to see each other in private until their wedding day, but they'd laugh about this in years to come, late at night, a passel of children abed in the chambers upstairs. He looked to Sera. "We shall marry."

There wasn't happiness in her eyes, however.

There was something else. Something like . . .

Guilt.

Confusion flared, and cast a look about the room, surprised to find another woman there, in the doorway. Another set of eyes, these filled with regret, and ever-present disdain.

His mother. His mother, who should have been in London.

"What are you doing here?"

She did not answer, but Haven did not need to hear it. He knew. When he looked at the Countess of Wight, it was confirmed. There was no regret in the woman's eyes. No guilt. No anger.

Only strength.

It took no time to piece it together—it was the oldest tale there was. The countess had collected his mother and followed her daughter here, to Highley. Not out of some impressive maternal instinct for danger, but because she'd known what was to come.

Because they'd conspired to trap him. "No." He looked to Seraphina. To the woman he loved. Willed her to deny it. "*No.*"

He resisted the truth even as he knew it to be true.

And then she nodded, and it crashed around him.

He wasn't the catcher. He was the rat.

Chapter 11

TALBOT TAKEOVER; HAVEN HORRIFIED!

He should have known she'd bring reinforcements.

He might have even imagined that she would bring sisters. But it hadn't occurred to him that she'd bring *all* of them.

She had, however, and they were reinforcements of the highest order, as there were not four people in the world who loathed him more than his sisters-in-law.

Eventually, when he recovered his wits, he would not be able to blame her. After all, this was the place she'd been promised would be her sanctuary. The place that should have been her home, where her family was not only welcome, but grew. And, instead, it was a place that had left her with nothing but pain and anger. A place from which she had fled.

Reinforcements must have felt necessary.

He would understand it in a bit. But in that moment, Haven was not pleased. And that was before the most outrageous one deposited what appeared to be a feral cat into his arms and promptly vomited upon his boots.

He was an intelligent man, he liked to think, but he had not a single idea how to proceed from this precise course of events, except to narrow his gaze at the four women remaining in the carriage, each obviously resisting the urge to laugh.

Correction. *Three* were resisting the urge to laugh.

His wife *was* laughing. With what appeared to be immense pleasure, and damned if he didn't warm at the sound—one of his very favorites. Even if he didn't care for the situation that inspired it.

Haven adjusted his grip on the wild animal in his arms, setting one hand to the writhing beast's back with firm control and willing it still. "Enough, beast," he said for show, sending a silent, *Come on, cat, at least allow me this*, to whatever higher power managed felines.

Remarkably, blessedly, the power in question heeded his request, which left Haven able to turn to the cat's owner and say, "May I be of some assistance, Lady Sesily?"

Sesily stood and leveled him with a cool look. "A decent gentleman would already have proffered his handkerchief."

She'd never liked him. None of them had.

Not that he'd deserved their liking.

"I would not like to give you reason to find me lacking, but . . ." There was not much he could do with a wild beast in his arms.

"No need to worry, Haven," Sesily said, her spirits clearly restored. "I find you immensely lacking without any additional reasons."

He blinked. "I am heartened to see you are feeling so much repaired."

"Knowing I ruined your boots does help matters along."

"I see you are as charming as ever," he said dryly, lifting the animal in his arms. "And with significantly more cats."

The cat protested with a mighty yowl.

So much for the feline gods.

Sesily reached for the animal. "Only a monster would punish a cat for an unavoidable owner infraction."

"Oh, for God's sake," he said, "I'm not punishing the damn cat. If you take him from me, I shall find you a handkerchief."

"No. No one is taking the cat. The cat is going back into his basket until Sesily has a room." Sera stepped down from the carriage, basket in hand, heading directly for them. "And a bath."

With that, the other women seemed to fade away, dwarfed and diminished by Seraphina, tall and beautiful, blue eyes clear and calm even as he knew she must be thinking about all the same things he thought about in this place. She looked utter perfection, even with the perspiration that coated the bridge of her nose and the wide expanse of skin above the bodice of her dress.

Not that he was noticing the skin there. The slope of her breasts.

He was simply noticing that the carriage must have been warm, what with the way her flushed skin rose and fell. Straining against the heather-grey fabric of the frock. It was nearly too tight for her. Perhaps she should take it off.

For her own comfort.

He cleared his throat.

"Your Grace."

Haven swallowed sharply, his gaze immediately snapping to hers. She appeared to be waiting for him to act. Had she said something? He opened his mouth, willing words to come. What came was, "Er."

Which was not a word at all.

One perfect black brow rose.

He cleared his throat again, but refused to speak and thus make an additional fool of himself. Silence could not be criticized.

The youngest Talbot sister, Sophie, snickered from her place several feet away. She'd always been considered the quiet one. That was, until three years ago, when she'd planted him ass-deep in a fishpond and ruined his best boots. After that, she'd found a bastard of a husband and her own voice, which she did not hesitate to use in the moment. "Perhaps the cat has got his tongue?"

One side of Sera's mouth twitched. "A woman can dream."

His brows snapped together. "What do you want?"

Her red lips curved. "The *cat*, Haven." She extended the open basket to him. "I want the cat."

Of course she did. She'd said as much.

Miraculously, the animal accepted its imprisonment without argument, after which Haven extracted his handkerchief and offered it to Sesily, who took it without hesitation. It was only then, when silence fell in the span of a heartbeat or two, that Haven realized that his best laid plans had gone entirely to waste.

Sera seemed to notice it as well. "Where are they?"

He feigned ignorance. "Who?"

Her brow furrowed. "The girls, Haven. Where are my replacements?"

As though she could ever be replaced.

He ignored the thought. "It's a good thing they aren't here, considering we're going to have to find four additional bedchambers for today's unexpected guests. How long are they staying?"

"Where is your brotherly love, Duke?" the one married to Earl Clare asked.

He ignored the question. "How long, Seraphina?"

She smiled, all serenity, and patted his cheek. "There are thirty bedchambers in this monstrosity of a house," she scoffed. "I think you'll be able to find space for family."

"Monstrosity?"

"No one requires a home this large." The words were full of distraction as she looked to a massive old tree, heavy with summer. A single crow sat on a low-hanging branch, and it seemed Sera was watching the black bird.

"There was a time when you liked it," he said.

She looked back to him then and said, softly, "No longer."

Of course she didn't. He was an ass for making her come here. For making her remember all they'd lost.

She continued, unaware of the riot of his thoughts. "Are you saying you haven't the room?"

"Of course we've the room." He turned and began to climb the stairs, suddenly keenly aware that the last time Sera had been here, she'd left him. And he'd deserved it. He resisted the urge to turn back and take hold of her. To prevent a repeat of the events of the past.

"Where are they?" Sera repeated her question. She followed him into the main entryway, flanked by her sisters—each wilder and stronger than the next—and his plans for the evening were suddenly outrageous. Misguided. Impossible. "Why did you summon me here with such insistence?"

What if he told her the truth?

"Are they even here?"

What if he told her he'd expected her to come alone?

"Haven?"

What if he told her he had planned to win her back?

"And why aren't there any staff about?" He turned to face her, prepared to tell her the truth, but when he met her wide eyes, he saw that she already knew the truth. "Where is the staff?"

"I gave them the afternoon off," he said, injecting the words with enough ducal force to inhibit any further questions.

He failed to remember that the Talbot sisters had never been intimidated by ducal force. Five pairs of knowing eyes bored into him, seeming to lay him bare.

"Why?" Lady Sesily said, handkerchief still at her lips.

Malcolm ignored the question and looked away to the crow on the tree, now no longer alone. There were still black birds there, seeming to watch him in return. He straightened his shoulders, channeled his ducal line, and, focused, returned his attention to Seraphina.

Mistake.

His wife's gaze was narrow and knowing. "Where are the girls?" It was her tone that brooked no refusal in the end, however, all duchess, ironically.

"They arrive in three days." The house was prepared, every bed made, every meal planned.

She nodded, and he could see the question in her eyes, the one she held back. *Why are we alone?*

He wondered for a moment what she might say if he responded honestly. If he told her the truth that they all seemed to suspect already. If he said, *Because I wanted you alone. Because I wanted to undo it all.*

It seemed a ridiculous plan now.

And so, instead, he found his reply in the moment, a fabrication that, once spoken aloud, thankfully seemed legitimate. "Our agreement was that you would play hostess and matchmaker, no? With that in mind, should you not be here in advance? To do whatever it is hostesses and matchmakers do?"

Malcolm was proud of the dismissive tone he somehow mustered, a tone that seemed to grate upon his sisters-in-law even as his wife remained unmoved.

"This is madness, Haven, you understand that, do you not?" Sesily said.

"Having her here will only set the other girls on edge," the Marchioness of Eversley spoke.

"No one has ever been comfortable around the Talbot sisters—and that is before one of us is *married* to their potential suitor." This, from Mark Landry's wife. Or maybe the Countess of Clare. He could never tell them apart.

"Good Lord. Even saying that aloud sounds like insanity," said the other. He'd forgotten what chattering magpies his sisters-in-law could be. But whichever one said that last bit wasn't wrong. The entire plan was mad.

He did not look to the assembled women, instead focusing completely on his wife, who watched him for a long moment before saying, "Well then. I imagine there is a great deal to do."

Seraphina lifted her skirts in one hand and, clutching the cat basket in the other with all the grace she might have if she were carrying a scepter, climbed the steps of the home to which she was mistress. He remained on the drive, watching her, transfixed by her smooth, fluid movements, even as she stilled on the threshold, turning to look down to him. "Why is your mother not playing this role?"

He did not hesitate. "The dowager is dead."

Seraphina revealed no emotion. "I am sorry."

"Are you?" He couldn't help himself.

"Not really, no."

Her sisters let out a little collection of surprised breath at the frank reply and, for the first time since he'd seen the carriage turn up the drive, Malcolm understood that even they were unsettled by this new, strong Seraphina.

But he, too, had changed. He was no longer afraid of the truth. He nodded once. "No, neither am I."

He didn't know what he expected her to say. He didn't know what he expected from her at all—actions, words, both, neither. She did not speak. Instead, she took what seemed to be a long, full breath, and turned her back on him, entering the house.

And Malcolm realized that she might never do what he expected ever again.

*S*he should have chosen a different bedchamber.

In the moment, with her sisters chattering like magpies, it had been the most natural thing in the world to climb Highley's wide center staircase and turn left into the massive family wing, assigning them each one of the manor house's most luxurious chambers, as richly appointed as she remembered.

It was only once she was finished with the task that she realized that the only room left in the cradle of her sisters' security was the chamber that she had been assigned years earlier, when she was duchess.

When she was duchess. Sera always thought of the title in the past, as she did everything to do with Haven. After all, it had been two years, seven months since they'd last seen each other, and more than three since they had actually shared civil conversation, and so the past seemed the best place for them.

Even now. As she stood in the window of the rooms reserved for the Duchess of Haven, watching the sun creep up over the eastern edge of the estate, chasing black sky to grey that might have been lavender, if someone wished to call it that.

Seraphina preferred the safety of grey.

And the room was grey, after all, with memories,

muted and aged, as though decades had passed instead of years, and with them, promise.

It had been a mistake to choose this bedchamber, because it had once been hers. And she was no longer that woman. In fact, in mere weeks, she would be free of that woman, and this room would belong to another.

The room. The house. The husband. The bed.

But three nights of fitful sleep in that bed had done little to dissuade her from the fact that she should have chosen another room.

"You are awake."

Sera started, whirling toward the words, spoken from the connecting doorway to the ducal bedchamber, where Haven stood as though she'd summoned him with her thoughts, perfectly turned out, looking like it was midmorning instead of dawn. Looking like color in the grey. She narrowed her gaze on him. "That door was closed, Duke. You are not invited to use it."

He raised a brow and made an elaborate show of straightening his shirtsleeve. "I was not aware I required an invitation, as it is my door."

"As it is the door to *my* chamber, I prefer you think of it as belonging to me."

One side of his mouth kicked up, and she hated the way he looked. Handsome and young and entirely too dangerous. "What say you we share it?"

Something shot through her at the teasing in the words. Something like memory. The echo of what seemed like an eternity past, when he was a man and she was a woman and that was all that seemed to matter.

What was his game?

She straightened her shoulders. "I say you are out of your mind if you think I am interested in sharing anything with you. Particularly close quarters."

"You chose the room, Angel," he said, his voice low and still tinged with the disuse of sleep. "Did you forget that it had the door?"

Her lips flattened into a thin line as the words threaded through her with an emotion unwelcome and long out of use. "Do not call me that."

"There was a time when you liked it."

A lifetime ago. "I never liked it. It's a silly name."

"The seraphim are the highest order of angels," he reminded her. "You're named for them."

"You understand enough of my mother to know that she has never in her life had a spiritual thought, and you think she named me for an angel."

He leaned against the door frame, folding his arms across his broad chest, as though it were perfectly normal for them to converse first thing in the morning. Casually. Like husband and wife. That half smile flickered again. "I think it, nonetheless."

She gave a little laugh and returned her attention to the window. "I assure you the angelic was not in my mother's mind when she named me. She thought it sounded aristocratic. That was her goal. Always." She stopped, then added, "You know that goal intimately."

The silence that fell between them should have been uncomfortable, full of that day long ago in this very house, when she and her mother had landed a duke. But it was not uncomfortable, not even when it summoned the memory of the horror on his face as he realized that they'd set a trap for him.

And they had trapped him. She'd trapped him. Because she'd never wanted anything more than him, and she'd believed that he wouldn't have her without it. That he was too high and she too low, and happiness was not for them.

And happiness, it seemed, was not for them.

I would have married you.

We could have been.

The words had crashed around her, filled with his fury and betrayal. And the past tense. Everything with them, always in the past tense. Ephemera.

"Why are you awake?"

The change of topic did not unsettle her. It had been the hallmark of their short-lived relationship, quick movement of thought, rarely without the other easily following. "I wake early." It was either that, or stay abed and let memory rattle. "And your future wife arrives today."

"Not for hours."

The sky had edged through grey and into pink, a deep, magnificent color that seemed too bright to be natural. "It's going to rain," she said, regretting the words the moment he moved, coming to stand behind her and follow her gaze to the sky.

"Not for hours," he repeated.

He smelled the same. Like fresh earth and dark spice. She tried not to breathe too deeply, afraid of what that familiar scent might do to her. "Soon."

The weather. They discussed the weather.

"Come riding with me." They'd never ridden together. There had been talk of it, a hundred years ago, promises that they would spend the summer here, at Highley, on horseback, discovering it together. And then they'd married, and they hadn't been able to stomach each other.

Or, rather, he hadn't been able to stomach her. She could not blame him for that, she supposed. Except, she had blamed him. Even before he'd turned to another whom he could stomach better.

She looked at him. "Why?"

He lifted a shoulder. Let it fall. "Because you like to ride and it is not raining yet."

She shook her head. "What game you are playing?"

"No games," he said. "I ride in the mornings."

"Enjoy yourself," she said. "I'm to have breakfast with my sisters and prepare for your suitors." She paused. "Suitors? Suitesses? Is there a word for young women vying for the attention of a duke?"

"Wisteria."

She raised a brow at the word, the kindest of the whispered names she and her sisters had been called. *Pretty, smelled nice, and very good at climbing.* "Not so quickly, Duke. We haven't seen or scented them, yet."

He did smile at that, full and handsome, and she hated the hint of pleasure in the curve of his lips. Hated that it ghosted through her, there and gone so quickly, she'd never have noticed it if she weren't so aware of him. And why? He was nothing but a barrier between her and freedom.

"Your sisters cannot protect you all the time, you know. We shall have to interact at some point."

She'd cloistered herself with them after their arrival the other day, attempting to forget that he was in the house even as they prepared for what was to come. "We don't have to be alone to interact."

He raised a brow. "Are you afraid to be alone with me?"

"Being alone with you has never worked out quite the way I imagined," she said, knowing the words would be a blow.

The blow did not land as expected. "I think it worked out rather well, once or twice."

Who was this man?

She tried again. "Oh, yes, Your Grace, being married to you has been the great wonder of my existence."

He looked out the window. "Need I remind you that four women want a life with me so badly they are coming here to compete for it?"

She gave a little laugh. "You think that they want it? They don't. They simply think they haven't any other choice but to vie for your attention." She hesitated, then, "How did you select the poor things?"

"It's not so difficult to find unmarried women with an interest in marrying a duke."

"Not even a duke who has been tied to scandal for years?"

"Not even that, surprisingly."

It wasn't surprising, though. He was handsome and young and rich and titled and any woman of sound mind would want him.

Not that she did. "And they were willing to wait until you had me declared dead? Husband hunting takes more patience than I recall."

"You were a superior hunter."

He didn't mean the words the way they came, she knew. But they stung nonetheless, the reminder of the trap she'd lay. The mistake she'd made.

She looked away, back to the sun, edging over the fields. "Little do they know that in a matter of weeks, your attention will wander elsewhere."

She hated herself for the bitterness in the words. After all that had happened, how was it that stumbling upon him with another woman was the only thing that seemed to matter?

Hated him even more when he said, "You left me—"

"You sent me away!" she said, unable to keep her voice from rising. "You stood in the house where we might have built a home, our wedding breakfast barely over, and you told me to leave you." When he opened his mouth to reply, she found she was not through. "And do you know what is the great irony of it? The whole world thinks you ruined me before you married me, when the truth is that I was not ruined until after the fact. You ruined my hopes. My dreams. My future. *You ruined my life.* And I've had enough of that. I am here for one reason only, Your Grace. I want my life back. The one you stole."

She was breathing heavily, full of anger that she rarely allowed release.

And damned if it didn't feel good.

Even as she met his gaze and recognized his frustration. His anger. *Good.* She preferred him angry. Preferred to see her enemy. And they were enemies, were they not?

"If I stole your life, what did you do to mine? You disappeared, leaving all the world wondering where you'd gone. Imagining that I might have driven you away."

She turned away again. "You did drive me away." It was a lie, but she said it anyway, hoping it would hurt him.

Silence fell, and she ignored it, refusing to look at him, even when he said, "I worried you were dead. The doctors told me you might die. Do you have any idea how it felt to know you might have *died*?"

She did not hesitate. "I can only imagine you met the possibility with hope, considering you already had such a clear plan to replace me."

She expected many responses to the smart retort—anger, sarcasm, dismissal. She received pure, unfettered honesty. "I never wished you dead."

The words sent a wash of embarrassment through her before she could stop it. Even as she resisted the idea of allowing him to embarrass her. "No," she said. "Only gone. So, let them come. And I shall give you what you wish. With pleasure."

Only then did she realize that a small part of her wished he would acknowledge it, the fact that he'd breathed a sigh of relief on the day she'd disappeared. He did not.

"After you left, I—" He stopped, then began again. "That last day, when—" He stopped the moment Sera closed her eyes against the words and the memory that came with them. The keen sense of loss. The child she could not forget. The future she had lost. The love. She should have thanked him for stopping, but he did not give her time, instead changing tack. Repeating himself. "I never wished you dead."

She knew that, of course. "You made me angry." It was the closest she would come to apologizing for lashing out at him.

Malcolm laughed then, the sound low and full of charm, just as she remembered. "I've always done that rather well."

She couldn't help her answering smile. "That much is true."

"Come riding with me," he repeated himself. "Before the others arrive."

He said "the others" as though it were perfectly normal that a passel of young women was about to descend to vie for the role of duchess—the role she currently held. She shook her head once more. He was too tempting, even now. Even when she knew the way this ended.

"I could insist," he said. "Make it a condition of the divorce."

"You could," she replied. "But you shan't."

"How do you know that?"

"Because I don't want to. And you won't force it."

"I forced you to come here and find your replacement."

"Which benefits us both. But spending time with you

is a fool's errand. We've always liked each other too much in the moments, Malcolm. And they were never enough to make up for how we hurt each other."

He looked away, out the window, and she silently begged him to leave her. He didn't. Instead, he said, all calm, "We cannot ride, anyway."

She followed the direction of his gaze to the spot in the distance where a carriage appeared, massive and black like a summer beetle, pulled by four matching horses and a pair of matched outriders. Her heart began to pound. "The first arrives."

The words were barely out when a second carriage turned into the long drive. "And the second."

Seven more vehicles trundled down the drive, black and serious, like mourners at a burial plot, and Sera turned to her husband. "Do they all know each other? Or are they exceedingly punctual?"

He cut her a look. "I assure you, I had no intention of the day beginning at seven o'clock in the morning."

"Then they've consulted each other on arrival time."

He harrumphed at the words. When she raised an inquisitive brow, he added, "More likely, the mothers knew that the early bird gets the worm."

Sera couldn't help her smile. "Well, Your Grace, you must admit, you are a terribly plump worm."

He ignored her. "But why eight carriages? I only invited four." His confusion turned nearly instantly to horror. "Dear God. You don't think they brought sisters as well, do you?"

"They wouldn't dare. Sisters are my weapon. These girls shall need to find their own."

"Is that what this is? Battle?"

She cut him a look. "It's marriage, Duke. Of course it's a battle."

One side of his mouth kicked up. "It always was with us."

She turned away at the soft words. "From the very start." She watched the line of coaches approach. "The second carriages come with assorted necessities. Our belongings should arrive today, as well."

His brows knitted together. "It's the largest and best appointed home in Britain. Are they afraid I shan't feed them?"

"No. They're afraid you won't have ladies' maids who are expert coiffeuses. And that you shan't have dozens of perfectly tailored evening gowns. And shoes. And underthings."

"They're correct about that."

"Of course they are. You're a bachelor. This home requires . . . feminization. Which is one of my tests for your . . . let's settle on suitesses for the time being."

"It most certainly does not require feminization." She'd never heard him so affronted. "And you have tests?"

"You asked me to find you a second wife, Duke. Considering what a hash you made with the first, I should think you'd be grateful for tests."

"What, like foot races? And dressage?"

"You're not far off, as a matter of fact." His brows rose, and she rewarded his curiosity. "Lawn bowls, certainly."

He nearly chuckled, and Sera was nearly pleased. Nearly remembered how handsome he was. Nearly remembered how wonderful it was to be the focus of his pleasure.

Nearly.

A firm knock sounded on the door, followed instantly by Sesily's bellow. "Sera! Haven's harem has arrived!"

Her lips twitched, and she was quite proud of herself for the serious look she gave her husband. The duke.

This would be much easier if she stopped thinking of him as her husband. He wasn't, after all. Not really. Not since their wedding. Not since before.

Not that it would be difficult for her, either way.

She was merely thinking of the other women. Of her replacement.

She cleared her throat, and called out, "Yes! I see them!"

"Well, we should go down and give them a look, don't you think?"

"I do, rather," Sera replied, enjoying Malcolm's discomfort.

"Right then!" Sesily said, cheerfully. "I'll just tell Sophie to squeeze into whatever frock still fits round her ever-expanding midsection."

"Oi! I'm standing right here! Wearing a frock that fits quite well, thank you very much! And you're one to talk, covered in cat fur. You're not bringing him, are you?"

"Of course I am. It shall be the first test of their mettle! Also, Brummell has discerning taste."

"As the beast enjoys your company, I can't say I believe that." Seline had arrived in the corridor beyond. "Come along, Sera!"

"Good God, there are a lot of them. And you think the house is not feminine enough?" Haven asked.

She smiled. "Not nearly, no."

He growled his frustration, turning for the door to his chamber. "Don't scare them off."

"My sisters?" she asked, all innocence. "They don't scare easily."

"You know precisely whom I mean. If anyone can terrify a group of debutantes, it's you lot."

"They don't call us the Dangerous Daughters for nothing, Your Grace."

He did not laugh, and she realized the retort was not funny. Not for him. Not for her, either. Not when he turned back, time stretching with impressive weight, and said, "You never came with things."

She stilled. She hadn't come with things. Not with a trousseau, or a maid, or anything, really. None of those things mattered when she married him. But he'd been too angry to notice. "I was different."

She hoped he'd let the answer stand without reply.

He didn't. "Because you came for me."

Every time.

She could have lied, but she didn't wish to. She didn't want to be someone she was not ever again. "Yes."

He nodded and crossed over the threshold, closing the door behind him.

Only then did Sera say the rest. "I came for you. Just as I left for you."

She smoothed her skirts and went to meet the women who hoped to marry her husband.

Chapter 12

SCRUMPTIOUS SCANDAL!
SERAPHINA TO SELECT SUCCESSOR!

The Talbot sisters met Haven's suitesses in the drive, along with a collection of their secondary players—four mothers, one father, and three miniature dachshunds who did not care for Brummell, who hissed with fervor from the safety of Sesily's arms.

Beyond the collection of guests, in the frenzied backdrop of the manor house courtyard, servants from within and without already rushed about, unloading trunks and hatboxes and saddles and—was that a bathtub? Why would they require a bathtub?—as the quartet of girls was thrust forward for Seraphina's inspection, each with seemingly less understanding of the protocol required for the situation.

Not that this particular scenario was common enough to receive attention in *Mrs. Coswell's Book of Ladies' Manners*. Indeed, Sera thought Mrs. Coswell might summarily perish if she were apprised of the goings on at Highley.

There was no reason why they could not make the best of a strange situation, however. If these four were all that stood between Seraphina and her freedom, she was certainly willing to play her part. With a wide smile and even wider arms, she said, "Good morning, ladies." The girls froze, eyes wide, looking first to each other and then to their respective mothers, clearly not knowing how to reply. Sera let her smile reach her eyes. "I am Lady Seraphina." She deliberately used the address she'd had prior to her marriage.

The smallest of the four, a diminutive brunette stepped forward, dressed in shell pink and with features so small and delicate that they reminded Sera of a mouse, though not altogether unpleasantly. "Do we call you Your Grace?"

It was decided. She liked this one, who had no trouble getting right to the point. "I confess, I would prefer you not. After all, we're all here to ensure that I am not Her Grace for any more time than is absolutely necessary."

The assembled mothers and daughters tittered. "This is highly irregular," one of the maters harrumphed. "Where is the duke? It's wildly inappropriate that he send you lot to greet us."

"I beg your pardon?" Sera said. "You *lot*?"

The older woman lifted her chin and sniffed at the air. "You take my meaning."

"I'm afraid I don't."

One of the other women waved a hand in the direction of her sisters. "You and your sisters aren't exactly good *ton* these days."

"I'm a countess!" Seleste protested before pointing to Sophie. "And *she* is Marchioness of Eversley and the future Duchess of Lyne!"

"Yes," the woman allowed, as though speaking to a child. "But none of you have come by your titles . . ."

Sesily's brows snapped together. "Say *honestly*, and get back in your carriage, hag."

The words were punctuated by a wild yowl from Brummell, and Sera resisted the urge to smile at her sister's undying loyalty, which had its place, but in this instance, was not entirely helpful. She looked to the older woman as her brows shot up, mouth forming a perfect O. Before the furious mother could speak, Sera leapt in, placing herself between the two women.

"Their titles are not of interest, however, are they, my lady? Mine is. You would do best to remember the prize you are here to win."

The woman hesitated, then acquiesced.

Sera turned back to the young women. "Well. As you know, I've been out of town for several seasons. Shall we begin with introductions?"

Another mother tittered, "Simply not done."

Sera lowered her voice and leaned into the girls conspiratorially. "You'll find I have little interest in what is done. Instead, I prefer getting things done."

Four sets of eyes flew to meet hers, myriad expressions chasing surprise in them—shock, confusion, amusement, and, in the last, admiration.

Sera made a mental note to investigate Admiration—at first blush, the plainest of the bunch, and clearly not plain at all.

Malcolm might like her.

The thought did not bring the satisfaction she might have wished.

Amusement—the minuscule mouse—was first to speak, taking a firm step forward. "I am Lady Lilith Ballard, youngest daughter of the Earl of Shropshire." She pointed to the pursed-lipped woman who had spoken earlier. "That's my mother, the countess." She lowered her voice. "Well done with her, by the way."

Sera grinned. Yes. She liked this one very much. She

nodded, "It's a pleasure." She looked to Admiration, who watched with keen eyes, but showed no interest in introducing herself.

Which worked out well, because the duke took that moment to arrive. "Welcome to Highley, ladies." His voice was deep and lovely, filling the early morning with aristocracy.

Sera stiffened as the assemblage turned their attention on him, the only father in the bunch taking that moment to move, coming forward with a too-loud throat clearing. "Haven. Bit odd all this, don't you think?"

Malcolm shook hands with the man. "Brunswick." Baron Brunswick, poor as a church mouse, Sera recalled, but with a proper, respectable title. "Has anything about my recent past been less than odd?" He waved to Sera. "You've met my soon-not-to-be wife, I see, and you must know her sisters."

The baron grunted his agreement and pointed to Confusion, a redhead with enormous green eyes. "That's my girl."

It did not escape Seraphina that the *girl* in question remained unnamed. As though one girl were the same as the next, and so why bother giving them unique names? Malcolm rectified the situation. "Lady Emily, it is a pleasure to meet you."

Lady Emily, for her part, did not appear to feel similarly. Indeed, she looked as though she might burst into tears.

She was saved from the embarrassment, however, by the loud, insistent, "*Mary*," from one of the other mothers. Shock seemed to come alive then, stepping forward and virtually throwing elbows to stand in front of Haven. She was blond and lovely as a porcelain doll. And it seemed her name was Mary.

Malcolm took the moment in stride, all gentleman. "You must be Miss Mary Mayhew."

Sera tilted her head in surprise. *Miss.* The Duke of Haven even considering a woman without blue blood was a shock, considering how disdainful he and his mother had been about her father's coal mining roots. "Her father is one of the most powerful men in Commons," Sophie whispered at her ear.

A politician. Even worse.

"Your Grace," the beauty said, dropping into a deep curtsy, her voice breathless and winning and very likely the most feminine thing Seraphina had ever heard.

She couldn't help herself. Her gaze flew to Haven's face, to where he looked down at Shock with polite interest. There was nothing about it that indicated anything more than common courtesy, but Sera did not care for it.

No. She did not care, full stop.

Let him appreciate the other woman. There was absolutely no reason whatsoever that Sera should mind if he thought her beautiful. No reason for her to even notice.

In fact, she hadn't noticed him looking at all.

She snatched her gaze away, the far-off sound of clattering wheels distracting her as another black coach came up the drive. Apparently one of the girls hadn't been able to fit all her belongings into two conveyances, and required a third. It seemed slightly unnecessary, but Sera knew better than most that catching a duke required commitment.

Not that she had needed anything extravagant to do it.

She cleared her throat and looked to Admiration, immediately regretting her sharp tone and the way it hinted at her unwelcome thoughts. "And you are?"

The girl did not flinch. "Felicity Faircloth."

Sera blinked. "I beg your pardon?"

Admiration smiled. "Ridiculous, isn't it?"

"A bit."

The smile became a smirk. "Does it help if I tell you I'm Lady Felicity Faircloth?"

Sera gave a little chuckle. Admiration was her favorite. "It does not."

"What a pity," Felicity said, showcasing absolutely no disappointment. "And if I told you my father was Marquess of Bumble?"

Sera tilted her head. "There's a Marquess of Bumble?"

"Indeed there is. Old and venerable."

"Well, since Haven brought you here, I'm unsurprised by that."

Felicity looked to Sesily. "That's a lovely cat."

Brummell howled and Sesily preened. "Thank you."

"Is it feral?"

Sesily blinked. "No."

"Pity. I had hoped it might take care of my mother's dogs." The three dachshunds were beneath a nearby hedge and, in order, digging a large hole, relieving itself, and ingesting a twig. Felicity followed Sera's gaze. "They're horrible."

"Then I assume you don't come with dogs?"

"Good God. No. Only my mother."

"But you do come with her."

Felicity winked. "She's so desperate for me to be a duchess, that might be negotiable."

Sera laughed. This girl had absolutely secured first place, and she wasn't yet within the walls of Highley. Sera would have her divorce in no time. She ignored the way the thought settled, slightly off, instead thinking of the Sparrow, and her future.

Divorce meant freedom.

If Haven liked Lady Felicity Faircloth, or any of the ladies, honestly, freedom was hers.

That thought settled slightly better.

She looked to Haven, who was watching her carefully. "Duke. Come meet Lady Felicity Faircloth."

As he did, the final coach arrived, stopping just past the assembled group, and Sera turned to the rest of the assembly, arms wide, attempting to move them to the entrance to the manor house, out of the path of the conveyance. "My lord and ladies, and Mrs. and Miss Mayhew, welcome. Let's get you all settled, and we shall plan for a lingering lunch during which we may all get to know each other better. There shall be games and, of course, decent drink." She had Lord Brunswick's attention then.

The words set the group in motion, one of the women saying in a loud whisper, "It's a bit of cheek to pack *three* coaches, don't you think?"

The question, meant to undermine others, put Sera on edge, serving as a keen reminder that she loathed these people and this life, and that she could not wait to be rid of it, and the man who tethered her to it.

She wouldn't have the backbiting. This gaggle of climbing, scheming titlemongers could bite in full view, or be civil. Seraphina remained mistress of the house and owner of the title, and so she would set the rules.

"As a matter of fact, I think the extra carriage shows a marked preparedness that is admirable in one who will run such a far-reaching household." She looked to Malcolm. "Don't you, Your Grace?"

He did not hesitate to lie, which was surprising, considering the fact that minutes earlier, he'd expressed the exact opposite feelings about the mass of coaches trundling up the drive. "Indeed." Mrs. Mayhew's cheeks went red as the duke looked to the young women. "And which of you is so thorough?"

The girls, for their part, looked to each other with a mix of curiosity and regret on their various faces. Finally, Lady Lilith spoke. "It seems none of us pass this particular test, Your Graces."

And as if to prove the woman's point, the door to the ninth carriage burst open, ricocheting off the coach and bouncing back to nearly slam shut before it was caught and controlled, and one large, long, buckskin-covered leg came to the ground.

"Oh, dear."

"What does that mean?" Malcolm's question came harsh and quick.

Sera did not have time to elaborate when a dark head popped up above the carriage door, followed by wide shoulders in a perfectly tailored navy blue coat.

Those assembled seemed to hold their breath at the appearance of this brash intruder.

What was he doing here?

"Ding-dong," said Sesily, at which point Sera was fairly certain she heard Haven growl.

This was not the plan.

Something had gone wrong.

"That had better not be—" Haven left the sentence unfinished when the man turned, revealing a face battered and bruised with what Sera could only imagine was wicked skill. Caleb Calhoun smiled, revealing his teeth, somehow still unscathed, and closing the door with a single, smooth movement. He approached as though this was all perfectly normal.

She was already moving toward him. "What are you doing here?"

"Good morning to you." Removing his tall hat, he

said, "I say, this place is busier than Faneuil Hall fish market at half past five."

The women assembled gave a little gasp at the words.

Well, most of the women assembled.

Sesily gave a little squeal of glee. "The American is coming!"

Sera slid a look to Haven, only to discover he was glaring at her, without even an attempt at subtlety.

"I'm afraid not for long, sweetheart." Caleb swept the hat from his head and bowed low with a grand flourish. "What a beautiful group of ladies. I'm not sure I could pick the prettiest among you." He looked up at Sera, eyes twinkling even as one of them was shining black and nearly swollen shut, and said, "Well, besides Duchess, of course."

She raised a brow.

This was not going to make things easier.

Chapter 13

―――――――― ❧ ――――――――

SPARROW FLIES THE COOP!

"*If* you'll excuse us for just a moment?" Sera said too brightly before opening the nearest door and pushing Caleb into one of Highley's numerous receiving rooms.

Murmurs of "This is all highly irregular," and "Who is that man?" mingled with her sisters' attempts to herd the entire group to their respective chambers.

Sophie's voice came above the rest. "Surely you all would like a moment to freshen up after your early travels."

"I don't wish to freshen up!" one of the mothers replied with affront. "Your Grace! I will not have my daughter so poorly influenced by your . . . wife!"

"Ugh," said Sesily from closer range than Sera would have expected. "Can we eliminate the Mayhew chit from competition as soon as possible? Her mother does grate."

Sera spun to face her sister. "Sesily!"

"What?" Sesily feigned innocence. "I thought you might need a chaperone." Applying her prettiest flirt, she switched her attention to Caleb. "One never knows with Americans."

Caleb sent her an appreciative look. "If one is lucky."

Sera huffed her displeasure. "Both of you are insufferable." She whirled on her friend. "What in hell are you doing here? And what in hell has happened to your face?"

"You should see the other men." Caleb smirked, then winced as the expression tugged at his lip. "Ow."

"That serves you right for thinking you could charm your way out of this," she replied, the words without sting. "What happened?" she repeated, lifting her hand to her friend's strong, swollen cheek, delicately feeling about his eye.

He inhaled sharply at the touch. "You can't come back. Not right now."

Sesily gasped. "You planned to sneak off to London? How exciting!"

Sera looked to the ceiling and asked her maker for patience. She'd planned for a clandestine night or two, just to check in on the Sparrow. "It's not exciting, Sesily. It's business."

"You say that like it doesn't sound exciting as well," Sesily replied. "Which it does. It's not every day a woman has a—"

"Stop." Both Caleb and Sera cut Sesily off before she could say *tavern,* Sera looking to the door to be certain no one was close enough to hear. Malcolm was in the foyer beyond, and he met her gaze, but the fury in his eyes likely had more to do with the clamoring gaggle of mothers objecting to the entire morning, and no doubt a great deal more. Like Sera, in general.

He hadn't heard, which was all that mattered. If he knew what she had, he would have altogether too much power over her.

As though he did not have enough of it as her husband.

"The point is," Caleb went on, "you must stay here."

She blinked. "Why?"

Sesily knew when she was not required. "I shall go fetch something for the American's eye."

"I've a name, you know."

Sesily winked. "But 'the American' sounds so much more ominous, don't you think?"

"Go," Sera said.

Sesily did and Caleb said, "That one is trouble."

"I shall be far more trouble if you don't tell me what is going on."

"Don't worry about it."

"If only men understood the rampant fear that particular quartet of words instilled in women's hearts." She whacked him in the arm. "Tell me."

"Oof!" he groaned, clutching his shoulder and going pale.

"Now she's hit him!" came a pearl-clutching gasp from the hallway beyond. "You must send her away, Your Grace. This is no place for a proper young lady!"

Sera ignored the words, overcome with concern for her friend. "Caleb. What's happened to you?"

"It's fine. It was a touch dislocated, but I found a decent butcher who put it back in. It's just a bit tweaky right now."

Her brows shot up. "*Who* dislocated you?"

"The Bastards."

The Bareknuckle Bastards, the pair of brothers who ran the Covent Garden underground. Until now, they'd left Caleb and Sera alone, but it hadn't been long since the Sparrow was up and running, and Caleb and Sera had expected their success would soon be noticed—and the Bastards wouldn't like it. "Did something happen to the Sparrow?"

"Nothing that can't be fixed in a day or two." She did not like the sound of that. "They wanted a trade. Money for protection. I told them I didn't need protection from a bunch of redcoats."

"And they set out to prove you wrong."

He tried for another smile. "I got a few good punches in."

She shook her head. "You're a child."

"We're not paying them fear money."

She narrowed her gaze. "Of course we're not."

"Excellent. Then consider this business meeting adjourned. You are staying here to get your divorce, and I shall take care of the rest."

Frustration flared. If she hadn't been forced to the country, she'd have been able to help in London. She'd have been able to protect the Sparrow. Ironically, she hadn't been at the club to protect it from its enemies because she was too busy protecting it here. From a different enemy altogether.

If she lost it, she lost the only reason to have returned to Britain. All that she was fighting for. She was here for the Sparrow's promise of freedom. For its future. And for hers. But there was no point in protecting the tavern in theory if she couldn't protect it in practice. "Like hell. I'm coming with you."

"No."

She cut him a look. "Tell me. What, precisely, makes you believe you can tell me what to do?"

He sighed. "Certainly not history."

"No," she agreed. "Certainly not."

"And if you do return, then what?"

"Something!" she insisted, frustration flaring. "The Sparrow isn't anything without its namesake."

"Bollocks," Caleb said. "You stay here. I'll take care

of the Bastards. Hire security, make sure they see I won't stand for them getting in our way. Don't worry your pretty head about the bits and pieces."

She narrowed her gaze. "I shall club you in *your head* if you continued to treat me as a precious dove. I'm coming back."

"Why?"

"Because it's *mine*," she whispered. "Held in trust by you."

"Until you get your divorce, which is why you're here."

"Which will mean nothing if I don't have a tavern standing at the end of it."

He looked to the ceiling and exhaled his frustration. "You want your nose in the business."

She nodded. "Now, more than ever."

"Fine. Then I shall spend days here."

It was such a terrible idea she laughed. "No, you will not."

"For once, we agree, wife." Haven stepped into the room as though he owned it. Which she supposed he did. Irritating man.

"I'd thank you not to eavesdrop on my conversations," she said.

"As we remain married, conversations you have with unmarried gentlemen are my business, pet."

Men were insufferable. "Call me 'pet' again, and see what happens."

He did not flinch. "What? You do to me what your American scoundrel had done to him?" He looked to Caleb. "Bad luck. I only wish I could have done it myself."

"If it had been you, Duke, you'd be looking a fright, not me."

Haven grinned at that. As though it was funny. "History would suggest otherwise, Yank."

Sera paused. *What did that mean?*

It did not matter. "Haven, I must return to London."

"No." She imagined neither man much liked agreeing with the other.

She could not contain her groan of frustration. "Neither of you get a say in the decision."

"We have a deal, Sera," Haven said. "And that deal does not include sallying off to London with some American."

"I'll sally wherever and with whomever I like," she retorted, suddenly incredibly irritated by everything. "You don't own me."

"But he does," Caleb said.

She blinked. "I beg your pardon?"

Haven was set back on his heels as well. "I beg your pardon?"

Caleb's gaze found hers, and she hated the meaning in it. "He does own you, Duchess. You're his wife. He owns you, and all of your belongings. He owns your very future."

The message was clear. To keep the Sparrow safe and hers, she had to stay here. She had to secure her divorce to secure her future.

She scowled at her friend. "You're a damn traitor."

"We do what we have to. Don't worry, Duke. She's not going back to London." Sera swallowed back her urge to do additional damage to Caleb's face, and he added, "And I'll be spending some more time here, it seems. We shall all become fast friends, I'm sure."

What nonsense. They had a plan, she and Caleb. He was not staying here. She opened her mouth to tell him as much, but Haven interjected, looking as though he might do Caleb severe harm. "I assure you we will be no such thing. And you are not welcome here."

She'd been certain Caleb wasn't setting foot at Highley again, until that moment. And then it became a point of pride. Just as everything between she and Malcolm always had been. "He stays if I wish it."

"You've wished quite enough, Seraphina. I'm not of a mind to continue to coddle you like a child. There's no room for him."

"Like a *child*?" To whom, precisely, did he think he was speaking?

"Oh, now you've done it, Duke," said Caleb.

Sera turned on him and raised a finger. "You tread upon very thin ice, Calhoun." Caleb spread his hands wide and she returned her attention to Malcolm. "There are a dozen rooms for him."

"They are under construction," he said.

She smirked. "Then he may share *my* room."

Sera might have considered the twitch in Haven's jaw signaling his fury a proper win in their battle, but she could not celebrate it, because it was punctuated by a collective gasp from the hallway beyond. When she turned to the sound, it was to discover a collection of wide eyes watching from several feet away.

"Well, this is already the best country house party I've ever attended," Sesily said, large slab of beef in hand. After handing the meat to Caleb with a whispered "For your eye," she turned to the rest of the women. "Don't you agree?"

"I most certainly do not," said Mrs. Mayhew. It was always Mrs. Mayhew, it seemed. "This is utterly improper."

"Oh, please," Sera said, exasperated by the misplaced pompousness. "Then you may go, Mrs. Mayhew. But you won't, will you? Because you want a dukedom as much as any other mother in London. And this is the closest you'll get to one."

Mrs. Mayhew shut her mouth.

"Now. As I remain mistress of Highley until one of your daughters assumes the position, I must insist you find your chambers and settle in. I very much look forward to seeing you for luncheon. Seline, dear?"

Her sister immediately leapt into action.

As the assembly filed further into the manor house, Sera turned and stared down her husband. "He stays."

"He is not welcome."

"*He* is standing right here," Caleb said.

"*Now* do you prefer 'the American'?" Sesily asked.

Caleb grinned. "You know, I might. I'm happy to stay, Duchess. But who is going to deal with your man? Not that I couldn't," he rushed to add. "I'm in fine fettle."

Haven was not paying attention to anyone but Sera, though. He approached, coming close enough to unsettle her.

But she did not feel unsettled. She felt something else, entirely.

Her heart thrummed and she met his gaze with pride before answering her friend. "*I* am going to deal with him."

Haven watched her for a long moment, making her feel as though she were the only person on earth. Finally, he spoke. "It's going to cost you dearly."

"Of course it will," she said. "That is the game we play."

She surprised him, but he recovered almost immediately. He did not look away when he spoke to Caleb and Sesily. "Leave us."

The words sent a panic through Sera.

Or perhaps it was a thrill.

"Uhh." Sesily did not seem to know what to do.

"Duchess?" Nor did Caleb.

Sera was not backing down. Without looking at them, she spoke. "Sesily, please see Caleb to a room in the family quarters."

"No," Haven negotiated, strong and firm, all ducal power. "Fourth floor. West wing. On the end."

As far from her chambers as possible. She smirked. "I am able to both climb stairs and traverse corridors, husband."

He ignored the words, instead repeating himself. "Leave us." Sesily and Caleb looked to her, and Haven's irritation came on a growl. "Call off your dogs, wife."

She nodded, and they followed the direction, Sesily closing the door behind them with a quiet *snick*. Sera inhaled deeply, willing herself calm enough—strong enough—for whatever was to come. "And now we are alone. Be careful, husband, or you shall set tongues to wagging. The mother of your future wife won't care for the appearance that we remain . . . sympathetic."

"I don't care what they think."

For a moment, she believed him. But she knew better. It was a pretty lie, but a lie just the same. She faced it with all the strength she could muster. "Nonsense. You've always cared what the world thinks."

He lifted a hand then, and her breath caught in her chest at the anticipation of his touch. And then he was touching her, his warm fingers finding purchase on her cheek, as though they belonged there.

She exhaled at the heat of him. The strength.

He exhaled, as well. Long and wonderfully ragged, as though he were as ravaged by feeling as she was.

As though he were ravaged worse.

She closed her eyes, resisting the urge to lean into the warm cradle of his palm. *Please,* she begged silently, to whomever might be listening. *Please, let him be ravaged worse.*

Because even now, years later, after the irreparable events in their past, she could not help but be drawn to him, this man whom she had once loved so thoroughly.

"I did care," he said, and his voice was ragged, like wheels on gravel. "I once cared too much what they thought. And now, I seem to care too little. I seem to care only what you think."

She couldn't resist looking at him and, as ever, she was instantly in his thrall. She shook her head, barely. Enough for him to see. "Mal," she whispered.

"What is it, Angel?" His whisper tempted her like nothing she'd ever experienced as he leaned closer. "I shall give you anything you ask. I have never been able to refuse you."

It wasn't true. There had been a time when she'd begged him to forgive her. When she'd ached for him to believe her. And he had refused.

But she was no longer that girl, and he was not that boy. And now, he promised not to refuse her, and she found she could not refuse him, either. It was her turn to lift her hand. Her turn to set palm to cheek. Her turn to ravage.

And she did, feeling more powerful than ever when he exhaled, loving the edge of breath that whipped over lips like memory. As though she'd burned him. And she might have. They'd always been oil and flame. Why not let it happen? Just once? Just for a moment? Just to see if the combustion remained.

She leaned up to him. Or he leaned down. It did not matter.

He was whispering at her lips, and she did not know if he spoke to her or to a higher power. "Forgive me," he said. Whom was he asking? For what?

She found she did not care.

The kiss unlocked her, breaking her open, letting light and air into the dark, dank places in her. It thieved the protection she had built over months and years, casting it out and leaving her with nothing to keep him away.

And still, she did not care.

Just as long as he did not stop. She was not ready for him to stop. It had been years since he'd touched her, and longer still since he'd touched her like this—with desire and passion and a commitment to nothing but pleasure.

She sighed into the kiss, and he, too, was unlocked, moving, his strong, warm hand sliding back, fingers threading into her hair, pulling her closer as he pressed his mouth to hers, somehow turning the clock back to another time, when all that was between them was this—nothing.

He tasted the same, like some mysterious, tempting spice, and she could not stop herself from wrapping her arms about his neck and pressing closer. Licking across his lips, bold and desperate to relive him. He growled at the sensation, the sound low and wicked, and then his arms were around her waist and he was lifting her, turning her, pressing her up against the closed door—thank God it was closed—and she was his.

As though years had never passed, and they were here, in love, once more.

Dear God, how she'd loved this. She'd believed she'd been broken all those years ago, ruined by pain and loss. And perhaps she had been. But she was no longer. Somehow, in his arms she found it all again.

Except it was not a surprise. She'd always found herself with him.

She tore her mouth from his, reaching for air, and he pulled back to watch her for a long moment, his gaze raking over her face, taking her in. "My God," he whispered. "You're more beautiful now than you've ever been." And then he was tilting her chin up to expose her neck and setting his lips to her flesh, before she could blush or turn away.

She gasped at the sensation, so delicious and familiar, and was rewarded with another deep, animal growl, as though he were unable to keep his desire at bay. Her fingers threaded into his hair, pressing into the curls at the nape of his neck, stroking in slow, encouraging circles—just as he liked. Another growl.

Lord, how she loved those growls.

And then his hands were at her bodice, pulling at the buttons of her pelisse, spreading it wide and finding the scalloped edge of the gown, lower than it might have been, and altogether too tight as she fought for breath. At her ear, he said wicked, wonderful things. The kinds of things she would not let herself remember in dark, lonely nights.

"I remember how pleasure finds you, Angel . . ." Long, deft fingers found their way into her bodice, sliding like a delicious promise. "I remember how you reach for it." He stopped just beyond one straining nipple—making her want to scream. "I remember how you hem and haw, doing everything you can to avoid telling me what you want."

The words shot through her, reminding her of the woman she had been even as he took the soft lobe of her ear between his teeth and bit gently, threatening to destroy her with pleasure.

He was right. She had been nervous around him, afraid to tell him too much for fear of being wanton. Of losing him.

But she had lost him. And he already thought her a wanton.

He'd already made her one.

So when she pulled back to meet his eyes, wild beneath lids heavy with the desire she knew coursed through him, she did not blush. And she did not hesitate. She tugged on the little bow that kept her gown tight to her skin, loosening the fabric just enough. And then she pressed her hand to his where it remained still and full of promise, and moved him. Pressed him to her. Urged him to take what she wanted to give.

Another growl, sending unimaginable pleasure straight to her core.

"Sera," he said, disbelief and desire at war in the word.

She brushed her lips over his cheek as he lifted one breast, testing its weight. "I remember how pleasure finds you, Duke," she repeated his words. "I remember how you reach for it. Shall I tell you what I want this time?"

He cursed, low and wicked, and she took that as a yes.

"I want your touch." He gave it to her, a long slow slide of his thumb. "I want your kiss."

He did not hesitate, leaning down and taking the tip of one breast into his mouth. Working it with lips and tongue until she thought she might perish from the pleasure of it. Sucking until she was gasping and writhing against him, one leg wrapped around him as he pressed her into the door.

When his hand came to her ankle and he slid to his knees, she knew she should stop him, but it had been so long—so long since she'd been touched. So long since he'd touched her. And then her skirts were raised and her leg was over his shoulder, and her fingers were in his hair and his mouth was on her with glorious certainty.

She cried out at the touch, at the force and pleasure of it, at its promise, not just in the moment, but for all the moments that were to come. Her cry was punctuated by his groan there, against the soft, wet center of her, where she was so tender, so ready, so desperate. His tongue—how many times had she lay in the dark and thought of his tongue?—stroked, sure and firm over her, finding all the places that had ached for him, and her fingers tightened in his hair. "Malcolm," she whispered. "Dear God. Yes. There."

"I know, Angel," he said against her. And he did. He'd always known.

In this, nothing was changed. He was back, this man whom she'd loved so thoroughly, this man who had always made her pleasure the most important piece of their lovemaking. Even at the last.

He pulled back at that, as though he heard the thought, turning his gaze to her, his beautiful eyes finding her, capturing her as one finger slid deep into her, finding her wet and willing. They both groaned at the sensation, and when Malcolm began to move, to wring pleasure from her most secret places, she was unable to keep her eyes open.

He stopped. "No."

She opened her eyes. Fairly begged. "Mal."

"I'll give you everything you want, love. But you give me what I want."

He moved again, and she lifted toward him. "Yes."

"You keep your eyes open," he said. "I want to watch. I want a new memory."

He was close enough that she could feel his words on

her, where she was open and aching. She wasn't even certain that there was sound to match sensation, but she understood him nonetheless.

She'd give him anything he wanted as long as he didn't stop.

And he didn't. He blew a long stream of air where she wanted him most, teasing and tempting and making promises on which she knew he could deliver.

Deliciously.

He wanted to wreck her with temptation. To punish her with the pleasure of the wait.

But she'd waited long enough.

She slid her fingers into his hair again, letting them tighten against his scalp until he looked up at her again, met her gaze. The universe had given him such power over her beyond that room. Beyond that moment.

But in this, they were equal.

In this, she reveled in her power.

"I want, as well," she said.

She took her pleasure.

He gave it, not hesitating, knowing just how to make her writhe and cry, slow, then fast, flexing fingers and tongue until she had lost her strength and he was holding her with strong hands and shoulders, wringing every inch of pleasure from her.

It was an age before she returned to the moment. It was an instant.

He sensed the moment, turning, pressing his lips to the soft inside of her thigh, lingering there until she pushed him away, removing her leg and lowering her skirts, smoothing them with careful precision as she willed her heart to stop beating.

Willed him to stand. She hated him there, on his knees, as though he gave penance.

As though he wanted her.

As though she was for having.

As though he was.

"Sera—"

"No." She cut him off. Unable to let him finish.

Afraid of what he might say.

"No," she repeated. Louder. Clearer. "No, Duke. This changes nothing."

Chapter 14

A MODERN "MEET DUKE!"

After making him desperate for her, his wife avoided him for a full week. Oh, she sat at breakfasts and luncheons and dinners, and she took her sherry and played croquet on the lawn. She did her requested duty with no sign of hesitation or distaste.

She even saw dossiers delivered to him with clockwork regularity—the ladies' respective qualities and interests outlined with impressive thoroughness. Indeed, once she received her divorce, Sera could easily find work as a professional matchmaker.

Of course, she wasn't receiving a divorce.

He'd never planned to give it to her, but now there was no way it was happening. Not when he'd touched her again. How often had he tried to remember that exact sound she made when she found her pleasure. The exact taste of her. The exact feel of her lips against his, of her fingers in his hair, of the weight of her in his arms.

It was all the same, and somehow, none of it was. She was entirely different.

This changes nothing, she'd said.

She was right. It changed nothing.

He still wanted her. He was still going to win her. The

only difference was the urgency of his desire to do so. He'd been patient as Job, dammit. He'd given her a week to find him again. To seek him out. He'd sat at meals, the proper duke at his end of the immense dining table. He'd greeted the suitesses—they were going to have to find a better descriptor—pleasantly when he passed them in the hallway.

The times he had gone hunting for her, he'd been way-laid by a collection of cloying mamas, and once commandeered into going hunting for an easier prey with Lord Brunswick, a man who was decent with a shot, but altogether too gleeful at the prospect of shooting things.

For the last seven days, Haven had done his best to stumble upon his wife accidentally. Or, rather, to ensure that she stumbled upon him.

And she hadn't.

It was as though she had eyes and ears throughout the house, and perhaps she did, considering her mad sisters seemed to be everywhere. The Marchioness of Eversley had taken up residence in his library, Landry's wife couldn't stop telling his stable master how to do his work, and that morning, when Mal had dressed, there had been an uncanny amount of white fur on his trousers from Sesily's damn cat. Not to mention the ass Calhoun, marauding the grounds like a damn pirate, tipping his hat at anything in skirts.

Calhoun.

Even at meals, Sera and Haven were separated, regularly seated at opposite ends of the formal dining room—a room in which he could not remember the last time he'd been—and she disappeared immediately following dinner.

Mal was ashamed to admit that he'd spent three nights listening to the silence on the other side of the adjoining door to their rooms before he'd given up and interrogated the servants about his wife's evening activities—desperate to know if she was, in fact, spending them with Calhoun, who made himself as scarce as his wife did in the evenings. It was only then that he was told that Mr. Calhoun left the house after the evening meal, and returned the following morning at dawn, before most of the house had rung for tea and toast.

Which meant Sera was alone at night.

In the next room.

Her silence was making him mad.

He'd given her space, dammit, sure she'd return to him. Sure she'd seek him out for—if nothing else—pleasure. She'd come apart in his arms, hard and fast and with an intensity that had brought him with her. That had left him on his knees as she'd straightened herself and turned tail.

And it had been turning tail.

She'd hied out of that room as though Lucifer himself had been on her heels. Coward.

Of course, he had not chased her.

Resisting the thought, Haven stood from the desk in his private study and went looking for his wife. This time, he would find her. And this time, she would not be able to avoid him.

She was in the kitchens, surrounded by his possible future wives and their mothers, as though the women were not houseguests, but rather sightseeing in Bath.

"Now," she was saying. "As mistress of Highley and Duchess of Haven you will be expected to arrange meals for the duke and any of his guests."

As Seraphina Bevingstoke had never once played the duchess, Malcolm couldn't contain the little grunt of surprise that came at her words; the sound was louder than expected, clearly, as it attracted the attention of the entire assembly.

Sera's face was all calm, even as Mal noted the way her eyes flashed with anger. "Your Grace? Do you require something?"

Yes. You.

"No," he said. "Please. Go on."

There was a pause, and he could see she wanted to argue. He raised a brow in invitation. Let her argue. If that was what he could have of her, so be it.

Her lips pressed together in annoyance, and he wanted to kiss her again. He wanted to kiss her always, honestly, but particularly when she was annoyed.

She began anew. "The duke enjoys game, lamb, and duck."

He did laugh at that. What a ridiculous play in which they all performed.

Sera's annoyance became anger, and she turned on him again. He took it back. He wanted to kiss her particularly when she was angry. She was most beautiful then. "Your Grace," she said, not hiding the disapproval in the words. "Again, may we assist you in some way?"

"No," he said, crossing his arms and leaning against the doorjamb. "In fact, I'm finding this supremely edifying."

"You are surprised to find that you enjoy duck?"

"I'm surprised to find that you are aware that I enjoy duck."

She raised her brows. "Am I incorrect?"

"No," he said. "But you've never planned a meal for me in your life."

He knew he goaded her. But if this was what he could have of her, he would take it.

She smiled. "Considering we're in the process of

divorcing, I would think you'd be happy I haven't attempted to poison you."

He blinked. The girls assembled tittered. Amusement? Surprise? Mal didn't care. All he cared was that Sera was moved. Moved enough to challenge him. This was familiar. And welcome. God, she was welcome as the sun in English spring.

As she drew closer, Mal's heart began to pound, his palms itching to lift her in his arms and carry her away. Find a bed and keep her there until she agreed to begin again. Instead, he willed himself still, even as she stopped, scant inches from him, and said, loud enough for the room to hear. "Shall I tell you which foods I would happily lade with arsenic?"

He raised his brows. "You realize that if I turn up dead now, we've a roomful of witnesses."

"A pity, as I realize I should have considered this course of action before. A widow receives a third of the estate, doesn't she?"

Christ, he loved the way they sparred.

She continued. "Duck with sour cherries. Vegetables turned in the Portuguese style. New potatoes with a salted cream sauce. Lamb with jelly made from Highley's own mint."

Until that moment, it had never occurred to him that his favorite foods might be used against him in battle.

"Sprouts roasted with pear, fig and pig cheeks. Vinegared artichokes. Neither beef nor poultry are of particular interest. His Grace does not care for sweets, but if he must choose a dessert, it is raspberries with a drizzle of fresh cream." She raised a brow. "Do you have anything to add, Duke?"

He'd been given a culinary set-down.

He cleared his throat. "I quite like asparagus."

She saw the lie. He loathed asparagus. But she inclined her head and said, "How edifying. He *quite likes* asparagus. Do remember *that*, ladies." He noted that several of the mothers were scribbling notes, as though she were giving a lesson in gross anatomy rather than meal planning. "If you're through, Your Grace, we are in a bit of a hurry, and you are a distraction."

She turned her back on him, and he was dismissed.

As though he weren't master of the house and lord of the manor.

As though he were a minor, petty, irritating distraction.

Dammit. *They* were the distraction. He had no intention of marrying any of the girls, and so Sera was not only wasting *their* time with discussions of food and table settings and linen treatments and how Highley soap was made, but also wasting *his* time. Time he could have been spending wooing her. Which was the plan.

Though the plan appeared to be falling apart, and it had been only a week.

It was an idiot plan, obviously.

With a bow and the most gracious "Good day" he could muster to the women assembled, he returned to his study, feeling insultingly bested and not a small amount responsible for it.

Ignoring his sister-in-law's cat, which had taken to napping on his desk, Malcolm attempted to throw himself into the estate, which he'd done halfway decently until a knock sounded on the door and his sisters-in-law entered, promising to make a bad day worse.

"There's Brummell!" Sesily swooped over to lift the disgruntled animal from its perch and smother it with an embarrassing amount of affection. Once she was done, she returned the cat to the desk, where it proceeded to bathe itself upon a stack of farming reports.

Mal scowled at the beast, to no avail.

"Oh, you look like you're in a sulk." No one had ever accused Sesily Talbot of beating around the bush.

He sat back in his chair. "Not at all."

"Mmm," she said. "It looks like it though, doesn't it, Sophie?"

Sophie, his nemesis, grinned and said, "I wouldn't know, as he seems to be in a perpetual sulk around me."

He searched for a retort, but all he could come to was, "I object to the word *sulk* on the grounds that it makes me sound a petulant child." Sophie gave him a look that easily imparted her belief that he was, in fact, a petulant child. He scowled. "I'm not sulking."

She spread her hands wide, brandishing a square of ecru. "Far be it from me to say otherwise."

The scowl deepened. He waved at the paper. "What is that?"

She looked to her hand, her features instantly softening. "A letter from my husband." She handed it to him. "For you."

"Why?"

She feigned ignorance. "Who can say?"

Haven sighed and accepted the missive, reaching for a letter opener and tearing it open to reveal the message:

Haven—
    As it is, I'm less than thrilled that my wife
has decided to spend the summer with you and her
sisters instead of with me, but I am loath to argue
with her when she is in her condition, and what she
wishes, she gets.

Haven looked up to find Sophie, hands over her expanding midsection, serene smile upon her face. He returned to the note.

> *So, I shall settle for this, knowing that there is little love lost between you. Upset her, and you shall answer to me. I shall take pleasure in it.*

And then, below, parenthetically:

> *(Upset your own wife and answer to her sisters, who are—en masse—as fearsome as I could ever be.)*
> *Eversley*

"He makes an excellent point."

Malcolm looked up from the note to find Sesily at his elbow, reading over his shoulder. He snatched the paper back. "You're rather rude."

She smirked. "Oh, and you've always been the portrait of good manners?" She turned back to Sophie. "King loves you madly."

The Marchioness of Eversley lifted a shoulder as if to say, *I know that bit.*

Sesily rolled her eyes and turned back to Malcolm. "We were sent to tell you that dinner is at eight."

He looked to his watch. There was enough time for him to shave and dress. He nodded. "Thank you." He moved to come out from behind the desk, aware, if unsettlingly so, that he was all too eager to leave these women. It wasn't that they scared him. Of course not.

They were women, for God's sake. He'd barely reached the corner of the great oak desk when Sophie shook her head. "You aren't to leave yet, though."

"First, we've something to say," Sesily added.

He took it back. They were terrifying.

"It's clear you've some idiotic plan afoot here."

Mal shook his head. "I don't know what you—"

Sophie slashed a hand in the air. "Don't waste our time, Haven."

His brows shot up. "To think, everyone called you the quiet one."

She grinned. "Well, you've got a pair of ruined boots that proves otherwise, do you not?"

He did, indeed. In fact, when he thought carefully on it, he could still remember the keen embarrassment he'd felt at being put on his ass by this woman. Not that he was going to tell her such a thing.

"At any rate," she continued, "we're all wondering what the plan is."

He wasn't about to say, but it seemed he did not have to.

"We've started a betting book." Sesily announced as though she were discussing the weather. "Would you like to hear about it?"

He leaned against the side of the desk, feigning disinterest. "By all means."

"Seline thinks you're after Father's money again."

"I wasn't after it the first time."

"No," Sophie said. "You were after his ruin."

He wasn't proud of it. He'd been blind with anger and frustration and betrayal, thinking that she'd never cared for him. Desperate for her to care for him. And he'd gone after her father. Would have paupered him if not for Eversley, who stepped in and settled him down. "I'm not after either, this time."

Sophie looked unconvinced, but Sesily continued. "Seleste thinks you're a spy."

That was unexpected. "To what end?"

Sesily put down the paper and waved a hand in the air. "Something to do with Mr. Calhoun and their tavern. It doesn't make any sense." Later, he'd wonder about that reference to the tavern. He'd think on the *their*. But Sesily was still talking. "Now I . . ." She paused with unsettling gusto. "Call me a romantic, but I think you're trying to woo her back."

His heart nearly stopped at that. He steeled his features as his sister-in-law soldiered on, thankfully unaware of the effect she'd had upon him. "Which is a terrible idea, I know. I mean, it doesn't take a brilliant mind to see that she'll never ever take you back."

The words were so matter-of-fact, he couldn't help but feel their sting. And say, "Even if I've changed?"

"You haven't," Sophie said.

"I might have," he found himself defending like an imbecile. "It's been years."

"Time is irrelevant," Sophie said. "Leopards and spots."

He opened his mouth to argue again, somehow unable to stop himself from the futility of the action, when Sesily interrupted. "It's worth saying at this point that Sophie thinks you're trying to exact further revenge."

Sophie nodded and waved in the direction of the letter now open on his desk. "Hence, the missive from King."

Malcolm resisted the urge to remind her that threatening husbands were rendered less so when they made their threats via post. "I'm not exacting revenge."

"That's exactly what you would say if you were exacting revenge, though," Sesily pointed out.

It really was no wonder that she remained unmarried. She was straight from Bedlam. Haven ignored her and looked firmly at Sophie. "I'm not."

She narrowed her gaze. "You forget that I witnessed

your anger, Haven. I saw the things you did. Heard the things you said."

All things he would give anything to take back. "I was—"

"You were an unmitigated ass."

He blinked. Sesily snickered. And then he conceded the point. "Yes."

Sophie watched him for a long while, and then said, "I feel I should tell you I loathe you. More than the rest of them do."

He nodded. All of Sera's sisters were forthright, but Sophie was the most honest. Always had been. He was going to have to win her back, as well. "Do you know what they call me now, Sophie? Since our last meeting?"

She smirked. "The Dunked Duke. I'm quite proud of it."

He inclined his head, unable to forget the way she'd set him on his ass in a fishpond. Unable to forget the fact that he'd deserved it. "As well you should be. It's a sound, embarrassing name."

That long assessment again. And then, "I see what you're doing. It won't work." Maybe not. But it was worth a try. "And besides, it's not me about whom you should worry. I don't loathe you more than Sera does. So, if Sesily's right, and you're trying to woo her back, you're going to need quite a bit of luck."

He rapped on the adjoining door to his wife's room sharply at a quarter to eight that evening. She opened it instantly, as though she'd been waiting for him on the other side, pulling it wide and stepping back to let him in. Keeping her distance even as she made it easy for him to look at her.

For a moment, he found he could not breathe.

She was more beautiful than ever, in a stunning amethyst gown, devoid of the wide sleeves, frills and frippery that graced every frock in existence these days. In its simplicity, the dress devastated, tracing her shape down her torso to her waist, where it dropped in magnificent lines, not a spare crease to be found.

She'd always been able to steal his breath. And now was no different.

She filled the silence he'd brought with him.

"I see my sisters delivered my message about dinner."

Why hadn't she told him herself?

Her sister's words echoed through him. *I don't loathe you more than Sera.*

He pushed the thought aside. "Yours, and their own."

She was already across the room at her dressing table, lifting a button hook. It was then that he realized one long amethyst glove was unbuttoned.

She extended one long arm to the light, revealing a long line of buttons, and began working to fasten them.

"I heard there was a message from King," she said, nearly absently. King was the Marquess of Eversley, a man whose infuriating superiority had been instilled with the name at birth.

It grated that she used the informal name without hesitation.

"He threatened harm should I hurt your sister."

She smiled at that, not looking up from her glove. "He loves her quite thoroughly."

The words were soft and full of warm satisfaction. And he hated his brother-in-law in that moment. Hated him because *he* wanted that satisfaction. He wanted to give it to her.

He took a step toward her. She stiffened, and he stilled. "Shouldn't you have a maid for that?"

"I am sharing Sesily's. I didn't bring one of my own."

She was the duchess. The entire house was at her beck and call. "You needn't share; there are a dozen girls belowstairs who—"

"I don't need one," she said, deftly buttoning the glove. "I've become quite skilled at dressing myself."

"For stage."

She nodded. "Among other things."

He didn't like the reference to her past without him. Didn't like the way it made him want to ask a dozen questions, none of which she would answer. He tried for something lighter. "Did you know your sisters are taking bets on why I brought you here?"

She did not look up from her task. "I thought I was here to get you married?"

"Seleste thinks I'm a spy."

She gave a little chuckle, and he was suddenly warmer than he had been in years. "Seleste reads a great deal of adventure novels."

"It's the best theory of the bunch."

"What are the others?"

Suddenly, it seemed like the topic was a poor choice.

Sera heard his hesitation. "Shall I guess?"

Perhaps she'd get them wrong. "By all means."

"Seline cares a great deal about our father, so I would expect she thinks you're after Papa's money. Which of course you're not."

"How do you know?"

"Because you were never after his money; you've always been rich as a king. You were after me," she said, lightly, as though they were discussing anything but her family's ruin at his hands. "Sophie thinks you are lower than dirt, so she likely believes you're out for revenge."

He hated the way his cheeks warmed with embarrassment. And with shame, for the way she said it, as though it was a perfectly reasonable thing for Sophie to think. Which it was. But dammit, it wasn't reasonable. If he could take it all back, he would.

He cleared his throat, but before he could speak, she said, "Of course, she's wrong, too."

"She is?" he said, his voice an octave higher than he would have liked.

"You're not trying to punish me. You know that it's impossible." She looked up then, blue eyes meeting his. "You can't punish someone who has nothing to lose."

The words stung. They had when she'd spoken them in his office at Parliament, and they stung now. Except here, he was closer. And he was looking more carefully. And that's when he saw it. The truth. The lie.

She *did* have something to lose.

But what?

"You're right. I am not out for revenge." She looked away then, as though she knew he could see into her, and she wanted to protect herself. He pressed on. "Would you like to know what Sesily thinks?"

She missed the button she was working on. "No."

He watched her grip the hook more firmly. Try again. Miss again. He stepped closer, taking the hook from her hand. Turning her toward him. She snatched her arm away. "I don't need your help."

"Of course you don't," he said. "You've never needed me."

It's always been I who needed you.

He left that bit out, instead extending his hand to her. "Dinner awaits." Not that he cared. He'd stand here next to her, breathing her air, for the rest of time if she'd let him.

She exhaled too harshly and slapped her arm into his outstretched hand. "Fine."

He worked the button hook, ignoring the irritation in her voice. "Sesily thinks I want you back."

She shook her head. "Sesily doesn't know anything about marriage."

He rather thought she knew quite a bit. He finished the buttons and ran a thumb across the soft silk. "Finished." He did not release her, but he did not hold her, either. Instead, he reveled in the feel of her, of this woman for whom he'd searched for years. For whom he'd longed for years.

I want you back.

What if he said it? What would she do?

Her eyes lifted to his, her black lashes impossibly long. For a moment, he thought she would say something. Something important. Something that might change everything. But she didn't. Instead, she took her arm from his grasp and said the least important thing she could say. The thing he'd just said himself. "Dinner awaits."

They never said the things that were important.

They were descending the great central manor stairs when she spoke again. "It's time you participate in this process, Mal. You've a choice to make."

You, he thought. *I choose you.*

He swallowed back the words. "The competition begins in earnest tonight then?"

She nodded. "It does."

"With what? Fencing? Fighting? Cutthroat charades?" Her lips twitched in a little smile, and he was quite proud of himself.

"Nothing quite so . . . on the nose."

"No rounds? What a pity."

She snickered. "We begin with food. She must be able to keep your house."

He didn't give a damn about food, but he could pretend. "Ah. Hence the duck."

They made for the dining room. "I know you like duck."

He shot her a look at her insistent words. "I shouldn't have said what I did."

"I spent months learning what you liked. Before we were married and after, even when I was not welcome in your house." He couldn't look away from her, even as she stared ahead, refusing to meet his eyes. "I had every intention of planning your meals. Of keeping your house. Of being your . . ."

She trailed off, but he heard the word. *Wife.*

And he also heard the past tense.

Why were they always in the past?

"Also, I know you loathe asparagus," she said, and the words were injected with something akin to smug triumph.

"I do," he said.

"You just wanted to undermine me."

"You've been avoiding me." Not that it was an excuse, but it was the truth.

"You never said we had to interact." He sighed, and she misunderstood it for irritation. "You know, you brought this upon yourself, Haven. *You* decided you wanted a new wife. *You* decided you wanted me to select her. This is the process. Imagine. You might even like one of them."

But he wouldn't love one of them.

"I don't need to like them to marry them," he said, knowing he sounded like a beast.

"It helps, don't you think?"

"I wouldn't know," he replied. "We never liked each other."

"Nonsense," she said as they approached the dining room. "If we hadn't liked each other so much, perhaps it all wouldn't have gone so wrong." Before he could reply, she said, "I've put you with Miss Mary. Be kind," and nodded to the footman standing guard outside the dining room. The boy opened the door, revealing the motley crew of houseguests, who all turned to see the duke and duchess arrive.

"Wait," he said, and she had to turn back else risk censure for ignoring him. There were benefits to being a duke. He lowered his voice and said, "What do you think I brought you here for?"

They'd discussed her sisters' theories. But he cared only for hers.

She watched him for a long moment before she said, low enough that only he could hear, "I think I am here to be your toy."

"What on earth does that mean?"

"You don't want me, but you don't want anyone else to have me, either. You never have." They were not true, but the words stung with brutal honesty, because she believed them. And then she added, "You don't want any part of a life with me."

The words sent a chill through him, evoking a memory he'd forgotten. A memory he wanted to expel immediately. Hang dinner and everyone at it. "Sera—"

She shook her head. "Your Grace. I have been in this particular position before." She was already turning to the room, where a collection of fresh-faced women was waiting.

At a table laden with asparagus.

He looked to his wife, knowing smirk on her lips.

She was wrong. He did want her. He wanted the life with her.

And, this time, he would not stop until he had it.

Chapter 15

⁓

TICK TOCK TALBOT TRIUMPHS!

April 1833
Haven House, Mayfair

He heard her the moment she entered the house.

If Haven were honest, he heard her the moment her carriage pulled to a stop in the street outside the door. The moment she stepped out, like a goddamn queen. He couldn't see her from his study, but he could feel her, changing the air in the square beyond. Thieving it.

He heard her in the sharp rap of the knocker on the door, and for a heartbeat, he considered telling the footman not to answer.

But therein lay the problem that would always exist between him and Seraphina Talbot—he would always answer her call. Like a damned sailor to a siren. It had been three days since they'd been caught, with another week to pass before they were tied together forever. And it would only grow worse after they married.

"Where is he?" The question was fairly thundered, the frustration and anger in the words rocketing through him on a flood of similar emotions. And anticipation. And desire.

Shame flooded him with the last. He shouldn't want

her. He should want to be rid of her. He should want never to see her again. He should want her punished for what she'd done—trapping him into this farce of a marriage, which was no farce at all because the entire aristocracy and every gossip rag in Britain seemed to know the truth of it.

"I shall stay here all day until he *is* receiving, so you'd might as well bring me to him." Haven stood at that, telling himself he was heading for the door to his study because he wanted to protect his servant from her wrath and not because he was tied to her like a dog on a lead.

"M-my lady," the footman stammered beyond. "I sh-shall see if the duke is at home."

"No need," she said.

"My lady! You cannot simply . . ."

But no one had ever successfully told Seraphina Talbot what she could and could not do, and she certainly wasn't going to begin taking instruction from a footman when she did not take it from the footman's master. "Oh, but I can! Don't you read the papers? We are to be married!"

Anger flared at her words and Mal set his hand to the door handle of his office, preparing to summarily exit her from his property.

He opened the door as she arrived. "We're not married yet, Lady Seraphina. I've still a week before I put my special license to use."

One mahogany brow rose in a perfect arch. "I assure you, I am well aware of my ever-tightening yoke, Your Grace."

It was his turn to look surprised. "It is *I* who limits *your* freedom, then?"

"That is the way of men and women, is it not?" She smacked him in the chest with a newspaper. "You punish me all you like. That is the bed in which I lay. But you leave my sisters out of it, you bastard."

He took the paper. "I'm sure we are both a bit saddened by the fact that I am not, in fact, a bastard. If only I were, we wouldn't be in such a situation." When she did not reply, he looked to the paper, instantly knowing to what she was referring. Still, he could not resist irritating her. "The king is vacationing in Bath."

"I should like to dunk you in a bath," she said, setting a finger to the paper. "There."

He'd read the story earlier in the day. *Haven Hooked by Huntress!* Irritation flared as he was returned to it. Irritation and hot embarrassment.

She did not wait for him to recover. "Shall I recite it from memory? *Men!*, warn the clearly deeply concerned editors of the *News. Mind yourselves! Lowborn ladies lurk London-wide, longing for largesse!*" Mal grimaced at the alliteration. She noticed. "Oh, you do not care for the overwrought language? Let me move on, for it gets significantly worse! *Heed the harrowing tale of the Duke of Haven! Do not fall victim to wicked, wanton Wisteria . . . no matter how willing! These are Dangerous Daughters, all!*"

He looked to Sera. "Do you wish me to disagree?"

She looked as though she wished him dead. "You don't even know my sisters." She raised her voice. "You never even came to my home to attempt to know them."

"I do not know them," he said. "But as it is my name being dragged through the mud and you who is doing the dragging, I am not predisposed to trust them with unmarried men."

"Oh, yes. Poor unmarried men, weak-willed, doughy boys with neither control nor intelligence. So easily marked and ruined by women—ever more powerful.

I wouldn't be surprised if we were all descended of witches."

He raised a brow.

She continued, "Poor, sad men, so kind and blameless, fairly wandering the streets in their impotent impressionability. How well they must be protected from the wiles of women, who want nothing but their destruction." She paused. "That is our tale, is it not? You, the tragically heroic Samson, and me, the temptress Delilah, thieving your power?"

Malcolm's gaze narrowed. "You tell me. Delilah took money and land."

"I took nothing from you."

"No," he said. "You did worse. There was no honorable thievery in your actions. You made a trade for your spoils."

She gasped. "Are you calling me a whore?"

"Your words, Sera. Not mine."

He should never have said it. For a moment he thought she might strike him. He would have taken it. Would have deserved it, even. But she didn't. She straightened, her shoulders going stiff and square, and her fingers curling into fists. He stood, prepared for the blow. Knowing he deserved it and somehow unable to apologize for his behavior. He was too proud and too angry.

As was she. "Someday, you shall have to listen when I speak, Malcolm."

"But not today."

"I apologized."

"Forgive me if three days is not enough for me to come to my senses about my soon-to-be wife trapping me into marriage."

She did not look away. "You were there as well, Your Grace."

"Yes. But with different intentions." He turned away, not wanting to have the conversation again. Not wanting to remember. He waved at the door. "You are welcome to leave."

"We do not have to marry." She'd said it a dozen times in the hours following their discovery. Another dozen the day after. Of course they had to marry. "I made a mistake," she added, softly. "I should never have agreed—"

"Stop." He didn't wish to hear it, the confirmation that she'd trapped him. He did not wish to relive the moment of realization.

She did not stop. "And if I told you it wasn't a trap? Not at the start? Not in any of the days leading up to the end? Because it wasn't a trap, Malcolm." Christ, he wanted to believe her. "It was all real. I was me and you were you and everyone said it couldn't be—"

"*Stop.*" He could barely contain his rage. "Still, you weave your pretty tale. *I don't care.*" He took a breath, forcing himself calm. "You landed your duke, as my mother landed my father before me. I thought you were in it for me, and you were in it for a title and I should have seen it coming and that is that."

Silence fell, thick and unpleasant as she considered her next words and he willed them to be anything but another lie. He did not think he could stomach another lie. Not from this woman who had seemed so much the truth for so long.

Finally, she spoke, something like panic in her words. "I've thought about this; if I leave—if I disappear, I give my sisters a chance at futures unencumbered by my scandal."

"You can't cleanse the scandal from them," he said. "They own it as they own your name. They are—forever—

Dangerous Daughters. Just as I am always Hoodwinked Haven."

She swallowed and looked away. "I never intended for this. I simply thought they would find us and we would marry. And we would be happy."

He could not contain the humorless laugh at that. "That's the irony, is it not? That we would have been happy."

Her eyes went wide. "And why can't we be? I made a mistake! I love—"

"No." The word, cold and full of anger, stopped the words. *Thank God.* How long had he told himself love was not a thing he would ever have? How long had he believed it was not real? And then he'd met Sera, and everything had changed. Everything, and nothing. He crossed the room and poured himself a drink at the sideboard. "Don't ever say it. Not to me. There is no room for that here. Not anymore."

"Malcolm," she said, soft and achingly beautiful, and he refused to face her for fear of what he would find. He did not have to turn. He could hear the sorrow, despite its silence. Christ, he wanted to believe it. He wanted to believe her.

She inhaled, a little sniffle the only hint that he might have upset her. "If you let me go, you shall have . . ." She paused, considering the rest of her words. When she resumed speaking, he heard the truth. "I should like to give you a future, as well. One that might have happiness. Surely you cannot wish for a marriage to punish us both forever."

"Don't you see?" he said. "I am the product of this marriage. I watched my parents punish each other for years. My mother the huntress and my father the hunted.

And me, the prize in the balance," he added, ignoring the pain that threaded through him as he spoke. "That is marriage to me. And it seems it will be marriage for me, as well."

"Then why choose it?" she asked, frustration and confusion in her words. "Why not find another?"

There was no other. Didn't she see that? This was how it ended, the sins of the father, revisited upon the son. "All marriage is unhappy," he said. "That's what you taught me."

Her eyes went wide. "How?"

There was no reason to lie to her. "When I met you, Sera, I had hope for something different and new. I had hope that we would forge our own path through marriage and destroy what my parents had wrought. I trusted you to help me do it—God knows I've no idea how to make a marriage happy. My parents could not stand to be in the same room with each other."

"Mal," she said, softly, and he loathed the sympathy in the words. The pity in them. He didn't want her kindness. He wanted to remember her betrayal. It was easier that way. And then she said, "I don't want that for my children," and it did not seem easy at all.

"There shan't be children."

She gasped. "What?"

Children were no longer in the cards. They had not been since the afternoon at Highley, when she'd trapped him. He wasn't interested in bringing another child into the life he had lived. "I've cousins. They may have the title."

"You do not wish for an heir?"

He looked to her then, meeting her beautiful blue eyes, wide and honest. How many times had he been lost in those eyes in the last few weeks? How many times had he believed what he saw in them? "I do not. I'm not interested in a child who is nothing more than a pawn in his parents' chess match."

She was silent for a long moment, her throat working as she searched for words. "Is this your way of punishing me?"

He raised a brow. "You wish for children?"

"Of course. They are part of life."

He imagined them, her children—a line of them with mahogany curls and bright, blue eyes, long frames and wide smiles. She would make beautiful children. *They would.*

Except they wouldn't.

He turned away, toward the window that looked out on the rolling estate beyond. "I don't want any part of that life." Three months ago, it had been truth. Three days ago, it was a lie.

He did not know what it was today.

"With me," she clarified. "You don't want any part of a life *with me.*"

"No." It felt like a lie. He had wanted it. He'd intended to marry her—this vibrant, funny, beautiful woman who seemed to know more about joy and love and family than he ever had. And then he'd realized she wasn't real, and neither was what they had.

"Then why not let me go?"

Because I still want you. "Because this is the bed in which we lie."

She was silent for a long moment—long enough that he thought to look back at her, even as he refused himself the gift of it. The pain of it. This was the battle they fought.

"What do you wish? Do you wish me to get on my knees? To beg you for my freedom?"

He did turn back at that. "Would you do it?"

Her eyes, cerulean and stunning, slayed him with their shock. She'd meant it as hyperbole. And now, suddenly, it hung between them. "Is that what it would take to win my freedom? To win my sisters'?"

"If it were? Would you beg?" He hated himself for the question.

And then he hated her, when she said, "I would." She would do anything to be rid of him. And he could not blame her.

"Get out," he said, turning back to the window.

"I could leave. I could run." She spat the words.

He waved his hand at the door once more. "By all means."

She couldn't run, however, not without bringing down her sisters, and she knew that. He did, too. Sera had always been the noble one. Even in deception.

Her skirts rustled against the carpet, and for a moment, he imagined that she might have done it, lowered herself to her knees. Offered him a plea like a serf to a king. Instead, she spoke all too near. "Do not ever imagine that I do not see what you do," she said. "You play the dog in the manger. You don't want me. But you don't want anyone else to have me, either." He faced her, hating the guilt that threaded through him at the words. "You are punishing me. And doing a superior job."

She was right. It was one or the other. It might have been both. But he was so blinded by betrayal and anger that he couldn't have said which. All he knew was that he wasn't letting her go.

Even as he knew it made him the worst kind of man.

She seemed to see it, though, taking a deep breath and closing in on him like a huntress, setting a single finger to his chest, strong as steel. Just as she always was.

"Fair enough. You do what you must to me, Malcolm. You blame me for my betrayal, and for the shattered remains of what was once promised to us."

"I do blame you," he said, backing away from her. "Make no mistake."

She pursued him. In this, unwilling to let him hide. "Then blame *me*. *They* have nothing to do with it. And I expect you to fix this."

It was an impossible request. Once the gossip rags had their teeth in a tale, they held on until it was dead. She knew that. She and her sisters had been called the Soiled S's since her coal-baron father had come down from Newcastle with five beauties in tow. "Perhaps you should have thought of that before, Sera."

The words were a mistake.

She turned on him, and he saw the rage in her face. "*Before?* Before what? Before you stumbled onto the balcony that night? Before you urged me to dance? Before you kissed me? Before you sent a carriage to fetch me to your country house? Because, as I recall it, there were two of us on the floor of your study, Duke. Not just Delilah, with her wicked blade."

His anger rose, too, along with guilt and frustration and—goddammit—desire. And he approached her, pulling her close. "You were Delilah," he growled. "Delilah and Salome and Diana . . . goddess of the damn hunt." He paused. "And I the blind, fat bull."

"What nonsense," she spat back, meeting him without fear. "You think I do not remember? How you opened my gown? How you lifted my skirts? Who begged then, Duke?" She laughed, the sound a wicked sting. "I wish I could take it all back. What a mistake I made."

He pulled her close, and she bent backward, over his arm, his lips lingering at her skin, loving the warmth and the scent and the feel of her even as he hated himself for being drawn to her. For wanting her so desperately. For being unable to give her up. Even as he hated her for wanting to go. "You say you made a mistake."

The words were air at her throat, and he imagined he could see the proud pounding of her pulse beneath them. "The worst of them."

"Tell me precisely what it was. Was it the trap that was your mistake? Or the fact you were caught setting it? Would you do it again if you could be certain I'd never know what you'd planned? How you orchestrated it? How you lured me in?"

Her gaze flew to his and he saw the pain in her eyes the instant before she confessed. "Of course I would."

For the rest of his life, he would wonder why he kissed her then, crushing her mouth beneath his until they were both gasping for breath. Until her arms were wrapped around his neck and she was matching every touch, every groan, every caress. And he would wonder why she kissed him back instead of pushing him away and leaving him forever. Perhaps it was because in passion, they saw the truth—that they were perfectly matched in strength and power and desire. Perhaps it was because, in those moments, there was a tiny thread of hope that they might find each other again, when their anger had passed and there was space for something else.

Or perhaps it was because he loved her, and she loved him in return.

Chapter 16

LAWN BOWLS? OR COURTSHIP GOALS?

"*C*ome along, Emily, toss the kitty!"

"Oi! Don't rush her! You take your time, Lady E. Get it just right."

"Oh, for heaven's sake, it's lawn bowling, not surgery, Em."

"All right!" Lady Emily found her voice, and Sera could not help but smile. "I'm throwing it."

"Tossing it," Seline corrected, quickly adding when the entire assembly looked to her, "What? That's what it's called." She added under her breath, "It's not my fault I'm married to a sportsman."

Sera resisted the inclination to suggest that lawn bowls were not precisely *sport*, and most definitely not when played by eight women in the gardens of an Essex manor house.

A cheer went up when Emily tossed the small ball the ten yards or so necessary to start the next round of bowls, punctuated by a cacophony of barking from the Marchioness of Bumble's dachshunds and Sesily's "Cor! That's a good arm, Emily!"

Lady Emily blushed prettily and dipped her head, uncomfortable with the praise. "Thank you," she said softly. "It is a good throw, rather, isn't it?"

"No one likes a lady with confidence, Emily," her mother called out from where the older women were assembled beneath several large shades nearby, fanning themselves and watching the game with frustrating focus. "You shall never win the duke's attentions if he thinks you prideful."

Emily's face fell. "Yes, Mother."

"If we ever *see* the duke, you mean," Mrs. Mayhew said before barking, "Shoulders back, Mary. He could arrive at any time."

Sera did not think Malcolm would come anywhere near lawn bowls, but she avoided saying so, turning her back to the mothers with a bright smile for Lady Emily. "I thought it was a terrific throw."

"Toss," Seline said again, following the groans that ensued with, "I agree. Also, don't ever listen to your mother, Emily. Decent men like a woman who knows her value." She paused, then said, "Though I'll grant that we've seen no evidence that Haven is a decent man."

Sera sighed. "He's a decent man."

"I should demand proof of it before I agree to marry him, girls," Sophie said from her place near a stack of blue bowls.

Her sisters were dangerous, indeed. If they did not stop with their snide comments, Haven might well be without a betrothed in the end, which would render this entire exercise moot and leave Sera without a divorce.

She would be damned if she was spending weeks at Highley, with its memories around every corner, for a moot exercise. "He is a decent man," she said, sending warning glares at her sisters. "You shall just have to take my word for it."

"Not to be contrary, my lady," Lady Lilith piped in, "but did you not leave him?"

"Lilith!" Countess Shropshire barked. "That's quite enough."

"You're the one who said I should do my best to understand the man," Lilith pointed out.

"Not like this!" her mother protested. "Be more subtle!"

Lilith grinned in Sera's direction. "Subtlety has never been my strong suit."

"Not to worry, Lady Lilith, Duchess isn't very subtle herself." Caleb had arrived, looking freshly rested and freshly washed. He raised a brow in Sera's direction. "After all, she nearly brought down Parliament several weeks ago."

Sera cut him a look and did her best to change the subject. "Mr. Calhoun! How kind of you to join us. I do know how you enjoy outdoor games."

"I prefer things where there's a bit more of a threat of danger."

"You haven't played lawn bowls with the Soiled S's," Sophie said cheerfully.

"Fair enough." He looked to the field. "An excellent toss." He winked at Lady Emily, who immediately blushed.

"Emily!" Countess Brunswick barked again, and her red-faced daughter moved to join her team.

"Stop it," Sera said, approaching her friend. "You'll chase them all away."

Caleb's masculine pride was palpable. "If you think that girl wants to run from me, you're losing your understanding of young women in your old age."

"I beg your pardon," she said. "I'm barely nine and twenty."

"Practically one foot in the grave," he replied.

She huffed her irritation. "How is my tavern?"

He raised a brow. "*My* tavern is fine. Repaired. The entertainment is passable." He'd been heading to London nightly to oversee the business of the pub, to ensure the entertainers were safe and the liquor well stocked.

She nodded. "But?"

He tilted his head. "But without the Sparrow, it's a watering hole."

A pang of regret threaded through her. She missed the place, the smell of freshly worked wood and liquor, the smoke of the candles and tobacco, and the sound of the music—the best in London, she was certain.

But mostly, she missed herself there. The way she lost herself to the music and became herself. The Sparrow. Free.

"How's your divorce?"

"If he'd spend time with the girls, it would help."

"Maybe he doesn't want the girls."

"They're his selections."

"Maybe he only selected them because he didn't think you were an option."

She scowled. "I'll be back as soon as he picks a wife."

Caleb grunted, and she did not like the meaning imbued in the sound. "What?"

He rocked back on his heels, fingers in the waist of his trousers. "Nothing. Only that I'm not certain you're coming back at all if you can't stand up to your duke."

She narrowed her gaze with an angry whisper. "What does that mean?"

"You think I don't know what happens whenever you are alone?" her friend said, all quiet casualness, as though they discussed the weather.

"I think you don't know a thing about it, as a matter of fact."

"Sparrow, that duke has had you since the moment you met. And you've had him. And neither years apart nor a divorce will change the way he looks at you. Or the way you don't look at him."

"You don't know what you're on about," she said, turning away and clapping her hands, marching to the place where the small white ball lay happily in lush green grass. "Which team shall go first?"

The way he looks at you.

He didn't look at her. He didn't want her. He never had. And if she didn't look at him, that was because she had barely seen him since they arrived. Not because she didn't want to see him looking at her.

How did he look at her?

No. Nonsense. Caleb didn't know a damn thing about looking.

Thankfully, one could always trust Sesily to distract. "As we *won the last round* . . ." She paused triumphantly— the words punctuated by a collection of cheers from Sera's sisters, laughing jeers from the four candidates for duchess, and barks from the hounds at the sideline. "We shall go first! Prepare to be *bowled over*!"

Several of the mothers harrumphed at Sesily's brash performance, but as they had quickly learned that complaining about the presence of the Talbot sisters wrought nothing but Sera's irritation and the sisters' increased impropriety, they remained tight-lipped.

It did not help, she imagined, that their daughters seemed to like the Soiled S's. Lady Lilith and Lady Felicity Faircloth—no one seemed to be able to refer to her as anything but her full name—appeared to more than like them, even. They appeared to be influenced by them. Sesily bent to fetch a heavy blue lawn bowl, and Lady Lilith called out, "I, for one, am already bowled over by that frock, Lady Sesily."

Sesily stood and canted one hip in the gown that might have been called too tight by some, and was certainly called such by the older women assembled. "I am happy to recommend you to my seamstress, Lady Lilith."

"Perhaps for your trousseau!" Sophie teased.

"Now, now," Sesily said, after the laughter died down. "Everyone knows Haven has an affinity for women who can command a bowl course."

"Is that true?" Miss Mary said, concern in the words.

"Very," Sesily said. "Ask Sera. She knows all about his interest in . . . orbs."

A septet of women laughed on a spectrum ranging from choke to guffaw. Caleb made it worse when he tipped his hat to Sesily and said, "I'm right. You are trouble."

Sesily winked. "Only the very best kind, American."

He laughed, full and welcome, and Sera couldn't help but join him, forgetting, for a moment, the true reason for their assembly.

Until Mrs. Mayhew reminded them all, slapping her fan shut and rapping it against her thigh. "Really! This is too unacceptable!"

Sesily blinked wide-eyed innocence at the older woman. "I don't know what you think I am referring to, Mrs. Mayhew. Haven likes bowls." She looked to Sera. "Doesn't he?"

"Very much, as a matter of fact," she said, rather proud of her ability to steel her expression. Sesily Talbot did not simply live up to the expectations for the Talbot sisters— she exceeded them. And Sera had always adored her for it.

Perhaps they could grow old together, partners in ruinous sisterhood.

"And what of the fact that she's a wicked flirt?" Mrs. Mayhew prodded in ear-piercing outrage.

"I see no reason why that should impede a game of lawn bowls," Sera said with a shrug.

"Excellent!" Sesily said. "It's decided, then! If I win, I get the American."

"And if someone else wins?" Caleb said with a laugh, "Not that I do not expect you to trounce them, Lady Sesily."

Sesily smiled wide. "Of course you do, future husband. I don't know . . . if someone else wins, they can have Haven. Isn't that what they're all here for?"

Sera's sisters laughed, as did Lady Lilith and Lady Felicity Faircloth, while Mrs. Mayhew and her poor daughter looked as though they might be sick. Lady Emily did not respond at all. Sera had just decided to step in and stop her sister's performance when Sesily set her eyes on a point beyond Sera's shoulder, and she smiled wide. "Don't you think it a capital idea, Your Grace?"

"It certainly would make things easier." He stopped behind her, his warmth all she could feel. "Good afternoon, ladies." The suitesses dropped into curtsies in a bloc, and Haven added, "I feel as though I should apologize for my distance since you arrived. An estate of this size requires more than a little attention when I return from town."

It was a proper lie. Haven had the best land steward in Britain working for him—an older gentleman with immense skill and virtual sovereignty over the land. Haven cared about nothing but the architecture. Sera had never seen a man so proud as when he spoke of the unique rooms of the main house, of the dower house, of the folly that stood in the eastern pastures.

"At any rate, I should enjoy spending a bit of idyll with you. Lawn bowls sound lovely." He was close to her—far too close considering he was speaking to an assembly of a dozen. And then he turned to her, the question he asked brushing over her skin like a caress. "Is the duchess playing?"

Sesily's eyes lit up. "Would you like her to?"

Sesily thinks I want you back.

None of this business. She stepped away from Haven, taking her place behind the ball Lady Emily had thrown, doing her best to pretend he was not there, no doubt looking poised and perfect. "I am not," she said. "I am the referee."

He nodded and made a show of looking over the field. "And the teams?" he asked, loud enough for everyone to hear, and she couldn't stop herself from turning to look at him. He sounded—content. As though he'd been looking for something to do with his time, and lawn bowls seemed a perfectly reasonable option.

Suspicion flared, and not a small amount of panic.

What was happening?

Seline leapt in to answer. "The unmarrieds versus the marrieds. And Sesily."

Sesily sighed dramatically. "Always a bridesmaid." She looked to Caleb. "American bride?"

Caleb laughed loud and brash, and Mrs. Mayhew harrumphed again from the sideline. Haven ignored the interjection, instead straightening his sleeve and considering the teams in question, which, to any bystander who happened along, would appear terribly unevenly matched.

On the left of the playing field stood four fresh-faced,

pretty young women in shades of pastel, each with some combination of hope, excitement, and terror in her eyes, each likely more eager than the next to impress the Duke of Haven and make herself a proper aristocratic match.

And on the right stood their opposites. In every way. The Talbot sisters had never in their lives worn pastel—they did not follow fashion so much as invent it themselves. They wore bright, beautiful colors that seemed captured from the summer gardens nearby, their hair in elaborate designs—they believed in brash honesty above quiet politesse, and together, they had the grace and tact of a runaway carriage, a fact underscored when Sesily called out, "Oi! Haven! I'd move if I were you—before my poor aim sends a bowl right into your shin."

"Here's to happy accidents!" Sophie called out from the table nearby, where lemonade and lunch had been served.

"She does loathe me," Haven said quietly.

"Indeed, she does," Sera replied, and she was surprised by the pang of discomfort that came at the thought.

"Is anyone else perishing from hunger?" Sophie added.

"We're not eating, Sophie," Sesily groaned. "We're playing."

"Don't think that this obsession with luncheon is about pregnancy," Seline opined to the suitesses. "Sophie has been hungry for every moment of her entire life."

"Truth!" Sophie added, popping a tart into her mouth. "No one minds if I start, do they?"

The mothers in the gallery seemed unable to decide if they were more affronted by Seleste's reference to Sophie's increasing state, or to Sophie's willingness to begin eating without permission from the duke or duchess, a fact that only served to remind Sera of how much she adored her sisters.

"I shall do my best to be a gentleman and join you," Caleb interjected. "I am, after all, a growing boy."

"Capital!" Sophie replied. "As it is possible I am growing *a* boy, we shall be a fine match."

The mothers whispered behind fans as the Marchioness of Eversley once more proved her reputation as a woman with a penchant for brashness.

Haven watched Sophie for a long moment. "Can she be won over?"

"Sophie?" Sera looked to him, shocked. "Why do you care?"

Something flashed in his eyes, something that looked remarkably like truth. "Can *you* be won over?"

Her heart began to pound.

He was doing it again, trying to win her when he did not want her. Trying to keep her when he did not wish to have her. When she did not wish to be kept. She'd been his possession once before. And it had not ended well for either of them.

She met his gaze. "No." The word shuttered the openness in his gaze, and she ignored the disappointment that flared in her, saying for all to hear, "I wouldn't worry so much, Duke, Sesily's rather terrible at this game. She's unlikely to hit you."

"At least, not on purpose!" Seleste pointed out from her spot down the field.

Haven raised a brow. "Now I'm not sure where to go."

Sesily answered without hesitation. "I could always *attempt* to hit you, Haven. If that would make you feel better."

Sera smirked and looked to him. "It is your decision,

which team you'd like, of course, as master of the field."
She waved a hand over the collection of bowls.

"Just throw the ball, Sesily," he said.

Sesily nodded once and did as she was bid, the ball
careening down the lawn and landing, quite beautifully,
by the small white kitty. A smattering of applause came
from Haven's suitesses, but the Talbot sisters were not
nearly so polite. "Oh!" Seleste gasped.

Seline blurted out, "Dear God! She nearly hit it!"

"Have you been practicing?" Sophie cut Sesily a skeptical look.

"I haven't!" Sesily crowed. "But I'll be damned if
I'm not a natural at this game!" The mothers went into a
flurry again, one that only increased when Sesily added,
"I told you we were right to bet on ourselves. I am clearly
a savant."

"Oh, clearly," Sophie said dryly, as Sera laughed.

And then Mrs. Mayhew said, "I beg your pardon, did
you say *bet*? Surely you are not wagering on the outcome
of innocent girls' lawn bowls."

"Surely you couldn't have imagined we wouldn't have
done whatever necessary to make innocent girls' lawn
bowls more interesting, could you, Mrs. Mayhew? Besides, you shall be quite happy with the results should
your daughter come closest to the kitty."

Haven was immediately suspicious. "What does she
win?"

Sera lifted one shoulder and dropped it.

"No," he said, and suddenly it felt as though they
were alone in the gardens. "No shrugging. What does
she win?"

"Well, if the sisters win, the one who gets closest to
the kitty gets to return to London," Sera said.

"Won't she be lonely? Best send the whole lot home with her." She scowled, and he added, "And what of the suitesses winning?"

"A private excursion."

"With whom?"

"With you, of course."

"Oh." Mrs. Mayhew spoke for all the mothers and, by the look on his face, for Haven as well.

Sera thought she would get more pleasure from his shock. She lowered her voice. "You wish a wife, Your Grace. This is how you get one."

He watched her for a long moment, and then said, "You're wearing lavender."

The change of topic threw her. "I am." The words came out more like a question, as though she did not have eyes in her head and a grasp of the color spectrum.

"Yesterday was amethyst. The day before, a grey like heather in winter."

She went cold. "I like purple."

He shook his head, his eyes dark with secrets. She knew it, because hers held the same. "No, I don't think so."

She didn't want to discuss it. Not then. Not as they stood there with what seemed like half the women in London watching.

She didn't want to discuss it. Ever. And she hated him for pointing out her clothing. Purples and greys. The colors of mourning.

Malcolm said no more, turning to face the girls at the other end of the field, and Sera had the distinct impression that this was what men looked like marching into battle. "Then I think I should stay at this end, and make sure you are impartial."

She forced a smile. "Afraid I'll rig the contest to keep my sisters?"

He lowered his voice. "Afraid you'll rig the contest to get rid of me."

She stilled. That was the point, was it not?

She'd been too lax with the girls and with him. He had to find a wife. One of these women was going to take her place. And Sera would restore her own freedom. She would get her tavern and her future and walk away from this place and this man and all the memories they wrought. She looked to him. "Haven," she said. "You must see—"

He cut her off, turning away. "Mrs. Mayhew. I see something must be irksome if you have come out into the sun."

"As a matter of fact it is," said the irritated woman. "Your Grace! I must object! These—" She waved a hand at Sera's sisters. "*Women*—I suppose one must call them—they are terrible influences. You've been positively invisible for nearly a fortnight and—frankly—this is all seeming like a terrible waste of time."

"Mother." Mary was in the mix now, calling from her place with the other unmarried women.

"I suppose I should take my shot," Lady Lilith said.

She hefted the ball high as Mrs. Mayhew pushed on. "My husband is quite powerful and Mary is quite in demand. We've passed up numerous invitations to other parties with other eligible men who—you'll have to admit—are far more eligible considering *your* circumstances."

Sera had to admit, Mrs. Mayhew was an excellent mother. She knew what bull she wished for her daughter and was not willing to stand by when she might seize it by the horns.

It was difficult not to see echoes of her own mother in the woman.

And, in those echoes, hints of what would either be a great success or an unmitigated failure.

"Mrs. Mayhew," said Haven, "I think perhaps—"

"Mother, please!" Mary was marching across the field.

Mrs. Mayhew was having none of it. "I should think it would not be out of line for you to find time to walk with my daughter, so you might know her beyond her enormous dowry!"

The woman was impressive. And Sera would be lying if she said she did not enjoy Haven looking so hunted.

"Are you out of your mind?" Quiet Mary was quiet no more. Indeed, it seemed the apple did not fall far from the impressive tree.

Haven was in a bind. And, instinctively, he attempted to reverse any embarrassment that the elder Mayhew might have caused the younger. "I assure you, Miss Mayhew, your dowry is of no consequence."

Mary paid Haven little attention. "Mother! You cannot simply rage at a duke and hope it ends in the marriage you want for me!"

"Not just a marriage I wish for you, darling, a marriage you wish for yourself!"

The other mothers had stopped both fanning themselves and pretending not to watch. All three of the aristocratic ladies were watching with wide eyes and open mouths. Caleb, for his part, was feeding a piece of roast goose to one of the dogs.

"Oi! Out of the way!" called Sesily. "Lilith is throwing!"

"Tossing!" Seline interjected.

"Ladies, may I suggest we remove this conversation to inside?" Sera asked, attempting for calm. "Or at least away from the assembled audience?"

Sera heard Sophie's "Oh, no," in concert with Seline's "Look out!" and turned just in time to see the ball careening toward them. She leapt out of its path, but Mrs. Mayhew was not so lucky. The ball crashed into her foot and ricocheted toward the kitty as she cried out in pain and nearly toppled over on top of Haven.

"I am *so* sorry!" Lady Lilith cried from her place at the end of the field.

"Nonsense! 'Twas an excellent shot! Look how close you got it!"

"She hit a woman, Seline," Sophie pointed out.

"Oh, it's not like she didn't deserve it. I wish we could hit every woman who behaves so abominably. Lady Lilith, is it possible your services are for rent?"

Haven choked—Sera looked to him. "Are you *laughing*?"

He shook his head and coughed. Too obviously. He was laughing.

Sera reached for the hobbled woman, doubled over in obvious pain and embarrassment. "Oh, my," she said, unable to keep the surprised laughter from the words as she made to help. "Mrs. Mayhew, are you quite—"

The woman snapped to her feet. "Oh, shut up," she snapped. "*You're* the scandal here. We should have known you'd bring it down upon all of us. You should have stayed in America and left your poor husband to his future. With a decent woman. One with grace and honor and *fidelity*."

Silence fell as the last word came, a sharp and angry attack, and Sera could not resist the impulse to look to Malcolm, wondering if he, too, felt the shame she did. Hating what she had brought down upon them all. Her sisters, the girls, and him—him most of all.

Except it was not shame she saw in his eyes, nor even a hint of the laughter that had been there before. It was rage. It was protection. It was loyalty.

For her.

And, before she could steel herself from it, before she could keep herself from feeling it, pleasure and pride and something much much more terrifying threaded through Sera. Something with an echo of memory she had sworn not to resurrect.

The memory of the Malcolm she'd loved.

But before he could give his fury voice, Miss Mary spoke, her own ire given free rein. "I should like it noted that you ruined this, Mother," she said, raising her voice and one long finger to her mother's nose. "I was willing to play your silly game and come here and vie for this man's title because I've always done what you and Father think I should. But these women are different and they are interesting and they are brave and so I think I should be as well. I'm not marrying the duke—though I cannot imagine I was in the running, as I cannot imagine why a man such as he would tie himself to a mother-in-law such as you. I am going home. To marry Gerald."

Sera's eyes went wide. "Gerald?"

"Who's Gerald?" This from Felicity Faircloth.

"Felicity! We don't interject into others' personal business!" The Marchioness of Bumble found her maternal voice.

"I've never understood that rule, you know," Lady Lilith said to her friend. "I mean, this personal business is very public, isn't it?"

Mary ignored the other girls, instead turning to Sera. "I am sorry. I should never have come here. I've a love at home. Gerald. He's wonderful."

Sera could not contain her smile. This girl had such a *voice*. It was remarkable. "I imagine he is if he's won you."

"He's a *solicitor*!" Mrs. Mayhew cried.

"So was Father before he was in Parliament!" Mary pointed out.

Mrs. Mayhew began to mottle. "But now . . . you could have a duke!"

"But I don't want a duke." She smiled at Malcolm then. "Apologies, Your Grace."

Mal shook his head. "No offense taken."

"I'm sure you won't understand, but I don't care that you are a duke. And I don't care that he is a solicitor. I'd have him however he came."

Malcolm's gaze flickered past Mary to Sera. "Rat catcher."

Sera stopped breathing.

Mary smiled. "You understand."

"I do, rather," he said, and still he watched Sera, seeming to understand how she struggled with the echo of their past. When he finally looked back to Mary, he said, "I am sorry we did not get more of a chance to talk."

The young woman smiled. "I think you would not have liked me, anyway."

"There, you are wrong, Miss Mayhew. I shall watch the papers for the announcement of your marriage. And in exchange for you removing your mother from my land, I shall send you and Gerald a very generous gift to celebrate your marriage."

Dipping her head to hide her smile, Mary dropped into a little curtsy. "That seems like an excellent arrangement. With apologies, Your Grace."

It did not escape Sera that that particular *Your Grace* was not directed at Haven, but at her.

"There is nothing to apologize for," Sera said, eager to forget the scrape of truth in Mrs. Mayhew's words. To put the whole event behind them.

"There is everything to apologize for," Haven said, cold fury deepening his voice to a tenor that Sera knew all too well. She saw the fear spread across Mrs. Mayhew's face. "No one speaks to my wife the way you did, Mrs. Mayhew. You will leave this house, and you will never return. Make no mistake, you are never welcome under Haven roof again." The woman went white as a sheet as he finished. "There was a time when I would have set out to ruin you. I would have fought for vengeance. You should get into your carriage and thank God that time is passed, and that I find I rather enjoy the company of your daughter."

The older woman opened her mouth to speak— perhaps to defend herself, but Malcolm held up a hand and said, "No. You disrespected my duchess. Get out of my house."

And then he was turning his back to the women, and they were dismissed, summarily. Having been on the receiving end of that cool dismissal, Sera knew its sting better than any.

Particularly when he turned to the group and said, "Lady Lilith, I must say the physics of your throw were quite remarkable."

Lilith smiled and replied, "I wish I could take credit for them, Your Grace. It was very good luck." It was a lie; everyone could see Lilith had fought for her friend.

Lilith was a good match. She would be lucky to have Haven.

That was, Haven would be lucky to have her.

And still, the echo of his words consumed Sera. *My duchess.*

Of course, he meant his wife in the vaguest, broadest terms. He did not mean Sera. How many times had he made it clear he didn't want her? How many times had she said she did not want him?

And she hadn't. Not once she'd stopped wanting him. Not once she'd left.

She'd spent nearly three years not wanting him. Proudly not wanting him. Proudly planning a future devoid of him. And now . . . with a handful of words—words like *my duchess* and *rat catcher*—he was reminding her of the dreams she'd once had. The expectations, unrealistic in the extreme.

Women did not win love and happiness.

At least, Sera did not. Those prizes were well out of her reach. Far enough away that she'd focused on other, more attainable goals. Like freedom. And funds. And future.

Leave love to the others.

As though she'd spoken aloud, Malcolm acted upon the words. "Lady Lilith, one almost feels as though you should win the prize by virtue of succeeding in such a valuable mission. Not that I'm any kind of prize, as I'm sure Lady Eversley will attest."

Sophie smirked. "With pleasure, Duke."

Lilith dropped a curtsy. "I'm sure that's not true, Your Grace."

Sera hated the beautiful young woman then. Hated her for her confidence and her poise and her damn skill at lawn bowling. And she hated Haven for the way he took to her, the way he smiled down at her with aristocratic kindness, as though he had nothing in the world he'd like to do more than commend Lady Lilith Ballard on nearly breaking the ankle of a terrible old woman who deserved it. It was irrelevant that Sera herself had been willing to lift Lilith onto her shoulders in triumphant glory when it had happened.

But mostly, Sera hated herself, for caring whether Malcolm liked Lilith at all.

From the luncheon table, Caleb cleared his throat, drawing Sera's attention. He looked at her for a long moment before tossing another piece of goose to the waiting dogs below and raising one supercilious eyebrow in masculine braggadocio, as if to say, *I see what's happening.*

He was wrong, dammit. Nothing was happening. Sera had come for her divorce, and she was going to get it. She was coming to erase her past. And write her future.

A life Malcolm could not give her.

A life she had to take for herself.

Chapter 17

---~---

WOMEN'S WILES AWAIT!
MIND YOURSELVES, MEN!

"*D*o you love my sister?"

Caleb Calhoun turned from where he checked the final winch connecting his carriage to the four horses that, in minutes, would ferry him to Covent Garden. Sesily Talbot leaned against the coach, arms crossed over her chest—a chest beautifully showcased by a stunning gold dress that gleamed like fire in the sunset.

The dress was likely thought too low and too tight, but Sesily Talbot did not seem the kind of woman who cared what was thought. And it didn't matter, honestly, as it wasn't the fire in the fabric of her dress that made the girl dangerous, so much as it was the fire in her eyes.

No, *dangerous* didn't seem the appropriate word for Sesily. *Dangerous* seemed too gentle. She was positively ruinous. Which was a problem, because Caleb had always been partial to ruination. And being ruined by his dearest friend's sister was not an option.

Ignoring the thread of pleasure that went through him at the sight of her, he returned his attention to the horse, making a fuss over a perfectly fastened harness. "Lady Sesily, may I help you?"

"Are you not answering me because you think I will judge you for it? I won't. People have always loved Sera. She's eminently lovable. The most beautiful of the Dangerous Daughters, to be sure." Caleb wasn't sure at all, as a matter of fact. "I only ask because if you do love her, you've a problem."

She was right about that. Haven clearly desired Sera with an intensity Caleb had never seen. When they were near each other, the duke was unable to direct his attention to any but his wife. And Sera—well, she'd never stopped loving her duke, no matter how awful their past and how impossible their future.

And Caleb knew about awful pasts and impossible futures.

He owned one and was speaking to another.

"Of course I love her," he said. "But not in the way you mean. I've no interest in seducing her."

"Do you love another, then?"

No one had ever taught Sesily Talbot tact, apparently. "I don't see how that is your business."

"Ah, so that is a 'yes.'"

"Love is a fool's errand. One only need look at Sera and her duke to see it."

She seemed not to hear him. "Is it unrequited?"

Irritation flared, and Caleb turned to meet her gaze, clear and direct and—Christ, she had the most beautiful eyes he'd ever seen, blue with a magnificent ring of black around them. Beautiful enough to make it essential that he say the next out loud. To remind himself of where his loyalties lay. "Your sister is the best friend I've ever had." He paused. "Which means I've no interest in seducing you, either."

He meant for the words to sting, just enough to put her off him, but they didn't seem to. They seemed to glide right past her. Indeed, she smiled. "I don't believe I asked to be seduced, Mr. Calhoun."

He was a bull, and she was a stunning red flag. He couldn't have stopped himself from approaching her for all the world. "Of course you have," he said. "You ask every time you look at me."

"You mistake flirting for desire, sir."

"I don't mistake your bold flirt for anything but what it is, Sesily Talbot."

She lifted her chin, exposing a millimeter more skin. Tempting him with it. "And what is that? Diversion?"

He let a beat go by as he watched this girl who had never in her life faced a proper man. "Disguise."

He'd shocked her. She uncrossed her arms and came off the coach, unsettled by him. By his ability to see the truth. "I don't know what you mean."

"I mean you're a flirt, Sesily, and a good one, too. Most people don't see what you are when you're not full of swagger."

"And you do?"

"I do," he said. "I recognize it."

She blinked. Laughed, bold enough for a lesser man not to hear the nervousness in it. "What do you recognize, Caleb Calhoun? An unwillingness to compromise?"

"An unwillingness to risk."

She narrowed her gaze. "You don't know much about me, if you think I do not risk. I've done nothing but risk since I had my first season. I'm a scandal for the ages."

"Nah, you're only a scandal because they don't see that you're the least scandalous of the lot."

Her brows rose high. "Never tell a Talbot sister she's not scandalous, sir. You risk us taking offense."

He smiled. "I've spent three years with Seraphina, love. I know the truth. You wear your pretty clothes and talk your clever talk, but when it comes down to it, you want one thing. And it's not what you want me to think it is."

Her lips pressed into a straight line. "I do so like it when a man tells me about myself. It's positively aphrodisiacal."

"I'm an American, my lady. Don't flummox me with all your big words."

Her eyes flashed with humor then. "Shall I tell you what I think about you, then, Calhoun? Never fear. I shall use small words so you understand."

No.

He didn't want her telling him anything. They'd already taken this too far. Sera would have his balls if he even touched her. She'd burn the Sparrow to the ground just to keep him from getting his cut. And then she'd hire herself a ship to take her to Boston and do the same to every property he owned there.

The thing was, it might be worth it.

He was so distracted by how well it might be worth losing everything for one moment with Sesily Talbot that he forgot to tell her to stop talking.

"I think you're here with my sister—in the country, I might add, which is positively dull as dirt, which you know, because you flee to London every night to breathe in the glorious stench of adventure—because being with Sera keeps you safe."

His heart began to pound. "Being with your sister keeps me in constant threat of being pummeled by your brother-in-law."

"That may be true," Sesily said. "But better feel any

number of fists upon your face than feel something truly dangerous."

He'd had enough of her. "And you're an expert on the subject?"

"On avoiding emotion? I am, rather." He didn't know what to say to that. "And on the day one awakens to discover that their future is set."

"Please," he scoffed. "You are a child."

"I am twenty-seven years old. Unmarriageable for many reasons, the least of which is scandal and the worst of which is my tragic descent into old age."

If that wasn't some British nonsense, he did not know what was. Sesily Talbot couldn't take a step down a Boston street without half a dozen men making eyes at her. Even the thought sent Caleb into a fury.

He was done with this. "Well. This has been entertaining, Sesily, but—"

"You and Sera make an excellent pair. Both terrified of what might come if you actually worked for something."

He scowled. "You know nothing about me."

She raised a brow. "I know you're a coward, American."

She was baiting him. He knew it, and still he wanted to prove himself to her. He wanted to do more than that. He wanted to throw her into the carriage and show her precisely how lacking in cowardice he was.

Instead, he opened the coach door to throw his bag into the carriage.

Only to be attacked by a violent white projectile.

"What in—" He leapt backward, the furred beast apparently not realizing that he'd ceded the carriage, as it clung to his coat with a mighty yowl.

Which was when he realized that Sesily was laughing. And that it sounded like fucking sin. Until that precise moment, Caleb would not have imagined that it was possible to simultaneously be attacked by a cat and go hard as a rock.

But Sesily Talbot was the kind of woman who taught a man things, that much was clear. Including how infuriated he could get.

He grabbed for the animal as it began to scale him like a tree trunk, and Sesily instantly gasped, "No! Don't hurt him!"

And then she was close enough to touch him. And then she *was* touching him. If one could claim claw removal as touching. Which Caleb was finding he had to do, considering how the gentle movements and the soothing tuts she offered the little beast made him want to claw something himself.

He had to get away from her.

Which was difficult, as he had a cat attached to him.

Finally, she cradled the animal in her arms, and, from beyond the edge of his jealousy of the damn creature, Caleb heard the smile in her voice. "He likes you."

He met her gaze. *I like you.*

Well, he certainly wasn't going to say *that*. So he settled on, "Mmm. And why is he in my carriage?"

She lifted one shoulder and dropped it, her lips twisting in amusement. "In my advancing years, sometimes I forget where I leave things."

This woman was trouble. The kind for which he did not have time or inclination. "So this was your plan? Set your cat upon me and hope for the best?"

She blinked, wide blue eyes making him want to kiss her without consequence. That was the problem, however. There would definitely be consequence. "Is it working?"

"No." Too much consequence. He put his bag in the

carriage and closed the door. "Old maid or not, Lady Sesily, you want love. And I know better than to get anywhere near that. With or without your attack cat."

He thought she might deny it, but it seemed Sesily Talbot did nothing expected, and certainly not when it came to tearing men to pieces. "You know, Caleb," she said softly, his name on her tongue a particular weapon. "If you did decide to seduce me . . ." He turned from her, unable to remain still as she spoke, as the words etched pictures upon him—images that he knew better than to think of and that he could not resist. When she finished the sentence, it was with knowing laughter in the words. "Well, you see it as well as I do."

He turned back like he was under a damn spell, only to discover that she had resumed her lazy place against his carriage. Ruining it, forever, it seemed. Because he'd never be able to look at that door without thinking of the moment that Sesily Talbot, cloaked in sunset, baited him so thoroughly, even as she remained perfectly relaxed against the side of his coach, as though she had no interest in the moment other than to toy with him. "See what?"

And then she smiled, and it wasn't the way she smiled while flirting. It wasn't the way she smiled at dinner or when playing lawn bowls. It was private. Personal. As though she'd only ever smiled for him. As if she were his own damn sun. And when she spoke, it was with perfect simplicity. "You see how good it would be."

He felt his jaw drop, and couldn't stop it, not even when, without hesitating over the cat in her hands, she dropped into a perfect, pure curtsy that made him think imperfect, impure thoughts. When she came to her full height again, she said, "Travel safely, Mr. Calhoun," and made for the house, her long strides lazy and without care, as though she hadn't just destroyed a man in the drive.

Christ. He would spend the rest of the night imagining how good it would be. And he would ache with a desire that would not yield until he returned to her and got her the hell out of his thoughts.

Which was never going to happen.

Haven found Sera on the porch beyond the library that night, after the rest of the women had taken to their chambers. She sat at the top of the stone steps leading down into the gardens, where lawn bowls and dramatic revelations had owned the day, a glass in one hand, a lantern and a bottle of whiskey by her side.

The woman he'd met years ago had drunk champagne and happily scandalized Society with her tales of Marie Antoinette's breast molded into glass. She'd drunk wine and every so often sherry, though he could remember more than one occasion when she'd wrinkled her nose at the too-sweet swill.

It had never been whiskey, though.

Whiskey had come when they were apart. And somehow now, as she toasted the darkness, it made sense. She, too, was made better with the years. Richer, darker, fuller. More intoxicating.

Minutes stretched into hours and Malcolm watched her, avoiding the temptation to approach, choosing, instead, to take her in, his beautiful wife—the most beautiful woman he'd ever seen—as she confronted the darkness of the countryside, dressed in a deep eggplant silk that had gleamed in the candlelight at dinner earlier and was now turned black in the moonlight.

His chest ached at the vision of her, stunning and still, lost in thought.

There had been a time when he could have gone to her and she would have welcomed him. A time when he wouldn't have hesitated to interrupt those thoughts. To have them for his own. But now, he hesitated.

She spoke without looking back. "Do you have a glass?"

The question unstuck him. He approached, sitting next to her on the stone steps, as though he were not in a dinner jacket. As though she were not in silk. "I do not." He watched her moonlit profile. "You shall have to share."

She looked down the glass dangling from her long, graceful fingers, then passed it to him. "Keep it."

He drank, unable to hold back the thread of pleasure that came with the familiarity of the moment. "I did not think I would find you alone."

She looked to him for an instant, then away, returning her attention to the dark grounds beyond. "I did not think you would come looking for me."

"Or you would have summoned your American to protect you?"

She gave a little laugh, lacking humor. "My American is on his way to London."

No doubt to care for his tavern. Caleb Calhoun was many things, but he was not a bad businessman. "He should stay there."

She was silent for so long that he did not think she would reply. But she did. "He thinks I am unable to manage here."

His brows rose. "Manage what?"

"You, I imagine."

"Do I require managing?"

She huffed a little laugh at that. "I would never dream of trying, honestly."

"I think you could, without much difficulty."

She watched the darkness for a long stretch, then said, "Caleb is willing to play the lover for the divorce petition," she added.

Later, he would hate himself for saying, "He is a good friend," instead of saying, *There won't be a divorce.*

"He is," she replied. "He's willing to do a great deal for my happiness."

"He is not alone." She looked to him then, meeting his eyes, searching for something. Finally, she looked away. "What do you want, Your Grace?"

He wanted so much, and so well that he shocked himself with his answer. "I want you not to call me Your Grace."

She turned at that, her blue eyes grey in the darkness. "You remain a duke, do you not?"

"You never treated me as one."

One side of her mouth rose in a little smile. "Silly Haven. Didn't you leave me because I knew your title too well?"

He hated the words. Hated that even in this quiet, private darkness, they were cloaked in the past. But most of all, he hated the truth in them. He had left her because he'd thought she cared for his dukedom more than she cared for him.

By the time he'd discovered that it mattered not a bit why she'd landed him—only that she'd landed him at all—she'd been gone.

And with her, his future.

She finally spoke, as though she'd heard his thoughts. "I didn't intend to trap you, you know. Not at the start." She took a deep breath, looking up at the sky. "That is the truth, if it matters."

He set his glass down and took up the lantern as he stood, reaching one hand down to her. "Come."

Her reply was as wary as the look she slid his hand. "Where?"

"For a walk."

"It's the dead of night."

"It's ten o'clock."

"It's the country," she retorted. "If it's night, it's the dead of it."

He laughed at that. "I thought you liked the country."

"The city has its benefits. I like to be able to see the things that might kill me in the dark," she said with dry certainty.

He remembered this, the way it felt to banter with her. As though there'd never been a man and woman so well matched. "Is there something you fear sneaking up on us in the dark?"

"There could be anything."

"For example?"

"Bears."

His brow furrowed. "You spent too much time in America if you think bears are coming for you."

"It could happen."

He sighed. "No. It really couldn't. Not in Essex. Name one thing that might kill you in the dark in Essex."

"An angry fox."

The reply came so quick, he could not help his laugh. "I think you're safe. We haven't had a foxhunt in several years."

"That doesn't mean the foxes aren't seeking revenge for their ancestors."

"The foxes are too fat with grouse to muster much anger. And if they do come for you, Sera, I vow to protect you."

"Your vows have not held much promise in the past," she said, and he heard the way she tried to avoid the end of the sentence, as though she hadn't wanted to say it any more than he'd wanted to hear it.

Of course, he deserved to hear it. He ignored the sting of the words and faced them head-on. "Tonight, I turn over a new leaf." He extended his hand to her again, and she considered it for a stretch before she sighed, collected her bottle, and stood, coming to her full, magnificent height.

He lowered the hand she did not take.

"I'm not wearing proper footwear."

"I was not planning on giving you a tour of the bogs," he said, descending the steps. "Do not worry. I shall protect you from nefarious creatures."

"Who will protect me from you?" she asked smartly before adding, "And where are you taking me?"

"See? You should not have been so quick to malign the foxes. They might have been your only saving grace."

"So this is it, then?" she asked as they marched toward his destination. "It shall be you who does me in in the dead of night?"

He ignored the comment, slowing to allow her a chance to catch up to him. "We're going to the lake."

"In the dark?"

He extended a hand for the bottle she held. She relinquished it and he drank deep, wiping his hand across his mouth before saying, "I am seizing the bull by the horns."

She took the bottle back. "Is one of us to be a bull in this scenario?"

"Did you know that Lady Emily does not eat soup?"

Sera shot him a look. "I'm sorry?"

He smirked. He had her now. Sera had never not been interested in another person. "You seated her next to me at dinner. There was a soup. It provided some interesting conversation."

Sera blinked. "I cannot imagine how."

"Believe me, I was surprised, as well. I thought I might perish from awkward avoidance of Miss Mayhew's disappearance. In fact, the events of the afternoon did not come up. Thanks to the soup."

"Malcolm, forgive me. But are you quite all right?"

"I am, as a matter of fact. It is the lady who seems a bit . . . odd."

"Because she did not eat the soup?"

"Not *the* soup. Any soup."

She stopped. *He had her.* "She does not eat soup?"

"This is what I have been trying to explain. The woman doesn't eat soup."

"Doesn't eat it? Or doesn't like it? Or both?"

"This is the bit I cannot understand. She does not know if she likes it, Seraphina. She's never had it."

She blinked. "Is this some kind of joke? You take my whiskey, drag me out into the dark, and tell me ridiculous stories of people who have never eaten soup?"

He raised a hand. "Upon my honor, Sera—what little you and your sisters think I have left—Lady Emily has never eaten soup."

There was a pause, and Sera said, "How is that possible?"

"This is my exact point."

A beat. And then, magnificently, she laughed. Like heaven come to earth, the sound curling between them before it spread out into the darkness, Malcolm half expecting it to summon the sun.

Because it felt like the sun.

And all he wanted was to bask in her, even as the

laughter died away, fading into little breathy chuckles. She began to walk again, and he joined her, the two of them in companionable silence for the first time in—possibly forever. And it was glorious.

Perhaps there was hope, after all.

They climbed a small hill, Malcolm reaching back to help her navigate a rocky patch, Sera taking his hand as though it were the most natural thing in the world, heat flooding him at the touch, along with desire. And hope, a dangerous promise.

She released him the moment they came to the crest, and the disappointment that came with the action was keen. After a long moment, she turned to him and he held his breath, wondering what she might say.

"Do you think it is liquid nourishment she fears?"

The return to Lady Emily's strange trait summoned his own laugh, loud and unfamiliar. "I don't know."

"You did not ask?" She shook her head in mock disappointment.

"I did not."

"I suppose you thought it would be rude to pry."

"I *know* it would have been rude to pry."

She nodded. "You're right of course. But there really ought to be a special circumstance allowed for this."

He hadn't felt this free in years. Not since the last time they'd laughed together. Before they'd been betrothed. Guilt flared. He'd taken so much from her—so much life. No wonder she'd left him. No wonder she did not wish him back. He should let her go.

Of course, he wouldn't.

Unaware of his thoughts, Sera added, "Between the soup and the lawn bowls, it's been a bad day for your unmarrieds, Duke."

"You're right," he said, unable to hide his frustration. "Let's send them all home."

"Why do you make it sound as though I am responsible for these girls? You are the one who planned a house party to find my replacement. You summoned them without me. You would have been here anyway, choosing your next wife. I'm merely trapped here alongside them."

He couldn't tell her that these girls had been summoned in a frenzied twenty-four-hour period immediately following his commitment to winning her back. She would not take well to the revelation—that much he knew. "I may have made an error in judgment."

She chuckled. "They're lovely women, Malcolm. Good matches."

He looked to her. "One has never eaten soup."

She smiled. "Think of how you might change her worldview! Did you not always wish me less worldly?"

Never. Not once.

"Ah yes," he said, ignoring the thought. "What a lovely foundation for a marriage soup might be."

She laughed at that, and then said, "She's not your choice, anyway. She was never going to be."

Of course she wasn't. None of them would be. "I'm fairly certain Felicity Faircloth would rather have your American than me."

Sera did not hesitate. "He's not my American, and you know it."

He did. Sera would never have allowed him to touch her if she were committed to Calhoun. But it did not mean that—

Before he could stop himself, Malcolm asked, "Has he ever been?"

"Does it matter?" she asked, watching their feet moving through the grass. "Does it matter if there were a dozen?" She didn't give him time to answer. "Of course it would. This is the world in which we live, where I am required to remain chaste as a nun, and you . . . you are welcome to the wide world." She paused, regaining her reserve. Then, softly, "He was never mine. Even if I could have loved him, he deserves children."

Mal didn't hesitate. "Your love would be enough."

She was silent for a long time, while he searched for the right words, to no avail. And then she lifted the bottle and drank. "It doesn't matter."

It did matter. It mattered more than anything, and somehow, like all things that matter a great deal, he could not find the words to say so.

"And you?" she asked. "How many Americans have you had?"

He told her the truth. "One. The one you witnessed."

She laughed then, hollow and so different from her earlier happiness that he felt the sound like a blow. "I am to believe that?"

"I don't expect you to," he said. "But it is the truth."

"That is the problem with truth; so often you must rely on faith to embrace it."

"And you've no faith in me." He regretted the words the moment they were out, wishing immediately that he could take them back. He did not want her to answer. The silence that stretched out between them in the wake of the words was clear enough without her answer. Not to mention unsurprising.

And then she said, so soft that it almost seemed she was speaking to someone else, "God knows I want to."

"It was one time, Sera. Once."

"It was meant to punish me," she replied, the words

simple and empty of emotion as she looked down to the lake, spread like black ink below.

Regret and shame flared. How many times had he felt them? How many times had they consumed him in the darkness as he searched for her? But they had never felt like this. Without her, they'd been a vague, rolling emotion, present, but never truly there. And now, faced with her, with her tacit acceptance of their past, of his actions, of his mistakes, they were a wicked, angry blow.

What a fucking ass he had been.

"I cannot take it back. If there were anything in the world I could take back . . ."

The breath left her in a stream of frustration then. "Tell me, is it the act for which you lack pride? Or the consequences of it?"

He turned to her then, unable to find the proper words to reply. "The consequences?"

"My sister landed you on your backside in front of all London, Malcolm. You did not care for it. You meted out punishment on the whole family after that."

Shame again, hot and angry, along with a keen instinct to protect himself. To defend his actions. But there was no defense. None worthy of the blow he'd dealt. None that had ever dismissed his regret for it.

I'm sorry. The words were cheap escape. "I would take Sophie's attack a hundredfold. A thousand. If I could erase the rest of that afternoon."

Sera grew silent, and Mal would have given anything to know what was going through her head. And finally, she said, "As would I, ironically."

He closed his eyes in the darkness. He'd hurt her abominably. They were silent for a long while as he considered his next words. But before he could find them, she said, "And what of all the years since?"

He looked to her, the darkness freeing him in some way. Making him honest. "I would erase them, too."

She turned to face him, slow and simple, as though they discussed the weather. "I wouldn't." The ache that came with the confession was crushing, black as the water that spread out before them, stretched forever like the silence that accompanied it. Finally, Sera looked to the starlit sky and said, "So, was this your plan? To lead me into the darkness and revisit the decline of our marriage?"

He exhaled, looking to the water, black and sparkling in the moonlight. "It wasn't, as a matter of fact." He began to descend toward the lake, calling back, "I had planned to show you something."

Curiosity got the better of her—as it always had. "What?"

Could he tempt her away from the past? Toward something more promising? It was worth the try. "Come and see."

For long moments, he did not hear her, and he steeled himself for the worst. For the possibility that there was no hope for them.

And then her skirts rustled in the grass.

Chapter 18

SUNKEN STARCHITECTURE: HIGHLEY'S HIDDEN HIDEAWAY

"This is beautiful."

Sera stood just inside a small, stunning stone structure, fixed with six stained glass windows depicting a series of women in various states of celebration, stars embedded in the glass around them, as though they danced in the night sky.

Malcolm stood to one side, lantern high in his hand, revealing the glorious stonework stars and sky that climbed the walls between the windows and spread across the domed ceiling of the space. Sera tipped her head back to take in the moon and sun in full relief above as he said, "The windows are more beautiful in the daylight, obviously," he said.

She looked to him. "I believe it."

She hadn't known what to expect when she'd followed him, lantern in hand, as he descended the rise to the lakeside. She shouldn't have even followed him, for what was the point? Spending time with him only resurrected the past in ways she wished never to do again.

Spending time with him only reminded her that she'd once wanted to spend a lifetime with him.

And still, she'd followed him in the night, drawn like a moth to his flame. And, just like a moth, the fire of him threatened to consume her. As ever.

She'd never spent time on the grounds of Highley; he'd spoken of the lake a dozen times—it held a powerful place in his childhood stories—but she'd never had a chance to see it.

And now, as she looked from one of the women to the next—each so beautifully designed that it seemed as though they were trapped in glass—Sera wondered why he hadn't brought her here, to this beautiful room overlooking the lake beyond. She looked to him. "Who are they?"

He hesitated—just barely—not even enough for another to notice. "The Pleiades."

The Seven Sisters, daughters of Atlas. She looked back to the windows, counting. "There are only six."

He nodded and turned away, toward the circle of wrought iron at the center of the room. Opening a gate inlaid in the railing, he waved the lantern toward the dark circle below. "The seventh is beneath the lake."

Sera moved toward him, sure that she had misheard, her gaze transfixed by the dark, turning staircase there. There were no lights below, the first few steps giving way to immense blackness in no time. She looked back to Malcolm. "I'm not going down there."

"Why not?"

"Well, first of all, because the words *beneath the lake* sound properly ominous and, second, because it's blacker than midnight down there and I'm not an imbecile."

His lips twitched in a tiny smile. "I was planning to go ahead of you."

She shook her head. "No, thank you. I shall be fine here."

He ignored her, turning to the wall and fetching an unlit torch, opening the lantern he carried and lighting it with impressive skill. Sera took a step back when he lifted it over his head, casting his face into bright light and sharp shadows.

"If you think a burning club is going to make me feel better about going down there, you're very misguided," she said.

He chuckled at that. "You do not trust me?"

"I do not, as a matter of fact."

He grew serious. Or maybe it was a trick of the light on his face, making him seem as though he were never more honest than in that moment. "I will keep you safe, Sera."

Before she could answer—before she could slow the instant, panicked beating of her heart—he was gone, heading down the steps into the darkness. She came to the edge of the railing, watching as his light circled down the narrow steps. "How far down does it go?"

"Don't worry, Angel, I shan't lead you into hell."

"All the same, I prefer not to follow," she called.

"Think of yourself as Persephone."

"It's summer," she retorted as a brazier came to life, revealing the bottom of the staircase. "Persephone is aboveground in September."

He looked up, his beautiful eyes turned black in the darkness, a wide grin on his face. "You'll follow."

She huffed a little laugh. "I have no idea why you would think such a thing."

"Because this is what we do," he said. "We follow each other into darkness." And then he passed through a dark doorway and out of view.

And damned if he wasn't right.

She followed, lifting her skirts and inching her way down the winding staircase, grumbling about bad decisions and irritating dukes the whole way. At the bottom, she looked up, the circular opening at the top of the stairs a great distance away, the stone and stained glass windows seeming, suddenly, as though they were a frieze painted on the ceiling rather than an entire room above.

It was beautiful artistry—a mastery of perspective like none she'd ever seen.

Air teased at her skirts, a cool and welcome respite from the cloying heat above. It comforted Sera for a moment, before she realized the reason for the comfortable temperature. She was underground.

The thought had her looking to the teardrop-shaped doorway where Haven had disappeared, and where he stood, not a foot away, torch in hand, grin upon his handsome face. "I told you that you would come."

She scowled. "I can go just as easily."

He shook his head. "Not if you want to see it." He waved his light deeper into the space, revealing what appeared to be a narrow, teardrop-shaped tunnel, painted on all sides in the same motif as the windows above, dark sky and a starscape that gave competition to the night sky beyond.

Her eyes went wide. "How far does it go?"

"Not far," he said. "Take my hand."

She shouldn't. "No."

He looked as though he might argue with her, but instead he nodded and went ahead, lighting another brazier, and then another, each revealing a few more yards of the tunnel.

"We are under the lake?"

Another brazier. "We are technically inside the lake, but yes."

"Why?"

And another. "Do you know the story of the Pleiades?"

There were moments when she could forget that Haven was a duke, and moments when his past, being raised in a constant state of aristocratic whim, showed without pause. Invariably, those moments were the ones like this, when he ignored questions and changed subjects without apology.

She did not hide her irritation. "I know they were sisters. I know they were daughters to Atlas."

Another light flared to life. "And once Atlas was punished, forced to hold up the heavens, they were left alone, with no one to protect them from gods or men. Seven sisters. With only each other."

She did not like the thread of awareness that went through her at the words. The familiarity of the story— her father, made aristocrat without warning, she and her sisters thrust into the world of the London aristocracy without aid. Never accepted for their low beginnings, never admired for the way they rose.

She affected a false bravado. "Dangerous daughters must stay together."

"One more than the rest." A flare of orange, casting his serious face in angles and shadows. He continued, his voice low and dark like the endless teardrop hallway. "The oldest six Pleiades were beautiful, and each tempted a god. Each married into the heavens. But the youngest, Merope—the most beautiful, most graceful, most valued—she caught the eye of a dangerous suitor— one who was earthborn."

"Isn't that always the way? Your sisters get their hearts' desire, and you get a mere mortal." Another brazier. This tunnel was endless. "Are we crossing the entire lake underwater?"

It was as though she had not spoken. "No mere mortal. Orion was the greatest hunter the world had ever known, and he pursued Merope relentlessly. And she was tempted."

"Of course she was. I'm certain he was handsome as the devil."

"He was, as a matter of fact." Ah. So he was listening. "She did everything she could to hide from him, knowing there was no hope for them."

She, too, was listening, the words *no hope* settling like an ache in her chest.

"She turned to her sisters, who banded together, working as only sisters can do to protect their youngest from the mortal hunter who would never be good enough. They began by blinding him—"

"And you thought *my* sisters were bad." He lit a final flame, revealing another dark doorway, the hint of something beyond.

One side of his mouth tilted up, even as he stood framed in darkness, watching her. He looked like a god of sorts—a modern one. Tall and beautiful, with a face chiseled from marble, rendered even more godlike in the flickering light from the torch he held, as though he could summon flame at will. "His blindness was no deterrent. He was a master hunter, made so by the gods themselves. And so he pursued Merope, ever more desperate for what they might have together. For the possibility of their future."

"You'd think he'd have given up on her, what with her clear disinterest."

His words were more growl than speech. "Ah, but it wasn't disinterest. It was fear. Fear of what might have been. And, as he was a mortal, fear of what she would most certainly lose if she succumbed."

Her heart. Him.

Sera remained silent, and he continued, his words soft and liquid in this private, untraveled space. They were as secret as the place itself. "Orion did not fear blindness. He only feared never finding her. Never having the chance to convince her that they were for each other. That mortal or no, he could give her everything. Sun, moon, stars."

"Except he couldn't," she whispered.

He hesitated at the words, and she noticed his fist clench around the handle of the torch, the way the light trembled there, in the dimly lit corridor, as though her words could manipulate it.

"The sisters went to Artemis, the goddess of hunters, thinking that if she called Orion off his search, he would listen. They pledged her their fealty. And she went to him."

"He refused," she said, suddenly knowing the story without ever having heard it. She drew closer to him, desperate for the ending. Knowing it would be tragic.

Wanting it to be happy.

"Of course he refused," Malcolm said, meeting her at a distance. "And that was his mistake."

"Never cross a goddess," she whispered.

He gave a little laugh then, and the years disappeared with the upturned lines at the corners of his eyes, his smile drawing her in, making her wonder at the way those eyes saw and knew and revealed. "As though I have not learned that lesson myself."

She watched the words on his lips, the memory of their smoothness and strength an assault. What if she kissed him? Not like she had the last time, with anger and frustration, but with pleasure? What if she kissed that smile? Could she catch it? Keep it for herself, for all the moments she was alone and wished she could remember it?

No. "Tell me the rest."

He lifted his hand, and anticipation consumed her as his gaze moved to the place where his fingers hovered above her skin, an unfulfilled promise. "Artemis went to Zeus."

It would not end happily.

Malcolm took a deep breath and exhaled. Sera felt the warm air at her temple. Ached at the touch. "She went to Zeus and asked him to hide Merope. To punish the man."

To punish them both.

"How?"

His gaze remained transfixed on his fingers, a hairsbreadth from her cheek. "First, he turned them into doves."

Her breath caught, and he looked at her then, as though he knew what she was thinking. She, too, had been turned into a dove. And it hadn't been enough to hide from him. But he did not know Sera had been a dove once.

"But finding his dove was no challenge for Orion, not even blind. Not even heartsick. He knew her song."

It meant nothing. It was a story.

"What's more, as a dove, Merope was all anguish. Doves, you see, mate for life. And so in asking for her to be saved from a lifetime with a mortal, Artemis had submitted her acolyte to the worst kind of pain—the pain of longing for her match. Orion knew this, and he did not rest, refusing to stop searching for her. He traveled to the ends of the earth to find her. To love her." He watched her in silence, and a long moment passed before he said, "And he did."

Her breath was shallow and uncomfortable, Malcolm had never found her. He'd never looked for her. She'd found him. It had been her on the floor of Parliament, no longer a dove in search of a mate, but a sparrow in search of her freedom.

"What happened?" she asked.

"He nearly had her. They were nearly reunited."

Sadness coursed through her. "Not enough."

His fingers finally, finally settled like a kiss on her cheek. Light and perfect and gone. "Never cross a goddess. Artemis returned to Zeus."

Sera exhaled, hating the way she missed that barely-there, barely-happened touch. "Damn Zeus."

"Zeus gave Artemis her wish."

"But not in the way anyone wanted."

He turned away. "Not in the way they wanted, certainly." He stepped into the dark room beyond, and Sera followed as though on a string, desperate for the end of the story. He crossed the room, torch in hand, pool of light following him, keeping him safe from the darkness beyond. The darkness that consumed her.

"Merope was not destined to marry a god, but Zeus placed her in the heavens nonetheless, alongside her sisters." The words echoed in the room, instantly unsettling her with their great, hollow sound reverberating against the walls. She turned in a full circle, looking up, disconcerted by her inability to place herself in space.

"Fixed to the firmament."

She looked toward him, and saw two of him, his back to her and his reflection in the wall of the room on the far side. It was a massive mirror. A dome of mirrors. She looked up. She watched him in the mirror, his eyes black as he lifted his flame to light another torch on the far side of the room.

"And Orion, desperate to be near her, begged to join her."

He lit another torch on the far side of the room. Not mirrors. Glass. Another. And another, until he finally set his torch in its waiting seat near the door to the room, reflections of light mirrored back and forth around the room, bathing them in the golden glow of each piece of thick, tempered glass, broken by ironwork the likes of which Sera had never seen. On the floor, the missing sister from the gazebo above—Merope, massive and glorious, writhing in stunning mosaic tile.

And beyond the glass, water, made starlit with her husband's fire.

Haven's words cut through her astonishment. "So it is that Orion chases her. Forever."

Sera was consumed in that moment by all the things she should not do. She should not have stayed, but how could she not? At the center of an underwater ballroom, like something out of the myth he'd just whispered to her?

Staying was one thing, however. Moving toward him was quite another. She should not have done that, either. She should have stood her ground on one end of the magnificent space, summoned her sense, and told him, categorically, that he should invite the remaining candidates for her replacement here, to win their hearts and minds. Because certainly, this place was magic enough to do just that to just about anyone.

Which was likely why Sera moved to him, summoned by this place that she'd never imagined. That she could barely imagine now that she stood inside it, intoxicated by its magnificence.

She resisted the idea of showing the others this place,

hated the thought of their sharing it with him, hated the idea of them seeing this version of him, manipulating water and air with his strength and purpose. Strength and purpose that had intoxicated her before. That intoxicated her still.

She stopped mere inches from him. Close enough that if he wished to, he could reach out and take her into his arms. If she wished to, she could reach out. Take him. Not that she wanted to.

Liar.

She shook her head. "This place . . ."

She did not have the words for what this place did to her. What his words had done to her. This room was myth made flesh, sticking her in the firmament as surely as if he was Zeus himself. Of course, he wasn't.

"I built it for you." The confession was so soft it almost wasn't there, followed by more, a rush of words he seemed to push out before he could stop himself. "I built it so there would be something for you when you returned. Something . . . new."

Something that was not weighted down with the past. With what had been lost. Their child. Their future. Sorrow came like a blow and she closed her eyes, letting it wash over here before she took a deep breath and looked up at the magnificent dome, hundreds of black squares of glass reflecting her. Turning her into starlight.

And him, too, the top of his head reflected dozens of times, his mahogany curls the only glimpse of him as he spoke, the whispered words echoing around them in acoustic perfection. "The day it was finished, I stood here, alone, thinking of you." He looked up then, to the perfect black mirror of the dome, finding her eyes instantly. Holding her attention as he said, "I dreamed of you here. In song."

She snapped her gaze to his without the safety of the mirror. "You built me a stage."

He lifted one shoulder and let it fall. "You loved to sing," he said, simply, as though it was enough. "And I loved to listen to you."

She knew what he wanted. Could hear the echo of the song in her head that she'd sung to him an eternity ago. Before their mothers had arrived and he'd discovered her silly plan—one that had never been so nefarious as it had been misguided.

And damned if she didn't want it, too.

"I miss it."

"Singing?"

Singing for you.

The thought shocked her, and she cast about for a different reply. "Performance becomes addiction. One finds oneself craving applause like affection. Song, like air." Her heart began to pound and she immediately regretted the words. She knew well the craving of the latter. How much had she dreamed of it from this man?

"And so the Sparrow is born."

She nodded. "In song, freedom."

"Are you so caged? You've only been here for three weeks."

I've been here for three years.

She did not give voice to the words, instead saying, "Three weeks is an eternity without approval, Your Grace."

For a moment, she thought he would fight her—push her for seriousness. But instead, he took a step back from her. "By all means, then, sing."

"And you shall approve?"

"We shall see." He was magnificent in his arrogance— had always been able to win her with it.

She grinned and lifted her skirts, showing her ankles as she did a small jig. *"Long live the ladies, lovely legs to the floor. Long live the duchess, the Sparrow, the—"*

He closed his eyes before she reached the end of the ditty, and she stopped, the final word hanging between them, at first jest and then jab, and she regretted evoking it, that word that had hung between them before, too many times.

She dropped her skirts, and Malcolm opened his eyes when the echo stilled around them. "And so? Does the space suit?"

He had built this place for her, he claimed. For the future and not the past. And even as she knew that it was impossible to forget the past that lay between them, she found herself unable to try.

She nodded. "It's perfect."

"Would you sing for me?"

She knew what he wanted. "I don't think that's a good idea."

"Likely not," he said. "But it does not change the desire."

And like that, she realized she wanted it, too, as though singing the song she'd sung to him years earlier would somehow free her. Free them. For something new and fresh. She hadn't sung it in three years. Not since she'd sung it to him.

But she remembered every note, every word, as though it were a prayer. And perhaps it was. Perhaps she could exorcise the past with it.

She closed her eyes, and sang, full and free, the perfect dome sending the sound curling back to them. *"Here lies the heart, the smile, the love, here lies the wolf, the angel, the dove. She put aside dreaming and she put aside toys, and she was born that day, in the heart of a boy."*

When she opened her eyes, he was watching her with gleaming pleasure, color on his cheeks and breath coming harsh. He approached her, the last notes swirling around them, and reached for her, pushing a loose curl back behind one ear. She should have stepped back from him, but found herself riveted by him, so close. So present. "Tell me, Seraphina. If there were no one—no sisters or god or goddess to protect you, no American, no aristocracy to watch and judge? What would you do if I pursued you?"

His eyes darkened with his words and she could not look away. How many times had he spoken to her like this? In liquid, languid poetry? How many times had she dreamed it?

He pressed on. "If I promised you sun, moon, stars? If I vowed to always hunt you, would you take flight? Or would you choose to be caught?"

He was close enough that she could give in. That she could reach up and press her lips to his. That she could throw caution to the wind and take what he offered. That he could catch her.

But he wouldn't, not without her consent.

"What if we could have it back, Sera?" The whisper destroyed her, the ache in the words matching the ache in her chest. "What if we could start anew?"

She shook her head. "You should never have brought me here."

He took a step toward her. Ignoring the words. "Would you take it?"

She swallowed, knowing she shouldn't.

He saw the hesitation. Leaned in, willpower alone keeping him from kissing her. How did he stop himself when all she wanted was to let herself go?

He stopped for her. "Take it, Angel."

One time. This one time, and then she would end it. Pass him on. Let him find a new wife. Let herself pursue freedom.

But this one, single time, she would take what he offered. What she desired.

She would get him out of her mind forever.

One time.

She came up on her toes, closing the distance between them as he whispered—more breath than sound—a single devastating word, a word echoed in her heart.

"Please."

Chapter 19

HAVEN HOOKED BY HUNTRESS

There was nothing soft about the way they came together, nothing quiet or tentative. They crashed into each other as though the dome around them might implode and wash them away, and if this was to be their last moment together, why not let it be one of power and passion and devoid of regret?

Why not have one, single moment when there was nothing between them—no plotting or anger or frustration or clamoring for something else—nothing between them but the desire that had always consumed them? The pleasure they had always wrought?

Sera's hands were instantly in Mal's hair, threading, pulling him to her, her lips already opening for him as he sent her hairpins flying, bringing her hair down around her shoulders before his arms came around her, lifting her high against him as he stole her breath.

As she stole his, as she claimed him.

There had been a time, long ago, when she would have followed him where he led. But not now, not when she'd dreamed of him for so long and changed so much. Now, she was his equal. Each led, each followed.

And it was glorious.

His hands were at the ties of her bodice, unraveling her even as she set to work on his coat, shucking it over his shoulders. He paused in his work at her gown, flinging the garment across the room even as he refused to release her from their kiss. Her hands chased over the lawn of his shirt, reveling in the hard, warm muscle beneath as he tugged at the silk cords keeping him from her.

After a long moment, he lifted his lips from hers. She opened her eyes, intoxicated by their kiss and desperate for him to touch her again. It was her turn to plead. To feel his desire shudder through him when she did.

With a wicked curse, he clutched the edge of the fabric where the ties seemed to flummox him, and he pulled, hard and fast, rendering the silk cords unnecessary as the fabric split in two, baring her to him.

Another curse. His. Perhaps hers, lost in their groans as his broad warmth pressed to her and they kissed again, long and rough and full of everything they had spent years denying.

And then he tore his lips from hers and set them to her jaw, her cheek, her ear, down the column of her neck, giving her all the words she'd ever dreamed of, wicked and wonderful. "I have ached for you for so long," he confessed to her skin, his lips playing at the secret places to which only he had ever had access. "It has always been you, every night, Angel."

His tongue came out, swirling a little circle at the place where her neck met her shoulder, and when she gasped, he said, "I have lain awake every night, visions of you haunting me until I have no choice . . ."

He trailed off, those lips sliding down the slope of her chest to the place where her breasts strained at the top of her corset. "Visions of your skin—miles of perfection—of your beautiful lips. Of your eyes, like sin. Of your breasts," and then he was there, lifting them from her corset, sliding his lips over the delicate, desperate skin of them, drawing little, teasing circles around her nipples. "You used to love it when I suckled you here," he whispered, the filthy words sending heat and heavy desire coursing through her.

"Do it," she whispered.

"Anything you wish," he whispered, his tongue finding the straining tip of one breast. "Everything you wish, love."

Love. The endearment thrummed through her, and she pushed it away, instead, setting her hands to his impossibly soft curls and showing him just where she wanted him. "I wish this," she said, his lips coming to take her nipple into his warm, glorious mouth. He shook beneath her touch—or perhaps it was she who trembled. He stilled until she said the filthy word herself. "Suck."

He did, giving her everything she'd ached for on her own nights. In her own darkness. Pleasure coursed through her at his touch, at first one breast and then the other, until her knees were weak and he was catching her, lowering her to the tiled floor.

He made quick work of the fastenings of her corset even as she tugged the shirt from his waist, her hands finding the warm, hair-roughened skin beneath, and tears threatened at the feel of him beneath her fingertips.

She had forgotten. It had been an eternity, and she had longed for him so well, and so thoroughly, and still, she had forgotten the feel of him. And now, the memories returned and she could not hold the glory and the ache and the thrill at bay.

She did not wish to.

Neither did he. "How often I have dreamed of this," he whispered, pulling his shirt over his head and sending it to the floor where his coat already lay, before spreading her corset wide and placing kisses between her breasts, down the soft skin covering her ribs, speaking to her body in a way he might never have spoken to her face. "How many nights have I taken myself in hand, thinking of this," he went on, the words echoing around them in the starlit dome, the shock of their truth setting her aflame. "How many have I spent alone, ashamed, desperate for you?"

"Not more than I," she whispered, immediately regretting the confession.

His head shot up, his eyes finding hers in the darkness. Refusing to let her go. "You have dreamed of me?"

It was one night. One night of truth. One night to exorcise the past and pave the way for a future free of their demons. Her hand slid to his face, to the shadow of his beard on his strong, firm jaw. "Every day."

His eyes closed at the confession, as though it had struck him like a blow. "Sera," he whispered.

"You haunt me," she said, the words unlocked. "You have haunted me every day since I left."

"I wish I had," he said. "I would gladly have been made spirit to watch over you. Christ, I ached for you. I ached for this."

He pushed her gown over her hips, following it with his kisses, and she recalled the marks there, on the place that had once been taut and smooth and ideal. She covered the soft, round swell of her belly with her hands.

Silently, he kissed the backs of her fingers, running his tongue along the seam where she hid herself from view, tickling there, just enough for her to move, for him to find purchase in that private, secret place. And then he said, "You are so beautiful here, more than ever."

The tears threatened again at the reminder of how she

somehow belonged to him there, of how she would never be free of him where she was marked in white, puckered lines by their past.

He stopped, and she looked to him, finding his eyes, filled with the same emotions that consumed her—too many to name, and all overpowered by an intense understanding that she had never thought to find in another. But of course, she found it in him. It had always been him.

He rose over her, strong arms holding him, corded muscle in his shoulders reminding her of his immense strength. And he kissed her again, long and soft and beautiful, until her breath was caught in her throat and she was ragged with agony and pleasure.

She lifted her hands to his face, her soft touch ending his kiss, pushing him back to look at her, eyes dark and full of sin. "You are perfect."

She closed her eyes at the sting of the words. "I am deeply flawed."

He stayed still and silent until she opened them again. "Your flaws are perfect. A map of where we have been." She caught her breath at that *we*. At how much she wanted it to be true. He went on, "I have dreamed of you here. Look up. Look at us. Look at how beautiful you are. Watch how I worship you."

Her gaze flickered past his shoulder to the domed ceiling, black and bright with their image as he returned to his worship—to her worship—the scrape of his teeth and the silk of his tongue along that flawed place sending heat through her, agony and pleasure, regret and promise, the emotions crashing through her as she watched him in the domed ceiling, consumed by their reflection, her hair spread wild beneath her, her breasts and body bare, one hand spread wide over her ribs, holding her still as he moved lower, his broad, muscled back, hiding her stomach, then her thighs.

"Do you see it, Sera?" he asked, the words low and dark. "Do you see how we are together?"

She took a deep breath, air shuddering through her. Bit her lip. His words promised so much—they tempted her with forever. But this was not forever. This was tonight.

He nipped at the soft skin of her stomach and he soothed the bite with his tongue when she gasped. "Do you see?" he repeated.

"Yes," she whispered.

He moved lower, speaking to the dark hair that covered the place that had only ever been his. "What do you see?"

"Mal." The word came out sounding like she was begging. And perhaps she was. She simply didn't know what she was begging for.

He did, though, parting her thighs and settling himself between them. "What do you see, Angel?"

"I see—" His fingers came to her core, warm and firm, and she gasped again. "Mal."

He stopped. "Tell me."

She looked up at the ceiling. "I see . . . I see you."

He spread the soft folds of her sex then, like a reward for her honesty. "Yes," he said, the word licking like flame against her. She could not stop herself from lifting herself toward him. "And what else?"

Desire pooled, thick and desperate. "And me." He set two fingers to the center of her, sliding them up and down her sex, up and down, again and again, until she thought she might die of the pleasure of it. Of the teasing. She writhed against the touch, desperate for him to find purchase—to stay in one place—to give her what she wanted.

What she needed.

"Mal . . ."

He removed his hand. "Tell me what you see."

"I told you already, dammit."

He laughed at that, the bastard. The feel of it nearly did her in. "Tell me more."

"I see you," she said sharply, irritation and desire in the words. "I see you touching me."

And, like magic, he touched her. One finger, circling that magnificent place where she was desperate for him. She gasped her pleasure. "Dear God."

The finger slowed, and she instantly spoke, desperate for him to continue. "I see you touching me," she repeated. "Exploring me. Finding all the places I want you."

And he did, sliding one finger into the hot, wet core of her, the sensation sending her arching into him even as her eyes widened, riveted to the wicked, wanton image above.

That's when she saw what he was doing. "Merope," she sighed.

His grunt punctuated another long, languid slide, this one with a second finger, the sound deep and dark and demanding that she say more.

"I see her, as well," Sera fairly panted. "You planned this."

"I did," he said, and he was so close to her, whispering the words at the place she needed him most. "I wanted you here. As beautiful as she is."

"You wanted me naked with her."

"I always want you naked, love."

The words sent heat curling through her, pooling deep. "I see that," she said, her gaze sliding over the mosaic nymph, breasts bare as her own, twisting and turning in the tilework as though Malcolm touched them both. As though in bringing pleasure to Sera, he was pleasing Merope as well.

Sera believed it as his fingers worked their magic . . . that he might be enough to please a goddess.

"Mal," she whispered, unable to keep herself from lifting into his touch as he stroked deep once, twice, a third time. Unable to keep herself from saying more. From taking everything he offered. "I see you looking at me," she said, and he stilled, pulling back and looking up at her, finding her gaze instantly, waiting for her to say more.

The thrill of the moment was undeniable. Her power, unmistakable. She could ask him for everything, and he would give it to her. "I see you wanting me," she whispered.

Without breaking eye contact, he pressed a kiss to dark curls. "More than I've ever wanted anything."

She understood that—felt the same want coursing through her own body, aching for him. She canted her hips toward him, and still he waited, as though he would wait an eternity for her to ask him to touch her. For her to give him permission to take her. She whispered his name, and still he remained frozen, locked in rapt attention, waiting for her command. "I see you kissing me," she said, the words coming more firmly than she would have imagined.

That low groan again, like she'd given him the only thing he'd ever wanted. And then he moved his hand, spreading her wide, revealing the swollen, pink heart of her. She stopped breathing, the anticipation unbearable.

"Tell me again," he said. "I want you to be sure."

Her whole body went bow-taut at the words. At the promise in them. At the meaning in them—that he would never take what she did not give. That he would follow her, Orion after Merope, but only while she wished to be pursued.

The realization was like no freedom she had ever known.

She did not hesitate. "Kiss me."

He rewarded her with his glorious mouth, spreading her thighs wide and lifting her to him, his lips and tongue taking her with complete certainty and no hesitation. She cried out at the feel of him, the way he discovered every curve of her, his tongue exploring as his fingers stroked and she opened, widened, offered herself to him without pause.

He took her offering, closing his lips around her most sensitive place and sucked, pulling her to him with magnificent skill, until his name echoed through the space as she gave in to the pleasure, writhing against him, bucking into him, her fingers sliding into his hair to hold him to her, to show him where she needed him most.

His tongue swirled against her, giving her everything for which she asked, and she closed her eyes, barely aware of the tears that came with the sheer, wild pleasure he wrought. Her whole body bucked and writhed against him as he delivered his unrelenting worship, and she gasped, again and again, the emotion rioting through her until she lay beneath him and wept with it, unwilling to let him go.

This man, whom she had once loved so much, who had always known how to wring pleasure from her.

This man, who gave her power beyond her ken.

And even through her tears, he did not stop, slow

circles becoming faster, tongue working against her, licking and sucking in lush motions as he slid his hands beneath her and lifted her up to him like she was a feast. Redoubled his efforts. Claimed her.

She gasped as the feeling rolled toward her, stiffening, nearly fearful of what was to come—of how he might own her if she let it come. Still, he persisted, giving her no purchase, worshipping at the pulsing, magnificent place where she most wanted him, making love to her until she cried her pleasure on his name—the only word she could find the ability to say.

He held her as she returned to the moment, to the magnificent space, the underwater dome looming above them like sky. And when he lifted his head, his face flushed and his beautiful eyes wild, the keen, unbearable want she'd kept at bay threatened to consume her.

No. She would not want him.

She could not have him.

She knew better.

She scrambled beneath him, pushing him away, and he was off her instantly, releasing her as though he'd only ever existed to do her bidding. The realization threatened to shatter her as well as his touch had.

So Seraphina did what she could, reaching for her dress, scooting back across the floor with it clutched to her. "We cannot go further."

He did not move from where he sat, bare from the waist up, one arm resting on a bent leg, clad in dark, soft buckskin. "I did not ask to go further."

"But you wish to."

"I'm a grown man, Sera, and I have waited for this— for you—for years. Of course I wish to." His gaze was hot and honest. "But I shall wait for you. Until you are ready."

She hated the words. Hated the way they tempted her. The way they whispered a promise that he understood. Of course, he couldn't. "I shall never be ready."

"Perhaps not. But perhaps you will. And when you are, I shall be here." He said it as though he had nothing to do but languish here, in his underwater lair, waiting for her to wander in and ask him to make love to her.

And something about that, about the certainty in his words, as though he would wait for her forever, unsettled her more than anything else could. "That particular act has never served us well," she said quietly. "Or do you not remember?" She hated the words, loathed that she gave voice—even in a vague, small way—to their past. To the child they had not planned. That he had not wanted. And to all the others they would never have.

She stood, too bare and revealed to remain still, and turned her back to him, pulling her dress over her head and wrenching the two halves of her bodice together in a fruitless attempt to erase the last hour of her life.

"Take this."

She nearly jumped from her skin. He was behind her, close enough to touch, holding his coat for her, as though it were all perfectly normal.

She took the coat and willed herself calm as she pulled it on, the broad shoulders dwarfing hers. She crossed the fabric over her chest, and her arms over that, like armor. He stepped back, hands spread wide, as though to show her that he was unarmed. Of course, it was not true.

They had always been armed with each other.

"I remember, Sera," he said, and the words seemed wrenched from him, as well, impossibly so. She could still hear his vow never to have a child. She could still feel the sting of it now, years later, and the ache of it after she discovered he would have one, nonetheless.

Just as she could still feel the quiet happiness that had consumed her when she'd known she would never be alone, even if she never had him.

And then, the devastation when she realized that alone was all she'd ever be.

"Let me go," she whispered, the words ragged, shot through with fear that he might resist them. That he might try to keep her there.

That she might choose to stay.

He took another step back. And another, until the path to the exit was clear for her. "You are free," he said.

"We're neither of us free," she said. "But we can be."

Lie.

He watched her, unmoving, his beautiful broad chest gold in the firelight, his face all light and shadows. And then he threw his weapon. "I never asked to be."

His aim was true, thankfully, pushing sadness from her and filling her with anger, reminding her of her plans. Of the Sparrow. Of her future. Without him. Without the past. Without the memories that she could not escape here.

"What a lie that is." She narrowed her gaze on him, and let her anger fly. "It was you who ended us, Duke. Not I."

Before he could reply, she escaped.

Chapter 20

HOODWINKED HAVEN'S SHOCKING SURPRISE

Three Years Earlier
London

$\mathcal{H}$e sensed her before he saw her.

He should have expected that the Countess of Liverpool would invite them both to her famed summer soiree. Should have assumed that the Soiled S's would be welcomed at the woman's mad garden party with its China-themed decor and the hostess herself dressed like one of the fish in her famed fishpond. Lady Liverpool had never once shied away from the dramatic, and the Talbot sisters were nothing if not dramatic.

Not Sera.

He did not turn to face her, knowing that all the world watched and whispered beneath stiff brims and behind fluttering fans. Instead, he resisted the urge to tug at his cravat, too tight around his neck in the hot, humid summer breeze, knowing that he was too much the focus of attention as it was.

Hoodwinked Haven caught by a Dangerous Daughter, the laughingstock of the gossip rags, made example for the rest of the eligible men of the *ton*. Never be blinded by beauty.

God knew he had been blinded. Like damn Orion.

Doomed.

It had been more than two months since he'd seen her—having left her, summarily, after their minutes-long, barely-there wedding and thrown himself into his work, doing all he could to forget the fact that he had a wife.

A wife whose nearness shattered his calm, and whom he knew he would find more beautiful than ever, if only he would turn to face her.

Coward.

The thought spurred him to action and, steeling his emotions, he turned, his gaze finding her, as ever, immediately. She was several yards away, in a cluster of jewel-toned gowns—her sisters gathered around her like a protective shield. And Sera in red shot through with gold thread. Of course she wore red. There was nothing in the world more desirable than Seraphina Talbot—no, Seraphina Bevingstoke, Duchess of Haven, his wife, his duchess—in red.

It did not matter that he would give anything to no longer desire her.

He would sell his damn soul to forget her.

And then the hens fluttering about her parted, and he saw the gown in full, chasing the lines of her breasts and hips, falling in lush waves to the green grass below. He raked his gaze over her, breathing her in, a cool breeze on the summer day. And that was when the blow came, wicked and unexpected.

She was with child.

She was with child, and she hadn't told him.

The emotions that coursed through him were myriad.

Disbelief. Pleasure. Hope. And fury. A keen, unyielding
anger that she had once again hidden the truth from him.

He was to be a father. He was to have a child.

And she'd hidden it from him, like penalty for past sins.

He steeled his countenance, refusing to show her how
the truth consumed him. How it struck like a blow. A
devastating punishment. And then he turned on his heel
and went to find a way to punish her, as well.

September 1836

𝒯he next morning, Malcolm received word from his
matchmaking wife that he was to ride with Lady Lilith
and Lady Felicity Faircloth. No doubt Seraphina thought
that it was time he come to know the remaining two candidates for future Duchess of Haven—as Miss Mary had
left for Gerald's warm embrace, and Lady Emily's soup
aversion was too overwhelming a character trait.

Not that he had any intention of marrying either of the
women. Indeed, the notice from his wife—perfunctory
and without even the hint of reference to the night prior—
had him immediately considering storming the breakfast
room and summarily dismissing all the houseguests, finally jettisoning the stupid plan he'd concocted to keep
Seraphina at hand while he wooed her once again.

He was through with schemes. He was ready to have
his wife returned. He was ready to win her in earnest.
And that required being alone with her, dammit. He
needed time and space and honesty to make her believe
him. To make her believe *in* him. In *them*.

These women were simply in the way. There was no
doubt that, of the original quartet of unmarried females
he'd summoned to convince her he was interested in

another wife, Lady Lilith and Lady Felicity were best suited to him. Lilith was clever and droll, with a passion for travel, and Felicity had a brain in her head and would make any intelligent aristocrat a decent companion. But Haven did not want a decent companion. He wanted his wife. The woman he'd wanted from the moment he'd met her on that balcony a lifetime ago. And that was simply the way it was.

And yet, he could not be rid of them—not without it becoming clear that the entire contrivance had been just that, an unsavory ruse that would anger half of London's aristocracy and incur his wife's wrath in the balance when she realized the intentions behind it, or lack thereof, as he had no intention of giving her the divorce she so publicly desired.

A divorce she would soon see she did not want, if only he could prove to her that their past had nothing to do with their future.

And so, the only thing he could do when he received Seraphina's note about his companions for the morning ride was to reply, insisting that she act as chaperone.

He hadn't for a moment thought she would agree. Indeed, he'd expected to have to fetch her—an eventuality that had his heart racing with anticipatory pleasure—which was likely why she did not argue with his insistence.

When she exited the manor house at five minutes to eleven, clad in a beautiful aubergine riding habit, hat perched jauntily on her head and—Lord save him— riding crop in hand, he lost his breath at the portrait she made, strong and powerful, as though the night before had not happened, or, rather, as though the night before had imbued her with even more purpose.

He could see the determination in her beautiful blue gaze, and he instantly realized that purpose; she wanted him matched. And soon.

He resisted the urge to laugh at the fruitless plan.

And then the laugh was gone, because her trio of companions arrived, despite their not being invited. Of course. Seraphina came armed to the teeth, with her private battalion of warrior women. Minus one, because Sophie, the Marchioness of Eversley, was increasing and, therefore, did not ride.

Thank goodness for small favors.

He refused to show his frustration, instead turning his back on the band of sisters, moving to help first Lady Lilith and Lady Felicity into their saddles. Neither seemed to require his assistance, both clearly excellent horsewomen, and it occurred to him that he might have one day enjoyed a ride with them.

Instead, he dreaded what was to come.

After assisting his guests, he turned to help his wife, who had—of course—already found her seat. He did not miss the fact that she'd chosen one of his most prized mares—a mount he'd had saddled specifically for her.

He looked up to her, fingers itching to touch her, to slide beneath the hem of her habit and find the soft skin above her riding boots. "Your American guard dog does not join you today?"

She raised a brow and cut him a look. "Mr. Calhoun has returned to London for good," she said. "I can only assume he did so at your insistence."

Surprise flared, followed by quick relief that his wife's protector had disappeared. "As a matter of fact, I had nothing to do with it, though God knows I am grateful for it."

"Damn coward," Sesily interjected, and everyone turned to face her. "What? He is."

Haven ignored his mad sister-in-law and headed for his horse, taking his seat. "We are headed to the eastern folly."

"Isn't that what people call your marriage, Sera?" one of her sisters said dryly, snickers following the question.

Sera replied dryly, "Not to worry, my ladies—Haven will almost certainly prefer a marriage to you than he did to me, and I imagine he shall be quite the husband."

Malcolm's teeth clenched at the words that came so easily when last night he had laid himself bare for her and she had come apart in his arms. In frustration, he spurred his horse forward, the group following behind, far enough away for him to avoid hearing them. He'd take the women out for their ride, return them, and then find a way to get the girls gone.

After a half an hour of riding, he slowed at the great stone folly on the far eastern edge of the estate—a medieval tower that had been built several generations earlier. Dismounting, he moved to help the ladies down from their respective horses. Not Sera, however. Sera dismounted on her own, moving quickly away from the group, pulling her sisters with her as though they followed on strings.

Leaving him alone with Lady Lilith and Lady Felicity, both with handsome color high on their cheeks, the result of the ride. It occurred that they might be considered pretty if he cared to notice, which he didn't. He was too busy watching his wife.

Nevertheless, he was not a monster, nor was he interested in navigating the gauntlet of his sisters-in-law, and so he guided the remaining suitesses to the entrance of the folly, indicating they should enter. When they did, he pointed to the winding stone staircase that led up the tower. "There is a remarkable view of the entire estate at the top if you do not mind the climb."

Lady Lilith was already headed up the steps, and Lady Felicity followed quickly, Haven trailing behind. When they reached the top of the tower, coming out into the sunlight, both headed immediately for the stone parapets to lean out and survey the land that stretched in miles in every direction.

Haven took to the far edge of the tower, looking over the side to find Sera and her sisters below, deep in conversation. He stood, watching them, wishing he could hear their words as his companions narrated the view, largely to each other.

"Cor, this is beautiful," Lady Felicity said after a long sigh.

"The best bit of the whole house party, don't you think?" Lilith replied, excitement in her voice.

"It was built in the 1750s," he interjected, telling himself that if he was participating in the girls' conversation, he was not pining like a simpering boy after his wife three stories down. "A gift from my great-grandfather to the woman he loved."

Lilith turned. "Not your great-grandmother, I'm guessing?"

He smirked humorlessly at that. "No."

The Dukes of Haven did not marry for love.

Not until him.

And even then, he'd mucked it up.

The ladies had returned to looking at the estate. "There's a dower house! Did you know there was a dower house?"

"I didn't! And look at the lake. It's beautiful." A pause.

"Goodness, is that a statue at the center of it? How curious! Simply rising up out of the water! Is it Orion, Your Grace?" Felicity Faircloth looked to him for an answer.

Malcolm ignored the pang of disappointment that these women had discovered the statue that marked the underwater ballroom before Sera had. His gaze tracked to his wife far below, and he answered the question. "It is."

If I vowed to always hunt you, would you take flight?

She had taken flight last night and did so still, far below, earthbound, looking as though she might do it in earnest at any moment—turn into a dove and leave him, forever.

What if she did not want him? What if he could never have her?

He hated the questions that came with the harsh memory of the night before, when she'd lingered on the past, invoking without words the child that they had lost. The history they had never been able to make.

They could make a future, though. He believed it.

They had a chance, did they not?

Please, let them have a chance.

She looked up then, as if she had heard the unspoken thought from three stories below. He met her gaze and held it, unwilling to let her go.

She looked away.

Lady Felicity pointed to a manor in the distance. "And what's that over there?"

He looked up from his wife and followed her line of sight. "It's the seat of the Dukedom of Montcliff."

Felicity nodded. "I've never liked that man."

His brows rose at her frank assessment of his reclusive neighbor. "No, not many do."

"Not many people like you, either," Lilith said.

The honest words startled him, and he turned to face the girls—Lilith, with a knowing smirk on her lips, and Felicity, wide-eyed in what could only be described as joyous shock. He let silence reign for a moment before dipping his head. "That, too, is true."

"Why?" Felicity asked.

"Are you two banding together?" They looked to each other and shared a grin, and Haven decided that he liked them. "Is this the bit where I am put on trial?"

"It's a fair question, don't you think?" Lilith pointed out. "We should know precisely what sort of fish we are buying."

"If we wish to have fish at all."

Ignoring the odd metaphor, Haven spread his hands wide. "By all means, then. Ask away."

He'd never seen such glee. Lady Lilith actually rubbed her hands together.

Felicity lifted herself up to sit on the low stone wall, in the space between the parapets, then leaned forward with her elbows on her thighs, posture to the wind, as though they'd been friends for a lifetime. "They say you're a terrible husband."

He lifted his chin at the shocking statement.

"Good Lord, Felicity," Lilith said, low and full of wonder. "Your mother would perish on the spot if she heard that."

"My mother doesn't have to marry him," Felicity said, not looking away from Malcolm.

"It seems we're jumping right in," Lilith said, dryly.

No one would ever say Felicity Faircloth was not a worthy opponent. He leaned back against the parapet and confessed, the words coming shockingly easy. "I have not been the best of husbands."

"They say you are unfaithful." His lips flattened into a

long, thin line, but he did not scare away this young brave woman. Instead, Felicity Faircloth continued. "And that's why Lady Eversley knocked you into a fishpond."

"They are correct." Lilith's nose wrinkled, and he could not blame her. "It was once. I had just discovered that Sera . . ." He trailed off. It was not their business. "I was angry. I have never done it again."

They were silent for a very long time, and Lilith said, "You know, I think I believe him."

Felicity nodded. "As do I, strangely."

Miraculous. Now if only they could convince Seraphina to do the same.

Felicity pressed on. "Shall I tell you what I like about your wife?"

He did not need to hear a list of Sera's qualities. He knew them well. He had listed them more than once. More than a thousand times. And still, he wanted to hear them. He wanted to speak of her with another, as though invoking her here could summon her close. "I do not imagine I could stop you, my lady."

She grinned. "That is likely true. I'm terrible at keeping quiet. It's why my mother was so thrilled to receive your invitation. You are her last great hope."

"I've no interest in being coddled," he said. "Dukes get too much of that as it is."

Felicity nodded. "Very well, I shall tell you. I like that Seraphina knows what she wants. And I like that she is not afraid to pursue it. Even when it is most definitely not done."

Divorce was that. He nodded. "She's always been that way."

"Women are not always able to have what we want," she said, and there was a wistful quality in her tone. "We are too often judged for pursuit."

The words sent a chill through him. He had done that. He had punished her for pursuit. And then, finally, he had punished her for refusing to pursue him.

"Did she pursue you?" Lilith, this time.

"She did," he said, hating the fist that caught hold of him at the words. The way it twisted in his gut.

"They say she caught you unawares. Hoodwinked Haven and all that."

These women lacked fear, and Haven could not help but admire that. "That is what they say."

"But it couldn't have been for the title," Felicity pointed out. "Else why flee? Why not stay and flaunt it?"

How often had he asked himself the same question?

"For all that pursuit, she does not seem to like you very much any longer, Your Grace," Lilith added.

"No, she does not," he said. That much was clear to everyone.

"I like that about her," Felicity said quietly. "I like that when it became clear you did not want her, she did not stay."

Except he had wanted her.

He still wanted her.

Not that he had ever told her as much. Instead, he'd shamed her for her passion. For standing on her own. For reaching for what she wanted. He'd kept it from her. From them both.

"I like that she knows herself. That she believes in herself. That she did not allow herself to be less than what she deserved," Felicity added. "I should like to be more like her than not."

"Then perhaps you ought not marry the Duke of Haven," Lilith said, all dryness. "History would suggest he is not the most accommodating of men when it comes to helping his wife reach her goals."

The words were not meant for him at all. And still they stung like nettles. "Mmm," Felicity said, thoughtfully. "I think that might be the case."

Christ. Why did it take two unmarried women to teach him what he should have seen years ago?

"And that's before the *other* problem," Lilith continued, returning Mal to the moment.

"What other problem?" he asked, the question more forceful than he planned.

The women continued, as though he was not there. As though they were still discussing the estate. Or the weather. And not his personal flaws. "Oh, certainly, that bit is clear as crystal."

"What bit?" he demanded.

Lilith turned to him, considering him for a long moment. "As this entire scenario is uncommon in the extreme, Your Grace, I wonder if you might find yourself willing to answer a rather—inappropriate—question?"

He could not help the shock that played across his face. "More inappropriate than the rest of this conversation?"

Both ladies laughed, and Lilith smiled. "Likely not, as a matter of fact." He waited for her to find the proper words. "Do you wish a new wife?"

And there it was, his exit from this debacle. "I do not, as a matter of fact."

She nodded and looked to Felicity. "Well, that's that, then."

"Indeed." Felicity hopped down from her seat on the parapet. "Thank you very much, Your Grace. This is a lovely folly. The best I've seen."

"And estate," Lilith leapt to add, politely. "That statue of Orion in the lake is particularly beautiful."

Confusion flared, and not a small bit of hope. Were all

women everywhere so unsettling? Or was it specific to the women with whom he came into contact?

"Are you leaving?" he asked, fairly agog.

"We are," Felicity said, dipping a quick curtsy. "I'm sure you understand."

"I don't, as a matter of fact," he pointed out. "I've never in my life met women so willing to speak such truth."

Lilith smirked. "Perhaps you should meet more women. We are not so very uncommon."

"Certainly not here. There are five other women on this estate who also seem to have no trouble speaking truth to you, Your Grace," Felicity said. "And that's not counting Miss Mary Mayhew, who spoke such truth it ended in her going off to find Gerald."

Lilith smiled. "I wonder what sort of man Gerald is?"

And like that, he was dismissed, the two leaving in happy conversation, skirts brushing softly against the stone floor as they made their way for the stairs. "Wait," he called, the entire afternoon seeming to slip away from him.

They turned back. "No need to worry, Your Grace," Lilith said. "We shall see ourselves off. You stay here and do whatever it is men do when they are not required to play the willing suitor."

"You did not tell me the other problem." They turned back, curious twin smiles on their vastly different faces. He clarified. "The one that is clear as crystal."

"Ah," Lilith said.

"Hmm," Felicity added.

"Ladies." The word came out more threatening than he intended. "I imagine it's something like the fact that I'm a terrible husband?"

"You know, I'm not sure you would be a terrible husband at all," Lilith said thoughtfully.

"Oh, no. He shan't be," Felicity rushed to reply. "I mean, not as soon as he discovers how much he loves her."

He could have been ashamed. He could have been defensive. But instead, Felicity's words, filled with truth, made him relieved. *Finally*, he thought. *Finally someone saw it.* Someone who believed it. Two someones. Two someones, who listened when he said, "I *know* how much I love her. I've known it for years."

They looked at each other, then to him, their judgment plain. They thought him an imbecile. "You should tell her, then."

Frustration flared. Did they honestly believe he did not wish to do just that? Did they believe it was so simple?

A flash of color came behind them, a deep, rich aubergine.

Sera.

Dammit, he would do it right now if he thought it would change things.

He stilled. *Would it change things?*

His heart began to pound as she came through the doorway, interest in her eyes and curiosity on her face. "This is a lovely folly," she said.

He would do it now. Here, in this place that his ancestor had built for a woman loved beyond reason. He would do it in front of these women, and finish this idiot scheme. Had he not told himself this morning that he was through with schemes?

Awareness and pleasure and excitement and desire pulled the words from him, as though he was a too-eager schoolboy. "I shall do it now."

He did not see the instant surprise and clear doubt in Lilith and Felicity's eyes. He was too busy looking at his wife, who stepped through the doorway, into the conversation, a portrait of interest.

He did not see Lilith shake her head.

He did not see Felicity open her mouth to speak, or see the way her brow furrowed when Sera asked, "You shall do what?"

If he had seen any of that, he might not have said what he said in front of what immediately seemed like all the world.

He might not have looked her in the eyes and said, with no thought of what might come of it, as though it were the most ordinary thing in the world, "Tell you that I love you."

Chapter 21

CORRECT YOUR COURTSHIP: LOVE LESSONS FROM LEGITIMATE LADIES

*T*o be fair, he realized immediately that he'd made a mistake.

And, surprisingly, it was not when his wife turned tail and returned down the stairs from whence she'd came.

Nor was it when Lady Lilith let out a little, "Oh, no."

Nor did he require Lady Felicity Faircloth's quite frank, "Well. That was badly done."

He realized he'd made a mistake the moment he'd heard himself speak the words—so unfamiliar—and discovered that he'd never spoken them before. Of course, he'd said them a thousand times in his head. Into the darkness as he longed for her late at night.

But never to her face.

And now, as he followed her through the eastern pastures of Highley, he thoroughly regretted saying them in front of Lilith and Felicity, feet from Sesily, whom Sera had nearly toppled from the staircase as she pushed past, and Seleste, who pressed herself flat to the ground-floor wall of the tower as Haven tore out after his wife. And from Seline, whose loud, "Oi! Haven, what've you done wrong now?" was punctuated by Sera's leap into the saddle, before she gave the horse a mighty "*Hyah!*" and let the beast have free rein.

"*Goddammit, Sera,*" Malcolm called after her. "Wait!"

Of course, she didn't, and he was headed for his own horse, nearly there when a heavy object caught him squarely between the shoulders. He turned to face his sister-in-law, who was straightening, testing the weight of another projectile.

"What in hell? Did you just throw a rock at me?"

Seline appeared to be calculating the distance between them. "I don't know that I would use the word *rock*."

"Stone, more like!" Sesily Talbot called down from atop the tower, where three bonneted heads peeked through the parapet.

"Barely a pebble." Seleste appeared in the entryway of the folly, arms akimbo, ready to do battle like a damn Amazon.

He shook his head at the sister-in-law who was armed. "You realize that throwing rocks is unsafe."

Seline tossed her current stone up in the air and caught it. "Not for me," she said. "I've a good arm."

He shook his head. "You're mad."

"No, I'm loyal. Which is a thing you have never been."

An instinctual denial caught in his throat as the Countess Clare called from her place, "And amen to that! Hit him in the head this time!"

For a moment, he wondered if Seline might actually do it. He spread his hands wide. "You're all mad. And I'm going after your sister."

"Not yet, you're not." Seleste came to stand next to her armed sister. "It seems to me that you've made her quite unhappy. Unhappy enough that she does not wish to see you."

"He told her he loved her!" Sesily announced from her place far above, her tone the same one might use if one were discussing finding a rat in a drain somewhere on the estate.

All the other women grimaced. "You deserve another rock for that," Seline pointed out. "And four more for the young women you've been dancing about while you tried to woo our sister back."

"It's no trouble, Duke!" Lady Lilith called down.

"Of course it is trouble! You're only for market for so long!" Sesily said. "And now the two of you have been passed over by Haven."

"Which isn't exactly the worst thing in the world," Seleste pointed out. "As he's dreadful."

"And about to get a rock to the head," Seline added.

Malcolm gritted his teeth. "I love your sister," he said. "Perhaps I shouldn't have said it, though God knows why not, because it's the truth. And I'm damned if I'm going to let you harridans keep me from telling her properly."

"Ha! You do realize this means I win, do you not?" Sesily crowed from where she leaned over the tower wall. It occurred to Mal that she might have been leaning too far over the tower wall, as a matter of fact, but he found he could not find the energy or the inclination to tell her to be careful.

"We know, Sesily."

"Ten pounds each!" she called down. "Sophie is going to be *livid*."

"There was a wager?" Felicity asked.

"Of course! There are always wagers. You should see us in season!" Sesily paused, then turned to Lilith and Felicity. "You *shall* see us in season, soon enough! Our betting book rivals White's! And it's *much* more interesting."

"I'm happy that you are all finding friendship and funds while keeping me from my wife, but I'm through with this now." He looked to Seline. "I trust you won't knock me unconscious on my way to fetch your sister."

"I shan't," Seline allowed, "because if you use the word *fetch* with her, Duke, she's going to knock you unconscious herself. She doesn't want you, no matter how much blunt Sesily's won." Seleste's words were cool and unemotional, and unsettling with the way they rained truth down around them. "You ruined everything years ago, when you refused to acknowledge she existed beyond you."

He stilled at that. "I never refused that."

"Oh?" called Sesily from far above. "We must have missed all the times you came to luncheon and tea."

"And the time you asked our father for her hand," Seleste said.

"And the times you made your courtship public," Sesily added. "And here we were, thinking you were ashamed of your toy."

Blood roared in his ears. "She was never my toy." But Sera's words echoed through him. *You don't want me, but you don't want anyone else to have me, either. You never have.*

Christ. What had he done?

He looked to his wife's sisters. "I only ever loved her."

"But not all of her," Seleste said.

"Not enough," Seline added.

In another lifetime, Malcolm would have argued the point. He would have let his anger and frustration get the better of him. Instead, in that moment, he looked from one of her sisters to the next, and the next, and then said, firmly, "I love her. All of her. Duchess or Dove. With or without you harridans."

Seline watched him for an uncomfortable length of time before tossing her stone to the ground. "By all means, then. Go convince her of it."

Malcolm did not miss the meaning in the words, the clear disbelief that he would succeed at convincing his wife of anything of the sort.

And still, he'd taken to the saddle, and followed her at breakneck speed, his heart racing as he realized the direction in which she headed, desperate to get to her before she discovered—

She was off her horse and headed for the little circle of trees that marked the center of the northern edge of the property, and he was shouting her name on the wind, driving his own mount forward as she faced him, her shoulders stiffening, her spine straightening. She stilled, waiting for him, the summer breeze taking her skirts in long, languid movement even as she remained frozen in the lush green grass.

His horse thundered toward her, and she did not move, remaining in perfect pause, as though a thousand pounds of horseflesh weren't bearing down upon her. Fear crashed through him as he pulled hard on the reins, the horse stopping mere feet from her as though she'd stayed it with mere force of will.

He was down from the saddle before the horse even stopped, not caring as his hat toppled from his head and he closed the distance between them, wanting to reach her and touch her and—dammit—love her.

He was a hound after a fox, and he fully expected her to go to ground.

Except she did not. Instead, she let him come for her. And it occurred that he might, in fact, be the fox.

Because when he reached her, his fingers reaching for her, curling around the back of her head, she tilted her face up to his, her own hand reaching. Her own fingers curling. And, God in heaven, his lips were on hers and she was his—all breath and touch and long, glorious kiss.

He could not stop it, not even when he knew that he should. Because he should. Because this was neither the time nor the place to kiss her—not when she'd run from him and he'd run to her and they needed nothing more than to talk.

It was time they had this out.

She pulled away, just enough to whisper his name, and that small, soft *Mal*, was enough to slay him and tempt him and bring him to her again. Just for a moment. Just until he'd tasted her and touched her. Just until he was made strong again by her presence.

It had been too long since he'd been strong.

And then she was pushing him away, color high on her cheeks, lips stung red with his kiss, and she was putting distance between them. She shook her head, and he opened his mouth to say the words—once, just once, alone with her. *Here.*

Sera did not give him a chance to have the first word. Nor did she intend for him to have the last. She lifted her chin. "What then, I was to have dropped to my knees and thanked you for condescending to offer me your love?"

He froze, his mouth open, words lost. He never seemed to have the right ones with her. Too often they were lies, and when they were truth—they were never enough.

"Or, what?" she prodded. "To profess my own feelings?"

"That would not have been unwelcome. And I might remind you that seconds ago, your kiss made a profession of its own."

"Kisses have never been our failing."

"What then?" he pushed her. Knowing he shouldn't. Knowing he must. "What has been our failing?"

"What hasn't?" She spread her arms wide. "Honesty? Trust?" The words were a cold burn, landing with proper sting. And still she came at him. "When did you invite them here?" His hesitation was enough for her to know the truth, and still she pushed him. "When, Malcolm?"

"The day you came to Parliament."

She looked away, toward the manor house, rising like a lie in the distance. "You never intended to give me my divorce, did you?"

Of course he hadn't. He'd chased her across the world. He'd never in his life been so thrilled as when she stormed into Parliament and fairly set the place aflame. She was his. "No."

"Why lie? To me? To these women? To their families?" Before he could reply, she continued. "Was it punishment?"

"No."

"Of course it was," she said. "You remain the cat and I the mouse. And all you can do is toy with me."

"No," he said, coming toward her, one arm outstretched as though he could catch her.

She did step back then, recoiling from his touch, wrapping her arms about her waist as though she could protect herself from him—as though she had to protect herself from him—and Mal dropped his hand as though he had been singed, never wanting to give her anything that she did not wish. He cast about for the right words— the ones that would change everything. Simply. Perfectly.

Of course, nothing between them was ever simple.

"Shall I tell you how I feel, Malcolm?" He waited, and she continued. "I feel angry. I feel betrayed. I feel lied to and tricked. You remember those emotions keenly, do you not? You certainly hurled them at me enough."

He stepped toward her. "Not any longer."

She held up a hand, staying his defense. "I suppose it is ironic, is it not? Here we are, in the precise situation where we began—one of us trapped in a marriage we do not wish." It wasn't true. Not really. It couldn't be. Except she went on, their past coming like arrows. "Except this time, it's not you who questions my honesty, but the other way around."

"How much more honest can I be?" he asked, frustration edging into his tone. "I love you."

She closed her eyes and looked away. "I suppose you loved me then, too."

"I did," he confessed. "I've loved you from the start, and you never believed it."

"When is that? When you stole kisses and threatened my reputation feet from the rest of London?"

A fist knotted in his gut. "Yes," he said.

"And when you made love to me here? At Highley?"

"Yes—Sera—"

"And when I forced your hand?"

He'd been so furious then. But it hadn't changed anything. Not really. "Yes."

"You didn't believe me then. That I loved you. That I was afraid for my sisters and myself. Everything you and I had ever done had been so clandestine. And I'd loved it. But what would happen in the light?" She shook her head. "I regretted it all the moment I did it. I once told you that I would do it again if I had the chance. I wouldn't. If I could take one day of my life back, it would be that day, here. At Highley." She looked away, to the horses, the meadow, the estate in late-summer perfection. "I regret it."

He nodded. "I know."

She returned her gaze to his, clear and honest. "I told myself then that I did it for my sisters. That's how I kept myself sane. But I did it for myself, as well. I did it for myself, full stop. Because I loved you and I was afraid I would never be enough for you."

"You were," he said, reaching for her again, running his hands down her arms, taking her hands in his. "You were more than I could ever dream. I had spent so much of my life believing that love was impossible that when I had it in hand—I wanted every bit of it for myself, alone. And that greed was my downfall." He shook his head. "I loved you. I never stopped loving you."

She looked away, at the summer breeze rustling the meadow beyond. "Then it seems that love is not enough."

He loathed the words, because he could see where she was headed. A runaway carriage that would not stop. "It is."

Sera gave a little huff of humorless laughter and looked to the manor house in the distance, rising on the horizon like a lie. "It's not, though. You still do not know me well enough to see the truth, Mal. You still see the same girl from a thousand years ago. The one who thought she loved you enough to win you. Who thought she could convince you to forgive her."

"I did forgive you," he said.

"No, you punished me," she said. "You punished me for trapping you—and never once believed that I trapped you for *you*, dammit, and never the title, the fucking title that hangs like a damn yoke about my neck." The curse shattered him with its proof of the life she'd had without him. Of the years she'd had free. "You refused to free me, even when I came to you, offering you freedom, as well. Offering you a future. Even when I offered to get down on my knees and *beg you for it*."

Of all the things he'd ever done to her, that one was still the most shameful.

"And all that before you meted out the worst of your punishments."

He would never forgive himself for that moment—for taking another woman to exact revenge upon his wife. "I cannot take it back. I can only tell you that I—"

"I know." She cut him off. "You were angry."

"I was more than angry." He reached for her, trying to explain himself. She stepped backward toward the trees, and he stilled. If she did not wish his touch, he would not give it. "I was destroyed. You didn't tell me—Christ, Sera. I was to be a father."

She shook her head. "You didn't want her."

The words stole his breath. "I never said that."

"You did!" The accusation came on a flood of anguish. "You said you didn't want a life with me. You didn't want a family. You didn't want children."

"I was wrong. I was angry and I was wrong," He rushed to right it. "I wanted that life. I wanted that child."

Christ, how they had ruined each other.

He pressed on. "I wanted that child, and I wanted you. But I was too angry, too cowardly, too rash to see it. I've never wanted to hurt someone as much as I did that day. I thought it was a lie—everything between us."

She nodded. "It wasn't."

"No. It wasn't."

"She wasn't a lie, either."

"No. She wasn't." He ran a hand through his hair, the only thing he could do to keep himself from touching her. "Sera, if I could take it all back . . ."

She shook her head. "Don't. You can't take it back, and even if you could . . . If we'd stayed together, something else would have driven us apart. Don't you see?"

No. He didn't see, dammit.

"That's the point," she continued. "I've never not wanted to kiss you, Mal. I've never not been willing to beg for your touch. And it's never been enough."

He would never know why he chose that moment to tell her everything. "I came to Boston."

The words were so unexpected that they moved her physically backward, toward the trees. "What?"

"I came after you," he said.

She shook her head. "When?"

"Immediately," he said, the words coming fast and clipped, as though he was ashamed of them. "The day you left. But you left without a trace."

She did not agree, but he knew it was truth, nonetheless. She hadn't returned to London. Hadn't even said good-bye to her sisters. "I went to Bristol."

He nodded. "And then to America."

Disbelief and uncertainty threaded through her reply. "If you knew—if you came to Boston—why did not you not find me?"

"I did, dammit." He looked away, his throat moving with frustration and anger and years of regret. "I found you. It took me a year to get there. I started in Europe. Spent months chasing mad suggestions—many of which came from your harridan sisters—that you were in half a dozen places. I went all the way to Constantinople before turning around and coming back. And when I landed in London, steeped in filth and exhaustion, I heard the story of a beautiful Englishwoman in Boston. A singer. *The Dove*."

Her lips opened and he saw her surprise—the final confirmation that the American had kept his arrival from her.

"I knew before I booked passage on the damn ship that

it was you. And I found you the moment I landed—went to Calhoun's raucous tavern and made a fool of myself looking for you. *I heard you*, dammit. I heard you singing, and I *knew* it was you. And still, there was enough disappointment that you'd fled me and our life, that I believed them when they told me it wasn't you, I believed them." He looked away again. "It wasn't disappointment. It was fear. Fear that you might not return. Fear that you might not want to. Fear of where we are, now."

Silence fell, and then, "Caleb knew who you were?"

"He knew I was after you. He hid you from me. . . . Not before I broke his nose," he added, evoking the one moment of light in the darkness.

Her eyes went wide. "*You* were the toff."

"He never told you."

"No." She shook her head, and he could see the shock in her eyes as she added, softly, "It never occurred it was you. I had . . . admirers. We had a signal." She paused, lost in thought. "I left the stage when men became too . . . forcefully interested."

He wanted to murder someone at that, but he swallowed the rage. "You didn't know it was me."

She shook her head. "He never told me. If I'd known, I would have . . ."

His gaze found hers in the fading words. "What would you have done?"

The summer breeze was the only movement around them, her skirts whipping about her legs, clinging to them. To his, as though her clothing knew the truth she denied. He took the touch, a piece of her he could thieve.

"I don't know what I would have done," she said, and he clung to that honest uncertainty. She didn't say she would have ignored him. Didn't say she'd have sent him packing. "You were the past, and I wanted nothing to do with it."

"You left me," he said, spreading his hands wide. "You left me here, to live in the past, frozen in time, full of regret, and you took yourself off to the future."

"Full of regret because you could not win me," she said softly. "I was always a prize, Mal. Even when I was punishment."

That much was true. He would take a lifetime of pain with her for a moment of pleasure. He pressed on. "But you didn't find the future, did you?"

"Because I am not freed for it!" she argued.

Perhaps it was the memory of the past that made him say it. Perhaps it was remembering the way he'd ached for her. The desperation he'd felt. The desire to find her. To win her again. It did not matter. "For every moment I do not free you, Sera, there is an equal one in which you do not free yourself. You think I do not see you? I have *always* seen you. You have always been in vivid color for me. Glittering sapphire on the first night you found me. Emeralds and golds and silvers and red— Christ, that red. I am obsessed with that red. The red of the afternoon you came here. The red at Liverpool's garden party, when you stood like a goddamn queen and watched me ruin us like a goddamn fool." He stopped, cursing into the wind as he tilted his head back with the memory.

"We weren't ruined then," she said.

"No, we weren't. We were ruined long before."

"Before we even met."

A muscle ticked in his jaw as he watched her, as he considered what to say next. "Don't think for a second that I haven't seen you since you returned—that I haven't seen you in equally vivid color. In slate and amethyst and lavender and today, in aubergine."

Her breath caught in her throat. "Don't."

"Last night, you told me I consumed you. You think I am not consumed as well? By our past? You think I do not see that you ache for it? For what we were once promised?" He paused and looked toward the trees, and then, soft as silk, "You think I do not mourn, as well?"

He reached for her, then, taking her by the hand with firm, unyielding resolve and pulling her into the trees. Into the clearing they surrounded, where a beautiful little garden was hidden away in a golden pool of light.

He let her go, watching as she moved to the monument at the center of the clearing. To the stone angel there, seated on a platform etched with two simple words. *Beloved Daughter.*

Silence stretched forever, until he could no longer bear it. She crouched, placing her fingers to the letters. "You did this."

"I came to you after it was done," he said. "My hands still frozen from the cold. My boots covered in snow and dirt. I came to tell you that I wished to start anew. You were asleep, but no longer at risk. I told myself there would be time to win you. To love you."

She looked over her shoulder, urging him to go on.

"You slept most of the next day. And the day after, you were gone."

She nodded, tears stealing her words, harnessing them at the back of her throat. "I had to leave."

"I know," he said. "I think I half expected you to be gone when I returned. But when I discovered it—that my mother had given you the money to run—I went wild. I banished her from the house; I never saw her again." He approached, coming to his knees next to her. "It might be best I did not find you in those days. I am not sure I could have won you then. Your sisters saw it in me. They sent me east when I should have gone west. Calhoun, too, hiding you from me like a bone from a dog. And they all might have been right." He reached for her, one large, warm hand finding purchase at her jaw. "I wanted you. Desperately. I wanted this."

Her tears were coming in earnest now. She closed her eyes, the pain of the memories and the moment etched upon her like stone. "I am haunted by Januaries."

"I know," he said. He was, as well.

"I had to leave." She ached, beautiful woman. And he wanted nothing more than to stop it.

He pulled her close. "I know."

"I'll never have her. And never another."

The words devastated him. "I know."

Sera stayed rigid in his embrace for an age, her cheek pressed to his shoulder, her hands at her side, her only movements the little breaths that seemed wrenched from her. Wrenched from him, as well.

And then she gave herself to him, collapsing against him, giving him her weight and her pain and her strength and her sorrow. And he caught her and held her, and let her cry for the past—the past for which he, too, had ached.

The past that, together, they finally mourned.

His tears came as hers did, from a deep, silent place, filled with regret and frustration and an understanding that there was no way to erase the past. That the only possibility for their future lay in forgiveness.

If she could ever forgive him.

If he could ever forgive himself.

And so he did what he could do, holding her for long, sorrow-filled minutes, until she quieted, and their tears slowed, and they were left with nothing between them but the sun and the breeze and the past. He pulled away enough to look at her, enough to cradle her face—more beautiful than he'd ever seen it, tearstained and stung with grief—and look deep into her eyes.

"I was late, Angel," he said, the words coming on a near beg, unashamed. "I've always been too late. I've always missed you. I had no plans to come to Highley for the summer. I was headed to search for you again. I will never stop missing you." He took her lips, the kiss soft and lingering, a salve.

She had always been his salve.

He broke the kiss and pressed his forehead to hers, loving the long exhale of her breath, as though she'd been waiting for years for this moment. And hadn't he been waiting, as well?

"Don't make me miss you today," he whispered.

She closed her eyes at the words, and for a moment he thought she didn't feel it. The keen, unbearable need, as though there was air and food and them, now. Here.

And then she opened her eyes, and he saw it there. She needed him, too.

They needed each other.

He lifted her into his arms, and carried her home.

Chapter 22

MARRIAGE ON THE MEND? MAYBE!

They did not speak on the ride home, and Sera was grateful for it, grateful for the chance to stay in Malcolm's lap, the scent of him consuming her, fresh earth and spice, encircling her along with his strong arms, like a promise. She knew there was no possible way that he could make good upon that promise.

Promises were never theirs to offer.

Not even now, wrapped in each other, the movement of his horse beneath them the only reminder of the world beyond.

She turned her face to his chest, loving the warm strength of him there, loving, too, the way he pulled her closer and pressed his lips to her temple, whispering words there that were lost to the wind.

She did not care that they were lost—they were better there, because if she'd heard them, she might have loved them. And she might have loved him. But there was no room for that. Everything she had ever loved had been ruined. So she knew better than to let herself fall into the emotion again. They had loved each other at the start, and it had been a battle nonetheless. It would always be a battle between them. Always a game. And never enough.

But that afternoon, as they had unlocked their past and confessed their sins and their regrets, it did not seem to matter that love was not their future. Instead, all that mattered was that each somehow understood the other.

It was that understanding that spurred them toward Highley, Malcolm choosing the back entrance to the manor house, helping her down from the horse and following her without speaking and without hesitation, taking her hand and leading her through the kitchens, ignoring the servants pretending not to notice them as they took to the back stairs and down the long, wide, dark hallway to his rooms. To their rooms.

All without speaking, as though giving voice to words would give voice to the rest—the doubt and fear and the fight and the world beyond. But there, in silence, as she entered his bedchamber and he closed the door behind her, there was only the two of them. Alone, finally. Together, finally.

Just once.

She walked to the center of the room, her heart pounding, knowing that she should speak. Knowing she should remind them both of who and where they were and what the future held.

Except when she turned to face him, his back pressed to the closed door, his gaze unwavering, she did not want to speak. She only wanted to touch. She only wanted to love.

Just once.

And so she reached for him.

He was already coming for her, but he didn't do what she expected. He didn't take the lead, did not set her aflame with his kisses and steal her breath with the passion that too often consumed them both. Instead, he went to his knees, bowing his head to their joined hands—a knight pledging fealty to his queen.

And there, on his knees, he pressed kisses to their entwined fingers, and whispered her name until she could no longer bear it, and she took his face in her hands, tilting him up to face her, staring deep into his eyes before joining him, kneeling before him.

He kissed her then, his fingers threading into her hair, scattering hairpins as he rained kisses over her cheek and jaw and lips, eager for her, following one kiss with another, another, another until she was meeting him caress for caress, drawn to him, starving for him.

The kiss was beautiful and honest—nothing frantic or angry. A meeting of lips, a quiet silken slide of breath. Her name. His. Her sigh. His. He lifted his lips from hers, just enough to whisper, "I love you."

And, for the first time since the start of their time together, she let it come, let him wrap her in it. They shared the twin aches of their sorrow and pleasure, past and present, and she took everything she'd ever dreamed. And he gave it to her, as though they had never shared another life.

And it was glorious.

His fingers tightened at her waist, pulling her to him. Or perhaps she was pulling him to her. For all the days and weeks of chasing, of battle, of pretending not to want him, of him pretending not to want her, it was a gift to meet in the middle, here, on their knees, in their rooms.

Just once.

He tilted her chin up and set his lips to her cheek, to her ear, and following the ridge of her jaw to the column of her neck, following it down to the place where it met her shoulder, leaving soft, welcome kisses in his wake. His tongue swirled there until she sighed, her hand coming to his head, finding the soft hair there, holding him to her.

He lifted his head and took her lips again, long and slow and sinful, as though they had spent a lifetime kissing and had another lifetime to offer. She met him kiss for kiss, breath for breath, until he sucked her lower lip between his teeth, biting gently before following the little sting of pain with a devastating lick of pleasure.

She gasped at the sensation and he released her, kissing across her cheek to her ear, where he took the lobe between his teeth, sending a thrill through her. "Mal," she whispered, the first word since he'd lifted her onto his horse and brought her here, home. He stilled at it, then—dear God—he *trembled*, as though his name in that moment, on her lips, gave him immeasurable pleasure.

Which was possible, of course, as it gave her the same.

"Say it again," he said.

She did, whispering his name against his lips before it was lost in another wild kiss, this one accompanied by his hands working at the front fastening of her riding habit, shucking it to the floor as he consumed her with the caress. He lifted her with him as he came to his feet, turning her in one fluid motion, releasing her lips only to settle his own on the back of her neck, sending chills through her as his fingers found the long line of buttons at the back of the dress.

He began to undress her, her name a litany on his lips, as he loosened the frock with quick, efficient movements, until it came away in a glorious release, falling to the floor in a pool of linen and lawn. He set to work on her corset then, pulling the strings with long, fluid movements as his tongue swirled patterns across her skin, and then that, too, was gone, followed by her drawers, until she was left in her stockings and nothing else.

She should have been embarrassed when she turned back to face him, but the supreme pleasure on his face was like nothing she'd ever witnessed, and all she wanted was to bask in it. To bask in him.

He reached for her, his hand hovering a breath from her skin, his gaze transfixed on her bare body for what felt like an eternity. Finally, she whispered his name, unable to keep the pleasure and pride and self-satisfaction from her words.

His eyes shot to hers.

She smiled. "Are you planning to touch me?"

He swore, harsh and wicked in the quiet room, and moved with impressive speed, lifting her, carrying her to the bed and laying her on it, staring down at her wicked wanton intentions as he shucked his coat and cravat and pulled his shirt from his trousers, sending it flying across the room.

He followed her down after that, pressing her into the soft mattress, his chest warm and wonderful against hers, the crisp mat of hair there teasing her in all the places that had been constricted for a day. For a lifetime.

She opened her legs wide, eager to feel him between her thighs again. It had been so long. He found space there, hard and perfect at the notch of her thighs, and he gasped at the sensation, his eyes sliding closed at the pleasure there. Sera's, too, closed, and she lifted her hips up to meet him, her body aching for him. Asking for him. As though it knew where he belonged.

He let himself meet her movements. Let himself match them for a heartbeat. Once. Twice. They pulsed together. They rutted. The word, filthy and erotic, whispered past as the movement made her ache with need, and she found she could not stop herself from opening her legs wider. "Please," she whispered, "Mal."

He caught the words with his lips. "Anything you wish. Ask."

She tilted her hips to him.

He understood. Pressing into her. Thrusting. The hard ridge of him making wonderful promises.

She couldn't stop herself from leaning up and catching his bottom lip in her teeth, sucking at it until he groaned his pleasure. She released him and pulled back, as much as their nearness would allow, and asked him for the only thing she'd wanted since the moment they'd met. "I want my wedding night."

The words were out before she could imagine their impact, on them both. He froze above her, the truth of the statement, the promise of the moment, the memory of the past, all of it was there, between them, hovering.

She couldn't stop herself from continuing. "We married, but I was never your bride, Mal."

It was too late for it, of course. She was no blushing virgin, and had not been that night, either. But she wanted him, nonetheless. She wanted the night, with the hope and the promise and everything she would never have.

She wanted the fantasy.

He opened his mouth to speak, and she was instantly terrified of what he might say. So, instead of allowing it, she slid a hand up into his hair, playing at the nape of his neck as she lifted her hips to his, rocking against him once, twice, a third time before he growled his desire.

"Give me that night," she whispered.

Perhaps if she had that, she could find the courage to leave.

She pushed the thought from her mind as she took his lips again, mirroring his long and slow kisses, the ones that made her willing to do anything for him. It was a glorious, heady feeling, knowing that he would soon do the same for her . . . until he tore himself away and pushed off her, moving to the edge of the bed and sitting, back to her, ribs heaving with exertion.

No.

He wasn't going to leave her. Not after the afternoon. Not after his confessions. Not after undressing her and spreading her across the counterpane, making her ache for him. She scrambled to her knees behind him. "Mal?"

He bowed his head, holding it in his hands as he struggled for breath.

"Mal—"

"Will this matter?"

He was not looking at her when he asked, and for a moment she did not understand his meaning. "I don't—"

He turned back, his beautiful eyes nearly black with emotion. "I don't just want to fuck you. I want to love you."

Her lips parted at the word, the way it whipped around them. The way it sent wicked pleasure pooling through her. It should have shocked her, not stirred her.

But it only made her want him more.

"Am I not able to have both?" she asked.

"God help me, I don't think I would be able to stop myself," he said, and she heard the self-loathing in his word. "I think you could tell me it did not matter. I think you could tell me it meant nothing at all, and I would do it anyway. I've never been able to resist you."

She shook her head. "You don't have to."

She left the rest unsaid. *You matter. This matters.*

None of that had ever been at issue.

For a long moment, she thought he might stop, after

all. And then he moved, bending to remove his boots before he stood, his hands going to the falls of his trousers, unfastening buttons and sliding fabric down his legs, turning to her, hard and perfect.

Pleasure spooled through her like silk at the portrait he made. "You are beautiful," she said. "You always have been. From the moment I first saw you."

Color rose on his cheeks at the words, as though no one had ever told the Duke of Haven he was handsome. He made to reach for her and she shook her head, wanting to watch him more, wanting to explore.

Wanting to give of herself.

"Wait," she whispered, and the magnificent man did, a muscle ticking like mad in his cheek, the cords of his arms and thighs straining when she sat back on her heels and spread her thighs, testing his resolve, loving the way his gaze fell to the place she so brazenly revealed.

He tore his attention from it instantly, as though he was embarrassed to have been caught staring, but she saw the way he tensed. Knew what he wanted.

He nearly leapt from his skin when she touched him, running her fingers over the muscles of his chest, exploring the dips and rises of his warm body, reveling in the way he labored to breathe beneath her touch.

She let her fingers dance down the ridges of his torso, and he caught her hand in his before she could touch him where he strained, proud and stunning. "No," he said.

She looked up at him, twisting her hand from his grasp. "Yes."

He shook his head, something like pain chasing over her.

She came up on her knees and kissed him, long and slow and lush. "You said you would give me anything I asked."

He groaned. "You are too good at our game."

It was her turn to shake her head. "Not our game, Mal. This is our due." Her hand slid lower, finding him hot as fire and hard as sin, and they both sighed at the touch. "Show me," she whispered.

And he did, without shame, wrapping her hand in his, showing her just how he liked to be touched. She leaned forward, her lips skating over his chest, her hands learning his pleasure. Reveling in it until he released her with a groan. "No more."

She did not stop, instead looking up at him, capturing his gaze. "Do you not wish it?"

He laughed, the sound pulled from him in disbelief. "I have wished it for three years, love. For longer."

She stroked, long and lush, loving the way he responded, the way she controlled him. "As have I." She watched her hand working over him, riveted to the beautiful strength of him, to the smoothness, to the way she could command his breath. "I have wished for more than this."

She leaned down and pressed a kiss to the crown of him, never feeling so powerful as she did when he swore, harsh and angry and full of want, his hands coming to touch her, to slide into her hair. "You shouldn't—"

But he did not stop her, and if he had tried, she would never have allowed it. Of course she had to. If this was to be the only time she could take this pleasure with him— this power—of course she wanted it.

She could not stop herself, licking over him, breathing him in, and he was tight as a drum, his hands trembling as they hovered, barely touching her, as though he was afraid to let himself go.

She adored the barely-there edge of his control, reveled in it, played at it with her hand, her breath, her lips, sliding over him with a feather-light touch, claiming his size and strength and his desire. Marking him as hers.

So much so that she whispered there, "Mine."

"Always," he replied without hesitation. "Forever."

She ignored the last, knowing it wasn't true, but wanting to believe it in the moment. She licked over him, testing the salt and sweet of him, suddenly wild for it, for him, and he groaned, his hands coming to hold her more firmly even as he refused to move her, to take what he wanted.

She smiled against him. "Show me what you like, husband."

And the word undid him, as it did her, sending a pleasure pooling hot and heavy to her core as she parted her lips and took him long and slow and deep, hard and hot as he lost control of his words, cursing and praying in equal measure as she licked and sucked and drew him deep, wanting nothing more than to give him pleasure and to take her own.

There had been times when she had imagined being with him like this, imagining what it would be like to drive him mad, to send him over the edge. Imagined how they would have found all the ways to pull each other apart and then piece each other back together. Night after night. Just as he'd said. Forever.

But she did not have forever. She had now.

His hands tightened in her hair as he released another groan, louder and wilder than before, and a thrum of pleasure coursed through her. "Sera, Angel . . . I cannot . . ." He paused, breathed deep as she gentled, licking over him, tasting him. Thrumming with passion. "Love, I've waited too long. I want to be with you when it happens."

The words, honest and beautiful, stayed her, and

she released him, raking her gaze over his strong, lean, beauty—drinking him in, willing herself to remember every inch of him. "I want to be with you, as well," she whispered, coming up to her knees and kissing him long and deep. "I want every inch of you on every inch of me. Without hesitation. Without fear. Without sorrow."

"Yes." He caught her to him, cupping her breasts, playing at the hard tips until she sighed and rocked against him, making him groan. "God, yes. Whatever you want."

Those words, again. So different from what he'd offered her long ago. So different from what she'd asked for. "I want you."

His hands came up, cradling her face, holding her still so he could watch her. "You have me." So plain. So honest. So late.

Tears pricked with the past. With the soft, unsettling whisper of a question—what if he'd offered himself to her years ago? What if they'd had another chance?

"I love you," he whispered.

What if they had one now?

But they didn't. There was no way to overcome the past. To put away the way they'd slung weapons at each other. And there was no way to erase the most basic of truths—the life they could never have because their only chance at it had disappeared in the cold January snow three years earlier.

She kissed him, because she could not find another reply.

Because she did not want to think of one.

He pulled away almost instantly, his lips clinging to hers even as he pushed her away, as though he knew what she was thinking and wanted to discuss it. "Sera," he said, and she heard the intention in her name.

She shook her head. "Not now, Mal. Not here. Not when I've been waiting so long. And you, too."

And then she lay back, spreading herself on the bed, one knee bent, arms wide, welcoming. Wanting.

His eyes flashed with desire and his lips flattened. "After."

She nodded. "After."

She would have promised him anything then. Anything to ensure that he would make good on his promise.

Gloriously, he was on her then, just as she'd asked. Every inch of him over every inch of her, the glorious, straining length of him notched against the wet heat of her, pressing perfectly, teasing her. His arms came up to cage her between them, her hands stroking over his beautiful broad shoulders as he rocked into her, against the place she wanted him more than anything. Pleasure shot through her and she gasped at it and the sudden, desperate ache that came from it.

She wanted him. Immediately.

He repeated the motion, teasing her, the head of him hard and firm against the place where he had always been able to make her wild. "You like it, don't you, Angel?"

"I do." The words came on a moan about which she refused to be ashamed.

He kissed her deep and did it again. A reward for her honesty.

"Tell me how," he whispered. "Tell me what you wish."

And she did. "Harder," she insisted. "Again."

He did it, and it was perfect.

"Mal."

He rocked against her, pressing firmly until they found her edge, and he played there, lingering, pushing her nearly over and then pulling her back from it, until she was biting her lip and thrashing on the bed, begging for release.

"Mal. Inside me."

He did not obey. "No. I want to watch."

She opened her eyes, finding his gaze. "You can watch while you're inside me, dammit."

The bastard laughed, rutting against her, rude and perfect, as though she weren't dying of need to have him where she wished him. Immediately. "Now . . ." She panted. "Mal, don't you wish to have me around you?"

He closed his eyes and stilled above her. "Christ, yes."

She spread her thighs wider and said, "I wish it, too. *I will it.*"

And the glorious, wonderful man did it, pressing into her slowly, perfectly, a thick slide of pleasure that had them both sighing before he stilled. "Sera?"

The concern in the word was her undoing. She turned her lips to meet his, sliding her tongue deep, scraping her nails down his back, lifting her hips to him, forcing him deeper. He moaned at the movement, and took up the rhythm even as he took over the kiss, claiming her in every way possible, rocking deeper and deeper until she was filled with nothing but pleasure and him.

She tore her lips from his. "All the time we were apart—"

He nodded. "I know."

He didn't, though. "Everything I ever imagined this could be . . ."

"I know." He kissed her again, reaching between them, finding the spot just above the place where they were joined.

She came off the bed like a bow, and he caught her to him, pulling them both up to a sitting position, giving himself more access to her body. He leaned down, taking the tip of one breast in his mouth, sucking long and slow as his fingers worked magic, all in concert with the rhythm that was proving to be her slow, perfect destruction.

And then she was thrusting, moving against him, reaching down to clasp his wrist and show him all the ways he could touch her, all the paths to her pleasure. "Faster," she whispered. "Harder." Though she did not know if she was speaking to him or to herself, because she, too, was moving faster. She, too, was coming over him harder and more forceful, as though she could imprint this moment in her memories.

Forever.

And then she looked into his eyes, desperate for release, and recognized the edge in him, saw the way they catapulted toward it. "Mal," she whispered. "I love you."

The words wrecked them both, tipping them over that magnificent edge, deep and fast and powerful. She reached for him, her fingers sliding into his hair. "Look at me," she whispered. "Show me."

He did, and she watched as he found his pleasure before taking her own, throwing herself into it, not caring if she ever returned, because there was nothing in the world she would ever want as much as this magnificent, unbearable, terrifying release.

And for the first time since she'd left him, Sera found peace.

They collapsed against each other, breaths coming in great heaving gasps that made it impossible to know where she ended and he began, and perhaps it did not matter. It did not matter. Sera could not stop herself from basking in it, this single moment, when they were not simply the aches of the past and the imperfect promise of the present, but all the magnificent moments between.

Long minutes passed as their breathing returned to normal and Sera returned to the room and the day and the life they'd built. And the promise she'd made to herself—that after this, she would leave.

Because nothing had changed.

She remained too overwhelmed by him, by the feel of him, by the unspoken promises of him. Even now, as they clung to each other like partners, like lovers, as though the future was theirs for the taking, she struggled to find herself in it.

I love you.

He unwrapped himself from her, pulling her down to the bed with him, kissing her, long and lush before tucking her into the crook of his arm and whispering into her hair, "I want you mine. I want you forever. And, dammit, I have you. I've had you all along. I should never have hesitated. I should have given you everything. The title, the marriage, all of it. I wanted to. I want to, still. I want to go back and begin again."

She'd never imagined she could love and hate something as much as she loved and hated those words. At once, she wanted everything he offered, without hesitation. She wanted the promise of something new and fresh and untarnished by the past. And still, she could not trust it. Nothing beautiful had ever stayed such for her.

There was no beginning anew. They could not erase the past, and they could not change the future. They could not have the promise that had teased them. But she could close the door on it. And give them both a chance at something new.

She could have the Sparrow, and the freedom that came with it. And he could have a family—one that loved him as much as he deserved. Tears pricked behind her eyes, and she had no choice but to tuck her face into his chest and hide from him.

As ever, she hid from him.

Because he had always been able to see her.

He sighed, long in the fast-dimming light of the room, and it occurred to Sera that they had skipped dinner. That the mothers and daughters who had been a part of his elaborate ruse would once again be slighted.

She pressed her ear to his chest, listening as his breathing calmed. Evened. Until he slept.

And still, she lay there, rocked by her love for him. By the way it claimed her, just as it had years earlier. By the memory of what had happened then. By fear of what might happen if she allowed herself to love him.

By the temptation of it.

It was only then that she replied to him, whispering to his warm, welcome skin, to his arm, wrapped tightly about her, even in slumber. To this bed that should have been theirs in this house that should have been their home with a family that would never be. "Don't love me, Mal. There is no future for us."

The keen understanding of that truth had driven her across an ocean, and to the floor of Parliament. She had lost everything she had ever loved before—her child, her family, her life. Him.

First, by chasing him, and then by running from him. And perhaps there was cowardice in her waiting until he slept to voice the truth. No *perhaps*. There was cowardice. Angry and unbearable. But who was she if not the sum total of her flaws?

At least if she ran, they both had a chance at being free.

Chapter 23

_____

DÉJÀ VU? DUCHESS DISAPPEARS
(PART DEUX)

$\mathcal{M}$al woke to a sharp rap on the door of his bed-chamber.

He sat up, unsettled by the darkness—unaware of the time or the date or of anything but the deep, drugging sleep that had consumed him. It had been ages since he'd slept so soundly. Three years. Longer.

He might never have slept so well, as he had never slept with her.

He reached instinctively for Sera, displeased to discover that he was alone once more in his bed, the sheets cool to the touch.

With a little growl, he looked to the windows, the heavy darkness beyond indicating that he'd been asleep for several hours. He swung his legs to the edge of the bed, wanting to rise for one reason only—to seek her out and drag her back to bed. To make love to her again, and return to sleep with her in his arms until sunup. Sunup a week from now, if he could manage it.

The knocking came again, quick and urgent.

Shrugging into a dressing gown, Mal headed for the

door. He'd locked it when they'd entered, unwilling to risk being interrupted, and Sera had likely escaped through the adjoining door to their rooms. He was halfway across the room when the sound began anew.

"Yes. All right!" It came on a near bellow, one he attempted to contain, knowing that his irritation with waking alone and out of time was not the fault of whoever stood on the other side of the door.

And they clearly had urgent business, dammit.

He tore the door open, "What is it?" dying in his throat as he took in the somewhat strange reality in the hallway beyond. The three remaining candidates for his unavailable hand in marriage were fanned out in the dimly lit hallway, each looking more mortified than the next to be there. Not so, their respective mothers, who seemed committed to whatever plan was afoot, which apparently involved Lord Brunswick, two of Lady Bumble's dogs and—somehow—Sesily's cat.

As a partially dressed Mal came into view, the assembly offered myriad response: two mothers immediately moving to shield their daughters' gazes from Mal's state of undress; daughters in question doing their best to at once feign innocence and get a good look; and the final girl—Lady Felicity Faircloth, of course—watching with unabashed amusement, despite her mother's clear, "Good heavens, Felicity, look away!"

Felicity did not look away, and Mal noticed she was holding the cat, who blinked at him and offered a low yowl.

They'd never quite become civil, he and that cat.

Baron Brunswick, for his part, appeared to have been sent to do the knocking, but had little interest in whatever was supposed to happen once the door was opened. The other man blinked, took a step back, looked Mal up and down, and then said, "All right then, Haven? Have we disturbed you?"

"You have, rather."

It occurred to Mal that much of the work done by the aristocracy was in lying to people about how one felt, so much so, that now, when he answered a question directly, no one in the group knew quite what to do about it. Well, nearly no one. After a beat of silence, Lady Lilith and Lady Felicity laughed.

Mal made a note to do his best to get the girls well matched just as soon as they were back in town. He and Sera would host them for dinner. They'd introduce them to every wealthy aristocrat in town.

He was lost for a moment in the domesticity of the thought. The idea of spending the rest of their lives in town and country, building a glorious life of laughter and languish, entertaining their guests before retiring to their bedchamber to make love until dawn.

Which reminded him that he had to be rid of this collection of people.

"Well," the baron said, as though everything were perfectly in order. "Would you—that is—should you put on some trousers?"

Mal did not move. "As I imagine that anything that would bring a group of houseguests to the door of the master of the house must be terribly important," he drawled, "I wouldn't dare postpone whatever this is."

For a moment, it seemed as though no one would speak to him or acknowledge his words. And then, Felicity's mother stepped forward, clearly willing to sacrifice her own goodwill for that of her daughter. "Is it over then?"

Mal blinked. "My slumber? Yes."

The assembly harrumphed, but the Marchioness of

Bumble was not cowed. Indeed, it was not difficult to see from whence her frank-tongued daughter came. "The competition. You've selected a wife."

"I have, as a matter of fact." Not that he could see why the situation was so very urgent. He could only assume that Lilith and Felicity had apprised the rest of the assembly of what had happened between him and Sera at the folly.

Lady Brunswick huffed her displeasure. "You see? I told you it was done," she snapped at her daughter. "I told you he cooled to you. You could have worked harder."

Mal did not care for the baroness's words, nor did he care for the way she seemed to indict Lady Emily in the fact that Mal had chosen to love his wife and forgo finding a replacement altogether. Of course, it was odd that the girl didn't eat soup, but it wasn't grounds for cruelty. They would invite her to the dinner with Lilith and Felicity. He could find a man who didn't care for soup, he was certain.

"I assure you, Lady Emily, it was a pleasure to meet you."

Lady Brunswick continued on as though he had not spoken. "It's no wonder that the Soiled S's all departed so quickly, but you would have thought someone could have told us you'd chosen your replacement, so we were not all left alone at the evening meal, waiting for your decision to be announced."

He stilled even as she pressed on.

"Instead, you took to your bed in the middle of the day! Good riddance to you and the Dangerous Daughters. Our family deserves better." She took hold of Emily's arm. "Come along, Emily."

Emily looked as though she wanted the ground to swallow her whole, but that was not Haven's concern.

He lifted his hands to stay the conversation. "What did you say? The others departed?"

"Like thieves! Skulking off in the dead of night!" the baroness sniped.

The words unlocked the other mothers. "An hour ago. The Talbot sisters all climbed into their coach and hied off."

"Sesily left her cat," Lady Felicity added, as though it mattered.

For a moment, it didn't. And then Lilith added, soft and serious, as though she understood the implications of her words, "They were in quite a rush."

They had left.

Surely not Sera. Not after everything they'd experienced that afternoon. Not after promising they'd discuss it. *After*, she'd said.

He shook his head, looking from Felicity to Lilith and back again. "All of them?"

"Of course all of them!" the baroness squawked. "They got what they wanted, the madwomen!" She turned to her daughter. "Come along, Emily, *we* must to bed as well, as tomorrow our search begins anew." She tapped her husband on the shoulder. "You as well, Baron."

Brunswick grimaced at the summons, but followed it nonetheless; at least, Mal assumed he followed it. He did not linger in the doorway, turning on his heel and heading for the door connecting his rooms to Sera's.

He burst through it, half expecting her to be there, in the bed, asleep. At the dressing table, fiddling with a button hook. In the chair by the empty fireplace, reading. Laughing with her sisters. Something.

But she was not. The room was dark and empty of her. *She'd left him.*

He moved to inspect the wardrobe, finding it full of

her things, dresses in a dozen purple hues, shoes piled below. On the dressing table, powder and hairbrushes, pins and baubles, a bracelet she'd worn at lawn bowls. Earbobs he recognized from one evening's dinner.

She'd left him, and quickly.

Goddammit, she'd told him she loved him, and she'd sped from the house as though hell itself was chasing her. Like Merope and the Pleiades taking flight as doves. And Malcolm, blind and desperate Orion, forced to hunt her again. Like a fool.

He bit back the scream of rage that threatened to loose itself in the dark room and went to the window, open to let in the summer's night breeze. The room faced the drive, a long, lingering path that led to the main road and then to the London post road.

There was no sign of the carriage, no lantern light flickering in the distance, no indication that she'd ever been here.

He placed his hands on the windowsill, clutching it until the stone and wood bit into his palms, and whispered her name with all the rage and desperation and love he could find.

She'd left him, like a damn coward.

And then the thought came, cold and harsh and terrifying. *What if she'd run again?*

He went stick straight. She wouldn't run again. Not the way she had before. She'd left with her sisters this time. They wouldn't let her go, would they?

Words echoed, memory of the day she'd appeared in Parliament and asked for the divorce he never intended to give her. *I have no reason not to end our unhappy union. I have nothing to lose.*

No reason not to run. Nothing to lose.

And she didn't have anything to lose. She'd made sure

of it. She'd returned to London on the arm of the American, with whom she had friendship and nothing else. She sang in a tavern. Slung whiskey as what—a lady barkeep? She had money—her father's and his mother's—and nothing to tie her to London.

But she had him, dammit.

"She said she loved me!" His harsh, broken whisper cut through the darkness, and he closed his eyes, fists clenched at his sides. "How could she leave me?"

Love is not enough.

"Your Grace?"

He spun, heart in his throat, to face Lady Felicity Faircloth, framed in the doorway, a lantern in one hand and Sesily's damn cat in the other. He shook his head to clear it. He did not have time for these girls. "It was never real, Lady Felicity," he said. "You were a ruse."

She nodded. "I know. Anyone with eyes in their head could see that you and the duchess were for each other and no one else."

"Anyone but the duchess could see it, I think you mean." He could not keep the frustration from his tone.

"I think she sees it, too, you know," she said. "But far be it from me to get involved."

"You're standing in my bedchamber holding my wife's sister's cat, so I think you are rather involved already," he pointed out.

She nodded, a smile playing over her lips. "That may well be true."

"As a matter of fact, I cannot think of a less appropriate location for you than in my bedchamber holding my wife's sister's cat."

The smile broadened. "Are you planning to debauch me in some way?"

"I am not."

"Well then I think I am perfectly safe. Also, the cat seems to dislike you."

Mal looked to the white animal, who appeared perfectly content in Felicity Faircloth's arms. "I thought we'd reached a détente, honestly."

The cat yowled.

"Oh, yes, it seems so." She paused. "The point is, I think my person is quite safe with you."

"There was a time when I would have been disappointed with that assessment."

Felicity smirked. "I imagine you were younger then. And less besotted with your wife, which puts a considerable damper on a man's dangerousness."

"Definitely younger, likely not at all less besotted with my wife."

"That seems to be a problem for you."

"Considering I regularly lose her, I would have to agree," he replied, unable to find humor in the situation.

Felicity Faircloth took pity on him then. "I'm afraid I've something to tell you, Your Grace, and I do not think you will enjoy hearing it."

He moved to the low shelf by the window and fetched a flint box, lighting the lantern there, at once making the room more welcoming for the young woman and more devastating for him. There was a hatbox at the foot of Sera's bed, open and empty, as though she'd had neither time nor inclination to fill it and take it with her.

And next to it, a piece of paper. Folded haphazardly, a scribbled *M* its only adornment. He opened it, his heart pounding.

I cannot stay.
I await news from Parliament.
—S

He swore, harsh and unpleasant, and crushed the paper in his hand.

He looked to Felicity. "Is it more or less enjoyable than hearing that my wife has left me . . . again?"

The young woman's pause unsettled, he had to admit. And then, "Well, to be honest, it is less enjoyable, I'd imagine. Considering the events of the morning." She paused, rushing to clarify, "The ones I witnessed, that is."

Mal's stomach twisted. "Go on then."

She sighed and crouched, lowering the cat to the floor. With no hesitation, the animal leapt into the hatbox and sat carefully inside, watching the two of them with serious, unwavering eyes.

Mal did his best to ignore the creature, turning, instead, to face Felicity, who had fetched a piece of paper from somewhere, and was now unfolding it.

"Have you prepared a speech of some kind?" he said, knowing he was being intentionally difficult.

She cut him a look, but ignored the question. "This arrived via my lady's maid an hour ago."

Mal did not like the sound of that. His gaze flickered to the escritoire in the corner, where a blotter and pen were left in disarray, as though his wife had dashed off a letter before she fled.

A letter to this woman, for some reason. "Go on."

Felicity nodded, and proceeded to read aloud. "*Dear Lady Felicity, You must know I am very fond of you. You are intelligent and forthright and, most of all, strong. You have a mind of your own and are unafraid to speak it, all things that will serve you well.*" She paused and looked at Mal, and he read the nervousness on her face. Recognized it. Felt it himself, loathing the anticipation of the words that were to come. Loathing the words themselves even before the lady read them. Wanting to stop her. Knowing that whatever she had to say must be said.

She persisted. *"All those things will serve Malcolm well, also."*

"No," he said, unable to keep the word from exploding from his chest.

Felicity Faircloth looked to him, in clear affront. "Of course not."

"Then why . . . ?"

She lifted one shoulder and let it drop. Then, simply, "She doesn't seem to care how we feel about it, Your Grace."

That much appeared to be true. Felicity continued. *"He is a good man, Lady Felicity—one who knows about life and about love. One who has showed a remarkable loyalty to his wife."* Felicity stopped. "Then she corrects herself. *To his wives."*

"Goddammit."

"My thoughts, precisely," Felicity replied. *"He will make you a good husband—"*

Frustration turned to disbelief. "Is she *gifting me* to you?"

Felicity's brows shot up as she considered the letter in her hand. "It's unclear, honestly, as I rather fear she's gifting *me* to *you*." She paused, taking a deep breath, as though she had to gird her loins to speak the rest. *"Some things you should know: First, he loathes asparagus."* She stopped. "Your Grace, I'm sure you'll understand if I say I have no earthly idea why your affinity or lack thereof for asparagus is relevant in any way to a marriage—let alone relevant enough to be point number one on a list of important points."

"It's not," he said.

"Well, the others are just as odd, so . . ." Felicity returned her attention to the letter. *"He's fascinated by the Greek myths. Read and learn them. He will be grateful for someone with whom to discuss them."*

The words felt like a betrayal of confidence. Mal remained silent.

Felicity moved on. "And this one is the strangest. *Find yourself a red frock and do your best to get him alone once you're wearing it. If you can do that in his private study, all the better."*

That's when the rage came. He moved for the letter, as though he could somehow use it to turn back the clock and stop her from the madness that had clearly consumed her. "What in hell?"

Felicity looked up, eyes wide at his proximity. "I agree," she said. "I don't understand what she's trying to do."

"I do," he said, the memory of the last time she wore red in this house—in his private study—etched keenly. How many times had he recreated that moment in his mind? How many times had he taken down her bodice? Taken up her skirts? Made love to her? How often had he imagined doing it again? He snatched the letter from Felicity Faircloth's hand, enjoying the release of anger that came as he folded it and began to tear it into pieces. "She wants you to seduce me."

She blinked. "Well, I don't wish to."

"Which works out well, as I have no intention of being seduced by anyone but my wife." Just as soon as he stopped being infuriated by her.

Felicity nodded. "That sounds eminently reasonable. Though, if I may . . .?"

He nodded. "Please."

"It seems your wife remains uninterested in being your wife, Your Grace."

The words should not have crashed over him. Should not have made such a powerful point. And still they did. Mal turned away from Felicity Faircloth then, hating that she understood the interplay of his marriage even better than he did.

No. She didn't understand it better. She was simply more willing to accept it. But Felicity Faircloth had not been married to Sera.

He could not stop himself from walking to the bed where he'd stood nearly three years ago, and willed his wife to live. Where he'd pulled her back from death. Where he'd come, vowing to fight for her. To love her. To chase her, into the sky if need be . . .

Only to find her already on the run.

It was then that Malcolm realized she would always run from him. Away from love. Away from the promise of a future. And he would always chase her.

Blind and broken.

His punishment for never being worthy of her.

He'd be damned if she was getting a divorce.

Chapter 24

SUCCESSOR SELECTED? DANGEROUS DAUGHTERS TURN UP IN TOWN!

The Talbot sisters had been stuffed into the carriage for more than two hours, the night roads requiring more time than usual to get them back to London. But it was not the stuffing of the sisters that was noteworthy. After all, they'd spent the lion's share of their traveling lives stuffed together.

It was their silence. The five sisters had never gone any length of time without speaking. Not even church services were sacred.

And so it was that when Seleste finally broke the silence with a frank, simple, "Well then," the sisters had been more silent than ever in their lives—something Seraphina appreciated, even as it ended.

"It was interesting, was it not?" This from Sesily.

"I, for one, did not expect it," Seleste replied. "I would have thought that Haven had a better shot at convincing her to stay."

"He was willing to take a rock to the head for her," Seline pointed out.

If she weren't so desperate to be out of the carriage, Sera might have found the energy to look up at that. But instead, she remained focused on her fingers, tightly entwined in her lap, ungloved, still ink-stained from the note she'd dashed off for Lady Felicity.

The note designed to encourage Mal's next wife.

If only he could see that their marriage was doomed, he could be happy with another. The thought sent a shaft of pain through her, constricting her heart and making it difficult to breathe. She willed herself calm, inhaling deeply, and returning her attention to her sisters.

"It's a good thing the wager was on Haven's intentions, Ses, and not Sera's actions, else you would owe the rest of us quite a bit of blunt," Seleste pointed out.

Sesily shook her head. "Oh, I never would have wagered on Sera wanting to win him back."

"I would have."

Sera snapped her head up, her gaze instantly finding Sophie's. Sophie, who had been watching her since they entered the carriage, concern and interest on her pretty face. "What did you say?"

"I would never have wagered that you didn't want Haven."

"Why not?" Sera asked.

Sophie raised one shoulder and let it drop. "It was not long ago that you taught me a lesson about love, sister."

The memory came from far away. Sera, laden with child on the Scottish border, sitting with Sophie, lovelorn and desperate for the man who would eventually become her husband. But that night, the Marquess of Eversley had been an impossible catch—until Sophie had gone to him and told him the truth. At Sera's bidding.

Sophie seemed to have the memory, too. "Did you tell him?"

"Tell him what?" Sesily interjected, but no one answered her.

I never told Haven I loved him, Sera had said, trying to convince Sophie to do the same. *And look at the mess I've made*.

She looked out the window, into the inky blackness beyond.

Sophie would not allow the silence. "Sera," she prompted. "Did you tell him?"

I love you.

She nodded, and her youngest sister reached for her, taking her hand tightly, without hesitation. Sera looked to her. "And?"

Sera shook her head. It didn't matter. It didn't change anything. It was all still a mess. She removed her hand from Sophie's. Steeling her emotion. "And love is not enough."

Silence fell in the wake of the words, until Seleste huffed a little sigh and said, "It may not be enough, but it's something, indeed, if we all had to scurry home in the dead of night." She waved a hand in the air. "I spend half my marriage sparring with Clare. It makes things interesting."

Seline rolled her eyes. "You and Clare are not quite a suitable comparison for others, you know."

"And you and your horseman are?" Seleste defended her marriage. "No two people in the world should share similar interests the way you two do. It's dreadfully boring."

Seline gave a little shrug. "It isn't boring to us." She leaned forward to look out the window. "Nearly home." Sera did not miss the excitement in her sister's voice. She was happy to be returning to her boring marriage and her too similar husband. "Mark shall be so surprised."

Seleste sighed happily and leaned her head back against her cheek. "Clare as well," she said. "He'd better not be at his club. I've a use for him tonight."

The sisters all groaned at the words, Sesily giving a grinning Seleste a quick thwack. "Please. Not while I'm busy attempting to hold in my accounts."

"What?" Seleste laughed. "Are you surprised by the fact that I'm looking forward to a night with my husband?"

"No," Sesily pointed out. "But you could be a touch more discreet about it."

"Pah," Seleste said. "Women are present during the act, Sesily. It's only fair we enjoy it."

"Damn right," Seline added.

"We all know you enjoy it, Seline. I recall an opera we all had to leave because Mother discovered you and Mark *in flagrante* behind a curtain."

Seline grinned smugly. "At least we were *behind* it. And besides—you're one to talk—everyone knows what happens inside that bookshop of yours when King arrives and you lock the door for hours and hours of *midday luncheon*."

Sophie's cheeks flamed red, and Sera could not help the little smile that found its way to her lips. This was why she had returned to London. Not for Malcolm, or for the family they'd once been promised, or for the title or the life she'd once led. But for these women, loyal and dear and bold and better than all others. And hers.

And so she would insist upon her divorce. And she would be free of her past and Mal could marry Felicity— who was an excellent choice. She'd be a good companion and make him pretty children.

The whole idea didn't make her feel ill at all.

The queasiness was from the carriage ride. Sesily's ailment was obviously catching.

Indeed, that queasiness did not come on a flood of longing for her husband. She didn't long for him. She had a plan, and she would keep to it. She would have her tavern. She would sing. And it would be enough.

It would have to be.

Something in her life had to be enough.

"It doesn't seem fair that we were all shipped off the country for a month, and Sera was the only one allowed to have . . . you know," Seline said.

Four sets of eyes sought Sera in the darkness, and she did her best to keep her attention out the window, suddenly desperately riveted to the passing buildings.

"Well, we don't know that she did have it," Seleste pointed out.

"No?" came the reply. "What else might have happened to send her fleeing him in the dead of night?"

"I've never wanted to flee it, have you?" Seline asked.

"Well," Seleste said, smirk in her tone. "Then we return to the original theory on Haven."

"What's that?" Sera could not stop the question.

"That he's terrible at it."

Everyone laughed. Everyone except Sera, who reached up and drew a slow, purposeful circle on the window. "He's not terrible at it."

The carriage went quiet again before Sophie sighed and said, "Sera—why are we here?"

Irritation flared, hot and unreasonable, but Sera did not care. "Because contrary to the rest of your beliefs, the fact that my husband is a superior lover does not make for a perfect marriage." Four sets of eyebrows shot high into hair, and the response made Sera even angrier.

"You needn't look so shocked. Not one of you has any idea what it is to be in my situation."

"Would you like to tell us?" Sophie was always so calm. So unflappable.

And she'd never been more enraging than she was then. "What would you like for me to say? There is nothing *to* say!" she said, her voice elevating to a fever pitch. "Your lives are perfect. Your marriages? Perfect. Your children—" Her voice caught, her heart constricting, and she swallowed, pushing past it. Refusing to allow sadness to come. "They are perfect. And I shall never have any of that."

"Sera—" It was the gentlest she'd ever heard Seline.

"No." She spun on her sister, one finger raised. "Don't you dare feel pity for me. I've made my choices. I might have run then, but I returned, stronger than ever. I don't need your pity."

"Are you sure?" Sophie snapped, and everyone turned to look at the youngest, quietest Talbot sister—the one everyone called the least interesting. Everyone who didn't know Sophie, that was.

Sera leaned toward her sister. "What does that mean?"

"Only that you seem to require our support—our protection—when it is convenient. And we have given it. Our undying loyalty. Because the Soiled S's stick together. But you've never once offered us your honesty. So my question is this—" The carriage began to slow, quieting as it arrived at Eversley House, where Sophie would disembark. But not before she drove her point home. "Is it simply that you refuse to be honest with us? Or because you refuse to be honest with yourself?"

There were things that only sisters could say. Ways only sisters could make a woman rage. "I've never not been honest with you."

"What utter swill," Sophie scoffed. "You left us. Without a *word*. What was honest in that? You lost yourself, Sera. You were in mourning for the man you loved and the child you lost. And you threw everything away. Including us. And I was inclined to be understanding. But now—it's time for you to see that you do yourself a disservice. Lord knows I've never had much love for Haven, but the man adores you, and he is willing to give you anything you wish. Anything you require. Though right now I cannot imagine why." Sera sat back on her seat.

"Oof. That was a bit harsh," Seline said quietly.

"Well, perhaps she needed to hear it," Sophie snapped.

"I didn't, as a matter of fact. Because it isn't true." Sophie raised a brow as Sera went on. "I asked him for one thing. A divorce. My freedom. His as well, I might add, and he hasn't given me that."

"Perhaps he won't give it to you because you have some kind of bizarre fantasy of what freedom is."

Sera narrowed her gaze on her sister. "And I suppose you know?"

"I do, as a matter of fact," Sophie said as the carriage stopped. She smoothed her skirts and her hair as a liveried footman approached to open the door. She looked to Sera before she took his hand and stepped down from the block.

Turning back, she said, "I love you, you know." Tears came, instant and unwelcome, and Sera looked away, which was best because they spilled over when Sophie added, softly, "I only wish you could find a way to love yourself in the balance."

Consumed with anger and sadness and frustration she could not voice, Sera did not look at her sister, until the door to the carriage closed with a soft *snick*.

With one hand low on her back, Sophie headed slowly

for the door to the town house, which stood open, a warm orange glow welcoming her inside. Guilt flared low in Sera's gut. Her sister was with child, and would have very likely been happier in a bed than crammed into a carriage in the middle of the night.

But Sophie was home now, and her husband was soon silhouetted in the golden doorway, pausing for the barest of moments before he came to fetch his wife, lifting her high in his shirtsleeved arms and kissing her thoroughly. The servants lingering nearby were either impeccably trained, or they were so used to the affection showed between the marquess and his wife that they were immune to the scandal of it. Sera imagined it was the latter.

And then King was carrying Sophie over the threshold and into the house, pausing only to kick the door closed behind them.

The carriage lurched into motion, and Sera put her head to the back of her seat with a frustrated, "Dammit."

Her sisters did not reply, and she knew why.

They agreed with Sophie.

Sera opened her eyes and looked to them. "I suppose you want apologies as well." She knew she was being difficult.

"I don't much care, honestly," Seline replied. "But if given the choice between you being here and you not being here, I prefer you in London. So, if you are planning to repeat your past actions and my opinion matters, please refrain from doing so."

"Are you? Planning to leave?" Sesily asked from her place in the far corner of the carriage.

Sera was quiet for a long moment. She shook her head. "I don't know. I was planning for my life. My business." She looked away and said the next to the window. "That is all I wanted."

Seleste and Seline did not reply, and Sera took their silence as tacit approval. Perhaps it was merely loyalty, but she would take the silence. It was better than the truth. But once the carriage had deposited them at their respective homes, to their respective husbands, leaving her alone with Sesily once more, Sera grew nervous.

Sesily was the most forthright of all the Talbot sisters and, in light of the events of the carriage ride, that could be a particularly unsettling truth.

"I would prefer you not leave," Sesily said, as the darkness of the carriage closed around them, the wheels clattering on the cobblestones as the carriage toddled through Mayfair toward Covent Garden.

Sera took a deep breath. "I hadn't intended to."

"And then Haven?"

She nodded. "He does not wish a divorce."

"Do you?"

Yes. No. She ignored the question, hating the strange, imprecise answer that came with it.

"If I may?"

"I don't suppose I could stop you."

"No, likely not," Sesily said, unmoved by the tart reply. "But Sophie isn't wrong, Sera. Freedom comes in many shapes. And even Sparrows must rest."

Sera looked out the window. "The carriage will take you home to Mother and Father when it has dropped me."

"Do you wish to join us? Mother will be thrilled to see you."

The topic should have been safe and easy. But, instead, it brought memory of their mother who, despite her terrible schemes, loved her daughters beyond reason.

She shook her head.

"She's learned her lesson, you know," Sophie said.

"Hardly ever looks at me with disappointed pity. I suppose I should thank you for that."

Sera forced a smile. "You're welcome. I shall come and see them another day, but tonight I must return to my place."

To herself.

To the woman she'd been when she'd arrived in London weeks ago, before Malcolm had changed everything. Before he'd tempted her with a different future than the one to which she was committed.

And so she would go to the tavern, and she would sling her drinks and she would sing her songs and she would hope for the night to drown out the day.

"I'll join you," Sesily said.

Sera looked to her sister. "No, you won't."

It was too dark to see her sister's face, but Sera knew that nothing would keep Sesily from getting what she wanted. "Why, because you are planning to leave, after all? You don't want a witness? Or you don't want someone to whom you'll have to say good-bye?"

"I'm not leaving, Sesily. Not tonight."

"I'm not sure I believe you," Sesily replied. "Running from Highley seems to be catching."

Sera noticed the irritation in the words. "Running from Highley?"

"This week, it's been a sport of sorts."

Sera's eyes widened in the darkness. "You mean Caleb?"

Sesily sniffed her disdain.

Good Lord. What had she missed? "Ses—has something happened?"

"No," Sesily said. "I simply wish to see this legendary tavern."

It was a lie, obviously. "You know Caleb owns it."

"Oh," Sesily said vaguely, "does that mean he will be there?"

Sera could not help her little laugh at the terrible performance. "You're not coming with me."

"Why not?"

"Well, largely because you are an unmarried, recognizable lady."

Sera could hear the pout in her sister's voice when she replied, "There are large swaths of London that would disagree with the *lady* portion of that sentence. I'm the last of the Dangerous Daughters, Sera. The former paramour of the most notorious actor in Drury Lane."

"Nevertheless, I'm not letting you be ruined. Not even by Caleb."

"This has nothing to do with Caleb."

"You're speaking to someone who pined for a man for years."

Sesily cut her a look in the dim light of the passing pubs and theaters. "And so? You would have allowed him to ruin you without question?"

"In fact, that is exactly what I did." *And this afternoon, again.* She left off the last bit.

"I've no intention of being ruined."

"That's excellent, as I've no intention of allowing it to happen."

"You cannot simply return to London and take on the role of proper guardian."

Sera lost her temper. "For God's sake, Sesily. One of us will have a happy life!"

"Yes, and at this rate, it shall be you, for at least you have a man willing to give you a tumble!"

The words came flying out of Sesily's mouth, shocking Sera into an unexpected reply. "You know, tumbles aren't always the solution."

Silence fell, and Sera was consumed with curiosity. She waited, knowing Sesily would not be able to leave it. She was right. Finally, her sister said, full of honesty, "I have plans."

"Involving Caleb?"

"Yes."

"Has he arranged some kind of assignation?" It was difficult for Sera to avoid sounding shocked.

"No. Worse."

Good Lord. She'd murder him. "What has he done?" Sera was suddenly properly displeased with the man she'd called her friend for so long. It was one thing to meddle in her life, but another thing entirely to seduce her sister.

"*Nothing.*" A little sigh. "That's the problem. He fled Highley when I asked him to do something."

Good God. "Sesily—he's—"

"You said you'd never played with him. You said you weren't interested."

"And that is all true. I was going to say that he's old."

Sesily smirked. "Not that old."

"Not old in body. Old in spirit. And he's a bastard." One who deserved a sound punch to the nose, apparently.

"Yes, I've sensed that last bit."

"And so?"

Sesily sat back in the seat, the flash of her white grin barely there in the dim light. "And so I think he deserves a bastard in return, don't you?"

Hang all men for making women feel.

Sera appreciated the simple, ideal vengeance of the moment . . . and the punishment it would mete out for Caleb's interference in her own life—keeping Mal's presence in Boston a secret. He did deserve a bastard, and Sesily was more than enough woman to play the part. But her sister did not deserve a man who had such a cold view of love. "Caleb . . . Sesily, Caleb is not the kind of man who is forever."

Sesily looked out to the darkness beyond the carriage for a long time—long enough for Sera to imagine her sister might not speak. She did, finally. "No one is forever until they are."

The simple statement impacted Sera more than she imagined it might. It lingered in the air between them, wreaking quiet havoc, until Sesily looked at her and said, "Are you forever? Is Haven?"

The questions shattered her—and she found herself unable to reply.

Terrified of what the reply might be.

Instead, she looked at her sister—the one who had taken London by storm and stood, brave and tall and beautiful and bold, willing to accept the life that came her way, as long as she had chosen it. A heroine among women.

Sesily deserved a crack at the life she wished, scandal be damned.

Didn't they all?

Sera might not be able to have the future of which she'd once dreamed, but she could help her sisters have it. If this was her role—helping them to have the future they wanted—then that would be enough.

It would have to be.

"Then the Sparrow it is."

Someone should find her future there.

Chapter 25

TOWN'S TORRIDEST TAVERNS!

"American, there are ladies—"

Caleb did not look up from the whiskey he was pouring. "Tell them to find another place. We're not a brothel."

The guard he'd hired to man the door of The Singing Sparrow several weeks ago tried again. "They don't look whores, American."

Caleb gritted his teeth at the moniker, which he seemed unable to shake. Indeed, he seemed unable to convince anyone in the country to call him anything but the American—including the man in question, a Samoan hired away from his cargo hook on the London docks, along with a half-dozen other men, decent and strong. "Well, then let them in," he said. "Women's money spends as well as men's."

Fetu grinned, white teeth showing bright in the shadows. "They're already in. I didn't think I could turn away the Sparrow herself."

The words caught his attention. Caleb looked toward the door, unable to see much in the crush of bodies stacked deep, with no care for the summer heat—not when there was entertainment and booze to be had. Instead, he set the bottle down and leaned over the bar. "She's back?"

"Beautiful, tall, and angry as a fox when I questioned her identity."

He had no doubt of that. What the hell was she doing back in London? Had the duke picked a wife? That's when the other bit sank in. *They.* Sera wouldn't have done it. Wouldn't have risked her sisters' reputations.

Her *sister's* reputation.

He smacked his hand on the bar. "You said *they.*"

Goddammit. Sera hadn't brought her here.

"There are two of them."

"What's the other look like? Plain and bookish?" Perhaps it was Sophie. "Tall as a tree?" Or Seleste. "Dripping in jewels?" Seline, maybe.

"Female."

"What does that mean?"

Fetu's grin again, this time, enhanced by enormous hands tracing an outrageously curved figure in the air. "Female."

Caleb grabbed Fetu's shirt in his fist, jerking him close enough to see the ink in the tattoo covering the crown of the man's bald head. "You don't notice that. She's not female to you."

The other man's brows rose high on his bald head, but he was interrupted before he could reply. "Am I female to *you*?"

Caleb released Fetu and spun toward the words. Toward the woman.

Dammit, he didn't want her to be female.

"No. You're a nuisance."

She laughed. The sound sin and sex, and welcome as the damn sun.

But she wasn't welcome. He didn't want her here.

Even if she was like a cool breeze in the hot, smoky room, hair up in pins that had worked too long a day, letting long, errant curls twist and cling to her neck and shoulder, the tip of one sneaking its way into the line of her dress. There was color high on her cheeks, a dewy sheen over the beautiful smooth skin there, and those lips, pink and full and perfect.

She raised a brow. "You can't escape. Not unless you're willing to leap over the bar and crash through a few dozen people clamoring to get a decent spot to watch the Sparrow perform."

He pointed to Fetu. "Go back to the door."

Fetu executed a short bow in Sesily's direction. "A pleasure to meet you, Sparrow's sister."

She smiled at him and dipped into a little curtsy. "And you, American's protector."

Caleb wanted to break something. "He's not my protector," he said, hating that he felt the need to say anything at all. He didn't care what she thought. Her thoughts were not for him to care about. "I don't need a protector."

She turned to him. "Oh? So why do you employ him?"

"Because he needs a protector," Fetu said with a smirk.

"Go back to the door," Caleb said, picking up a bottle and pretending to pour whiskey for men who were not waiting for drink. Once Fetu sauntered off, he tried for casualness, looking at Sesily once more. It was not easy, as she was far too beautiful to look at without fearing repercussions. "You shouldn't be here."

"I wouldn't have had to come if you'd been less of a coward."

He grew hot with frustration. "A man would become acquainted with my fists for such a suggestion."

She smirked. "Well, as we've already established, I am not a man. So I think I shall take my chances."

With a near growl, he tossed the bottle onto a low table and came out from behind the bar, taking her by the arm and guiding her through the throngs of people, into the back room of the pub, where there was nothing but whiskey and gin to play witness. He released her and closed the door behind him.

Sesily was too surefooted, already taking one long step toward him, and Caleb had to work not to back away. She was distilled danger. And that was before she said, low and sultry, as if she were testing the depths of his wildness, "Perhaps not so much a coward, after all. What do you intend to do with me here?"

The question produced so many vivid, stunning, devastatingly wanton answers that he required a moment to wrap his mind about them. Of course, he did not intend to act upon even one of those answers, even as he quite desperately wanted to.

He was, after all, a man with a pulse.

Clearing his head, he searched for a safe topic. Seized upon it. "Where is your sister?"

She stepped closer, her deep cerulean skirts now brushing against his legs. Not that he felt them. Not that he ached for them. "She left the moment we arrived. Argued with Mr. Fetu, gained entrance to the main room, and left to the stage, muttering something about entertainment."

"She should not have brought you."

"Are you afraid I shall be ruined?"

"Someone should be."

She tilted her head. "Hasn't Sera told you that my sisters and I are ruined before we begin? We are the Dangerous Daughters. The Soiled S's. Interestingly, we are

so ruined that we cannot shock Society. We can run from
our husbands. Toss dukes into fishponds. Horserace. Hie
off to Scotland in carriages with men we do not know.
And all we do is prove the world's point. One of my
sisters is a duchess. Another a marchioness. Another a
countess. And the last richer than the other three combined. Ruin has served us quite well."

He narrowed his gaze. "Not you, though."

Something flickered in those eyes, blue as the shimmering fabric of her dress. Something that he would
have called sadness if he were willing to pay attention.
Which he wasn't.

"No, not me. But perhaps I simply haven't given it
everything I have."

And then she laid hands on him, one palm high on his
chest, flat against the buttoned linen vest he wore over
shirtsleeves when he worked. The touch was like fire.
He reached for that criminal, glorious hand, certain he
was going to lift it from his person. She was a flirt—the
worst kind—the kind that made a man want to sit up
and beg.

He didn't move the hand. Instead, he pressed it tighter
to him.

Those blue eyes captured his. "Your heart is pounding, American."

"Incidental," he said. "I thought I made it clear that I
am not for toying."

"Tell me why, and I shall allow it."

He couldn't help a little laugh at that *allow*. As though
the entire world bent to her whim. As though she and
her kind ruled it like queens. And perhaps they did. "Because I've vowed off women like you."

Her voice went soft and smooth. "Women like me?"

"The dangerous kind." Was he leaning down to her?

"Is that not all of us?" Perhaps she was stretching up to him.

"Lord knows it's most of you." She was right there, lips parted like a promise. Like a secret.

"You seem a man who likes a bit of danger." The words were a breath against his skin, that hand sliding up to his shoulder, to his neck. He fisted his hands at his sides.

"Not the kind that lands me married."

She watched him, beautiful defiance in her eyes. "I never said I wanted to marry you."

He deserved a damn medal for not kissing her then. For not accepting the tacit offer she voiced—the kiss. The touch. And whatever else Sesily Talbot, the most dangerous of the Dangerous Daughters, wanted.

He deserved to have President Jackson walk into the damn room and present him with a cabinet post. He deserved to be knighted by the damn king. Riches and power beyond his dreams. All of it. Because, surely, stepping away from her was the single noblest act anyone had ever performed. Arthurian in scope.

Made even nobler when he said, "Go home to your cat, kitten."

Sesily's lips flattened in something like disappointment, and then she sighed. "My cat is still at Highley."

"Why? Decided you did not require a feral sidekick?"

She replied, dry as sand. "Brummell went into hiding after you skulked off."

"I didn't skulk."

She ignored him. "He longed for his American scratching post."

He scowled. "Perhaps you should go fetch him, then. I don't much care what you do, frankly, as long as you find yourself another tree up which to bark."

"Your skill at mixing metaphors truly is unparalleled," she said.

"Seems a good enough reason to find yourself another man with whom to toy, Sesily," he said, steeling his tone. "I am not green enough to be tempted into the game."

He'd made her angry, if the color that flooded her cheeks was any indication. But before she could reply, the air changed. From what seemed like an immense distance, in the room beyond, quiet fell, soft and heavy with anticipation.

Sesily looked to the door, hearing the silence. "What's happening?"

"Your sister is about to sing."

She turned to him. "I'm not leaving without hearing her."

"Stay if you like," he said, affecting disinterest. Hoping for it. "But don't expect me to stay with you."

She lifted one brow and straightened her shoulders. "And so I was right."

"You were wrong. I am not another man to be ensorcelled by you." Perhaps if he said it, she would believe it. Perhaps he would.

She did not. Indeed, she seemed utterly unmoved by the words. By the insult he'd intended in them. Instead of turning tail and making an exit, she smiled, bold as ever. "No, Caleb, I was right. You are a coward. Unwilling to see the truth."

She'd said the words before. In the country. He didn't have to ask her to clarify, as they remained etched in his memory.

How good it would be.

He shook his head. "Go home, little girl, before you get yourself in trouble."

She watched him for long enough to unsettle him

before she smirked. "I don't think I am in any danger of getting into trouble, American."

"The world shall think I've ruined you if you're not careful."

"And they shan't think it at all if you are careful."

He hated the way he responded to her bold brashness. To her words, so shocking and so damn welcome. He hadn't felt this way—this awake, this on fire, this *hard*—in years. Attempting to ignore all that, he spoke, steeling his voice. "What do you want, Sesily? I must return to the tavern."

"I want you to kiss me."

He shook his head. "No."

She moved toward him. "Why not?"

"Because I don't kiss girls."

"As I've told you, I'm not a girl."

He clung to the emotion, hoping to push her away— far enough that she'd never return. "But you're young and spoiled, aren't you? Always have been."

"Then I should get what I wish, no?"

"I'm not interested."

"In spoiling me?"

"In kissing you."

The words landed and stung. He saw it in her beautiful blue eyes for a barely-there moment before she shuttered the emotion and nodded. "Then I shall find someone else."

"To spoil you? That's an excellent plan." He didn't care. She wasn't his problem.

She turned without a word and headed for the door, opening it and turning back before she replied. "No. To kiss me." She was into the throngs of people beyond before he could catch her.

He stared after her for a stretch of time, long after

she'd disappeared into the crowd. She was safe, and not his concern.

She wouldn't leave without Sera. Indeed, she'd probably make her way behind the stage to find her. She was safe, and not his concern.

There were half a dozen men in that room who had been hired to keep the peace. She was safe, and not his concern.

He'd just convinced himself of that fact when the brawl began.

*M*al rode straight to Covent Garden, making up much of Sera's head start, arriving outside The Singing Sparrow to find lanterns ablaze, throngs of raucous revelers blocking the street beyond, cursing and shouting from pleasure and drink.

Hitching his mount outside and tossing a coin to a boy nearby to ensure the beast's protection, he headed for the door, desperate to get to Sera, whom he knew without question was inside. Mal pushed past the large doorman—grateful for the American's obvious good sense at least in the matter of hiring the fellow for security, as few would risk the wrath of such brawn—and into the room, dark and smoky and rank with the smell of London in summer. The room was oddly quiet, anticipation and excitement in the air. His gaze went immediately to the stage, empty but perfectly lit, the candles long and flickering, as though they, too, trembled with the excitement of the room.

"I hear she's back," a man announced to a group seated at the table immediately to his left.

"Cor," came the scoffing reply. "They've been saying that every night since she left. I heard she's flown back to America. Sparrow didn't like the pickings here."

Another chimed in. "Aye, they say she came looking to sign on as mistress to some rich toff, and none of them want her."

"Would *you* want her? It's not as though she's a lady."

Haven gritted his teeth, loathing these men and this place and everything it represented—the life she'd chosen over him. How she must have loathed him to pick this life. He had to get to her.

Before he could, the first man spoke again, punctuating his words with a rude hand motion. "All the more reason to have her. Chit knows how to do."

The men laughed uproariously as Haven turned toward them, taking note of the large tankards of ale on the table as he crouched low and took a shoulder in hand. "Say it again."

The words were low and ominous, and the men just drunk enough not to see the danger ahead. "Wot, that the Sparrow seems a good plow?"

It was the hours of frustration, riding alone in the dark, desperate for her. It was the weeks of frustration, wishing for her with him even as she stood inches away, impossible to reach. It was the years of frustration, knowing that he'd made every possible mistake. Fearing that he might never find her.

Without all that, perhaps he might not have flipped the table, sending the quartet flying backward, out of the way of furniture and fury.

Perhaps he might not have grabbed a tankard of ale virtually from midair and cracked the most vocal of them on the side of the head, enjoying the mighty thud that came with the blow more than he should.

The man landed on the ground with a wild curse, the throngs that had seemed dense and immovable scattering to clear a wide space, someone calling out "Brawl!"

The room exploded with activity, the razor-edge anticipation of Sera's return performance translating into a wild curiosity about the fight that had broken out. Women shrieked and yanked their skirts out of the way as men began to call out wagers.

Mal did not pause to hear the over-under on his success, however. He was too busy fighting, his fists connecting quickly and powerfully, punishing the remaining three members of the foul-mouthed group with his fury. "You do not speak of her that way," he said, bloodying one man's nose before turning to block a chair wielded by another.

The furniture crashed over his arm, and he turned away from the shower of splintered wood before landing a massive blow to his attacker's jaw. "You do not speak of women that way," he roared.

"Sod off!" came the retort from the first man down, now once more on his feet, blood on his cheek. "I'll say what I like, where I like!"

Mal went for him again, taking him by his grubby shirt and tossing him, bodily, toward the enormous guard, who appeared less interested in the disgusting refuse of a human at his feet, and more interested in getting to Mal, no doubt to stop his bout of fury.

Mal raised his hands in surrender. He was not after the men who protected Sera. "I am not here to—"

He was unable to finish the thought, however, as a feminine screech sounded behind him. He turned, uncertain of what to expect.

He certainly did not expect to find his final foe mere inches from him, arms flailing, fists diverted from their original path by the woman who had attacked the cretin from behind. Sesily. His sister-in-law, who looked directly at him and said, "Go on then, take your shot!"

He did. One wicked jab that would have made his boxing instructor at Eton immensely proud. The man fell like a tree, Sesily atop him.

She sat up remarkably quickly, and with an impressive flourish, as though wrestling beasts to the floor while wearing skirts were a particular talent. She grinned up at him. "We're in a bit of trouble, I'd think."

Sesily was, as ever, superior at understatement.

The room was riotous, hooting and harrumphing and cheering and hissing consuming the group, money changing hands, and one enterprising bookmaker calling out, "As no one wagered that a girl would enter the fray, no one wins!"

Suffice to say, those assembled for their winnings were unsatisfied.

As they waged war among one another, several large men emerged from the woodwork to remove the four offending men. Mal reached down, offering his sister-in-law a hand, helping her to her feet.

She smirked. "I knew you would come, but I did not expect such an impressive entrance, I confess."

He scowled. "I don't know that she'll feel the same way."

She shook her head. "Don't be silly. Women love a grand gesture."

Mal wasn't certain that destroying a tavern and bloodying four men was quite the same as a roomful of hothouse roses, but the guard reached him before he could argue the point, massive hands coming to Mal's shoulders and yanking him back toward the entrance. "Time to go, toff."

"Wait!" Sesily said, coming forward. "He's—"

"What in ever-loving hell were you thinking?" Mal had somehow forgotten the American, which was a shock, honestly, considering how thunderous the man was at that particular moment, spinning Sesily to face him. "Did you just throw yourself into a goddamn bar fight?"

There wasn't even a hint of a cower in Sesily. Indeed, it appeared that his sister-in-law was pleased beyond measure with Caleb Calhoun's rage. Understanding dawned as she turned with utter calm. "What business is it of yours?"

It appeared the Talbot sisters had struck again, and for the first time since he'd woken hours earlier and realized that Sera was gone, Mal found himself thinking of something other than winning back his wife.

Calhoun rounded on him. "What are you smiling at, Red?"

Mal smirked. "Only that it's nice to see you laid low by one of them, as well."

"Leave," Caleb said, jabbing one finger in Mal's direction before waving it in front of Sesily's nose. "And take this one with you."

Her eyes went wide. "This one?"

"You destroyed my tavern, harridan!"

"I did no such thing! There's barely a scratch." Mal cast a look about their wreckage. "And besides," she said, "it's not your tavern. It's Sera's."

Mal went still. "What did you say?"

Caleb cursed, and Sesily's eyes widened, as though she'd just realized what she had said. The implications of it. She immediately retreated. "Uh . . . that is—"

"It's not Sera's," Caleb said.

"It's not," Sesily lied. Too quickly.

Mal struggled to make sense of the moment through the events of the last ten minutes, the last twelve hours, the last four weeks. Through the ache in his arm where he'd been struck with a chair and the one on his jaw where he'd been struck with a fist, and the one in his chest, where he'd been struck with the truth.

And then the room went silent, impossibly so, considering the fight and the drink and the heat and the sheer mass of humanity, all eyes on the woman now at the center of the small, bright stage, masked and beautiful. The fight was forgotten.

She stood in perfect stillness, as though she had simply materialized there, in a pool of golden candlelight, like a goddess.

"It's her," someone breathed, adoration in the words.

Adoration Mal understood, because there, on the stage, was the woman he loved.

He would have known her, masked or no, covered in paint or no. He would have known the long lines of her, the curving shape of her, the breath of her. Like light and air and sin and love.

She wore a stunning gown in the deepest purple, somehow impossibly vibrant in red and blue, shimmering like the metal of her mask, delicate filigree twisted in an elaborate, impossible pattern, an echo of the feathers of her namesake, low over her nose, leaving barely any space between the edge of the mask and her perfectly painted lips, full and stunning.

The dress was too tight in the bodice, too low in the neck, and perfection.

And then she raised her arms in the silence, turning her hands out to her audience, all grace, as though she were inviting them in, so she might tell them her most private secrets, so she might love them, as they deserved.

So they might love her, as he did.

The entire room seemed to tilt, leaning into her, and Mal with it, pulled on a string. There was nothing that could move him from that room in that moment. Nothing that could take him from this woman.

She was magnificent.

"Welcome loves," she said, her lips curving around the full, proud words, her voice low and languid. Familiar, and somehow entirely foreign. "'Tis lovely to be free with you tonight."

And that was when Mal realized the truth.

This might be a part she played, yes. And it might be something he'd never seen and never known, but it was *she*. A part of her. And it was not by requirement. She basked in it. She was elevated by it. And then, when she opened her mouth and began to sing, he realized that they were all elevated by her.

It was no surprise what she sang. Even there, in the dark, where he knew she could not see him, he knew she would sing for him, that song that had echoed in his memory for years.

"Here lies the heart and the smile and the love; here lies the wolf, the angel, the dove. She put aside dreaming and she put aside toys; and she was born that day, in the heart of a boy."

But he did not know there was more to it, additional verses that were melancholy and beautiful, and that made him ache. *"Gone is the flower and gone is the crow; gone is the future that promised to grow. Farewell the past, the present, the now; farewell the ship, the anchor, the bow."*

And then, she found him in the dark room, turning toward him, connected to him now, as ever. As they had been that first night, a hundred years earlier, a thousand, on the balcony in the darkness, destined for each other. For this night. Forever. *"So we lie down and pillow our heads; so we lie down in the cool of our beds. We put*

*aside dreaming, and we put aside toys; and remember
our days in the heart of a boy."*

The tavern was still and silent as snowfall, the notes
filling every corner of the room, the entire assembly en-
raptured by her beautiful voice. But only Mal was devastated by the song.

Because he finally understood.

The Sparrow was no sparrow. She was a phoenix.
Risen from the ash of the past. Of *their* past. None of
the things they'd broken were here. None of the things
they'd lost. How often had she spoken of freedom? Here,
in this room, she was free.

He finally understood.

When the music ended and she bowed low, the room
erupted in deafening applause and thumping hoots of
approval that set the walls shaking. She did not linger in
the glow of the applause, however. Instead, she turned
and pushed through a little curtain at the side of the
stage, barely noticeable if one wasn't interested.

Of course, all the men assembled—and several of the
women—were interested. He moved to stop them from
following her when a hand stopped him. "There's security," Calhoun said. "She's safe."

Two massive men took their place at the curtain, prepared to do battle for the Sparrow, their Queen.

He didn't care. He wanted to protect her.

"Perhaps you should wait," Sesily added.

Mal heard the meaning in the words. *She doesn't
want you.*

He turned on the duo. "This isn't her tavern, *yet.* That's
what you meant to say."

"I didn't mean to say *anything.*" The American scowled
at Sesily.

Sesily lifted a shoulder and let it fall. "You made me

angry. And besides, it's time someone chivvied them along."

"Along, where?" Caleb growled.

"He's not divorcing her, American," Sesily said. "He loves her quite thoroughly."

She was not wrong, but nothing in the conversation was helping. Mal resisted the urge to tell them both to shut up and said, "I'm right, am I not? The tavern is to be hers."

The answer was wrenched from the American. "It's hers when she can take it."

Mal shook his head. Married women could not own property. And they could not own businesses. "Which can never happen. Not as long as she is married to me."

The American did not have to reply.

To have her future, she had to forget her past. Which was impossible, if he was with her. He looked to Sesily, the only sister who seemed remotely willing to forgive him. "Why didn't she tell me?" Calhoun did not have to reply to that, either. Mal answered for him. "She did not trust me not to play games with her." She did not trust him, full stop. And he had done nothing but prove her right, scheming and planning and throwing a damn house party to lure her to him instead of telling her the truth. And risking everything.

Everything he'd lost anyway.

He'd never given her reason to trust him.

Her words from that morning—had it only been that morning? Christ, it felt like an age—echoed through him like her song, sweet and honest and melancholy. Final.

Love is not enough.

There had been a time when it would have been. When he had been all she'd ever wished for. All she'd ever needed. But he'd been too blind to see that everything she'd done had been for him. For their family. For their future. And by the time he'd understood, she'd already been fixed to the firmament.

He nodded, knowing what was to come next. Knowing that if it did not work, he would lose her forever. And knowing that he had no other choice.

He turned to leave, and Sesily stopped him. "Wait! Haven! What do we tell her?"

He replied without looking back. "Tell her I'm not marrying Felicity Faircloth."

He crossed the street outside, needing air and a moment to think. Turning his back to the curved cobblestone wall, he closed his eyes and took several deep breaths, the tight ache in his chest threatening to consume him.

When he opened them, it was to find two brutal men standing in front of him, one tall and lean with a wicked scar down his cheek and a walking stick that looked like it was no more designed to assist in balance than it was to assist in flight, and the other shorter, broader, and with a face that would evoke Roman sculpture if he didn't look a portrait of cruelty.

They looked too turned out for pickpockets or drunk blades, but it was Covent Garden, so he said, "If you're looking for a fight, gentleman, I should warn you that I'm more than willing to give it. Find another bear to poke."

The tall man didn't hesitate in his reply. "We're not here for you, Duke." Mal was unsurprised that they knew him. They seemed the type of men who knew a fair amount. "At least, we didn't come for you. But now that we've seen the way you fight . . ." The scarred man tutted his approval. "Don't suppose you'd be interested in fighting for us. Good blunt in it."

"I'm not."

The other one—the one with the handsome, cruel face—spoke then, his voice low and graveled with what sounded like disuse. "Nah. You'd be rubbish at it."

"Why is that?"

The tall one again. "My brother means that there are two kinds of fighters; the ones who excel at the fight no matter what, and the ones who only excel when something they love is on the line. You're the latter."

Like that, he knew who they were. "You're the pair that pummeled Calhoun."

The tall one tipped his cap, wide grin on his face. "Just a little how'd'y'do, welcome to the neighborhood. Calhoun fought back, and well. We're friends, now."

Mal nodded, even as he doubted every word. He paused, considering the two men and all the ways he might ruin them if they dared even look at his wife. Finally, he gave a little growl and leaned in. "You are right, you know. I am single-minded when something I love is on the line. And I assume you can tell that because you are cut from similar cloth."

The men watched him carefully, but said nothing.

Mal held his fury and frustration in rigid control. "You listen to me. Everything I love is inside this place. If anything happens to it, I come for you."

There was a beat of silence, after which the quiet man grunted and the tall man said, "Christ, I wish we could get you in a ring. Think of the money he'd make us!"

"He's other bouts in mind."

God knew that was right. Until that moment, Mal had fought for himself.

It was time he start fighting for her.

Chapter 26

DUCAL DIVORCE: DECISION DAY!

October 12, 1836
House of Lords, Parliament

"*I* don't see him."

Sesily leaned out over the railing of the observation gallery and stared down at the procession of parliamentary members filing into the House of Lords, and Sera ignored the pang of disappointment at the pronouncement, which was validated with a longer, hanging look. "No, I don't think he's there."

"Well, everyone can see you, so that's what matters," Seline pointed out dryly as Sesily righted herself and turned her back to the speaker's floor.

"I'm not inclined to show deference to a passel of ancient, venerable men, you know. Not unless they give Sera what she wants."

"Which won't happen," Seleste replied, putting her perfect bottom to the railing and crossing her arms over her chest. The position placed her posterior on full view below, not that she seemed to mind. "Clare says he has it on good authority that you haven't the votes, Sera, which you know. Though, of course, you've Clare's."

"And King's," Sophie chimed in.

Sera knew she wasn't getting her divorce. Indeed, she was still surprised that there was a vote at all on the matter. After all, Mal had spent weeks playing at plans for the dissolution of their marriage, ruining the summers of a half-dozen women and Sera's, as well.

Lie.

She ignored the whisper and the truth that came with it. It was easier if she imagined the summer ruined. If she pretended she didn't care for him. Then, perhaps, it would not hurt so much when he did as he'd always promised—kept the marriage and stayed away.

For three weeks, he'd stayed away, with no contact and no message other than the one he gave to Sesily at the Sparrow after nearly destroying the place. He wasn't marrying Felicity Faircloth.

It seemed he was not marrying Lady Lilith, either, considering both women were returned to London and the marriage mart with the new session of Parliament, along with Lady Emily. Surprisingly, *The News of London* gossip column had already claimed them three of the brightest jewels of the Season.

So, it seemed, Mal would not marry another and, therefore, had no intention of divorcing her.

Three days after Mal left The Singing Sparrow without a word, Sera received word from the Lord Chancellor, indicating that that "the matter of the dissolution of your marriage to the Duke of Haven, by divorce" was to be taken up on the floor of the House of Lords. She was neither asked to make a statement about her request nor was she permitted to engage a solicitor for the proceedings. Wives were not legal entities, and so she was simply given a date and time.

October the twelfth, 1836, at half-eleven in the morning.

"Well," Seline had declared when Sera had told her sisters of the missive. "At least we shan't miss our morning ride."

And so, here they were, each of the Dangerous Daughters having been allowed into the viewing gallery to sit beside their sister as her fate was decided below, by nearly two hundred men born into pomp and privilege. Well, nearly two hundred, and their father, who'd won his title at cards, which, if one thought too much about the current situation, might easily have been the reason they were all sitting there, in the current situation.

The men below milled about, seemingly unaware of the futures that hung in the balance of their legislative work, filing in and out of two doors, one on either side of the chamber. The door on the left led to the Content Lobby, where lords in favor of the Duke and Duchess of Haven's divorce cast their votes for "Content." To the right, the Non-Content Lobby, where the opposite occurred.

"You've at least two votes in favor of the divorce, though," Seleste pointed out. "King and Clare are standing on your side. The problem is, not one of those crusty old titled men are interested in unhappy wives being able to simply beg off marriage. Our husbands, however, they are loyal to a fault."

"I've never considered it a fault." Sophie smiled, peering down over the viewing gallery. "And, besides, I've no interest in begging off marriage." She paused, then breathlessly, "I haven't ever seen King in his wig. It's quite . . ."

"Stirring?" Sesily offered.

"I was going to say curious. But stirring is an interesting option." She tilted her head. "Am I *stirred*? It's possible."

"Wigs will do that," Seline said, dryly. "Powdered horsehair passed down through the generations. Very handsome. And fragrant."

The sisters dissolved into laughter. All the sisters, that was, but Sera, who could not ignore the pressing question of the day. Which made sense, considering the question was to directly impact her future and freedom.

It did not matter that suddenly, with Mal disappeared from everywhere but her thoughts, she was far more interested in one of those than the other. "You're sure he's not down there?"

Sesily turned and considered the men below once more. "It's difficult to tell, what with all the wigs and robes, but I don't think so." She looked back to Sera. "Don't you think he would look up here? Or even better, come and fetch you? I mean, this whole procedure seems designed to put you on display. He's not giving you the divorce, so what's the point of it?"

"He promised me a vote."

"He promised you love and honor, too, and that did not work out so well."

"Seline," Sophie said sharply. "She doesn't need reminders of their past."

"I promised him those things, as well," Sera pointed out.

"Pah," Seleste waved a hand. "We promised obedience, too, and have any of us followed that one to the letter? The point is, this is humiliating. If he insists on keeping you to wife, then he should have canceled the vote instead of making all the world watch as you lose it."

Sera could not disagree with the statement, but it was little matter if he intended to spend the day gloating over his win if he did not turn up to gloat over his win.

"Well, in either event, you'd think he'd be here," Seleste replied, joining Sesily to look down on the floor of Parliament. "Surprisingly, Sera, you look as though you've received more votes than simply our esteemed brothers-in-law—Oh! There's Father coming from the Content Lobby. Good work, Papa!" she called down with a wave, drawing the attention and clear disapproval of the lion's share of the House of Lords. "Papa voted for you, Sera."

Sesily added to the spectacle, calling down, "Vote Seraphina!" She turned back. "We should have made hats. Carried signs. Marched."

Sera resisted the urge to hide her face in her hands when Seline added, "I don't think a march would have helped."

"One never knows," Sophie said, hopefully.

"One knows," Seline said, voice dry as sand. "No one likes a fearless woman."

"Well, there are our reputations out the window and into the Thames, then," Sesily said, dry and droll, taking her seat next to Sera and adding, blandly, "Whatever shall we do."

The Dangerous Daughters snickered en masse.

"For all the grabbing Grab-hands does, you'd think he'd be a bit more in favor of a divorce," Seleste said, a touch too loudly, drawing a collection of harrumphs from below for her inappropriate and exceedingly apt assessment of Lord Grabeham. She also drew a wink and a smirk from her handsome husband. "Oh, yes, I do like that wig."

"Seleste!"

Seleste lowered her voice to a whisper. "Well, it's true."

"Which bit?" Sera asked.

All four of her sisters turned surprised eyes on her for a beat before Seleste replied, full of honesty, "Both."

Their collective laughter echoed through the hall, and

Sera found she did not care. If Malcolm couldn't find it in himself to turn up for the damn vote, she could spend the morning enjoying herself. After all, he would still win in the end, would he not?

You might win, as well.

She swallowed the thought, disliking the way it sent unease rioting through her.

"My Lord Chancellor!"

"Oh! Look! Heiferbetter's something to say!" Sesily narrated, lowering her voice. "Odious man."

Sera did not disagree with the assessment.

"The Chancellor recognizes the Lord Hoffenbetten," the man presiding over proceedings intoned.

"I humbly request that those in the viewing gallery be reminded that we are in a place of grave importance, deciding upon a question that impacts one of our members gravely, and may well influence the rest of us in a manner that might only be described as—"

"Grave?" Seline asked, the word carrying down to the floor like lead.

Lord Hoffenbetten looked up to Seline with pure irritation, and said, "*Serious.*"

The Lord Chancellor responded in utter boredom, "Quiet please, from the gallery."

The quartet of sisters did as they were told, remarkably, taking their seats in a surprisingly quiet, colorful line of women, watching the members of the House of Lords file in and out through their respective doors to cast their vote, and possibly end their sister's hope for a future that was not lived in the shadow of the past.

After long minutes of observational silence, Sesily said quietly, "Sera—there are far more men voting Content than I would have expected."

Seleste leaned in and whispered, "I have been counting, and . . . well, I don't wish to give you false hope . . . but I think you might have a fighting chance, Sera."

Sera nodded, unable to tear her attention away from the door to the Content Lobby, where a seemingly endless stream of peers—most young enough for her to recall from her early seasons—were returning to the floor of the House after having voted in favor of her divorce.

Her heart began to pound. "It might happen," she said softly, more to herself than to the others, but the Talbot sisters had always been connected by some kind of unbreakable bond in times like this.

Sophie reached for her hand, squeezing it tightly. "Sera."

And that's when she saw the Marquess of Mayweather. Memory crashed through her—so weathered it seemed as though it had happened decades earlier and not only three years prior. The night she'd met Mal, on the Worthington House balcony, he'd been with Mayweather, bemoaning the state of marriage-minded misses, berating the marquess for falling in love.

She looked to her sisters. "Is the Marquess of Mayweather married?"

Confusion bloomed on their faces before Sesily said, as delicately as Sesily could say anything, "Perhaps you should wait until you're actually divorced before"—she waved a hand in the air—"setting sights?"

Sera shook her head. "I don't want to marry him, Sesily. I'm just curious."

"Oh. Good then."

"He is married," Sophie offered. "The marchioness frequents the bookshop."

"Helen," Sera said. "Her name is Helen."

"Well, I've only ever called her Lady Mayweather, but yes, I think it is. Did you know her? Before?"

She shook her head, barely speaking above a whisper, distracted by the man far below. "I knew of her. I knew that he was besotted." She was distracted by the fact that he entered the Content Lobby. The Marquess of Mayweather voted for divorce. Why? Wouldn't he side with his friend? "She likes cats," she said, vaguely. Nearly unaware of what she was saying.

If Malcolm wanted a divorce, wouldn't he ask his friends to vote with him?

"I also like cats," Sesily said. "Has anyone seen Lady Felicity since she returned to town? I was so happy she returned Brummell. Someone should have her to dinner."

"You could have her to dinner," Seleste said.

Sesily shook her head. "No one will let their unmarried daughter befriend me." After the events at the Sparrow, Sesily's name had been plastered throughout the papers, and their parents were threatening to send her away from London to restore her reputation. As though such a thing were possible.

"Sophie should host her. She's the most respectable of the lot of you."

"Oh, yes," Seleste smirked. "She's never done anything scandalous."

"Well, her scandal ended in a marquessate."

As Sera watched, another man exited the Content Lobby far below, stopping to speak to several others in a tightly knit group. She couldn't place them, but they were terribly familiar.

"Sera?" Sophie said, quietly, as though she could sense Sera was thinking.

"Who is that man?"

Sophie turned to look. "The big one is the Duke of Lamont. The tall ginger is the Earl of Arlesley. And the handsome one is the Marquess of Bourne. They own a club."

Not just any club. They owned Haven's club.

And they were voting for divorce.

Something was happening. Her breath came fast in her chest. Something was afoot, and she could not work it out. Where was Mal? Would he not cast his vote? Why not? Why let her sit in the gallery and wait for the results as though she were waiting for the guillotine?

It had been three weeks since she'd left him, sleeping at Highley, and he'd left her at the Sparrow. She'd seen him there, in the audience. It had been impossible not to see him, and not only because he and her sister had colluded to destroy a table and several chairs at the Sparrow, and sent four men battered and bruised to the ground.

She'd seen him the moment he'd entered.

But Mal had disappeared, as though the night had never happened. Which was, Sera supposed, what she had always hoped for him to do. Except, once it was done, she seemed not to want that at all. He'd disappeared and, somehow, all she wanted was to see him.

Why wasn't he here?

"Sera," Sophie said her name a third time. When Sera looked, it was to discover her youngest sister, watching her carefully. "Do you still want it?"

The question was nearly too much. Of course she wanted it, didn't she? She'd wanted it for years. It had been the thing she'd promised herself in the years she'd had nothing. After she'd lost everything—the marriage of which she'd dreamed, the husband she'd loved, the child she'd birthed, the future she'd imagined. And when she'd run, she'd even lost these women, her sisters.

Divorce was to close the door on all that loss and give her a chance to begin again. "Everything I've ever loved has turned to rubbish. Everything but the Sparrow."

For nearly three years, the only time Sera had ever been happy was on the stage, first, in Boston as the Dove and then here, as the Sparrow. In song, she had always found herself.

And if she had nothing else, she at least had that.

"I cannot be the Sparrow and the duchess. I never wanted to be. But now . . ." She let the words trail off.

"But now . . . ?" Sophie always saw the truth before the rest of them.

Sera looked to the floor far below, absent of Mal. Thought of the past three weeks, absent of Mal. Where was he? Had he decided not to be here? Not to chase her? He'd spent the last three years chasing her. He'd traveled the Continent. He'd sailed to Boston. He'd searched for her.

He'd loved her.

Even as she'd believed she'd lost everything, he'd loved her.

And now, he was gone.

And it felt, somehow, like she was losing everything all over again, and this time, she was not certain the Sparrow would save her.

"My lords, the votes are tallied," the Lord Chancellor boomed from his place at the far end of the floor. "And I am surprised and not a little amazed that the result is a tie. Eighty of my lords have cast a Content vote, and eighty a Non-Content vote."

Sera caught her breath in shock as the collected aristocrats hemmed and hawed and harrumphed, several calling out their vocal discontent for the scenario.

"A demmed tie?"

"As though it weren't enough that we wasted a day voting on a dratted divorce!"

"The man should take his wife in hand is what he should do!"

"Who said that?" Seline leaned over the edge of the railing. "I want to be certain to invite your poor wife round for cake—perhaps we can convince her that marital dissolution is a worthy goal!"

The men below thumped and bellowed, disliking the brazen women above. "One wonders why Haven would want anything to do with you lot! How any man would throw in his lot with such a horrid group!"

Sophie's husband leapt into the fray, the Marquess of Eversley coming to his feet, robed and wigged and not a bit lacking in intimidation. "Say it again!" he thundered. Shouting ensued, the room gone wild with the restrained madness that comes only from parliamentary antics.

And all the while, Sera was consumed by the vote. "How is it a *tie*?" She looked to her sisters. "We were assured I did not have the votes!" Her gaze fell to the Marquess of Mayweather, who looked perfectly calm. As did the owners of Mal's club and several other members of the Content Lobby.

Sesily Talbot was not content, however. She stood up, grabbing hold of the railing guarding her from toppling over into the throngs of lords below. "Oh, for heaven's sake, Lord Chancellor. Get to it! What happens now?"

What happens is, Mal comes.

And as though Sera summoned him with her thoughts, the enormous doors at the far end of the room burst open, the sound echoing through the quiet hall, quieting the chatter. There was Malcolm, calm and unflappable, as though this were a perfectly ordinary day, and his wife weren't sitting in the gallery waiting to hear of their future.

"If I may, Lord Chancellor?"

Sera drank him in, marveling at how she could have gone years without seeing him and now, three weeks had made her desperate for him.

"You are late, Duke Haven," the Speaker called. "Which is not a small amount strange, considering the business of the day. Additionally, your inappropriate attire insults the circumstance of the House of Lords."

He wasn't wearing his robes. Or his wig.

"I do apologize," he said. "I was whipping votes."

Sera went cold at the words, then fiery hot.

"Well, you've done a poor job at it, as the count is a tie."

Was that a smile on his lips? She could not look away from that expression—not happy and not sad. What was happening? "Ah. Well. Perhaps, as I am here, now, I might be able to cast a verbal vote?"

The Speaker paused. "That is unorthodox."

The room erupted in a chorus of pounding fists and hissing. "Let the man speak," came a cry from somewhere below her.

And then Mayweather spoke up. "He's got a right to vote on his own marriage, doesn't he?"

"He does," she said softly.

Her sisters heard her. Sophie turned to look at her. "You want him to vote."

If he voted, it would be to keep their marriage intact. *Yes.*

Shock coursed through her, and she nodded, the movement barely there, so small that no one should have seen it. Of course, her sisters saw it, and they set to hooting and shouting themselves, banging their hands on the observation railing, and drawing Mal's attention to the upper level of Parliament. When he found her, he met her gaze without hesitation, and she saw everything there. Love. Passion. Conviction.

He wanted her, and he would do anything to have her.

And in that moment, she realized, she felt the same way.

"I don't think you're getting your divorce now," Sophie said, squeezing her hand.

"But it does seem like you might be getting a grand gesture," Sesily said happily. "I told him we like a grand gesture."

"All right then, Haven, get on with it," the Lord Chancellor said with more than a thread of irritation in his tone. He seemed to have eschewed parliamentary formality.

Haven moved to the center of the floor, his gaze riveted to her, and somehow, all Parliament fell away, as though it were the two of them somewhere private and perfect. The underwater ballroom at Highley. The stage of the Sparrow in the early morning. Somewhere the world could not see them.

She caught her breath, waiting for him to speak.

"I love you."

A chorus of irritated harrumphs sounded around the room as peers from across Britain realized what they were in for, but Sera found she did not care a bit. She stood, clutching the rail of the observation gallery for support, wanting to be as close to him as possible for whatever was about to come.

Especially when he pressed on. "I have known I wanted to marry you since the moment I met you, when you gave me a dressing down for insulting women's motives in marriage. You were magnificent." He pointed. "Mayweather was there. He would have thought so, too, except he was in love with Helen already."

Her sisters all offered little sighs of pleasure, so Sera assumed the marquess did something lovely at that, but she was too busy watching her husband, who was moving toward her, as though she weren't ten feet in the air. "Do you remember what I said to you that night?"

"You said that love is a great fallacy."

Several of the men assembled seemed to agree.

Mal nodded. "I did. And not ten minutes later, I had tumbled into it."

Her heart pounded. She had, too. She'd been planning to seek him out, this legendary eligible duke, and then she'd stumbled upon him, and he'd been perfect. And she'd almost been disappointed that he was the same man she'd thought to catch.

"Do you remember the first song you ever sang to me?"

Of course she did. And he knew it. She'd sung it that last night at the Sparrow. "I do."

Mal had reached the first of several rows of seats separating them, all populated by robed, wigged lords. "Careful, Haven," one of them grumbled.

He didn't seem to hear. "*She was born that day in the heart of a boy.* I always thought it was about you. That you found yourself in me." Tears pricked at her eyes. "But as the years passed, I realized it was a fool's thought. Because what of him? What of the boy, born that same day, in the heart of a girl?"

The words were thick with emotion, and Sera's knuckles turned white with the force she used to clutch the railing. "What of the boy who hadn't seen the sun until he'd seen her? The moon? The stars?" He stilled, staring up at her, his gaze tracking every inch of her face as she did the same, wishing he were closer.

He must have wished the same, because he moved then, climbing up onto the heavy benches below, caring neither for the venerable furnishings, nor the venerated aristocrats who had to lean out of the way or find themselves trampled by the Duke of Haven. He seemed to care only for getting closer to her.

"Here it comes," Sesily whispered.

Sera leaned over to watch him as he reached for the inlaid pillars in the wall beneath and, without hesitation, began to scale the wall.

The room gasped in collective shock, a dozen men on the floor bursting into angry censure, and two directly below reaching for him, as though they could stop him.

They couldn't. He was too fast, and too strong, and too damn perfect, throwing one leg over the rail as Seleste and Sophie backed away to make room for him while Sesily squealed her excitement from several feet away.

At least, Sera was fairly certain it was Sesily. She wasn't about to look away from Mal to be certain. And then he was standing in front of her, breath coming harsh from the exertion of—Dear God. He'd scaled a wall.

He reached for her, his fingers trembling as he pushed a curl behind her ear, leaving a trail of fire in the wake of his touch. When he spoke, his voice was thick with emotion. "What of the boy who couldn't let her go?"

Tears came, hot and unexpected. "That was always the problem," she said to him. "You wouldn't let me go." Or perhaps it was that he wouldn't keep her close. Nothing made sense anymore. Except this. Him, here, touching her.

He shook his head. "I was a bastard. I didn't see that the closer I held you, the farther you'd fly. I didn't realize you could take flight. And I was young and stupid, and God knows I did young and stupid things, not the least of which is vowing never to let you go."

He paused, and she ached for the people they'd been, for the young, beautiful, restless people who had done everything wrong. "Even when you returned, I swore I'd never let you go, Sera, because I never stopped wishing that you'd stayed."

But she'd had to go. She'd ruined so much.

It was as though he could hear her thoughts. "I know you think we failed, my love, but we did not. I failed. I failed you."

She shook her head, tears coming hard and fast. "No."

It wasn't true, of course. They had both failed, and they had both succeeded. They were better for their losses, for their risks, for the world they had left behind and the new ones they had built.

They had not failed.

They had loved.

Did love.

He lifted his other hand, holding her face firmly in his grasp, speaking as though the whole world weren't watching. "I thought that if I chased you long enough and far enough, and held you close enough, I could convince you that I had changed. That we could start anew. But I can't do that and give you your freedom, which is all you've ever asked me for, and all I've ever refused you. Because I've been a bastard from the start. Never once deserving of you."

"No, Mal."

"Yes, love. I'm through chasing you. I shall have to be happy with finding you in the stars, at night." He paused, and she gasped, realizing what he was about to do. "There will never be another for me. But it is not my choice that matters; it is yours. And if you do not want this, then I would rather you be free of it, as you've wished since the start. To begin anew. To choose your happiness somewhere else. With . . ." He paused, began again. ". . . with someone else. Someone you can trust. Someone you believe."

He'd stolen her breath; her tears were coming in earnest now, streaming down her cheeks, and she could not stop them any more than she could stop herself saying his name.

I believe you.

This is enough. You are.

"We are yet married," he whispered, and he kissed her, in front of her sisters and Parliament, amid cheers and shouts of disapproval that faded away into the caress, long and lingering and beautifully soft. And sad. Because it felt like a last kiss.

It felt like good-bye.

When it was over, he pressed his forehead to hers. "I only ever want you to be free, love. I only ever want you to be happy. I only ever want you to choose your path and know that I shall love you better for it," he said, softly, as though he could release her, like a bird, into the sky. "I shall love you."

What was he doing?

And then he did release her, turning away with utter conviction and raising his voice to the House of Lords. "My Lord Chancellor, I vote Content."

And, like that, they were divorced.

Chapter 27

_____ ❧ _____

EVERY DUCHESS HAS HER DAY

*T*wo hours later, Mal entered his parliamentary offices to discover his ex-wife encamped within.

He stopped just inside the open door, handle in hand, and took her in, perched on the built-in seat at the window overlooking St. Paul's, knees pulled up to her chest, still and beautiful in the light of the perfect October day.

And here.

Thank God, she was here.

She did not look away from the city skyline when she spoke, her face in perfect, golden profile. "I imagine the members of the House of Lords are not thrilled with you today, Duke."

He closed the door and pressed his back to it, afraid that if he went any closer, she would disappear, and he would be alone again. She was no longer tied to him, after all. She could leave and never return.

"Many of them are not, no." Mal had spent the last two hours navigating the anger and disapproval of the eighty members of the aristocracy who had voted against the dissolution of his marriage. "They think we've disrespected the institution."

"The institution of marriage? Or the institution of Parliament?"

"A little of both."

Her little exhale might have been a laugh. "Only a little? You were shamefully, improperly attired for the floor of the House of Lords, Your Grace."

"Interestingly, no one seemed interested in that bit."

"I suppose they were most concerned that you scaled the wall and kissed me."

"Yes," he replied. "But you were my wife at the time, so I think they were more irritated that when the news got out, they'd all have to do something similar for their own spouses."

"I wouldn't recommend it," she said. "Such grand gestures too often end in divorce."

"Too often?" He would give anything for her to look at him. To turn and face him and tell him every bit of what she was thinking.

And then she did look at him, capturing him. As she had ever done. "One hundred percent of the time."

It took all his strength not to go to her. He'd vowed to stop chasing her. Vowed to let her make her own choices. "Terrible odds."

She smiled then, small and perfect. "You're a madman."

"You are not the first to have made that assessment today."

She turned away, lifting one hand to the window, tracing a circle in the glass there. She was silent for so long that he was not sure if she would speak again, and he realized he did not care if they lived here, forever, in silence, as long as they lived here, together.

And then, "The sailors on the ship to Boston called me the Dove." He inhaled sharply at the words, soft and lovely, hazy with memory. She smiled, wistful in the sunlight. "They liked me."

"Of that, I have no doubt," he said, hating those men for having her at a time when he was so desperately seeking her.

She shook her head. "Not like that. I was . . ." She trailed off, searching for the right finish. Then, "I was sad."

He could not have stopped moving toward her, not if he'd had the strength of ten men. But, miraculously, when he reached the window, he found a way to resist touching her, instead sitting in the chair next to her, wanting to claim her, knowing he shouldn't. Knowing that if he did, she might stop, and willing to do anything to prevent that.

She did not look away from the city beyond the window. "I was sad, and I barely slept, so I walked. The first few nights, they told me I couldn't be on the deck, that it was too dangerous."

"It was an Atlantic crossing in February." Even saying the words made him nervous. She could have taken horribly ill. Worse. He loathed the idea of her on that terrifying journey, tossed about by the sea, threatened by the elements. Alone.

He should have been with her.

She never should have been there to begin with.

If only he'd been less of a fool.

"You sound like them." She smiled. "I am not so fragile."

"No," he agreed. "You're beauty and steel."

She resumed her tale. "Mainly, they didn't want me topside because I was a woman, and women are bad luck near the sails."

"I imagine you weren't having any of that superstition."

She laughed then, low and soft, and he felt the sound in his gut. "I was not, in fact. I wanted to be in the air. I liked the numbing cold. And so, I persisted."

Pleasure thrummed through him at the words. Of course she had. Brave and strong, as always. "I also have no doubt about that."

"And I sang."

"The Dove." The name the sailors bestowed.

"They said it was because I only ever sang like mourning."

He closed his eyes, hating the words and the knowledge that came with them. Knowledge and memory and regret. He should have been there to hold her while she mourned. To love her through it.

They should have loved each other through it.

She went on. "When I landed in Boston . . . when I found Caleb—at the insistence of some of the sailors, who knew him, and knew he and I would make a good team." He opened his eyes, and found her gaze locked on his, stunning and blue, glittering with knowledge and something else. Something like promise. "Would you like to know why I kept the name?"

"Yes." More than anything.

"Because doves mate for life, and I knew there would never be another for me."

The words weakened him, sending him forward, toward her, desperate to be closer to her, and still, afraid to touch her. Afraid to rush her. His hands fisted—tight enough to strain the muscles in his fingers. He could wait. He would wait a lifetime if he had to.

She did not look away, seeming to draw strength from the truth. Freedom from it. "By the time we made the return trip, back to London, I was—happier. More confident. More powerful. And when I took to *that* deck—

ignoring superstition once more—and sang, my songs were not quite so melancholy. Those sailors taught me their sea shanties, the saltier the better."

"I should like to hear those." Truth. He wanted to lie in the grass at Highley and let the summer breeze wash over them and carry her lewd songs to the corners of the earth.

"I know one about a lad from Glasgow that will make you blush." She smiled wistfully and looked out the window. After a pause, she said, "They gave me a name on the return ship, as well."

"The Sparrow."

"They said I made them dream of the girls at home. But home isn't all the sparrow represents." She looked at him. "Young sailors often ink sparrows on their arms. For freedom." His breath caught in his throat. "Freedom to go where you choose and be what you choose. Freedom to close one door and open a new one, and make your home where you land." She paused. Then, softly, "Freedom to forget."

He waited, biting his tongue, refusing to speak, desperate for her to continue.

Finally, she did. "Good Lord, Mal. Don't you see? I didn't choose the Sparrow over you. Or America, or Caleb, or anything else. I chose all of it because I didn't have you. Because I didn't think I would ever have you again." He heard the tears in her voice when she added, "Because I didn't think you would ever forgive me, so I tried to forget." She sighed, long and trembling, as she battled the memory. "I tried so hard to forget all of it. And all I could remember was you. I told myself the Dove was the vestige of my past. And promised myself the Sparrow was the promise of my future."

She looked at him, then, eyes glistening with unshed tears. "When all the time, I was both."

He couldn't hold back any longer. He reached for her, hauling her into his lap, into his arms. And she came, without hesitation. "Mal," she whispered to his chest as he pulled her close, pressing kisses to her hair. "I'm so sorry," she said. "For so much."

She was crying and he couldn't bear it, tipping her face up to him, kissing over her cheeks, sipping at her tears as he whispered, "No, Angel. The sorrow is mine. The regret. I never told you how much I loved you. I never showed you how I ached to know you. I never even broke bread with your sisters—who I like more than I probably should, by the way."

She laughed through the tears at that. "They grow on a person."

He pulled back and met her gaze, serious. "There was so much I never said. So much I wish to say now. Forever." He told her then, whispering all the things he wanted to tell her. How beautiful she was, how perfect, how he loved her. He kissed her in between the words, soft and sweet, brushing away her tears with lips and thumbs, covering her in kisses, until he found her lips again, soft and sweet and perfect.

He lingered there, pressing long, sweet kisses to her lips between the vows that flooded him. "I love you," he whispered like a prayer. A kiss. "I need you." Another. "Stay." Another, and another, and another, until Sera's tears were gone and she was clinging to him, forcing the kisses to press harder, last longer, burn hotter.

Before they could consume them, however, Sera stopped him, breathing heavily, pulling away—as far as he would let her go. "You divorced me."

He nodded. "I wanted—"

She stopped his words with a kiss. "I know what you wanted. You wanted to give me my freedom. You wanted to give me my choice."

"And now, I want to get down on my knees and beg you to choose me."

She stared deep into his eyes and smiled, pure and honest, and sending joy and pleasure through him. "That is a beautiful, tempting offer. But I'm afraid I don't wish to choose. I want it all."

"You can have the Sparrow, Sera. It's yours now. Calhoun has the papers. All you need do is sign them."

She shook her head. "And what of you?"

"You don't need papers to own me. I belong to you outright." He kissed her again, long and lingering, until her lips were parted and clinging to his. "You have me. Here. Now. Forever. However you wish."

"You make it very difficult for a girl to chase you."

The words—their implication—thrummed through him. "You wish to chase me?"

"If you don't mind very much, Duke."

"Not at all, Duchess."

She pulled back instantly, tutting false disapproval. "*Former* duchess. Now, a mere lady. And even that is a questionable moniker." She lowered her voice to a whisper. "You see, I am a divorcee now. And I own a tavern."

"Ah," he said, going after her, nipping at her jaw as she wrapped her arms about his neck. "That does sound terribly scandalous."

"Oh, absolutely. Why, just this morning I scandalized the House of Lords."

"What a coincidence, I did, as well."

She grinned. "You'd be shocked what divorce does to a fine, upstanding person."

"I'm sure I would be," he teased, loving the smile on her lips. "Why don't you show me right now?"

"In due time. But first, I should tell you that I've been doing some reading since you left me."

"You left me first," he said.

"Yes, but you destroyed my tavern and then left me."

"I had to convince eighty members of Parliament to side with a duchess in divorce proceedings. That is not the easiest of tasks. The number of chits that I've doled out is staggering."

She laughed. "And we shall discuss all that at length later. But first, I wish to tell you what I've learned."

As she remained in his arms, she could read the minutes of last season's parliamentary session for all he cared. "Do, please."

"I have been torturing myself by reading about the Pleiades." And, like that, he was riveted. Her fingers played at his hair as she went on. "You see, Merope is the only one of the Seven Sisters who cannot be seen without a telescope. Did you know that?"

His heart began to pound. "I did."

"Of course you did. And first, I should like very much to get a telescope and have a look at her." He'd buy her a telescope that day. He'd build her a damn observatory. "They say she is hiding her face in shame because all her sisters married gods and she loved a mortal."

He nodded. "Yes."

"I think they're wrong. I think she is turned away because she looks in the wrong direction for her happiness. I think she is searching the sky, waiting for it to find her. And . . ." She paused, the words catching. ". . . if only she turned around, she would see that Orion has been there, waiting to make her happy, all along."

He nodded, the words thick in his throat. "He only wants her happiness."

Her blue gaze found his. Held it. "And her love, I hope."

"Christ, yes. Her love."

Tears glistened in her eyes. "I should tell you that I am here for more than that."

Anything. He'd give her anything.

She climbed off his lap and he mourned the movement, until she was standing before him, and he realized what she was wearing. His robes. How had he not noticed it before? And how was it that now that he had, he was certain he'd never seen anything so stunning in his life?

"I didn't want to go home to find something to wear."

"I recall you wearing a perfectly respectable gown earlier," he said, tilting his head. What was she up to?

A shy little smile played over her lips as she fingered the fastening to the robes. "Yes, but I thought red would be more appropriate."

And, like that, Mal was desperate for her, turning to face her, reaching for her, taking her by the waist and pulling her close, between his legs, and stealing her lips once more as he sought the opening of the robes. And then, growling, "I am reminded that I'm very angry that you told another woman about my love for red. You shall have to apologize for that, later."

She gasped at the words. Or perhaps it was the feel of his hands, stroking over the velvet of her robes, pulling her to him. "I am sorry," she whispered. Her hands came to his jaw and she tilted his face up to hers, kissing him. He took his reward, punctuating it with a long, slow slide over the soft velvet of his robes. "Does it help that I want to be the only woman who ever wears red for you again?"

His breath caught. "It does."

"It's true," she said. "I want to be the only woman. Forever."

The words roared in his ears. "Forever how?"

"Forever, as a partner. Forever, as equals." She paused. "Forever, in love. Forever, married."

He couldn't stop himself. "Are you sure?"

"I am," she said with a little laugh. "I was this morning, but then you divorced me before I could tell you so. But . . . it all works out well. If you'll have me."

He laughed, too, unable to stop himself. The idea that he might not have her was ludicrous. "I shall, I think."

She smiled, there and gone before he could bask in the warmth of it. "You are certain? You won't . . . we shan't . . ." She took a deep breath and released it, and he heard the tears in the sound. "You shan't have an heir."

He put his hands to her face then. "I shall have you. I shall love you. And I shall grow old in your arms."

She closed her eyes and a tear escaped. Mal chased it with his thumb. They kissed, slow and perfect, and he willed her to believe him. To understand that he was nothing without her, and she was everything he would ever desire.

She must have believed it, because when it was over, she backed away from him, fingers coming to the fastening of the red velvet robe. She loosened the tie, and the velvet pooled around her feet, stealing his breath.

She was naked beneath.

She was naked, and instantly in his arms.

He pulled her onto his lap, without hesitation, loving the way she straddled him, loving the feel of her skin and the sound of her sigh of pleasure. Loving her. "Lady Seraphina, you scandalize this place."

"What did you tell me the last time we were here? That this was a place for men of purpose?"

He was kissing her neck, making little circles with his tongue at the place where it met her shoulder, where she was sensitive enough that he could make her sigh with a mere touch. He smiled there, against that impossibly soft skin, his hands finding the round swell of her bottom as she pushed his coat from his shoulders. "I seem to recall such a description."

The coat gone, his hand stole to her breast, cupping it, testing its heavy weight, and she groaned softly at the touch. "And what have you to say about it?"

His lips tracked down the slope of that breast. "I have purpose right now, don't you think?"

She burst out laughing, the sound carrying down the staid, venerable halls of Parliament, out of place and perfect. And Mal set about making her laugh again and again, until she was making entirely different sounds altogether.

And then he was making them, too.

When they returned to earth, on the floor of his office, wrapped in his heavy velvet robes—robes he would never again be able to wear without summoning his wife to his offices to help him remove them—he pressed a kiss to her temple and said, softly, "I suppose I've got to get round to the news today."

She lifted her head, confusion furrowing her brow. "Whatever for?"

He smiled down at his former and future wife. "We should announce our engagement, don't you think? The Duke of Haven and The Singing Sparrow?"

That laugh again, beautiful and perfect and his. "Most definitely. We wouldn't want people to talk."

Epilogue

BEVINGSTOKE BABE:
HAVEN CAN'T WAIT!

Six Years Later

"*Y*our Grace, it simply is not done!"

Mal ignored the midwife as he pushed into the room, shucking his gloves to the floor and sending his coat after it, eyes only for his wife as he climbed onto the bed.

His wife, who appeared entirely too serene, considering she was minutes from giving birth. "You'll give the midwife the vapors."

"She'll be fine," he replied, taking her hand and bringing it to his mouth for a firm kiss. "I'm never touching you again."

She laughed, as though they were out for a stroll. "That's what you said the other times."

"This time, I mean it."

"You said *that* last time."

He didn't remember, but he imagined he did. Three months after their second wedding—a glorious spectacle attended by half of London at the insistence of his sisters-in-law—Sera and Mal had discovered that Sera

was increasing, to equal measures of surprise, delight,
and terror.

Miraculously, an easy birth produced a healthy son,
Oliver, now five and wild about horses and paints. Two
years later, they'd welcomed Amelia, as brilliant as her
mother, and full of opinions. Just that morning, at breakfast, she'd looked Mal dead in the eye and pronounced,
"If you and Mama can have a baby, it's only fair that
Oliver and I have a kitten."

Mal had spent the morning in the stables, selecting
the perfect pair of cats to live in the manor house. After
all, Amelia had pointed out, the baby should receive a
gift upon its arrival. That was only polite.

Needless to say, the doctor who had pronounced Sera
barren after the birth of their first child had been wrong.
And the happy life into which Sera and Mal had settled,
had become an equally happy chaos.

"Any word from the Sparrow?" Sera asked, as though
she were in the gardens playing lawn bowls and not preparing to birth a child.

"Caleb arrived yesterday," Mal replied. "Your tavern
is in fine hands while you attend to other business."

The family lived most of the year in London, close
enough to The Singing Sparrow that Sera could manage
the daily operations, and that the Sparrow herself could
find time to sing on rare, wonderful occasions, always
with the Duke of Haven in attendance.

But all of their children had been born at Highley, and
this one would be no different.

A wave of discomfort hit Sera and she gasped. "It's
time."

Mal rolled up his sleeves and moved behind his wife.
While he was properly besotted by his children, and
thanked God above for them every day of his lucky life,

it did not change the fact that he had no love for the getting of them. "I am reminded I don't like any part of this."

"You like the bits leading up to it quite a bit, husband," she said dryly. "As do I."

The midwife tutted her disapproval, and Mal raised a brow. "You know they say I am the scandal, now, don't you? And here you are, scandalizing the room with your talk of the bits leading up."

She smiled. "Considering my current state, Mad Malcolm, I'm fairly certain the room is aware of the bits leading up."

He laughed, wild for his wife, as ever beauty and steel.

A wave of pain hit her then, and Mal did his best to retain his composure as the midwife looked to Sera. "The babe comes, Your Grace." She looked to Mal then. "You are certain you wish to remain?"

Sera clasped his hand. "He is certain."

As though there were anywhere else he would be.

He offered his wife his hands and his strength as she did the immense, magnificent work of bringing their child into the world. Not that she needed him.

Indeed, it was Mal who required Sera's strength when, minutes later—the healthy cries of their second son filling the room and Mal's heart—she delivered their third daughter.

Hours later, as the sun set in the distance, turning the room a rich, golden hue, Mal entered the Ducal rooms to find his wife abed, looking every bit an angel, hair down about her shoulders, surrounded by their children.

She held one of the twins, the second asleep at her side, both blissfully unaware of the thorough inspections they received from their older siblings. Sera's gaze found him, blue and full of love, a smile playing over her lips before she said, restrained amusement in her tone, "We are considering our options."

He approached, feeling as though his heart might burst from his chest at the picture they made, these children, this woman. His loves.

Amelia was on her hands and knees, considering the baby on the bed. "I prefer this one."

Oliver shook his head, all seriousness. "I don't. Sisters can be very troublesome."

"That much is true," Sera agreed, speaking from vast experience. "But they can also be terribly loyal."

"And excellent in battle," Mal added, winking at his wife.

"Nevertheless," Oliver said, "I would prefer to keep the boy."

Mal's brows shot up. "I beg your pardon?"

Sera grinned. "It seems they only had one name selected, and so we must choose which to keep."

He matched his wife's grin. "Does the name help with the decision?"

She shook her head. "I'm afraid not."

He looked to his older children. "What is it?"

"Chicken," Amelia said, simply.

Mal laughed loud and long, before taking his place at the head of the bed, on the other side of his youngest daughter. "Well, I think we'll be keeping them both if you don't mind."

Oliver sighed. "If we must."

Mal leaned over to kiss his wife, soft and lingering. "You are magnificent."

"I am, rather, aren't I?" she said, happily.

He chuckled and leaned down to place a kiss on the

forehead of the boy in her arms, and another on little girl asleep on the bed.

"And me!" Amelia cried, launching herself into his embrace. He cuddled her against his chest and kissed her forehead, too, as Oliver scurried into the cradle of Sera's free arm.

The family lingered until the last of the golden sun had dissolved into red and purple streaks and faded to black, revealing stars and a sliver of moon in the night sky beyond. Mal carried his children to their respective chambers, settling the babies in the next room—the rooms once reserved for the Duchess of Haven had been turned into a nursery, as neither Sera nor Mal had any desire to sleep apart.

Once the children had been cared for, Mal returned to find his wife at the open window in their bedchamber, a nightingale singing in the darkness beyond. From behind, he pressed a kiss on the soft skin peeking above her night rail, wrapping his arms about her.

She leaned into the caress, giving herself up to it for long, lingering minutes. "You are going to catch cold in this window, wife."

"Do you see?" She pointed. "He's here."

He followed her direction. "Orion. Poor chap, always chasing."

"I think you mean poor girl, never caught." Sera turned to him then, tilting her face to his, sliding her hand up to pull him down for a kiss, deep and slow, filled with love. When they parted, she added, "She ought to take matters into her own hands. He'd never know what hit him."

"Nonsense." He lifted her high in his arms and carried her back to bed. "If she chased him, he'd do everything he could to get himself caught. And well."

She smiled at that, tucking herself against him. "And what happens after she catches him?"

He kissed her gently, marveling at this life they shared. "Happy ever after, of course."

She smiled, eyes closed, sleep coming fast. "Finally. Well deserved."

Author's Note

*H*aven and Sera's story has haunted me for longer than I can say—since long before they had names and took center stage in *The Rogue Not Taken* as the catalyst for Sophie and King's love story. *The Day of the Duchess* is a story of finding hope from sorrow—from a marriage that might never work and a loss that might never be overcome—and when I sat down to write it, I had no idea that it would become the story of so many women I've known, women who have amazed me with their strength and their ability to face an uncertain future. I could not have predicted that, over the course of writing this book, I would be so inspired by so many—friends, family, readers, strangers—all made of beauty and steel. Sera is for all of you.

While it may seem as though Sera and Haven's divorce was too easily obtained, the events in the story are a surprisingly close reflection of divorce proceedings in the House of Lords during the early 1800s. Until 1857, women were largely excluded from petitioning for divorce, as wives had no legal personage. What's more, wives were not allowed to testify on their own behalf in Parliament, which made divorce on the grounds of anything but female adultery tricky. In the late 1700s, however, a shift came in the way Parliament and society viewed marriage—as less a requirement for property and more a possibility for happiness—and divorce petitions rose significantly . . . along with spousal collusion. Essentially, men and women trapped in unhappy marriages worked together to achieve their common goal—usually with an unsuspecting bystander being dragged into the ruse as a witness to a wife's adultery. A quick (albeit expensive) Parliamentary vote resulted in the dissolution of the marriage, and everyone was free to head off and marry their lovers. I was shocked by how easily a rich and powerful couple might obtain a divorce—and fascinated by the idea that husbands and wives might work together to get it done. For a rich, riveting history of divorce in England, I recommend Lawrence Stone's *Road to Divorce*, which was a constant companion while I wrote—much to my own husband's trepidation. The extensive Parliamentary collections at the British Library were also essential to this part of the story.

A note on Sera's music: "The Spanish Ladies" is an old sea shanty, predating the 1700s when it was finally written down; I've also used Thomas Moore's "Oft in the Stilly Night" and "The Last Rose of Summer." "She Was Born That Day in the Heart of a Boy" is mine, with many thanks to a long-ago French café wall for the titular inspiration.

Sometimes, a piece of history grabs hold of you and won't let go. For several years (and several books), I've searched for a way to put an underwater ballroom into a story. The ballroom is real! There is a nearly identical underwater ballroom at Witley Park in Surrey, a massive estate built in the late nineteenth century by Whitaker Wright, an eccentric millionaire scoundrel. While Witley's underwater ballroom was built in the 1890s, there's no reason why it could not have existed in the 1830s at the hands of a man desperate for a monument to his love, as metal and glass submarines had existed for more than a century already. Though I swapped Witley's Neptune for Highley's Orion, I borrowed liberally from photos and first-person accounts of visits to the Witley ballroom, which, remarkably, remains intact. I'm deeply indebted to Atlas Obscura and numerous Reddit users for their commitment to understanding the physics and engineering of the ballroom.

As always, I am endlessly grateful to Carrie Feron, Carolyn Coons, and the outstanding team at Avon Books, including Liate Stehlik, Shawn Nicholls, Pam Jaffee, Libby Collins, Tobly McSmith, Carla Parker, Brian Grogan, Frank Albanese, Eileen DeWald, and Eleanor Mikucki. Thank you, also, to Steve Axelrod, who has all the best stories.

I am lucky to have a husband who has never once made me want to storm Parliament and friends who are the very best. Thank you to Eric for unflappable calm; to Lily Everett, Carrie Ryan, and Sophie Jordan for unwavering friendship; and to Bob, Tom, Felicity, and everyone at Krupa Grocery for keeping a table free for me.

And to you, wonderful readers, thank you for trusting me, for reading me, and for sharing so much of yourselves with me. These books are nothing without you. I hope you will all join me in 2018 for my next series, featuring the Bareknuckle Bastards, and some young women you'll find familiar.

Oh, and as for Sesily and her American, stay tuned.

*Three brothers, bound by a secret
they cannot escape . . .*

The Rake, all vengeance and vice

The Warrior, all fists and fury

The Duke, all power and past

*. . . and the women who bring
them to their knees.*

THE BAREKNUCKLE BASTARDS

A new series from Sarah MacLean
Coming 2018

Give in to your Impulses!

These unforgettable stories only take a second to buy and give you hours of reading pleasure!

Go to *www.AvonImpulse.com* and see what we have to offer.

Available wherever e-books are sold.

AVONIMPULSE

IMP 0811